Rick Can

(The Rick Cantelli Series)

Blood Ties

by

Bernard Lee DeLeo

*****

PUBLISHED BY:

Bernard Lee DeLeo and RJ Parker Publishing Inc.

ISBN-13: 978-1539636120

ISBN-10: 15396366127

As it will be with every novel I write from now until my own End of Days, I dedicate this novel to my deceased angel, wife, and best friend: Joyce Lynn Whitney DeLeo.

Chapter One

Nightmares

Lo and I perked up in our seats at the same time, glancing at each other with the 'are you seeing what I'm seeing' feature. Ushers escorted three African American men to seats in the reserved front section for the showing of Logan Heights. They wore white suit type hoodies, which personified the joke of racial profiling. Hoodies of any sort represented an absolute law enforcement nightmare if allowed into public businesses where they obstruct the identity of the wearer. Contrary to popular crap by the media, it has nothing to do with race, creed, or color. If an asshole gangbanger walks into a convenience store while concealing his identity with the usual hoodie uniform, it's common sense to make that a no/no.

On any other occasion, Lo and I would simply write this off as management stupidity and politically correct bullshit. We had a dog in the hunt on this particular movie 'Red Carpet' night. After the movie 'Here and Now', with all our very close family in it blew the doors off box office history, this release premiere of 'Logan Heights' cemented Temple and Jim into box office gold. With the young movie couple, Temple and Jim, trapped into a 'Logan Heights' action thriller, the plot gripped without overdoing intent. Jim, practically playing himself as the young white knight, martial arts kid, who helps a troubled girl in danger, grabbed any viewer by the throat. Caught in the horrid deaths of her parents in 'Logan Heights', Temple's character charted her way with Jim to the apprehension of her parents' killers. The plot had leaked out to the general public, including the newly formed cop hating, race baiters, Black Lives Matter.

"I'm not waiting for the movie to start, Peeper."

"Agreed, Sis. I thought the director of this had a tight rein on anything of a gangster flavor after what we cautioned him about. Now… they're letting fancy dressed gangsters into the reserved area? I don't think so."

"Nor do I," Lo agreed as we moved out of our very good seats behind the kids. They sat in a line with our entourage of Madigan and Cantelli employees and movie stars. We sat a couple of rows above our suspects. Lo motioned for them to stay put.

We approached with simplicity. Lo leaned down to the man occupying the primo seat at the aisle end. "You and your friends will have to come with us for a moment, Sir."

He took one look in Lo's eyes and began pulling the outrage card about hoodie this... and hoodie that... which Lo allowed to go on for a couple of seconds until she pressed an impressive stun gun against his balls. "Keep talking and I burn your balls into the seat. Tell your buddies to come along quietly if you value your ability to ever get a hard-on again."

Hoodie number one gestured at his buddies with trembling hand. "Do as she say!"

I stayed right with his exiting friends, watching hands, while Lo gracefully guided Hoodie one out stage right, with one hand on his arm, and the other with her blue light special ready for a sale. Out of the main seating venue, we ushered the three to the ushers who had escorted them in. Lo kept her finger on the trigger while discussing the facts of life.

"Which one of you dweebs decided to let hoodies wear their gangbanger gear inside?"

"We can't discriminate-"

"Are you stupid?" Lo didn't like the tone she was hearing. "I'd bet money you chumps brought these three in, bypassing the checkpoint too, didn't you?"

Silence, but the ushers were looking around. Bypassing checkpoints at one of these 'Red Carpet' movie debut events was a firing offense.

"How much did the Hoodie gang pay you to lose your job,

5

Dweeb?"

"Fifty. What's the big deal? They just makin' a political statement."

"Let's see about that," Lo fired off an arc right in the lobby as a demo, causing the Hoodie gang to jump. "Get your hands up on the wall while my partner does a pat down. Any objections, and I put you all down hard."

The two I watched looked ready to bolt until they saw my Colt .45 in hand. "Do as you're told or I pistol whip you."

"Man... this is wrong." Although Hoodie complained, he put his hands on the wall, nervously watching Lo's stun-gun. Real security police moved into position around us. His buddies followed suit.

I showed the security police my FBI/Homeland Security ID. "These three were escorted past the check point. My partner and I want to find out why."

One of the security group pointed at the ushers. "You two stand over by the check point. I'll want to talk with you in a few minutes."

I returned my Colt to its holster and did a professional pat down on the Hoodie gang. They carried 9mm automatics, stiletto knives I hadn't seen in years, with rolls of cash and an assortment of drugs filling separate pouches inside the jacket linings. The inside of those fancy white suit hoodies impressed the hell out of me. I grinned at Lo. The hoodie political statement meant something different than the initial trouble we figured on. I figured these three were carrying a stash in the tens of thousands dollar range. The security guys looked a bit stunned, not that they hadn't seen similar plays like this.

"Outstanding gimmick, guys," Lo said. "The very expensive white hoodies, worn in full sight over your heads, make you three beacons for the upper crust patrons, huh? There must be a lot of the audience in the know. They see the white hoodies marking your business presence. Then during intermission and hoopla, the rich and famous approach your jive-ass political statement selves for the recreational drug buy. Nice. What the hell's all the weapons for?"

"We pack for protection. We want a lawyer."

"We'll take it from here, Cantelli. I don't think you want to make this into a federal case. We'll hold them until the local police arrive. You two own Madigan and Cantelli P.I. firm, right?"

"Yes," Lo answered. "We protect the stars of this show amongst others. Because of trouble we had shooting the movie in the 'Logan Heights' area, Rick and I needed to make sure strapped gangbangers didn't get in. We work with Captain Bill Staley out of the University Precinct in San Diego on certain cases. He and his wife are guests in our section."

As his companions handcuffed the captured Hoodie drug pushers, the security cop with Bascom on his nametag moved nearer to Lo and I. "You've been in more shootouts than Wyatt Earp and Doc Holliday, Cantelli. How'd you ever get an FBI badge? More importantly... why aren't you in prison?"

Lo enjoyed my upbraiding. I was getting used to my infamous reputation only time would dull. I changed the subject. "Are you and your guys out of the Hollywood Station?"

Bascom grinned. "Yeah, we don't get the media attention you do. I'll call for pickup on these guys. Can we have the bust?"

"We were hoping you would," Lo agreed. She gave Bascom one of our cards. "Rick and I are going back to our seats before the show starts. If you need to contact us or a consult on anything, give us a call. I'll bring The Lone Ranger here with me and give you a hand. Thanks for the help."

Lo left 'em laughin'... at me, of course. We returned to our seats only a few minutes ahead of the opening of 'Logan Heights'. Lo was already texting answers to the fifty question pop quiz we were getting from our acquaintances. She downplayed everything, knowing our resident psycho, Trish, would have been depressed the rest of the night if she'd missed something sudden and violent. Stacy turned to me as I sat down again.

"I didn't hear any gunfire. You must be slipping."

I patted her hand. "I'm trying to quit. Did we miss anything?"

"Frank's taking movies of everything. The lights are starting to dim. The spotlight drifted over our star celebrity row. I can't believe how adult Jim looks. Watching him standing next to Temple on the red carpet took my breath away. Nothing phased him. He seems to absorb it all like a big sponge."

"It's a good thing he's eating like a horse. When he hit the six foot tall mark, coupled with the workouts, I was worried he'd look like a death camp survivor. It's good his coordination is keeping up with his growth, although the growth spurt slowing down helped a bit. Temple and Ellen on his arms looked gorgeous. With Ellen, that is a danger zone."

"You're damn right it is," Lo lurched into the conversation, her bat-like ears nearly vibrating as she extended her antennae. "Those three alluded my minions many times during the 'Logan Heights' movie production. Even Trish couldn't believe how often they dropped off the grid. Frank told me one of the celebrity wombats tried to join Jim, Temple, and Ellen while we were clearing the media press. She walked up and grabbed Jim's arm. Jim patted her shoulder and walked her away, gently whispering sweet nothings in her ear. Frank says when Jim turned to walk back, the young lady stared after him with more than celebrity need. The boy's dangerous, Rick. We need to put him in the iron mask in the dungeon until he's twenty-one."

We enjoyed Lo's description of Jim's coming of age gift of a dungeon. Frank leaned over to hug Lo. "She's so worked up over the three kids' potential, she can hardly sleep at night."

"Welcome to our club, Lo," Stacy replied. "Rick and I go over our scenario for each day, trying to find everything and anything we can fill Jim's days with. He works out, boxes, does martial arts, goes to school, plays intramural sports, and works at your office every chance he gets."

"The boy worries me," Lo said. "He's so talented, it's like watching a shooting star."

Uh oh, now Lo has me worried. "Easy, Sis. We have three shooting stars in our midst. You and Frank just returned from seeing your girls and the getting huge by minute new grandson, Mark Jr."

"Oh my God... he calls me Ma and hides behind me when Sarah yells at him. We're going to buy them a mansion down here to get them with us full time. Mark senior is working on a way to move south with us. He's a worker. Sarah being three months pregnant with a new baby has him thinking about local babysitters."

"He has common sense and logic on his side. Kim getting engaged must be putting you and Frank over the edge. Remember how she used to talk about marriage as if it were the third rail of hell on earth?"

"She's also talking about moving south," Lo replied, stunning me. "I never thought it possible. I've kept my distance because anyone not wanting to be around me, including my kids, get their space. I'm hoping for an even bigger extended family down here."

"Kim's fiancé served in the Marines with two tours in Afghanistan. I doubt anyone else could have even interested her."

"Kim worried me because she wasn't afraid of anything until we handled the MS-13 gang problem she had," Lo replied. "After that wakeup call, she's been a different person."

The movie started with lights lowering and Stacy gripping my hand. Watching my grandson act out an action adventure hero role nearly catapulted me into an alternate reality. After the success of 'Here and Now', Temple and Jim's picture graced nearly every media outlet in the world. Cheech Garibaldi, a former mob boss and now movie producer, requested the kids stay away from talk show

9

interviews because of the age difference questions sure to be brought into the interviews. We agreed. It would be nearly impossible for them to avoid the talking head media after 'Logan Heights'. Cheech's timing on the movie proved impeccable with it hitting the theaters shortly after 'Here and Now' began showing in Blu-Ray and DVD preorder sites. He had the funding and script ready for a third installment of the feel-good romance comedy series with Lo's half-sister, Karen, our former contract killer, Trish, and Temple with young Jim. Yes… it was all weird.

Business boomed. Everyone wanted to be escorted around by killer movie star, Trish. Lo kept her at a price only the very rich could afford. Partners, Trish and Meg, mimicked comedy central with the lines they blasted each other with. Since the Black Lives Matter creation by lies and media sheep, Bone and Steve were also golden in the escort gigs. All the fearful of public outcry, but very much wanting protected, chose Bone and partner Steve at a premium price. Having a huge black bodyguard, unafraid of anything or anybody, backed by an instant pepper spray/stun-gun enthusiast like Steve, always fit the bill. I worked installs now with Jim and Ellen, with Ellen's parents written and notarized consent. Working installs, with two young go-getters wanting to learn the criminal mind, coupled with high tech security, made a blessing out of a previously hated job.

I drifted in and out of movie plot, family, and present reality seamlessly until the movie credits rolled. A standing ovation brought us all to our feet. I spotted the black masked invader as he emerged from the side entrance Lo and I had escorted the Hoodies out of, aiming a shoulder strapped weapon with silencer. Thank God only Frank and Lois sat between me and the aisle as the masked man pointed toward our celebrity row of family and friends.

"Get down, Lo!" Lois questioned nothing. She reached for her own weapon while bodying Frank down on his seat.

The masked freak shouted, "Allahu Akbar!"

We can hesitate and lose everything in our world or we can

allow God to answer ambiguous question marks from eternity's end. I shoot to kill. I'm so damn proficient at it, the mayor of my city constantly searches for ways to exile me from it. No one wants me for a bodyguard, except the ones willing to be a pariah in order to make some kind of statement. Combat happened in the next moment within absolute silence. No crowd applause or noise of any kind interfered with my gentle first pad of index finger trigger pull. Twice the blast of my Colt banged into the crowd surround sound. All visual or audio input, other than my target's masked face, faded into nothingness. He had dark eyes I saw clearly through the eye holes. I pulped his head with my two hollow point hits. Masked man and automatic weapon pitched like a puppet with blunt force trauma propelling it to carpeted eternity.

Lo and I didn't freeze, wondering what the hell was happening, or a second in remorse over a dead stranger. We moved in practiced offensive combat toward the origin. Lo backed me amongst screams and panicked audience with Trish, Meg, Bone, and Steve in a semicircle around her, facing the milling crowd with gesturing hands and calming voices. Jim, Ellen, and Temple joined them. Lo and Trish carried heat as I sprinted through the exit, ready for anything. Death lay all around, except for two masked bandits guarding access to their designated hitter. I knew I had backup. I ran straight into the one on the right, carrying his surprised ass into the wall with pistol whipping attitude. The other clown died between shots from Lo and Trish at nearly identical firings. We needed a prisoner. I had him. Until the regular authorities took over the crime scene, we would protect the scene and extract information.

When my target and I landed, I cracked his face and head open with two professional pistol whipping beauties. I hogtied his ass with a plastic restraint so fast, it would have made any rodeo audience applaud. The hunt was on after that. Seconds passed, as I contemplated the driver or interrogation decision. I decided. I ran for the back entrance, choosing rightly the assholes wouldn't approach or exit from the media covered front. With Lo and Trish on my six, I broke into the street past the dead guard. I saw a black van with side door open, idling by the curb. I never hesitated. I charged into the open back and shot both front passengers through their open mouthed, questioning masked heads. I reached forward with care to turn the engine key off.

I sat down for a moment with Colt in my lap, head back, and murder in my heart. I didn't know what it would take to get our lone survivor alone to find out who sanctioned this outrage on everything I cared about... but I planned to find out. Lo and Trish peeked in, weapons searching for targets. When they saw me waving at them with a smile, they enjoyed the moment after, that intense close order combat brings.

"Well... Peeper, what the hell do we do with this?"

I shot from my lazy ass enjoyment of the moment. "We go take the survivor for a private interrogation session before the cops swarm us."

"Oh yeah!" Lo agreed as she and Trish moved out of my way.

I ran full speed to my survivor, searching for the right room, where we could find out who the hell sent these killers. I plucked the survivor over my shoulder on the run, heading for the front most security office. The bastards had killed everyone. Security police, ushers, and Hoodie gang lie in pools of red rivers, never expecting the silenced weapons assault. I passed Bascom's body. His open mouthed stare and drawn weapon, clutched in spite of the automatic weapons fire that killed him, gave testimony he died with his boots on. I planned to give him comfort in the afterlife.

By the time I slammed my burden into a chair, I had Lo at my side with stun-gun in hand and Trish at the door, gun in hand. I ripped the mask off my target with disdain for wounds, moaning consciousness, and any semblance of compassion. I smiled into his awakening face with angels singing in my head at the opportunity. Lois provided his wakeup call with a five second blue light arc special of hell on earth to his balls. Oh yeah... he screamed at our introduction.

12

"Hi," Lo said, patting his face while lighting off her blue light special tool. "You better start talkin' Porky, or I'm goin' to fry your nuts into bacon grease, baby!"

I grinned as he stupidly tried to play the lawyer card which earned him a trip into blue light pain hell for five never to be forgotten seconds. Lo pinched his chin in practiced iron grip I'd witnessed many times. He looked into her eyes with respect, horror, and recognition he could count on more of the same until he talked or died… realizing the woman staring into his eyes didn't care which he chose.

"Aga Saleh! Do not hurt me again! We… are Syrian nationals… with refugee status. You must return us to Syria."

"Great… this is what we get for ignoring the list," Lo said. "We can't let Saleh know we found out who sent these bozos. Where's Aga now, Porky. He had to have been relatively close in the recent past to round up you murdering scum."

Porky tried to pretend ignorance. Another blue light special convinced him to share. "He…he is at the embassy extension in San Francisco! That is… all I know!"

Lo watched his face during each revelation. After Porky's last one, she nodded at me. "I believe him, Rick."

"So do I." I grabbed Porky by the neck and finished him off. We set the scene with Porky holding his gun. "I fought him in the office, trying to take him alive, but I had to choke him out or be shot."

Lo moved back from the scene in the office, scanning the looks of the room and victim. She nodded. "This will work. We have to bring Floyd and Van in on this."

Floyd Randolf and Van Carmichael contacted us on behalf of Homeland Security and CIA to go back to work for them on a case by case basis. Van asked us to assess a threat at our embassy in Sana'a, Yemen. We did. We immediately evacuated all personnel. While Lo worked details in Riyadh, the embassy cleanup crew, Carl

13

Santiago and I, defended the embassy. Aga Saleh's son joined the assault on our Sana'a hotspot. He died with a shitload of his fellow peaceful Islam types until Lo could fly Santiago and me out of there.

In part, this assault on a movie debut night began during our escape from Sana'a. Saleh made one attempt to kill us already. The mutts he sent to do it this time, killed a lot of innocent people to get at us, and make it look like a terrorist 'lone wolf' attack. That term, made popular by our terrorist enabling media, to make citizens believe terrorists randomly jumped out of the woodwork to kill us, would have made a great cover story for this debacle if it had succeeded. Saleh would have to be dealt with, one way or another, hopefully with the covert blessing from HS and the Company.

"Put away your piece and join our group in the theater, Skipper. I don't want you taking heat for this. Rick and I will talk to the cops. Handle crowd control."

Trish hesitated, but she knew with her background, Lo was right. "This is going to be bad. Call me if you need me."

Lo and I tidied things in the office a bit to make it look like a fight for life took place. The sirens in the distance arrived a few minutes later. Another mob of fans and media were out front, waiting for the eventual chaos of movie stars being interviewed. If the doors hadn't been locked at the front, there would have been many more dead inside. I could hear them banging for entry, knowing the end of the movie time schedule. The paparazzi expected to be allowed in to mingle before the stars exited. We left the office, holstered our weapons, and waited in plain sight of the rear entrance with our hands also visible.

S.W.A.T entered in typical fashion for expected combat after seeing the dead in the getaway van. The initial interlude with law enforcement, followed by hours of nightmare afterward, ended in an interrogation room. A woman officer escorted Lo in with me. She sat down with an annoyed snort.

"Well, Peeper?" Lois Madigan and I spent decades together as one of the deadliest teams the Company ever enlisted. We were

14

family, not by our blood, but by the blood of our enemies. Our FBI and Company contacts, Floyd Randolf and Van Carmichael, would be around to see us in short order.

"Same old... same old, Sis." We knew the cops were listening to everything. "Van will be here soon. Did you ever reach Floyd?"

"Yep... about three minutes before they discovered I had a second mobile phone and confiscated it. So... how'd you like the movie?"

"It was excellent." We talked performances, plots, and movie attendees for the next forty-five minutes until Van and Floyd arrived in a huff. They sat down facing us with very worried expressions.

"Are we clear?" I had to ask.

"Did you just insult me, Rick?"

We got a chuckle out of that. "You know I needed to ask, Floyd."

"I know. I have a team of agents with me. No one has access to this room on any level."

"I can imagine how much fun the PD had questioning you two old buzzards," Van said. "We won't insult your intelligence with stupid questions. Tell us what happened and what we can do about it. We know there are five dead bad guys. The locals want to know why we're here and if we're responsible for the dead innocents."

"Those Syrian shitheads murdered the innocents," Lois retorted. "Aga Saleh sent them. They weren't going to stop with killing our friends and loved ones. They planned to rake the audience. Rick shot the first guy through the door pointing a gun. Otherwise, we'd have hell to pay in dead bodies. He led the charge out to the lobby area where he tackled the one we got the info from. I shot the other one. Rick restrained the live one and ran out the back for the escape vehicle. He dived inside and killed the two waiting. I questioned the live asshole. He talked."

15

"I'll bet he did." Van exchanged worried looks with Floyd. "We know you kept Saleh out of the explanations. I heard the sanitized version with Rick struggling to capture the informant. You're hoping if Saleh doesn't know we know about him, then he wouldn't try to flee the country yet."

"Correct." Lois leaned over the table. "He's in San Francisco. Rick and I are going up there and set things right. We need to know if there's any objections."

"The media knows you and Rick killed the terrorists," Floyd said. "Wouldn't Saleh figure you found out he was behind the attack?"

"Probably," I replied. "Lo and I figure if he thinks that and tries to run, you suits can stop him. If he waits, believing we don't know he sent the Syrian death squad, then we'll hatch a plan to take him out. We'll need full bore surveillance of his whereabouts. We also need a list of suspects from your watch list, Floyd. We need a patsy to take with us – someone you believe belongs to one of these terrorist shithead groups, but can't prove it."

Floyd leaned back in his chair. "I think I get it. You want a Lee Harvey Oswald to fill in as a dead primary suspect. Then you and Lois take the shot from the grassy knoll. The shit hits the fan when a sitting Yemen ambassador gets his head blown off, and he's officially done in by one his own peaceful Islam cultists, right?"

"That's our plan, although I'm not certain of the way in which Aga will be leaving this dimension," I told him. "I'm certain with all the Moslem ass kissers everywhere in government these days, Saleh must go virgin hunting in a plausible way, with a likely suspect fitting our needs."

"Surveillance won't be a problem," Van said. "If he's hiding in place, it will be difficult to catch Saleh away from the embassy."

"I would assume you would like one of our un-vetted Syrian refugees to be the fall guy since Saleh used them for this kill mission."

"It would fit our narrative. The Syrian refugees, the idiots in DC keep flooding America with, can be seen in the proper light, especially after the movie debut massacre," Lo replied. "Can you look into the matter of likely suspects without leaving a trail?"

Floyd nodded. "I can do it. As you surmised, we have a rather large database of people in this country from the Sand, who don't assimilate. Because of groups they belong to and the places we've traced them from, we keep track of them. There's a ten acre place off of Hollister Street in San Diego with a front man named Gabriel Paria. His compound has numerous guards. Local police have not been able to get inside when they suspected Paria of running a training area for Muslims of the Americas, giving a safe house for illegal crossings from Mexico of Middle Eastern origin. We have accumulated enough intelligence to raid the place, but the DOJ blocked our request and actually tipped Paria off."

"He sounds like just the guy we need," Lo said. "Focus some assets and find out where he hangs out when he leaves the compound."

"We know Paria visits the Muslim Community Center twice a week in search of recruits. He goes alone, dressed in a burka. We've managed to keep that information away from the DOJ. Someone in the Community Center hierarchy knows about it. That I'm sure of. Paria has one of those Isis beards with no mustache so he wears the Full Monte black burka."

"How sweet, a burka babe with a beard. Where did he come from?" This guy sounded perfect. Lo and I could snatch him and head for San Francisco. "Do you want him questioned? He won't be returning from our jaunt to San Francisco."

"Yes. We want intel making it mandatory we act on the compound," Floyd answered. "He trained at the Khan Eshieh camp in Syria. We're not sure where he came from originally. They let the asshole in as one of the first refugees, years ago."

"Send us the data on our private drop, including days and times he normally goes to the Community Center. I assume you

17

know how he travels. Paria doesn't travel with guards when he goes as a burka babe, does he?"

"No, which made us suspicious of a Muslim woman traveling alone and driving a late model Audi. He parks two blocks away so as not to be seen arriving or leaving suspiciously. Our guy caught him pulling the slave costume top away from his face to wipe away sweat on a hot day. Any recruit he interests who visits the Hollister Street compound automatically goes on our list of suspected potential jihadists."

"I'll key in assets on the compound in addition to what Floyd employs," Van added.

"How does it look for us getting the hell out of here tonight," Lo asked.

"Good. We called your lawyer we had on file. He was busy eating them alive out there when we set this interview in place. I'll check and see if he's done munching on them. We'll leave with our team now. Cleaver will have you two released immediately, I'm sure. They're keeping the shooting irons for now."

"We'll be in touch." Floyd stood. He gave us a small wave and led the way out with Van staying for a moment.

"Let me know when the window of opportunity opens."

"We will, Van. Thanks for coming out so quickly," I told him. He nodded and left. Lo and I became silent, stationary lawn decorations until Cleaver came with a detective to get us released.

Chapter Two

Killer Cantelli

"I thought after you and Rick tamed Logan Heights during the movie filming, all would be well for a while." Cleaver escorted us out of the precinct. "Even the police admitted a lot more people would have died tonight without you two in the audience. Why they put you through the wringer after they lost some of their own stinks of something else behind the curtain. Your friends' team helped immeasurably. Some of the detectives were at a loss explaining the interrogation and detention after initial statements."

"They mentioned keeping our mouths shut about the killer team's identity until they could sort out the facts," Lo replied, as we got into Cleaver's car for the ride home. "It's the same old Islam cover-up. Moslem mutants attack innocent people, kill cops, kill gangbangers, and theater ushers. The mayor and police chief get together after hearing about the rampage. Suddenly, it's the 'not all Moslem mutants of Islam are terrorists' show, where the politicos and media decide to create their own event facts. They blame everything and everyone else but the mutants that did the deed, including climate change."

Cleaver remained silent after nodding his understanding. I'm certain this kind of disgrace going on around the world bothered him as much as it did all other thinking human beings. Lo and I believed a deeper plot, involving corrupt world leaders, partnered with billionaire power fiends, worked the sacred globalist agenda worldwide. Cleaver knew we probably had a theory. He wanted to hear it, taking the chance he might get a verbal slap in the face from Lo. Such would not be the case this time. My partner Lois Madigan hated cover-ups and politicos. I could tell the way she fumed in the front seat with her fists clenched, it wasn't Cleaver's interest that upset her.

"Would I be wrong in assuming these terror acts all over the world share something more than a few fanatics going nuts at the same time?"

Lois patted Cleaver's shoulder. "No, Cleve, you and every other sane person on the planet suspects a conspiracy in spite of hearing the pathetic mantra of isolated incidents, global warming, and the maniacs just need jobs."

"I know you probably believe I only pay cursory attention to the frightening aspects you and Rick have dealt with in the past year. I deciphered the sequence of events surrounding the killing of Tonya Stuart. It ended in billionaire Jorge Boros' death. I don't need to hear a confession to know one of you killed Boros. I thought with him dead, a lot of the Islamic chaos would end. They proved he was bankrolling terrorist organizations around the world while influencing the Muslim refugee disaster."

"Use the term Moslem," Lo directed. "It means 'evil and unjust', rather than the bullshit Muslim word meaning 'one who gives himself to God'. The inbred zombies, following Islam's death cult act, out their insanity for no God. They have murdered each other and everyone around them for over fourteen hundred years. God had nothing to do with it."

"Agreed," Cleaver said. "Boros' death didn't slow them down much."

"Other power brokers filled Boros' place," I told him. "The vast fortune he controlled went into the wrong hands by his design. His inheritors continue the plot of world dominance Boros started. I hate conspiracies. People have been looking for scapegoats for centuries. I'm beginning to believe in the globalist, one world order, world bank crap more every day. I admit it fits all the incredible stupidity going on amongst so called world leaders. They sell out the citizens of their nations, their own nation's sovereignty, and the rights of their own citizens to protect themselves."

"Rick's right. The puppet masters place their own citizenry in deadly danger so they can ride in on the horse of totalitarianism. Europe illustrates the outcome daily. Even after the lessons of a

20

disarmed populace in world war two leading to disaster, the first thing Europe does after world war two is disarm their citizens again. They then found a rabid, mongrel horde of mutants to import into the midst of their populace, citing refugees from persecution. Bullshit!" Lo was steaming. "They put us peons at the mercy of a ravaging bunch of freaks, incapable of living amongst their own Death Cult worshipping confederates. The Moslem zombies don't assimilate into civilization. They destroy it. What better way to embrace the global policing of totalitarian dictators and money changers?"

"You two scare me."

"Cleve... if you're afraid to hear about it, then don't act like you want to know," Lo replied with quiet determination. "You're a great friend and lawyer. You're paid in full. I'm taking you off our pad. If you want to work for us, then fine, we'll pay top dollar as always. If you've had enough of our new clandestine entries into the real world, I'm giving you your ticket out right now."

Cleaver drove to the side of the road. He held out his hand which Lois gripped. "I'm in. I can't survive a totalitarian, liberal, brain washing experiment. I don't have any other skills except in defending our laws, so they'll execute me first, along with the rest of the 'useful idiot' liberals and politicians with no real-world skills." Cleaver smiled at Lois with a deep intake of breath. "I know many quotations, but this one hits to the core of our relationship: 'people sleep peacefully in their beds at night only because rough men stand ready to do violence on their behalf'. I know Richard Grenier originally said it in relation to both George Orwell and Rudyard Kipling in his Washington Times essay. I must add 'and rough women' to the quote, because as I know Rick would agree, you are one of the most dangerous women on the planet, Lo. You and Rick do what's right, and I believe in what the two of you have done for this nation. I am with you in all things until I am no more."

Lo hugged the bugger. "We're good, Cleve. I know I give you a hard time. That's in the past. You paid your dues. You're right about the situation which today's liberal idiots don't realize. If you don't have real-world skills, you have two options, death or slavery. Rick and I have obtained a few real-world skills, but mostly, we're killers. When the horde comes for us, we'll pile the bodies before they ever come close to getting us. If we get clear to form a resistance, the horde better kiss their asses goodbye. We won't hit the usual targets. Rick's the best long range assassin I've ever worked with. We will steal everything from them to use against their assault on America until we die... period."

Cleaver chuckled. "Would you take in a know-nothing lawyer and his family if the shit hits the fan?"

Lois turned on him, with hand shaking his arm. "You're family, Cleve. We don't leave anyone behind. Tacticians need support. I'll train you in whatever needs to be done. Let's work on making sure that never happens though. Rick and I haven't given up on our nation. We have enough imagination to foresee worst possible scenarios."

"I have to say... being around you two is a roller coaster ride. I thank God I crossed paths with you when I did, Lo. Me, and everyone I loved would be dead otherwise. Banchek would have executed me and everything I loved."

"Don't think about that anymore, Cleve," Lo replied, while settling back into her seat again. "That prick deserved to die. The financial morass you allowed yourself to get into took a bit more in the way of alterations to get you clear of the law. Luckily, there wasn't any fall out when Banchek and a bunch of his disciples went down the long, lonesome road into hell."

Okay, I was surprised. I remembered executing a Banchek and minions. I remembered the order, facilitated by my trusted partner, was Homeland Security ordered. I'm not shocked, because I have an odd relationship with Lo. I did what I was told because she sanctioned it... not because the morons in the alphabet agencies dictated it. I'm immediately thinking Lo had more imagination concerning future endeavors than I realized.

22

"I know what you're thinking, Peeper." Lo snatched my thoughts in a practiced mind meld of intrusion. "Let it go. Banchek would have made our list sooner or later. Remember how little fallout we encountered after ending them at the cabin in Tahoe? Cleve wasn't the only target. Banchek expanded his human trafficking into Las Vegas. He shipped the girls to the Middle East. Word reached me via our buddy Van there would be no repercussions if something unfortunate happened to the big B."

"I hired on with Banchek, thinking he was legit," Clever added. "I invested in his cover firm and transportation network. Then he hit me up to defend his hired help whenever they were stopped. I looked into his operation more closely, finding the links to disappearing women, and foreign venues marketing for sex slaves. He had me connected to it all. A friend in DC I called for advice gave me Lo's number. I…I didn't know the kind of solution the two of you specialized in."

Interesting story of how we came to involve Cleaver in our legal affairs and why Lo trusted him so much. I figured the whole operation was sanctioned. Lo had satellite surveillance, times, dates, and a likely spot for the hit. She spotted for me in the woods near Banchek's cabin retreat. He hosted a party meeting with his trafficker staff. I adjourned the meeting from five hundred yards with my old Barrett M82 with depleted uranium tipped ammo and silencer. Banchek died first. The rest scrambled around inside the cabin. They didn't make it. Lo and I visited to make sure. Done deal.

"You've sure gotten me out of the tank enough times to be off the pad, Cleve. The locals surprised us a little with this interrogation time. It didn't take a rocket scientist to see what happened at the theater."

"The episode caused ten times the media coverage because they did allow everyone to exit the front eventually. It wasn't exactly the red carpet event complete with smiles and waves." Lo busily went through her returned phone, scanning messages and pictures. "Our crew did real well, somber, respectful, and straight to the point.

23

The quotes in the media breakdown are exactly as they should be, honoring the fallen officers. They're still withholding any mention of nationality or that he shouted Moslem murder mantra, 'Allahu Akbar', before Rick blew his head off. The authority idiots couldn't keep all the people interviewed from the theater audience from informing the media, who had them on live news feed."

A few minutes later, Cleve drove in front of Trish and Sam's mansion where the after theater party get-together was still going on. Amazingly enough, midnight still awaited us with over half an hour to spare. The place looked like Disneyland with all the lights and colored fountain aura.

"I can't stay," Clever announced. "I will be in touch with you both the moment I'm informed about how well your handlers from the Company and HS did. It won't matter. The police know they have to contact me before they can even speak to you two. Goodnight. Enjoy the party. Those kids are incredible together."

"Yeah... they are," Lo said, kissing Cleve's cheek while hugging him. "It's good to know you councilor."

Clever shook my hand. "It's good to be the Madigan and Cantelli consigliere. No one... and I mean no one messes with me. I have your pictures posted all over my office with the movie stars and all of Rick's shenanigans. The gangsters who try to enlist my services do so politely once they see the 'Killer Cantelli' photos. I have a great one someone took of you sitting with Bill Staley in front of Dane Ramos and his crew's dead bodies."

Lois enjoyed Clever's office description with inappropriate laughter.

"Anything I can do to help, Cleve. Talk at you tomorrow." I exited the vehicle with the amused Gorgon. We watched him drive away. "I'm glad he's off your pad, Lo."

"He'll always be on my pad, Peeper. That was simply a verbal compliment to his ability. Cleve gets to feel like he has free will in regard to Madigan/Cantelli. He doesn't."

"How sweet. I feel a double Bushmills is in order to start my night away from the precinct. How about you, Sis?"

"Whoever stands in our way better be family with a sacred reason or armed and ready to shoot. Either way... I don't like their chances."

"Agreed."

We were mobbed at the entryway anyhow. I had dozed off during the time when they left us in the interrogation room to steam for a while. Our Captain Staley of the San Diego police force would never have tried that ploy. He'd know Lo and I would nap through it. Jim and Stacy assaulted me in a good way first, glad to see me in person. Stacy, dressed in a clinging, dark blue, off the shoulder evening gown, felt as gorgeous as she looked to her old first love. Temple hugged me after Jim shook my hand with solemn pleasure in seeing my old mug.

"Pop! You saved us all. What the hell did they take you and Lo into custody for?"

"Sometimes, kid, we have to ride the Karma train no matter which direction it's headed. All of you... safe in this house... is everything to Lo and I. My partner and I have to go pour a couple to sip. Interrogation by chimpanzees have a drying effect on our mental outlook, requiring sustenance of a mind numbing nature. You, and anyone else, can ask us anything... but only after I have a couple of sips."

Trish laughed and gestured at us while I shook hands with Frank. "Right this way, Hooterville. The only other time you've been here was to save our lives. Let me show you what a great bar we have."

"That's what Rick's talkin' about, Skipper," Lo said, arm in arm with Frank. "Lead on. Give me your weapon. At some point, the flatfoot up in LA is going to get two different ballistics results for the slugs they find. I'll tell them you gave it to me when the shooting started."

25

"We nailed him good," Trish handed over her weapon from the purse she carried even now. "I forgot about ballistics. I'm getting senile."

Lo patted Trish's shoulder. She accepted Trish's transfer of the weapon while shielding the action with her body. "We sure did. I thank God that Rick gave us a chance to drill him. Let's go get that elixir Rick and I need for any further discussion."

Sam stood behind his bar with a big smile. He already had two doubles of Bushmills poured with ice water back. "Let me know if you'd like something to munch on."

I shook hands with him. "That sounds wonderful, Sam. Any snack stuff you have floating around would be great."

Lo clinked her glass against mine. "You were damned good, Peeper. All this action, workouts, and family revved your old Hooterville ass up. I doubt you could have done any better when we first started together."

We sipped down half the Bushmills. After playing evasive games all night, this was heaven on earth. A man approached in purposeful strides that caught my attention immediately. His gait was familiar. I smiled and downed the rest of my Bushmills. Bone was on his tail, looking at me quizzically. I stood to greet him.

Lo took one look at my face and drew out Trish's Sig-Sauer 9mm. She spotted who I stood to meet and started laughing. "Speedy! Let me shoot him, Rick!"

"Calm down, Sis. You can't buy entertainment like this. I think Sam should fire his security crew. Bone's on his six. He sure is dressed nice. Maybe he got an invite."

"He didn't, Rick," Sam said while pouring me another.

I captured Eddie Tanner along the beach after he tried to make a run for it, hence our nickname for him: Speedy. He said a few too many things I had to address by cracking a few ribs for him. Speedy went along peacefully with Bill Staley after I finished with him. He looked hard and lean tonight. I don't know how the hell he got out of prison, but I planned to find out. Speedy stopped, giving me about eight feet of respect. Jim, Ellen, and Temple moved over next to Stacy. Lo had the Sig-Sauer under the cover of a bar towel. It was aimed at Speedy's nuts. If he reached for something, Eddie would be very popular with his cell-mates. The closer he had come, making his way through the large crowd of tinsel-town residents, the grimmer the look on his face became.

"Hi, Speedy. How the hell did you get out of prison?"

"Don't call me that! I've dreamed of this, Cantelli! You cheap shot me on the beach. I-"

"Stop and think, Speedy," I advised, watching his hands. They were balled into fists. "If you start threatening things, it won't end well for you. Watch your mouth. Start with how you got out of prison. That interests me and Lo."

"You set me up! My lawyer made sure I was separated from the other guys you screwed over. They had to let me go on appeal. I spent time in the joint because of you!"

"Boo hoo! Light a candle and move on, Speedy."

Speedy pointed a finger at me. "I remember what you and your partner said about some list. You best remove my name from it!"

Lo's familiar cackle made its audio appearance. "All you did coming here, Speedy, was elevate yourself to the number one slot. You were right, Rick. Speedy's a treasure. Can we keep him talkin' while we sip this second shot of elixir?"

"Sure, Sis. I'm going to talk Speedy down off that plateau of violent expression he's on. You're on the list until you die, Speedy. That ain't changin'. If you screw up in any way, Lo and I will have to pluck you off the list the hard way. We may anyhow." I reached around to take my refilled shot in hand, sipping from it with heartfelt relish. "I killed four more men tonight, punk! What the hell would I ever get from worrying about your cheap thug ass?"

27

Oh boy, did that stir the coals blazing in Speedy. He wanted some. "If we weren't here, Cantelli, I'd smash every bone in your body!"

"Rick made you cry the last time you talked big, you dumb pussy," Lo said. She turned to me. "You earned it tonight, Peeper. I can see you want to walk on the wild side. Don't break your hands."

"Thanks, Sis." I slipped off my very nice tuxedo jacket and eased off my bowtie. "Do you have a problem with this, Trish? You and Sam own the joint."

"Nope. I heard about the hoedown in the sand. The whole thing will mean more publicity. You okay with it, Sam?"

"I am indeed, babe," Sam answered.

"You can walk away now, Speedy," I warned for a final time. "Once you throw a hand, I will begin breaking things on you. Same rules as the sand. Try for a takedown and I put you down and kick your face in."

There were gasps of surprise all around amongst the party goers as Speedy quickly stripped off his jacket, tie, and shirt. He'd been working out in the joint. Speedy had all the big muscles and six-pack needed to impress. I could have taken off my shirt but I didn't plan on working up a sweat on Speedy. I remembered all the things he said about playing with Stacy and Jim before he killed them. I glanced over at Stacy's horrified face as Jim gripped her hands. I waved at her. Speedy intelligently picked that time to attack. Only one problem – this wasn't my first rodeo.

Eddie threw a powerful haymaker at my head with an impressive left hook. I ducked and pivoted with a full force left of my own to Speedy's ribcage. It was so good catching him coming in, multiple bone cracks sounded audibly like dry twigs snapping along a woodland trail. Eddy crumpled to the floor in a quiet, white faced, horror filled realization I wasn't done. He watched me move over him with purpose, his breath coming in short gasps. He held onto his ribs with one arm and waved a useless hand up in a play for mercy.

Not this time, Speedy.

"Please don't, Rick!" Stacy gripped me from behind, her face against my back. I glanced over at Lo.

"She's right." Lo sighed. "The police will not like another body, dead or maimed, appearing on our ledger tonight. Speedy's on the list forever. I can speak for Rick on this issue. Get out of town and don't come back. How did you get in here? Answer truthfully or I'll kick your face in."

Before Speedy could answer, Sam and Trish's uniformed security guy, Rob Buckner, stepped forward. "It was my fault, Ms. Madigan. He has a press pass. I'm sorry about this. It's a flaw in our security plan. I should have a list of all press people with legitimate entertainment media."

"Thanks for letting us know, Rob." Lo motioned for Bone. "Bone? Would you help Rob get Speedy on his feet and out to his car?"

"Gladly." Bone plucked Speedy off the floor without Rob's help as Eddie yelped in pain while clutching his ribs. Rob retrieved Eddie's clothing, rifling through the inside pocket. He handed the fake press pass ID to Lo.

"Damn… you're right, Rob. This looks legit. We'll look into it." Lo gripped Eddie's chin. "Give me a name. Who the hell made this swell ID for you?"

"Audrey… Mercal." Eddie kept his eyes focused sideways away from Lo's stare.

Lois released him and patted his cheek. She leaned in close. "Don't tip her off about anything, Speedy. Give Bone the phone number and address where you went for the press pass. You'd better keep an arm around that ribcage while you're driving to the hospital. I'm betting Rick separated a couple. If we get mentioned in your recounting of this visit, we'll come looking for you. No one will find you again. Understand?"

29

Eddie nodded. Bone gripped the back of his neck in a Vulcan death pinch. "I'll get the address and check Mercal out tonight when I get home. Right this way, Speedy."

I kissed Stacy. Then I took a deep breath and fixed my tie and suitcoat. "Never would have figured on him showing. What moron prosecutor couldn't keep Eddie in prison? Maybe we can find out. Here comes Bill."

Bill Staley gave his wife a hug. She split off to talk with Karen and Trish who were on patrol again for media opportunities after the Speedy incident ended. Bill stayed at Sue's side for a few moments, watching to make sure he didn't leave her hangin' by herself. "Stace… you, Jim, Temple, and Ellen go mingle. Lo and I need to talk with Bill."

"Okay, Rick. C'mon, Jim. We need to turn media attention on the movie and its stars. Rick will handle the rest. The media will turn all the tragic events into a white washed mess, using the stars of the movie to help. You kids can tell the truth about what happened."

"G-ma's right," Jim said. "We don't need to turn them onto the subject. They'll walk right into it. We can reveal the truth on live newscasts. We know what that killer shouted before Pa stopped him."

"Good one, Stace," Lo said, as she watched our white knight march away with his two willing accomplices.

Stacy nodded and followed.

"I'm going to marry her, Lo. I don't know if she can stay out of trouble or not. She deserves a real chance. For her own protection, I'm leaving everything to Jim. I'll have Cleve write the contract. If something happens to me, he'll see her through."

"I never thought I'd ever see the day when you marrying Stacy would be even remotely a hoped for event. I'm happy for you, brother. I think it best to do it exactly as you outlined."

Frank stuck out a hand to be gripped. "She's completely

different, Rick. You and Lo know people better than I could ever hope to, but to me, Stacy moved past all her acting bits. She stopped you tonight to prevent your usual journey into the tank. I saw your eyes, brother. Speedy was heading for the happy hunting ground."

I know my mouth tightened. "Take my word for it, brother, Speedy will be heading there anyway. I'm glad I didn't ruin this night's celebration but ending our goofy nemesis, Eddie Tanner, would have been worth it."

Frank grinned and nodded as Bill Staley joined us. Sam served us while enjoying his wife in her new element as contract killer turned movie star.

"Am I interrupting?"

"No more than usual, flatfoot," Lo bludgeoned Bill in her way of greeting.

"I didn't stick my nose in that business of yours a moment ago, did I?"

"Lucky you," Lo replied. "Why the hell is Eddie Tanner annoying us like a puss filled boil?"

"Alexis Setteridge," Bill answered. "Before we get into that, thanks for blowing the shit out of those mutants who killed the Blue tonight. I heard the real story. It could have been a hell of a lot worse."

"Lo fixed one of them special before he died so we could find the prick responsible," I told him. Bill was one of us. I know he didn't want to be, but he knew the downside of ignoring reality.

"Can I help?"

Lo gripped his hand momentarily. "If you can, we'll read you in all the way. For now, this has to stay between Rick and me. I've had a couple of jolts. Tell me the news about Saint Ally. I can take it."

"Tanner's lawyer, Gilbert Knox, knows how to shop for the

right judge. Apparently, Eddie had enough money stashed to enlist Knox. He researched the feud between you two and Saint Ally. Knox took full advantage of it. I testified at the hearing Knox instigated about a travesty of justice, where a confession was beat out of his client. Judge Ally ignored evidence, and my testimony Tanner's injuries occurred during his own assault on police assets. Knox interjected Madigan/Cantelli into his plea. Setteridge then nearly went into a coma inventing wording to legitimize her release of Tanner. Thank God the rest of the crew was nailed dead to rights."

"You're off the hook for this Setteridge canker sore," Lo said. "I thought we had that bitch backed off. Let's not discuss anything else about it. You did what you could. She should have been stripped of her judgeship after the last travesty she tried to pull off."

Setteridge's last attempt at taking a swipe at Madigan/Cantelli was a gift that kept on giving. "Ally sure got the surprise of her life letting Trish out of prison."

Lo toasted me. We finished off our drinks and Sam happily refilled them, glad to be in the know on our dealings. Sam was family now... no matter what.

"When she released Trish, Saint Ally had no idea the string of events she put in motion, all of which screwed her, but good. We hired Trish, knowing the only way we could control her actions depended on working in the rough trade legally." Lo paused, relishing the images of what Setteridge must be going through. "Ally hoped Trish would kill us all. I have no doubt about that. Now, she not only works for us, but she's a movie star, married to a billionaire. Karma's a bitch, kiddies!"

I smiled at Lo's cackling enjoyment of our legitimate triumph over a travesty of justice in the person of Alexis Setteridge. She and I knew we would have to deal with her now. Instead of showing in person with fists and bad attitude, Speedy could have picked a spot to spray everything we loved in automatic weapon's fire. Saint Ally's improvisation of the law cannot go unanswered any longer. She endangered everything in our reality. We should have dealt with her after she released Trish, a contract killer with a grudge reason to wipe out Madigan/Cantelli without a second thought.

"I see you and Sue are still getting along, Bill. I'm happy for you, pal."

"Thanks, Rick. We are together in everything now. I don't hide anything from her. She understands everything I could never explain before. Jenny returned to us from LA woke me to the fact I was never as smart as I thought. Rick brought Jenny home from that hellhole and my life fell back together. Parents take kids for granted, just as kids take us for granted. Jenny told me what you did to bring her home, Rick. I thought everything had to be done inside a travesty of justice. You blasted Jenny out of that hell on earth, for at that time a stranger. It's always pissed me off to the max we can't have justice inside our law."

"We used to, flatfoot. We back the Blue... period. In the old days, the politicos backed the Blue. In past times, you could have called the Blue in LA. They would have ripped Jenny out of there, along with kicking the shit out of every 'banger who got in their way." Lo smiled, and even in my Bushmills' feel good buzz I was waving her off. She ignored me. "We called in favors, Bill, and it was so good. You caught us at a good time. Rick and I were fading complacently into a retired sleep-fest of daily bullshit."

"Don't, Sis," I implored. Lo knew Sam lurked closely, wiping the bar, and screwing around to be close. Frank, grinningly listened, knowing the full story. I was beginning to acknowledge Lois had reached a point in her life where she was tired of pretending.

"We found that gang of assholes and their slave trade," Lo stated, straightening to finish off her drink. "They shipped the girls into the Middle East morass of death."

"Jen went to LA with a boyfriend she claimed was going to marry her. Sue wouldn't let me use physical force to stop her." Bill took a shot from Sam and drained it, sighing and pointing toward his better half. "Sue's driving tonight. I take it Sam behind the bar is in the know."

I glanced back at the suddenly wiping the bar Sam with a nod. "Sam's in, Bill. Forget about Jenny's extraction from LA. The only thing I feared was whether Jenny wanted to come home or not when I found her. She understood the situation she was in. Jenny had overheard her hosts taking bids over the Internet's 'Dark Web'. She wanted to come home... period. Done deal."

"She said you sauntered in, gripped her hand with a smile and pointed to the door, saying you were there to bring her home. Then... you killed everyone between you two and the door that tried to block your way."

I drained my drink then. I wasn't complacent enough to think spending my December years in prison would be a good idea. "I escorted her out with a minimum of violence. Lo threw a banger into the room the moment we cleared the door. Lo, Jenny, and I left LA, brother. I'm old. The details of our escape from LA are a bit foggy. Let's just say there was no follow up. Did the DA file an appeal based on Setteridge's actions?"

"Yes, and I thought they were holding Tanner until the appeal cleared one way or another," Bill answered. "Believe me, if I had known he was already on the streets, I would have warned you immediately."

"We have a name directly from Tanner - Audrey Mercal. She's a fake ID artist. The press pass Eddie managed to get by security with was as good as I've ever seen," Lo told him. "You can bet press passes aren't the only things she's making. I have an idea for taking her down if Rick thinks it's okay to use Stacy to entrap Mercal. Would you like the arrest?"

"This would be a good time for me, especially if this Mercal may be working an illegal alien processing plant. Would Stacy be willing to do something like this, Rick?"

"She's one of the best con-artists on the planet. Stacy wants to do more in our line of work. It helps her keep out of trouble too. We'll let you know what the address is."

"Good," Bill replied. "That way I can call the commander in whatever precinct she's working out of about the tip. Usually with a day's notice, I can be allowed into the bust on scene. I'm glad your FBI contact issued you both IDs. If it's a tough takedown we won't have to jump through hoops if Killer Cantelli here has to do his thing."

"Gee thanks," I replied. "Mercal's a counterfeiter, not a mob enforcer."

"In any case, at least you'll be covered if there is trouble. Do you have a plan or is it too early to ask?"

"I'm thinking Stacy goes in with her prison record, cons Mercal into believing she needs a new identity because she ripped off Cheech Garibaldi," Lo explained. "All points of the con have a basis in truth. You can bet Mercal will check on her background. She'll overcharge Stacy. We'll cover the seed money. Once we get Mercal recorded delivering the ID, we'll hand her over to you."

Bill nodded. "That's good, Lo. I have to get back with Sue. Call me when you get this plan hatched."

"We'll try and give you enough notice. Rick and Bone can work with Stacy to start setting Mercal up tomorrow. C'mon Rick. Let's eat and go check on the media with Sam. I'm curious to hear how the truth about the attackers went over live. Saleh will have heard about his killers' unexpected deaths."

Fifteen minutes later, with some food in us, we migrated to where the entertainment media interviewed our young stars. Sam rejoined wife Trish, who had backed away from the media circle along with Meg, Karen, and her husband, Danny. Our office manager Shelly and her husband Max were on the other side of Trish, with Stacy and Ellen. We joined them, watching Jim pose with Temple. The lighting and setting were perfect, making Jim look over twenty in his tux. Temple appeared younger than her nineteen years.

35

Stunning, with her long black hair and dark eyes, Temple no longer looked like the TV teen detective, Sally Waters. Even in high heels she was a head shorter than Jim. Stacy gripped my hand.

"They look so good together. The press people didn't ask one age question. Trish and Karen joined them for a time at the beginning, taking questions about a third addition to the 'A New Beginning' franchise."

"Jim looks old enough to drink. Did they speak at all about the theater shootings?"

"They asked," Ellen chimed in for Stacy. "When they received the truth, the reporters backed away for a moment. No follow up questions either. I heard one of them say 'oh shit, that was live' when she conversed with her cameraman."

At the moment, I didn't care. In spite of the food, I still had a buzz on. I could tell Ellen endured the Jim and Temple moments with teen angst still. She and Temple hung out all the time though now. I saw Bone and Carlene smiling over at me. Brother Bone had stayed in the background with his wife. He looked like 'Shaft' on steroids in his tux. You can bet he made an impression on Speedy when returning Eddie to his vehicle. When Bone puts that Vulcan neck pinch on you with attitude, you see stars, and get fitted for a neck brace. We had our own area out of the way, so I motioned Bone and Carlene over to join us. I didn't see our other gumshoe, Steve Ramirez and his wife Kris.

"Hey, Bone," Lo said. "Bring Carlene over to my house tomorrow. Frank and Rick will barbeque some steaks. We have a plan to nail the ID woman, using our ex-con, Stacy."

"Sure, Lo. That sounds good."

"Really!" Stacy lowered her voice, realizing we were in the middle of a crowd. "I get to work my specialty, huh?"

"Rick will explain it later. Text Mercal's number to Rick when you get a moment, Bone."

36

"Will do."

"There won't be any shooting over at your house, will there, Lo?" Carlene, a veteran of a few unexpected shootouts at our restaurant, wanted to make sure the barbeque tomorrow would be just that: a meal.

"No shootings, Carlene," Lo replied with a smile. "Where the hell is Steve, Bone? He and Kris were at the theater."

"After the cops questioned everyone, Kris yanked Henpeck out of there by his ear."

Lo nodded her understanding. "I don't blame her. Kris realized she could have died tonight. I hope Steve can calm her down. We need him."

"I like Steve partnering with Timothy," Carlene said. "They work good together without having to shoot anyone."

We all enjoyed that shot across my bow.

"Gary split on me after the interrogations were over too," Meg said. "I think the first date with accompanying gun battle turned him off a bit."

"You should have told Gary about your cheerleader costume and pompoms," Trish poked her partner. "He would have hung around then, especially if you admitted going commando to the theater."

Meg gasped. "I did no such…" she slapped Trish's shoulder, seeing Trish was screwing with her. "You're mean."

"Sorry."

"Liar. Are we all invited, Lo? Maybe I can get Gary to give me a second chance."

"Of course. It will be an office barbecue. If it wasn't January, we'd have it at the beach house. All the kids are invited too. I want to see my baby niece, little Lo. Can you and Danny come, Karen?"

"We'll be there, Sis."

Group affirmative murmurs made it plain Frank and I would be spending most of tomorrow in front of a hot grill. "I don't want to put an evil exclamation point on this, but please don't forget to set all your security systems."

"Yeah, Trish," Meg jumped right on the opportunity. "You, a contract killer, getting taken like a Brownie at her first campfire. Shame on you!"

Meg nailed Trish but good. Trish stammered a bit with Sam enjoying her discomfiture. I could tell the ex-partner Chet, taking her and Sam in their home, was an open wound that would not close any time soon. It had been a miracle Lo and I reached them in time to execute Chet and his crew before they got real busy on Trish and Sam.

Trish gave up any pretense of a comeback. "Okay... good one, Meg the peg-rider. The security system flaw will not be repeated. That was a hell of an entertaining reunion with Speedy, Rick. What's his life expectancy?"

"He's under observation for the moment. If not for Bill Staley showing up on the beach when Speedy and I had our first dance, we'd be talking about him in the past tense. Let's enjoy the rest of this evening without mentioning my unexpected party crasher."

Attention returned to our young present stars for the night. Unfortunately, my night was not over. After dropping off Temple and Ellen, Stacy drove Jim and me home. The glow of a pleasant evening on the heels of a tragic killing of cops and ushers seemed improbable and disturbing all at the same time. As we approached our house, I saw dark hooded figures wandering around in front of my place.

"Drive down the street, Stace."

She did as told with me eyeballing my cadre of sullen hoodies. Yep... they were looking at me too. They gestured at me threateningly. I smiled, gesturing at them in a wait one motion. "Park here, baby."

Stacy parked in the spot a block down from our house. She stayed silent. There would be no last minute pleadings. Jim grabbed my shoulder.

"Pa... you don't even have a gun!"

"Yeah, I do. Stay with G-ma, kid. This can't be ignored or witnessed."

"You're drunk," Stacy blurted out. "Don't do this, Rick!"

So much for the pleading pause. I reached over and gripped her hand. "Stay with Jim. Be ready to drive, babe. Don't think about it. Remember the meth lab I stupidly walked into. The ending was dead drug dealers and Bill Staley escorting you to jail."

Stacy giggled. "We are a pair... aren't we?"

"Hell yeah, girl. I'll be back."

I exited the GMC with murder in my heart. I didn't know how many the hoodies brought, but I knew it wouldn't be enough. It had been a long night. Luckily, I snoozed during the police holding cell excursion. I planned to round out my current death cycle with more bodies. I gave up long ago trying to bury the killer inside of me. Snipers don't appear by magic and learn the trade. We're cold blooded killers. We squeeze the trigger from half a mile away with the thrill of a kill enveloping us in a blasphemous euphoria we admit to no one. I kill close too... and I like it. I walked toward my hoodie greeting party while moving my tux coat away from the Ruger 9mm at my belt. I waved at the dark forms moving toward me.

"Hello there. Are you gentlemen waiting for me? I'm your Huckleberry. Come get some. I've had a hell of a night. It's morning now. I'm feeling refreshed. What's on your empty headed minds? If any of you reach, I'll kill all of you. I have a fourteen shot clip... eight more than I need for you boys."

The leader looked around at his compatriots. I could tell on his face he knew me and that I wasn't kidding. His buddies were his problem... not mine. They were easing hands toward places they shouldn't be. He noticed. "Don't reach!"

"State your case quickly. This is my home. I kill intruders around it without mercy. Choose your words carefully, Binky."

"We had brothers in the theater tonight, Cantelli! You got them killed. We know you and your shithead people were the target! Now... our blood is dead!"

"Boo hoo. How the hell would you know about this? More importantly... why should I care? You guessed right though. I plucked your homies out of the crowd and turned their drug dealing asses over to the security cops. I didn't kill them, moron. Terrorists did. Maybe you idiot gangbangers ought to concentrate on a real enemy."

"We ain't..."

Two in the back reached. It was on then. It made no difference what the hell Binky said, did, or thought of doing. I drew the Ruger killing machine with practiced ease and no mercy. Binky died first with one right between his horns. Then, it was the shootout at the 'Okay Corral'. After Binky dropped with the surprised look still on his face, I shot his two wing men behind him, center mass. Hollow point 9mm slugs don't have the knock down power of my . 45 caliber Colt hollow points, but they get the job done. To their credit, the other three were clearing their goofy slouch pants with weapons.

I fired into the one with his piece almost out. The next one nearly had his pointed. I shot him in the face to make sure he didn't get a pull on the trigger. The last of my hoodies got a shot off. It ruined my tux coat's sleeve, putting a gouge in my left arm. His next pull of the trigger resulted in a jam. Imagine his surprise. I shot him in his open mouthed face too. I then made sure there would only be one side of the story, dropping down on one knee and firing into each head with a second kill shot. I then had to move Binky slightly, extract his weapon with my hanky and lay it next to his hand. I called Stacy first. This would be messy. I'd already decided to have

Stacy drive immediately to Temple's house for the night with Jim.

"Rick? Thank God. My heart's bursting out of my chest."

"We'll catch up later, Babe. Drive Jim to Temple's house. You two stay there the night. Put Jim in handcuffs." I heard Jim protesting my order with Stacy giggling uneasily. "Go now."

"Okay, Rick. I love you."

"I love you too, girl. Get going."

I disconnected and Facetimed Lo. "Hi, Lo."

The wombat surfaced first on the screen. I could tell she hadn't gone to bed yet. She snarled – not a good look. "What have you done, Peeper?"

"Look who came to visit." I turned the iPhone, scanning the land of the dead.

"Who the hell is that bunch?"

I turned the iPhone to a face to face conference again with a grin. "They're friends of the three guys in the tuxedo hoodies that were dealing drugs at the theater. Someone tipped them off we were the target. They decided we got their buddies killed. My yard of the dead guys met me on the front lawn. I sent Stacy away with Jim to spend the night at Temple's house. Don't call Cleve. Can you call Bill tomorrow and have him look into any rap sheets they might have?"

"Sure. I hear resignation in your voice. You're thinking tank time, huh?"

"One of them gave me a scratch on my arm, so I'll get the cops to take me to the hospital if I don't like the way I'm treated. I'll plead for medical attention."

"Good one, Rick. Now you're thinkin', partner. Get a bit faint while you're at the hospital so they keep you overnight for observation."

"I'll give it a try, Sis. Talk to you in the morning."

41

"Are you sure you don't want me to come over?"

"Positive. I called you tonight 'cause I knew you'd give me a Tijuana Haircut if I didn't."

"You're damn right. Get some sleep if you don't spend the night in the tank."

"Will do. Tell Frank and Bill I'm in the death cycle again already."

"You sure as hell are." Lo disconnected.

Chapter Three

Death Cycle

I heard the sirens coming from a neighbor's call, I'm sure. My neighbors will be getting a petition to make me leave the neighborhood before the mayor exiles me from the city. I knelt under the streetlamp, with my Ruger on the ground, and fingers interlocked behind my head. I also had my FBI identification open in plain sight. It was real, thanks to Floyd. Maybe it would keep me out of jail. I figured by the time they processed the crime scene it would be dawn anyway. They turned off the sirens as two squad cars drove to my crime scene. The officers left their vehicles with weapons pointed at me. Once the lead officer put the cuffs on, I was allowed to stand, while he checked the FBI identification.

A few drops of blood from the gash on my arm found their way onto the handcuffs. The lead officer's partner, a young woman in her late twenties, noticed the tux sleeve. "Did they get you Cantelli?"

"One of them nicked me. They all drew at the same time so I'm not sure which one creased me. If you have a moment, you could pull my hanky out and tie it around my arm. I'm getting blood on your cuffs." I grinned. "It's clean. I had it stuffed in the pocket for show."

Officer Tabler smiled back. "Sure." She tied the hanky in place at about the right tightness. "How's that?"

"Feels good." I watched the other pair of officers roaming amongst my gangbanger flower garden. Tabler's partner, Officer Cantos had reached a number where he read off the information on my FBI wallet ID. He then disconnected.

"You're legit. How does a psycho gumshoe get an FBI badge? We know you killed four men in LA. You no sooner get home and you kill six more?"

"Those four in LA happened last night. It's morning now, Officer Cantos."

Tabler snorted laughter and turned away with her hand over mouth. Cantos didn't care for my off the cuff reply though. "You think this is funny?"

"I didn't think it was funny when those terrorist slime in LA killed the Blue from Hollywood Station. I met Officer Bascom there. He died with his boots on. I sent four of his killers to hell and my partner sent a fifth."

That remark sobered Cantos. He nodded. "Okay... take it from the top on this."

I told him my Stacy and grandson Jim staying at a movie star's house story. I came home to stay because I had a meeting tomorrow. "The 'bangers in the yard got tipped off that my partner and I caught their three drug dealing brethren at the movie premiere tonight. We turned them over to Officer Bascom. They were killed by the Syrian terrorists too. I explained what happened when the leader in the yard accused me of killing his cohorts. They didn't like my explanation and drew on me."

"How many shots did they get off?"

"One. I got creased in the arm."

"You do understand how this looks, right - killing six armed men? They only get one shot off before you killed them all. How many shots did you fire?"

"Twelve. It sounds as if you think it would have been better if I'd let them kill me, Officer Cantos."

One of the other officers exploring the garden of the dead joined us. "Each one has two kill shots in him, Sid."

"Twelve shots, Cantelli? Two kill shots in each man?"

"I was a Navy Seal sniper. I then worked in combat situations for the CIA for decades. My partner, Lois Madigan, was my CIA

44

handler. We still consult for them and the FBI. I don't miss with either hand. I'll bet money those six on my lawn have records going back to when they were babies."

Cantos ignored the explanation. "We'll have to bag your weapon. The coroner is on the way. Show me where you were standing. I'll try and find the slug and match it to the weapon fired."

That was good police work. I didn't know, considering the angle, how much luck they'd have finding the slug that creased my arm. I perp walked over to exactly where I stood. "If Officer Tabler could stand upright over by the bodies, I'll help look for the slug once we pinpoint the trajectory."

"Yeah… that'll work." Cantos took off the handcuffs.

I enacted how I stood when the one shot me. We glanced at Tabler's position on a slightly higher incline. After figuring a likely area on the street where the spent slug went, the five of us began searching. Surprisingly, one of the second team of officers found it after only ten minutes. They bagged it. The coroner arrived while the garden of the dead grew yellow crime scene tape decorating the lawn. Cantos left the cuffs off, gave me the formal reading of my rights, and handed me my FBI/Homeland Security ID back. We left then for the station where I knew the interrogation room awaited me. I was ready for a nap anyway. Besides, Cantos let me keep my iPhone. Since Cantos treated me with some semblance of respect, I didn't insist on the hospital stay.

Between going over my story a dozen times, and napping in the periods where they like to let us known criminals stew in our own juices, I managed to get a few hours' sleep. My final visitor before Lo and Clever arrived was a young white prosecutor. I figured she was probably in her mid-twenties. She resembled a lot of pictures I'd seen of Hillary Clinton at that age when she got fired from her position on the 'Watergate' mess in the seventies for unethical conduct. She plopped down in front of me all smiling and smarmy. Oh good.

"Mr. Cantelli… I-"

"That's FBI Special Agent Cantelli." I knew where this conversation was going and I wanted to at least get a dog in the hunt.

"Uh... yes... Agent Cantelli... you killed ten men in a matter of hours. We are getting calls insisting you be charged with hate crimes."

"Whose we? For instance, who the hell are you?"

"I'm Assistant DA Terra Flavion." She laced her hands on the table, leaning forward. "You need to take this more seriously, Can... I mean Agent Cantelli."

"I'm dead serious. Who is we? If you're thinking of railroading me, I'll wait for my lawyer. He doesn't take kindly to my being accused of incredibly stupid stuff."

"We have already heard from Black Lives Matter and the Council on American-Islamic Relations. They are demanding an explanation of the ten murders."

I smiled and leaned against my seat back, folded my arms, lowered my head, and began my nap process. Terra railed away at me until she ended her rant with a threat to see me held on federal civil rights charges along with hate crimes. I napped until Lo and Cleve arrived, escorted by Assistant DA Flavion. Lo reached across and patted my face.

"I can see you've been sleeping instead of convicting yourself on all the bullshit charges this young whelp thinks she can pin on you."

Terra gasped in indignation. "You have no right to-"

"Shut the hell up, ding-a-ling!" Lo turned on Flavion full throttle. "Rick's been doing the rough stuff, keeping flowery cunts like you sipping Starbucks and wine, getting paid for shitting on your country and our nation's laws, for decades. He's a former United States Navy Seal with more time in service to America than you've been alive! Explain her lovely parting gifts, Cleve."

Cleaver went to work on Flavion with facts, the law, federal

46

jurisdiction, Homeland Security Act, and the criminal jacket of every gangbanger in my garden of the dead. "If I even hear of you continuing with these bogus charges I will have you disbarred, Ms. Flavion! I know your boss personally. He never authorized you to proceed in this manner on the hearsay of gangbanger enablers. You've heard the cliché about 'you'll never work in this town again'? You go anywhere in public with any of this travesty of charges, and I will slap a suit on your head so pervasive, San Diego will have to go into Chapter Thirteen to pay it off. I want FBI Special Agent Cantelli released right now! Do you understand?"

Flavion, red faced in white guilt of God knows what, sat down heavily, and gestured at me. "You are free to go, Agent Cantelli."

I stood happily but Lo wasn't finished. She pointed the finger of the Harpy at her. "You're on my list, girlie. Make no mistake about this clown show you tried to instigate. I'll be watching you from now on. I live by the feud."

Lo startled the hell out of Flavion. "Are...are you threatening me?"

Lo leaned down in her face with the smile that can make a man's balls retreat into his stomach. "Threat is such a weak word, girlie. I'm old school. I deal with cheap little cunts like you in ways nightmares are made of. Think of me now as your mentor to do what's right and good from now on, because honey, I'm like Santa. I'll know when you've been bad."

We left her there to pout. After reacquiring my belongings, we quietly left the precinct. The three of us didn't speak until we were in the car. "How much trouble am I in, Cleve?"

"Flavion's right about C.A.I.R. and the BLM. It's incredible when we have groups allowed to exist, paid for by foreign interests tied to terrorism, who operate freely in America on lies and hate. They did file official protests demanding explanations. Bill was ordered to stay away from your case, but he made sure we received the arrest records. BLM won't get anywhere except possibly trying to riot. I sent the records of those six gangbangers out to all major news outlets, including major social media news sites."

"I've called Floyd," Lo added. "I want to find out what Homeland Security can do about the C.A.I.R. rats. They're nothing but terrorist enablers and facilitators. They've been busted before for terrorist connections. As to Black Lives Matter, they don't give a crap about the thirteen blacks dead and fifty-two wounded last weekend in Chicago, killed by other blacks. We've been around too long, Rick. Bill's watching out for you. If something happens other than the charges getting dropped, he'll be calling. He repeated his favorite warning for you, 'your next killing better be a suicide'."

"He's so cute. I'm glad I bought two extra Colts. I'd be down to my old Jennings otherwise. Did Flavion speak with you two at all before the interrogation room scene?"

"She wants to prosecute," Cleve said. "We kept our mouths shut until we could get in to see you. There were six guys on your property with drawn guns with assaults, armed robberies, rapes, and numerous gun charges. The DA told me there would be trouble, but not from his office. It's lucky there weren't any survivors. Our exposure would be worse with one of them lying through his teeth."

"It wasn't luck, Cleve," Lo told him.

"Is it provable, Rick?"

"Unlikely. I took care with the second shot to make sure. I'm glad you thought to flood the media with their records. It won't stop the BLM Gestapo if they decide to seek their peculiar justice. I wish C.A.I.R. would send some Moslem zombies over to the house. I'd be back in the interrogation room in no time."

"Don't even joke about that," Lo ordered. "I want you to move into the beach house for a while until this cools off. We'll keep your house under observation for the time being. The cops allowed Stacy and Jim to pack a couple bags this morning. They're at the beach house now. You already have stuff over there. I called everyone and told them we'd have the get together at the beach house."

"After all this, it would be good to bust the counterfeiter for our sake and Bill's." I forgot for a moment we would be filling Stacy in on our sting operation.

"How's your arm?"

"It's fine, Lo. They put a bandage and some antibiotic cream on it at the station."

"Get some sleep at the beach and the crew will come by around two," Lo replied. "You're welcome to come, Cleve."

"Not this time, Lo, but thanks. You two are the craziest semi-retirees I could imagine ever existing."

"Did you ever see 'The Shootist' with John Wayne," Lo asked.

"Sure… good movie."

"That's Rick and I. We're goin' out with our boots on."

"Understood."

* * *

My welcoming party at the beach house was impressive since Temple brought Ellen along with Stacy and Jim. It seemed the friendship with Temple meant a lot to Ellen, in spite of Jim being the completion of a young love triangle. I hugged everyone and pointed at Ellen.

"Do your parents know what happened last night and this morning, Mars Bar?"

"Don't call me that, Rick. Lois nailed me with it just because she heard from you about being a Veronica Mars fan." Ellen was annoyed. She better get used to it.

"I don't take orders from young neophyte detectives, Mars Bar. Answer the question."

She looked to the side of my Cantelli stare and knew right

49

away I was on to her. Ellen decided it wasn't worth it to try and keep the con going. "No. They know a terrorist plot with deaths happened at the movie theater which I explained. They hadn't heard yet about the six guys you wasted in your front yard. I can plead ignorance on that one until I see them again."

"Fair enough… the sun's out and the temps in the low sixties. I'm showering and getting some sleep before our barbeque. I would suggest you three young connivers take some lawn chairs and go out by the water. While you're out there the three of you can get your stories together about the guy you've been following."

Temple gasped, got an elbow from Ellen, and Jim simply shrugged. It's always neat to take these young punks unawares. Ellen was a dangerous commodity. She had wonderful instincts about people like her mentor, Lo. Unfortunately, the comparison ended there. Ellen didn't have Lo's instinct for danger yet. We had to keep the twerp under observation because she had Lo's power to browbeat her friends Jim and Temple into any plot she came up with.

"Sorry, Pa."

"Jim! What are you doing?"

"Calm down, Mars Bar," Jim retorted. "Think for a moment. Pa and Aunt Lo are already onto you. They're either having someone checking on us or they're doing surveillance themselves. Besides, no one's better than Bone. He's probably hacked every device we own."

"This is an invasion of our privacy!"

"No… Mars Bar… it's us old timers keeping you alive. You have good instincts but no sense. Did you think Eric Stargie wouldn't notice he was being watched by young punks? He did. We know he's already found out where each one of you live. Bone hacked him too. We know he's planning on invading Temple's house on Wednesday. He thinks he has a jammer that will work on her security system. He's wrong, but we figured to pick him up then."

Ellen went into full bore Supergirl pose, hands on hips and face jutted forward. "I was right. Stargie was hangin' out around our high school for abduction purposes. I spotted him, Rick! I should get some credit for noticing his weirdo presence."

"Lo and I are proud of you, Ellen. We're also worried. You don't seem to know when to hand over a perp you suspect to us. You enlisting Jim and Temple on surveillance put Temple's residence and life in danger."

Hands dropped from sides, clenching into fists. "I thought with Temple driving… oh crap… I screwed up again. I guess Lo knows."

I grinned. "Of course. Lo and I have agreed this will be your last warning, Mars Bar. You pull a stunt like this again and we collect your torch. You'll be officially off Cantelli Isles immediately. Say you understand, kid."

"I understand. I'm sorry, Rick. I know that doesn't mean crap to you and Lois."

"You're right… it doesn't. I'm sorry doesn't cut it if Temple winds up dead and Stargie begins stalking you and Jim."

"What happens now?"

"That's none of your business, Mars Bar. Lo and I will handle the threat to Temple ourselves. Keep those lips of yours shut about this or the torch will pass so quick it will make your Mars Bar head spin."

Ellen bit her lip, unwilling to simply accept the facts. "I know you killed ten men in less than ten hours, Rick. I understand what you're saying. I don't have to be a detective wannabe to know what's on the horizon for Stargie. Can you share what happens?"

"That's not the way our relationship works, kid. We'll encourage you to keep your eyes open, do some preliminary checks with our help, and then the case gets handed over to us."

"Am I in danger, Pop?" Temple only followed the Mars Bar and her minion, Jim, because she loved Jim. She had more survival instinct than Ellen, after the warehouse surveillance incident where

51

she nearly got killed.

"We'll handle it, Temple. I expect you to rat out your cohort, Ellen, at the first sign she's going off the grid from now on. That goes double for you, young Jedi."

"I thought I could call you in without endangering anyone, Pa. I screwed up. It won't happen again. That Stargie guy is dangerous. He back traced us, huh?"

"Yeah... he did. Let's not go into that right now. You have damn good survival instincts, Jim. You clued us in when Mars Bar went off the rail before. I'm not putting anything else on your head from now on."

Stacy spoke for the first time. She put an arm around Ellen's shoulders. "I went against Rick many times in the past, El. He and Lois are the best there is. I'm a con-artist from way back and I never stood a chance against those two. You're at the beginning of life. Take it easy. Use your instincts and logic within the boundaries. Otherwise... you'll end up dead. You can learn how to be like Lo. You'll never be Lo. Get used to it. Trish and Lo are poured out of the same mold, but even Trish knows better than to mess with Lo."

"Amen to that. I'm heading in to take a shower. You three idgits stay in sight from the window the whole time I'm napping."

"We'll be fine, Pa. I promise," Jim replied.

* * *

My first love princess joined me within moments of my lying down on the bed after showering, naked and unafraid. By the time I napped, I made her afraid for her sanity. Heh... heh. I did trust the kids to bond and be careful on their own for a time. They needed alone time to discuss how easily they were found out. It really wasn't that easy. I don't trust Ellen. Neither does Lo. We're hoping to guide her furtive mind in the right direction. Unfortunately, we had assumed she learned her lesson after the near catastrophe following the drug dealers at the school. Jim warned us that time. I'm not a slow learner. I had them monitored by either me or Steve

52

since then, with Bone doing all the computer foraging. This had proved to be the time to spring it on them. Stargie had been the only blip on our radar in a while, concerning the kids. I hated to admit it, but it seemed as if Ellen latched onto a serial killer. Eric Stargie was no joke.

* * *

"Sorry, Temple," Ellen said after they walked along the beach in silence for a ways. "Rick's right. I'm an airhead who doesn't consider danger. If Rick and Lo get this guy, Stargie, I'm never pulling a stunt like this in secret again."

"I know you're passionate about doing this detective work and surveillance," Temple replied. "I had a taste of my own stupidity showing up at a warehouse on a lark to be with Jim. I should have known better than to go along with your covert operations, Ellen. This Stargie may actually be a serial killer. I wonder what Rick and Lo will do with him."

"Best not to wonder about that," Jim said. "From now on, plausible deniability kicks in. I know when Stargie made us too. Outside of school, we should never have come within sight of him. You spotted Stargie at school right away, Mars Bar. From now on, that will be the time to let Pa know about a suspected perp."

"Don't call me that!"

"You've earned it," Jim replied. "You can call me Dodo for not going to Pa with your suspicions right away."

"I...I'm out of the detective business," Temple added. "I believe in three strikes. I've got two. One more strike and I'm dead. If you keep your eyes open for people out of place while we're going somewhere together, let me know, and you can play detective with Jim. Calling Pop right away is the first step no matter what."

"We can't be afraid of everything," Ellen said defensively. "I want to do detective work even more now. We have to at least follow through on surveillance until we know our suspicions are right. Like you said, Dodo, we can't let the perps spot us in different places.

That was a big mistake. I don't like calling you Dodo."

Jim shrugged. "It's better than Hooterville Jr. I'll only call you Mars Bar when you screw up. I like your full name, Ellen."

"I do too," Temple said. "Lo sure pegged me with the Shortcake tag."

"That's a lot cuter than Mars Bar," Ellen said. "Or Veronica Mars turd."

The three friends enjoyed Ellen's repeat of Lo's original derogatory nickname for Ellen.

"I could be like the TV show and Sherlock Holmes' declaration: Elementary. Temple can be Tempest. Jim can be Vanilla Ice."

"Gee... thanks," Jim replied. "I like the nickname business because we can key in our own sites on the Internet while exchanging private messages. I know Bone doesn't care what we say. He probably does some form of datamining when checking on us. We can make the nicknames into code for checking our messages on a separate site."

"That's really good, Jim! I'll work on an index for us. We'll make your nickname something simple to clue into the index code. How about 'Cross'?"

"Simple is good," Jim replied. "Whenever we use our tag names in a sentence, we'll know to go into conversation on private chat. I'm still not hiding anything from Pa and Aunt Lo. If that's what you think I'm doing, then say so, because you're wrong."

"I know you'll rat me out if I forget and start getting my butt in the wood-chipper," Ellen replied. "If you have a problem with what I'm doing, say so to my face first."

"I have. You ignored me and kept talking your agenda without a pause. If you ignore me again, I'll go right to Pa behind your back, and so will Tempest."

"Damn right, girlfriend," Temple confirmed Jim's threat. "Lo owns my butt. She can tell if I've done something stupid, or if I'm thinking of doing something stupid. I'm where I'm at right now because Pop and Lo care about me. Don't take Pop's threat about being voted off the Cantelli Isles as a joke. If they get your torch you're dead to me, Ellen. That's how much they mean to me."

"Ditto," Jim said. "Actions have consequences, Ellen. You've already seen that, especially in this goofball movie star world. I've lived life in a shit-pile. I'm never going there again... ever."

Ellen didn't like what she was hearing, because her friends agreed upon action, singled her out as generating dangerous problems. It only took another few seconds of analytical thought to know her browbeating style didn't work from a fourteen-year old. "I understand. I'm always looking for people and scenes out of sync. I need to put my natural instincts into line with reality."

"We can all be great friends with that in mind, Ellen," Jim said. "Pa and Aunt Lo are willing to teach us everything. They won't factor in stupidity when interacting with us. They're professional killers. Get that in your head and when you think of something off the grid, go to them first rather than last."

"Yeah..." Ellen walked along, kicking sand. "Eric Stargie ain't long for this world. I found him though."

"You did indeed, Elementary," Jim replied. "I like Mars Bar better. It fits you."

* * *

Stacy moved to where I aimed an electronic device toward the kids walking along the beach. "I thought you were taking a nap. It's a wonder you can walk after that perverted preliminary. What are you doing?"

I made wait gestures at Stacy, keeping my headset in place. Stacy smacked me on the shoulder. "If I didn't know you had those kids' safety first and foremost in my mind, I'd...I'd... oh hell, let me listen!"

I let Stacy pull away an ear muff for her own listening pleasure. After our nap, I began preparations for guests and a large barbeque with Jim's help. Although a chilly breeze from the ocean cooled the outside barbeque area, I liked it for the actual barbeque, with our enclosed deck acting as the area for serving. Jim set the table places while Stacy, Ellen, and Temple fixed our extras. Our barbeque proceeded without incident, other than a businesslike atmosphere of how Eric Stargie, Audrey Mercal, and Aga Saleh would be handled in our time frame.

The kids walked the beach along with our friends not part of the Cantelli-land death cycle. I began our talk. "We don't do anything at all until Stargie is in hell. Bone and I have eyes on Temple at all times until the threat is dealt with."

"If this guy is as bad as Rick and I think he is, we must have all assets in place to confirm what we learn about his victims," Lo added. "We'll find a way to give their families closure sometime in the future."

"How do we know about the victims or Stargie's connection to them," Meg asked.

"I found a list of suspicious disappearances in each place Stagie lived," Bone said. "It's too much of a coincidence. If the cops would have had even a suspicion, things would be different. He'd either be on death row or in prison forever. The list is all high school aged kids. Most got written off by the cops as runaways."

"Good," Trish said. "We'll have a list to check against when Lo gets Stargie talkin'. Do you still want me to be at his place once you have him?"

"We're covering all the bases, Trish," I told her. "The list is the ultimate, but these sick bastards usually take things from their victims. Finding his stash will be important and the first thing we'll make him tell us the location of."

"That damn Ellen is scary good," Meg said. "The brat was right, even though she nearly got Temple killed."

"Yep. Mars Bar is under observation from now on," Lo replied. "If we don't get her survival instinct working, she won't see sixteen."

"Jim won't give her a chance after this to screw up in his purview," I told them. "I've talked to him and he will rat her out in a heartbeat from now on."

"A good part about this near disaster is Hooterville Jr realized how Stargie put the finger on them," Lo said. "It was after the fact, but still good instincts. We'll go after Mercal right after Stargie. If we get a legitimate bust for Bill at nearly the moment Stargie disappears, it will shift suspicion from anything to do with us. Rick will be in hiding here at the beach house until we move on Stargie. I'm sure everyone's seen the 'Killer Cantelli' headlines back in the news. Everything he's involved in will be under the microscope. Rick and Bone will work with Stacy doing the set up work for Mercal. By Thursday, the only thing we should need to do is catch Mercal in the act handing over the fake IDs."

"I know this won't be for the rest of us, but what about Saleh? Have you heard any news on whether he's suspicious of the dead Syrians," Trish asked.

"So far, so good on him," I answered. "Lo talked to Floyd. He's lying low at the San Francisco embassy. We hoped for some time to pass before dealing with him. When he thinks he's safe and no one suspects his involvement with the Syrians, Saleh will start moving around town. That will be our best opportunity. An ambassador is a tricky deal we don't want anyone else in on at any level. Lo and I will figure out how best to take him."

"There's fallout from the BLM, Rick," Bone said. "The racist bastards are trying to make those six dead punks into saints. It's not working so far thanks to keeping their records on display in the media. Three of them have been identified in armed robberies the cops didn't know about. Steve and I are watching your house. It's under 24/7 watch along with Temple's place. They're lookin' for you, brother."

I'm more worried about Bone. "Understood. I heard the media questioned you about Madigan/Cantelli employment. Are you getting any heat over this?"

Bone chuckled. "I own the street. BLM don't move around here without me knowing. Lo gave me a small fortune to keep our information network on the street feeding us info on the BLM thugs. My guys watch Mom's house and mine. I've got workin' dudes from my time in the Army spreading cash amongst blue collar folks that know 'Black Lives Matter' don't care about no lives other than their two-bit paid off pawns runnin' it. I'll be fine."

"Take nothing for granted, Bone," Lo cautioned. "If you get any kind of trouble on the radar, we all move on it."

Bone shook his head while taking in a deep breath. "Who in the hell ever figured the race baitin' assholes would ever be allowed to take foreign money to act as terrorists targeting the police? It's insane!"

"Amen, brother," I said.

Lo pointed a finger at Bone. "I can't afford to lose you, Timothy. Your black ass matters to me. Don't underestimate the punks and get yourself killed. You call me or Rick without hesitation."

"Understood, Lo."

* * *

Eric Stargie allowed the thrill of a hunter obliterate all other thought. He sniffed the air around Temple Donavan's mansion, the early morning, 1 am air seeping into his consciousness with an added ecstasy of purpose. He crept forward without worry of dogs, guards, or alarms. Eric knew his security system jammer would render any security system the bitch had in place useless. At the front door, Stargie went to work with his digital code cipher. In minutes, he was inside Donavan's estate. This would be his greatest conquest of all time. *I'll have that tasty little bitch for a long while, maybe even days. I'll...* - the Taser needles embedded in his clothing

58

seconds later, and the last thing Eric could remember was a cackling escort into painful unconsciousness.

* * *

"Is he breathing, Sis," I asked. Man, that was a long electronic dance. It illustrated how much Lo cared for Temple. It didn't really matter though. Eric wasn't going to lockup. We planned to find out everything about his victims. Then we'd dump him alongside of the road somewhere in the salt flats near the Dumbarton Bridge. "I think he started getting rhythm by the time you finished baking him."

"I could almost hear his thoughts. This little weenie thought he would get Temple for an extended time in hell. Wake him up, Rick, and don't be gentle doing it. I'm going old school on his ass."

"Let me get him on the tarp, restrained and ready, Sis. We should do this here while Temple's staying at my place. If we take too long, we'll be in danger of someone else getting Temple. Stacy's a heavy sleeper."

I fixed Eric for questioning, without clothing or a prayer of ever living another hour, inside a big blue tarp. Lo waited patiently with pliers and propane torch in hand while chuckling at my reference to Jim and Temple in the same house without mishap. "There... that's got Eric nice and cozy. Wakey...wakey, little Eric."

My bitch slaps decorating his face in methodical expertise, woke our buddy painfully into cognitive understanding, he wouldn't be going to Disneyland after this. "Hello...hello... Eric the red-face. How you doin'? I'm Rick. I'm your facilitator into hell. My partner next to you with the pliers and propane torch is Lois Madigan. She's going to reawaken your memories concerning past victims."

"I didn't... do anything! I'm in the wrong house! What victims? I'm wasted. I-"

"You're in the wrong house, Elmo," Lo interrupted, clacking her pliers together. "I'm going to set your house straight. Rick's going to hold you tight while I introduce you to your pain threshold.

For a pussy like you, I figure your pain threshold somewhere between a two year old with an earache and a kindergartner scraping a knee on the playground."

I held onto Eric the bucking bronco while he tried to shake, rattle and roll into a different dimension. I pinched his nose off. When he opened his mouth to suck wind, Lo extracted a few teeth he wouldn't be needing anyway. I gagged him and Lo moved on with the propane torch. She gently stroked Eric until he was lightly toasted. We waited for our serial killing companion to downgrade from muffled screaming to simple sobs of abject terror. I removed the gag. Lo stroked his cheek with a big smile.

"I think we have the introductions over, Rick. I believe we've reached an understanding, right Elmo?"

"Yesssss... God yesssss... what do you want to know?" Eric writhed, searching for some relief from his mouth, gums, and toasted exterior not forthcoming.

"Everything, honey," Lo replied. "You're not famous. You're one of those hideous little creatures the True Crime novelists write about. I want every detail from your life concerning victims, including where we can find the proof. I know a perverted weasel like you will have trophies or souvenirs or whatever you call them, collected from your victims. We have someone to check on your place, or anywhere else you might stash them. If you don't have any information, I'm going to extract the rest of your teeth, and caress your worthless soul with my torch until you're crispy brown. Start talking, Elmo... right fucking now!"

It took a while for Elmo to sob his way through fourteen victims' whereabouts, complete with proving their number, and their taking times and places. He also provided the proof by telling us where he stashed the trophies collected. Trish called us to confirm number and hiding place. Lo and I aren't the touchy feely sort. Lo extracted the rest of his teeth and toasted Eric golden brown before I gave him the kill shot with my hypodermic eternity needle. I didn't like handling Eric inside Temple's house, but it couldn't be helped.

60

We dropped him off and went home to get some sleep before we captured our counterfeiter, Audrey Mercal.

                    * * *

Stacy had her part down in our sting perfectly. We spent a couple days helping her make contact, forward her information, and reach a price. Bone hacked and monitored all movements Mercal made after Stacy initially contacted her. Mercal checked Stacy's jail and prison record through a contact at the records office who would soon find herself out of a job. She also made sure Cheech Garibaldi owned Godfather's Cell where Stacy worked. Mercal settled for ten thousand dollars, half to be paid up front, and the other half on delivery. It was a rip-off, but we figured Mercal wanted a percentage of what she thought Stacy had embezzled from Cheech. He had been informed about our con. Garibaldi got a big laugh out of what had been a big fear in the past: a Stacy backslide into oblivion. Stacy acted out her big scene, talking live to Mercal with her usual excellent con-artist expertise, complete with tears and real fear.

Everything at the beach house, very quiet on the early Thursday morning, projected a wonderful panorama on the sand. I jogged along the beach, remembering 'Hell Week' in the Navy Seals entry program basics as usual. I had come a long way since then. Political situations and Lois Madigan's recruitment of my naïve ass into the CIA haunted my thoughts this colorful horizon morning. I counted my blessings first, with Stacy back in my life, bringing along grandson, Jim. Like the old 'Tale of Two Cities' by Charles Dickens, me and a lot of other folks around the world were living in Dicken's cogent line 'It was the best of times, it was the worst of times, it was the age of wisdom, it was the age of foolishness'. I would substitute 'self-indulgent suicide' for foolishness.

I jogged and I hated jogging. I feared if I only walked, my mind would infuse nightmarish visions of the way the leaders of this wonderful nation destroyed everything the original creators of America envisioned. I ran at a steady pace with tight lipped angst realization I couldn't hide, dispel, or alter the path of America. I figured a lot of citizens felt the same way, both liberal and conservative. Unfortunately, the feel good liberal method of running a country, ignoring laws, moral codes, and the right of a free people to not be taxed into obliteration had somehow become racist and xenophobic. Entitling terrorists, deadbeats, and illegal aliens to vote and be listed on our welfare lists, while for some reason embracing the death of common sense and logic, had taken over the liberal priority list.

I didn't leave my sanity or survival instinct at home. I spotted the rapidly approaching figure in full clothing. I had no idea who it was in the dawn beginnings of light. I knew the person's appearance directly in front of me had nothing to do with two ships passing in the night. I already had a wound. I didn't want another one. I drew my replacement Colt out of its snug holster at my back. I smiled as Speedy became recognizable. He started firing the moment after his identity became clear to me. Speedy thought with a fourteen round clip he couldn't miss me at twenty-five yards no matter what I did. He was wrong.

From the first recognition, I hit the sand to my left, away from the ocean. I felt the sand granules digging into my skin, my head, and all the unfavorable places I learned to embrace during my admission to one of the most elite forces on earth: the United States Navy Seals. Speedy fired and fired. He lacked the discipline to understand his target continued to move and he lacked the imagination to realize where I would logically roll to. It didn't matter. I'd envisioned the moment I didn't see sand kicking up behind me, I would reverse my roll. It was so funny. Speedy reached the end of his clip, pulling the trigger even after his slide told him the weapon was empty.

I smiled as I came into position to fire from the sand. Speedy threw his weapon down and put his hands up in the air. I shot him right between the eyes. When he collapsed, I annoyingly extracted myself out of the sand, which clung to the already sweated spots I incurred while doing my most hated endeavor of jogging. I sighed, brushed my ass off as thoroughly as I could and got to my aging feet.

I walked over to Eddie Tanner. I waited, watching him bleed out. Once dead, the corpse stops bleeding. I called Lo. She was already up.

"Okay... I know damn well you didn't call me to shoot the shit, Peeper. Did you hear from someone important that was stupid enough not to call me first?"

I smiled at my iPhone screen Facetime picture of Lois. "I unfortunately encountered a person of interest on our list who finally decided it was time to die. Speedy came calling during my jog on the beach."

Lo started laughing. It took many moments for her to regain speech. "Oh my God... Speedy thought he could come kill you in revenge! Good Lord... he had an out to disappear. Oh my! Okay... show me, Peeper. Quit teasing."

I gave her a head to toe close up viewing of Eddie. I focused it back on me. "Eddie died with his boots on, Lo. He pissed on his ending by throwing his weapon on the ground when he missed me with a fourteen round clip and held his hands up in the air."

I had to wait many moments while Lo enjoyed that word picture. "Neat... huh?"

Lo sighed. "I'll be over in an hour. Drag Speedy's ass to the beach house front. Do you have anything to put him in?"

"We haven't touched our body-bag supply here, Lo. I wish it were easier, but we'll have to take Eddie out for a burial at sea. His demise can't even be remotely mentioned anytime soon."

"Agreed. Frank's sleeping in. Let's do some fishing while we're out."

"I like it, Sis. I'll get the big thermos of coffee ready before you come."

"Make some sandwiches too while you're being such a homebody."

"Done deal. We needed to run the boat a bit anyway. I'll have to lie to the kid. I have a feeling Jim will be up."

"Why lie? Get Jim to help you. You told me he has the day off because of a teacher's conference. Cover goofball in sand until you and Jim can get to him again for bagging. That sucker weighs too much for you to drag him alone if you don't have to. Go on. Get movin'."

"See you." I disconnected, thought it over, and did as Lo ordered. At some point in the future, if he didn't already suspect it now, Jim would have to be read in on what Lo and I sometimes do.

I retrieved Eddie's personal effects and weapon before covering him with sand. I marked the spot with a circle of washed up kelp. I jogged back to the house. Jim was indeed moving around in the kitchen. He waved at me, noticed I tracked sand granules with every step, and took a closer look at my sand crusted face. Then he noticed Eddie's weapon and wallet in my hands.

"Did you fall down in the surf, Pa?"

"Nope. I'm glad you have your jeans on. Put on your shoes while I fetch a bag out of our storage cabinet, kid. I'll explain while we walk the beach."

Jim wasted no time. He went looking for his shoes while I located one of our three body bags Lo and I store there for emergencies. Jim followed me to the sand without questions. I brought along a collapsible shovel for cleaning purposes and my range finders. The beach was deserted at 6 am, but it wouldn't be for long. Anyone in the houses around us curious about what we were doing would need binoculars to see with.

"Eddie Tanner tried to kill me this morning while I was jogging. I killed him. I need your help bagging his big butt and dragging it to the beach house. Your Aunt Lo will be here shortly. I'll take a shower. We'll load Eddie in Lo's GMC and if you want you can go out on the boat with us fishing. We go out quite a ways."

"Do you weigh the body down?"

64

"We don't need to get into that, Jim. Tanner's heavy. Lo suggested you'll need to know the truth soon anyway. We can't keep everything we do from you. She thought it best to not keep you in the dark."

"Does G-ma know?"

"She knows everything about me. She doesn't know everything Lo and I have done over the decades in defense of the nation and our friends. Neither will you. We don't want you implicated in anything. I hope you can trust us to be on the right side of what we do."

"I do, Pa… without question. I'd like to go along with you and Aunt Lo."

"Okay then. I can give you the graphic details about body disposal at sea if you want to hear them." We arrived at my kelp marker.

I uncovered Speedy, using the range finders to keep tabs on company. Jim helped me with putting him in the bag. I showed Jim the easiest way to slide the body into the bag. I covered the blood pool, digging a hole beside it, stirring everything, and shoveling fresh sand all over it. I then cut my kelp in half. I arranged half over the blood grave. The other half I used every fifty yards we dragged the bag, to stir fresh sand over our trail. When we reached the house, Lo was standing by the gate, motioning to us. She had a throw rug next to her spread for Speedy's body-bag, which Jim and I rolled him up in. I went back with my kelp brush and did some final stirrings to make the trail much less noticeable. We carried the carpet bundle to the GMC cargo area Lo had a plastic painter's tarp covering. Moments later, we were walking inside the beach house.

I took a shower in minutes, made a huge thermos of coffee and a half dozen of my multiple layer sandwiches. Lo sipped a cup while talking with Jim about the facts of life in a bit more detail. I sat down with them after packing our picnic bag and getting some coffee for myself.

"Aunt Lo explained about situational times like these. The only thing, calling the police into the case would accomplish, is get your name on the front page again. I'm still interested in how you dispose of the body. Couldn't it drift back into shore like those bottles with messages that appear at times on beaches?"

"I cut the body down the middle as when a hunter dresses a deer, Jim. I take out everything inside, making sure to puncture all parts, before throwing them overboard. The intestines and stomach, if left in a body, bloat with gas. They will keep a body on the surface. With the body stripped of everything, it will sink below the surface to be nibbled by scavengers, and even sharks, because of the blood."

Jim never blinked. He listened intently. Lois watched the boy's face during my explanation. She nodded at me. "He's okay, Rick. That's the worst of it, Jim. Still want to go fishing with us?"

"As long as we don't fish near the body, I'd really like to go."

"Let's get started then. I'll leave a note for Stacy to let Ellen know Jim won't be over with Temple today very early. I know they wanted to be in on our final run through before Stacy meets with Mercal, but that can't be helped." In minutes, Lo was driving us toward the dock where the Madigan/Cantelli boat was docked. I called it 'The Harpy' but the boat title was Sea Breeze.

"I don't know how you two do it," Jim said. "It's like things just explode around Madigan/Cantelli suddenly, as if a bomb goes off."

"Your Pa and I have dealt with these times ever since I recruited him from the Seals. He was a sullen, disillusioned young buck then, deadly as hell, and wanting to do right. I wanted his ass with me at the Company. This crap with the BLM gang and Moslem morons will have to be dealt with one thing at a time. Speedy in the back was just plain stupid."

"Lo and I don't keep anyone near us who can't take the heat,

66

Jim," I admitted. "When your Grandma triggered a decision not to lie down and croak in peace, we ramped up to the way we used to be. We're older, in shape, smarter than ever, with a great team around us who know the score. We're enjoying life again. We never did take to that toned down version of ourselves where nimrods thought they could disrespect us like we were a couple of aging loons. We're back in the mix for good now with reestablished CIA and FBI contacts."

"All that… and just as deadly as ever too," Lo added. "We don't want you looking at us like we're a couple of superheroes on a binge. We're cold blooded killers. We'll torture and kill without a second thought. We want to train you. I don't know if you'll go anywhere with the training as we have; but in this day and age, the training will possibly save everyone you love one day."

"I want it all, Aunt Lo. I've seen all the perversion and crap from my foster home days. You and Pa handled those child predators like they were muffins, ready for the oven. Do you think Ellen can learn?"

Lois sighed. I knew she liked Ellen a lot. "I can't trust Ellen to do what needs to be done, whether it's sharing her gut feeling on a pervert like Stargie, or being aware of danger she puts loved ones in. We'll have to reserve judgement on her for now. I have no such qualms about you, Jim. That's why Rick and I are reading you into all this at your age. If any of this creeps you out, say so. We'd be arrested for exposing you to any of this stuff."

"Nothing creeps me out," Jim stated. "I'm glad you and Pa are honest with me. The movie business is exciting. Working with Temple in a setting like that where we're creating a vision someone writes for us makes me feel like I'm creating something. I like the thought of entertaining people. So does Temple. I want a part in real life where I can help make a difference rather than a fantasy. I've read where a few of those goofballs who starred in 'The Sopranos' actually thought they were in the mob and got themselves arrested. I know the difference between reality and fiction."

"I think you do, Jim," Lo replied. "We'll see how you take to this ultimate screw-up by a human idiot. Eddie Tanner had a chance to disappear into whatever rat-hole he desired. Instead, he emptied a fourteen round magazine at your Pa, sure he had a kill, and if he didn't, he'd throw his hands in the air, surrendering. Your Pa and I don't do surrendering. The difference between fantasy and reality is important for more reasons than you know."

"Lo and I don't leave people alive once they try to kill us, and sometimes when they just hint at killing us," I told Jim in matter-of-fact tone. "It's the main reason she and I are still alive. We don't do mercy, especially with a dangerous felon like Eddie. If you believe in second chances for deadly individuals, you should stay on the pier until your Aunt Lo and I come back to drive you home."

"I understand, Pa. I want to go. Besides, your old butt needs my help taking Speedy on board."

Lo enjoyed that poke far too much.

Chapter Four

Blood Ties

I am a butcher in a way. I have no feeling for my targets or respect for how I treat them after I take their lives in extremely violent ways. When I fix one for a burial at sea, I don't wrap them in a shroud, anoint them with oils, or even say 'Vaya Con Dios'. I take them from their body-bag, placing them on something I will discard later that will hold in the more slimy gel of dead life. I sliced Eddie and gutted him like a freshly shot deer with a scalpel. I sliced his entrails before depositing them in the water with his punctured lungs, kidneys, and liver. I felt no remorse or joy.

When the waters began stirring with scavengers, I deposited Eddie's empty carcass into the sea. It stayed atop the water briefly before a group of larger scavengers hit him. Jim remained motionless during the process. He didn't move until Eddie disappeared forever beneath the waves. We lived in a time when our most dangerous enemy taught their children to mutilate animals and smear the blood on their faces. Their own parents sent them out with suicide vests on to blow up other more innocent children. The creatures of Islam positioned their children to mutilate and kill hostages. Jim would never do any of those things; but after I trained him, he would be well equipped to deal with our enemy. Once shed of Eddie, we motored far away to fish, drink coffee, and eat my wonderful sandwiches, at least Lo and I ate.

"Here, kid. Drink this," Lo handed Jim a double shot of Bushmills while loading our coffee a bit with the same numbing agent.

Jim drank the whole thing down and held his glass out for more. Lo filled it a bit. "Sip that one, Jim."

He sat down, sipping while Lo and I drank our coffee and ate sandwiches. After a half more of his drink, Jim accepted one of the sandwiches and ate with slow deliberate consumption. I baited all the hooks on our poles after we finished. We fished for the next couple hours with short but detailed answers to any question Jim asked. His questions about covert operations were well thought out. I could tell they had been haunting him for quite a while.

"Ellen thinks like that," Jim said finally after catching a large sturgeon and reeling it in for my net. "She spots unusual details I dismiss when I first see them, explaining… sometimes with annoyance, what interested her about them in the first place. Over the last few months, I realized I wasn't missing details… I was ignoring them. I knew when Stargie glanced at us at the mall when we tailed him there that he made us. I didn't say anything because I thought he was another one of Ellen's games. I won't make that mistake again. He could have killed us right then."

"No… he couldn't. Bone was only a ways to your right. By then, we knew Ellen was on to something. What we do certainly isn't for everyone," Lo said. "Temple is in our care. Ellen is not. Everything done behind Ellen's parents' backs can backfire on us in very bad ways. Using her as bait is not an option. We would never do so on purpose but you and Ellen managed to become bait a couple times now on your own. That's unacceptable. There will be no more second chances for Mars Bar."

"It won't happen again unless somehow I don't know about it," Jim replied. "I can tell her parents are worried about her because of the way she acts. I'm worried too. She hangs out with Temple a lot. They like each other. Temple admitted during filming of 'Logan Heights' she missed having Ellen around. Are we going to workouts and the restaurant this week? Monday seemed quiet at both places. You were sure getting eyeballed, Pa."

"Believe me… I noticed." Our regulars in both Jadie's Gym, and the restaurant, rightfully felt uneasy being in the same zip code with me. "We'll go. I'll keep a low profile. I figure if we arrive early, things might quiet down a bit. I'll miss playing Rick from Casablanca out front with the customers. It can't be helped. I admit to letting bad habits overcome common sense lately. I should have been varying my patterns everywhere. Complacency in this business is a killer."

"We better get back," Lo said. "Will you be okay to accompany Temple over to Ellen's house to pick up Mars Bar?"

"I'll be fine," Jim answered. "I texted Temple we would be later than agreed on. Will the Mercal meeting still take place at three?"

"Yep. Do you remember the ingredients for a successful sting we went over with you and Ellen?" I received a taste of what we explained to Jim while jogging this morning.

"Only allow a select few know when and where an operation will be conducted." Jim thought for a moment, deciding to let me know he did consider my brush with Speedy this morning. "You're wondering how Eddie Tanner knew where the beach house was, right?"

"I sure am. In answer to your original question, outside of Bill Staley, no one knows about today's Mercal sting other than the participants. Bill will gather officers to take Mercal into custody only when the meeting is due to happen."

Lo started the Sea Breeze's engine, moving us toward our home dock while Jim and I iced the sturgeon. "I bet you're worried about something else too, Peeper."

"I am, indeed. I'm thinking someone's been tailing us. With all the people we've had over to the beach house as of late, I guess Eddie followed one of us. It could be he did a record's search too. The beach house is listed under Madigan/Cantelli."

Lo steered us slowly around. "Those are my thoughts as well. There's no use in pretending we're moving around in secret anymore. We can hone down who accessed what digitally, but in the end, it won't matter. I hate giving the 'watch your back' lecture, knowing if someone wants to hit one of ours, they will be vulnerable no matter what we do. We'll have to go old school."

"Agreed."

"What's old school in a case like this," Jim asked.

"We round up the usual suspects and shoot them all in the head," Lo replied.

I chuckled inappropriately. "What Aunt Lo means is we'll have to do a sweep of all likely parties interested in us. Then, we begin finding out if they're getting into our business for reasons detrimental to our health. Right now, we have the Council on American-Islamic Relations and Black Lives Matter interested in us. C.A.I.R and the Muslim Brotherhood are joined at the hip, both with each other, and terrorist organizations like Isis. We parted on decent terms with the Logan Heights crew except for the guy Lo toasted, Leroy Adkinson. We know where he hangs out and lives. He's the only common thug we have on our list."

"So, everyone is stuck with heightened awareness, huh?"

"It does boil down to that. Our sweep of the interested parties should help. We don't underestimate these people but we don't overestimate them either. After we get Mercal today, we'll go to work on our own surveillance case. Going to Jadie's for a workout, followed by the restaurant bash for Casablanca night, will provide a lot of HD data from our cams in the parking lots and inside both places. We already have all the houses, office, and wide angle on the neighborhoods around all our places. You and I can start checking all our feeds from the last few days and nights. We'll enlist Ellen too. She needs to find out about the less exciting part of surveillance."

"What if we miss something though?"

"You won't, Jim," Lo assured him. "We have Company facial recognition software with database access to all the world law enforcement digital data, including Interpol. You and Ellen will be looking for suspicious movement of any kind – people without purpose, all vehicle license plates around our dwellings, and anyone hanging out inside a vehicle. Besides, Rick and Bone will be overseeing you two."

"What will you be doing, Sis?"

"I'll tell you what I won't be doing: peep work."

* * *

Stacy entered CiCi's Pizza place furtively enough, mixing the right amount of criminal angst with harried concentration. She dressed in her manager's outfit from Godfather's Cell for the meeting as if on break. We knew Audrey Mercal entered the pizza restaurant twenty minutes ago with two bodyguards. Trish and I worked behind the counter. We promised the owner a complete picture shoot with Trish, Jim, and Temple if he'd get his staff to serve while we took orders. The counter, a ninety degree serving center, enabled us to always be out of the way with our black ball caps with a big C on them. The red and blue pullover shirts worked well for the small holstered weapons at our backs. Lo had the duty out in our van. With Bone next to her, watching computer images of everything, Lo listened intently to Audrey and her bodyguards speak in low whispered tones. They ordered a small pepperoni pizza and a salad for the counterfeiter.

The location in University Square suited Bill, who placed his unmarked vehicles within attacking distance of the entrance. We planned on the exchange being made and Stacy walking out in the clear with everything recorded. Our perps would follow. Bill and his crew would make the arrests well away from the restaurant. We already knew what car they arrived in. It would be a quiet takedown. I watched Stacy enter. The terrified image she presented struck Audrey just right. Mercal nonchalantly motioned Stacy to their table, where the bodyguards seated her between them. Our networking provided loud and clear audio of every word. Trish and I wiped down the counter, then moved to the tables, taking our time clearing them.

"Money first, Alden. Give the envelope over to my associate on your right."

Stacy glanced around the inside structure with the grace of an acting pro while taking the envelope full of cash from her purse with slightly shaking hand. She passed it under the table to Audrey's cohort. Mercal pleasantly nodded when her associate gave her the high sign that the money was all there.

"Keeping Cheech off your ass should be worth more than ten," Mercal said. "I read where you clung onto celebrities and shit. What the hell did you do to screw up that gig?"

Uh oh. I watched Stacy slip into her shattered persona with ease as Lo cackled in my ear.

"I ripped Cheech off big time," Stacy professed in tight lipped hushed tones. "I hacked his account records one night at his house. I have the transfer ready to… the Cayman's. It means more money than my con I have going with that dumb-shit old gumshoe with the celebrity connections. He can't get it up to save his fuckin' life."

I had to do some acting then while wiping down tables. I could hear every voice stifling amusement, including Bill Staley. Trish dropped a plate on the floor on purpose to get below table level with her wiping cloth. Mercal and her buddies he-hawed for a few moments at Stacy's throwing me under the bus. We had anticipated the ploy for more money. To make it seem manageable, she carried another couple thousand on her.

Mercal leaned over the table, pushing the food dishes aside. "We figure another five would suit us."

Stacy's outrage without overly done emotion hit perfectly. "Five! Jesus… I have to get out of here right now," she told Mercal in hushed, wide-eyed assertion. "We made a deal! You're highly recommended. Look… I don't want trouble… I have two on me. Screw me… and I make you famous before Cheech cuts my throat!"

"Maybe we'll cut your throat here, sister!" Mercal grabbed hold of Stacy's wrist.

"Hold," I said quietly.

Stacy let the cold, calculating bitch surface as she stared

74

down at Mercal's clutching hand. "Take it or leave it... shit for brains. You're not cutting my throat here. You picked this place because you probably have it memorized for location and escape route. Make up your mind! I ain't giving you spit until I see the product. It better light my eyes up, or I make a scene in here you won't cover with these two bozos. You feel me... bitch!"

Mercal sat back in her seat, motioning for her minion to show Stacy the goods. "You'd best have two big on you more or you walk with nothin', you old crone!"

I peeked while Stacy did a very professional inspection of the fake IDs.

She smiled. "These are damn good, kid. I'm goin' to the Cayman's. Keep that to yourself and I wire you ten more as a bonus."

Stacy poked around, producing the other two thousand. She passed it to the cohort. "Pick your poison. I walk first or you do. How do you want to conclude?"

"You go," Mercal ordered. "You better make good on what you promised or I fix things so you won't enjoy a damn penny of what you took."

Stacy stood and leaned down on the table with both hands planted after accepting the fake IDs. "I have the money. You'll get yours when I reach the Caymans in one piece."

After clearing the bodyguard blocking her exit, Stacy walked with poise out of CiCi's and around the corner to where one of Bill's unmarked cars waited for her. She passed the goods over to them. Steve walked her to our vehicle and helped her inside with Jim, Ellen, and Temple. Trish and I made sure no one followed.

"Clear," I told Bill.

We waited then, listening with amusement as our sting targets spoke about getting the ten thousand bonus. Mercal confided she would find a way to get Stacy if she didn't pony up the bonus.

75

Little did she know that an old con just ate her lunch and stiffed her on the tip. We all waited in position. Trish and I went in the back and ditched our costume gear. We were to follow our perps out to their vehicle where Bill and his crew would take them. Our targets finished eating, did a restroom break, and walked out to their Dodge Charger. They were feeling pretty good, until the intercept vehicles shut off their escape before they could get into the car. Bill had two he could count on, our old friends Officers Jamile Crosby and Terrance Stanley. The other two officers looked a bit new to operations. Bill stayed with them.

Trish and I followed the complacent, newly rich perps, without them even giving us a backward glance. We looked completely different. I had thrown my shirt, tie, and jacket on while Trish evolved from pizza waitress to hot movie star in unbelievable time. In Cantelli-land, everything that can go wrong, usually does. Such was the case here. The unmarked cars cornered the Dodge Charger. It was going nowhere. We were ten feet behind the perps when they knew their money transfer had gone terribly wrong. One of the bodyguards went for a damn Uzi under his jacket.

Don't get me wrong. I think the Blue are trained, mentally prepared, and equipped to handle everything in today's society... except killers. I had spotted the dangerous one in CiCi's while he watched Stacy with every intent of killing her on the spot. No way was I going to let him pull that damn Uzi. For one thing, I was unsure whether even Crosby or Stanley would shoot in time. I charged into his back, taking him for a facial into the car trunk. He slammed face first into the trunk surface with audible thump. Unfortunately for me, the Blue on my right fired, making a nice groove over my right ear. Before the blackness descended, I dragged my Uzi pal to the pavement with a final elbow to the side of his head. My last memory was Trish's fading image, her weapon out, and pointing away from our perps. I latched on to her shooting arm.

"Don't... kid-"

I sure didn't have any pleasant dreams in wonderland. The

curtain of darkness receded to a dull, aching image of an EMT smiling at me. "Can you hear me now?"

I smiled with crooked acknowledgement of medical humor. "Yeah... I can. How'd I do?"

"Fairly well. You're on the way to the hospital, Mr. Cantelli. Can I go through a few basics with you?"

I noted I wasn't strapped into the gurney. I slowly pushed to a sitting position, waving off his attempts at keeping me lying down. "Let me sit. I'll go back down if it feels bad."

I felt the bandage on the side of my head. "No one else got shot, did they?"

"No, Sir," he answered. The EMT took me through a number of exercises with my eyes and physical reflexes. The worst was the needle light that felt like he stabbed through my brain. "Your pulse, blood pressure, and reactions are very good."

"Any chance of getting a couple of Vikings for the headache, kid?"

He chuckled at my homemade nickname for Vicodin. "I'd do it in a heartbeat but I can't."

I felt around in my pocket, found my iPhone, and called Lo. I knew she'd be on my trail. Her image swam into view. "Hi, Lo."

"Hey Peeper. Good to see you upright. Is this a courtesy call?"

"Do you have a couple of Vikings on you? My head feels like it's ready to bomb out of the dimension."

"I'm right behind you. Make the kids pullover."

"We can't do that, Sis. Pass them to me on the way in to hell."

"Will do. Trish is drivin'. She wants to know if you really can't get it up anymore."

77

I listened to the amusement at my expense going on in our trailing vehicle. "See you soon, Sis. How's Bill liking the bust?"

"Believe me... he's in heaven, especially when I told him you wouldn't mention anything about the idiot that shot you. She's on suspension and desk duty when brought back in."

"That's cold. At least she shot something. The guy I tackled was a killer. It's possible she would have shot him in the head if I hadn't tackled him."

My partner Lois enjoyed the assessment from a professional killer perspective. "You're right, Peeper. We don't even exist in this takedown arrest, so maybe we can put in a good word for the young newbie."

"That would be my call. I have to get off the phone, Lo. I need the Vikes. Please don't pay any attention to my attentive EMT saviors."

"You're golden with me, Peeper. Tell the kiddies not to get in our way or I light them up."

"Bless you... dear one." I disconnected and returned to a prone position with hands on my head. "If you value your safety, young man, please don't try to interfere with my partner passing me a couple of pain killers. I'm too old to await relief from your drug window."

"I did two deployments in Iraq. I can allow anything you deem necessary. Your partner told me you're an ex-Navy Seal. I trust you to not throw me under the bus."

I reached out to grip the kid's hand. "No way do I rat you out, brother. Thank you for your service, my friend."

"Thanks for yours." He added his additional hand in recognition of my words. "I followed your adventures with interest, including the Sana'a adventure. You're a celebrity with us grunts."

"Sana'a... that was one righteous op I won't forget for a long time. We..." I fell asleep. I guess the morning's adventure had dulled my pain somewhat after all.

Apparently, my sleep deepened into a coma. I returned from La-La land in a nice warm bed with a tube dripping fluids into my arm. My head didn't hurt. I thought maybe I had taken a couple of Lo supplied Vikes and went nighty-night. Not so – Stacy, Jim, and Lo sat in a semi-circle around the bed. The fact darkness outside my window informed me time passed while I snoozed, made my visitors excited welcome to consciousness a bit scary.

While Stacy hugged my arm and sobbed, Jim held on to her. "I told G-ma you'd be okay. That was a great tackle on the guy with the machine pistol."

Lo patted my hand. "Don't keep us in suspense. Does your head feel like it's still attached?"

"No pain. How long have I been out?"

Lo looked at her watch. "Just over five hours. They already checked you in the tube gizmo. The Doc said your readings looked good. He took a look at your arm too while you've been out. He told us it's healing well. I told Bill you don't want the kid written up for shooting you. Jamile and Terry said to say thanks. When the Uzi hit the pavement, they knew why you stepped in. That clown you took down's a contract killer, suspected but not charged in numerous murders on the East Coast. Makes me wonder what a two-bit counterfeiter's doing with a contract killer on the payroll, no matter how high end she is."

"I hope Bill pretends the shot didn't happen. We were assisting on the bust. It was bad luck I became part of the bust."

"Are… are you really okay, Rick?"

"I think so, babe. I'll know more once I get on my feet. See if you can find someone to give me permission to get out of bed. Stay with her, Jim. I'm trying to turn over a new leaf. I will be the conservative, well mannered, and cooperative Cantelli."

Lo snorted at that remark while Stacy and Jim went in search of my doctor. "The second bodyguard's done a nickel in Folsom for armed robbery up North. All three go on our list. Mercal nearly blew a gasket when Bill explained the evidence against her. Except for your headshot, this really was exactly what we needed."

"We've had a hell of a time this past week." I made the bed go up so I could take stock on whether I really wanted to get out of bed or not. "I feel okay sitting up."

"They'll want to keep you overnight. Concussions can kill you, partner. We can take you out if you want to go. I'm not going to talk you into staying. I hate hospitals. If you get a blood clot, at least you'll go out with your boots on. We have Aga Saleh on the radar too coming soon. We'll have to move on him if we want to get him before he leaves the country."

"I guess since we made Speedy disappear, we'll have to hold off on our talk with Ally too. She won't be going anywhere though."

Lo's brow furrowed into her Gorgon look. "I hate that bitch. That idiot Tanner could have went after us with a machine gun. She had no business letting him out. This is personal, Rick. Tanner's release had nothing to do with the law. St. Ally's after us, brother. She thought she killed us, releasing Trish. We have to work out something soon for her. You worried me, tackling that killer. Police brownie points or not, you should have shot him in the head."

"I won't argue with you. It was a judgement call." I rotated my feet off the bed and onto the floor. "I thought Trish and I were too close to fire amidst adrenaline charged cops. I would have tackled him lower but I had to make sure he would lose control of the Uzi. It worked out, although I'm sorry I got a rookie into trouble for doing the job. Have you heard anything about what the kid said? Maybe she fired after catching a glimpse of the Uzi."

"She already told Bill she thought you were another bad guy. She was so into the actual bust, she forgot you and Trish were there to guard the back door. Jamile and Terry said the opposite. They admitted to me that they're hesitant to shoot anyone lately, thanks to these fairy tales concerning the cops out of control, shooting

80

unarmed people. Talk on the street is the BLM thugs and gangbangers are baiting the cops with BB guns and other crap so if the cops shoot, they can sue in court or beat a criminal charge."

"Those two better get their heads out of their asses and fire. We'll do what the mob does and hunt down all witnesses to any justified police shooting a bad guy." I stood away from the bed, waiting for nausea or equilibrium problems. "I think I'm good to go, Sis. My head feels swollen; but according to you, it's always swollen anyhow."

"You have that right, Peeper."

"I'm going in to take a pee on my own. If Stacy and Jim return with a Doc, tell him or her I'll sign the release papers or whatever to take the blame if I'm wrong about how good I feel."

"Okay. You'll have to drag your drip bag tower with you though. Be careful and hang on to it."

"I will. Here I go, motoring on into the winter of my life."

The cackle sounded like music to my bandaged ears.

* * *

I awoke the next morning in my own bed with my mature maiden of choice stroking my head. I could tell she hadn't slept much. It is comforting I could now sleep with my first love princess without wondering whether I would awaken in the afterlife or without valuable pieces of my anatomy missing. I reached over to pat her leg.

"I'm okay, babe. If my inner alarm clock and temperature gauge are still working, it's 5:15 am and sixty-three degrees in here."

Stacy glanced at the clock. "Jesus…"

Stacy rolled out of bed to check our hallway thermostat. She stomped back in, hands on hips in annoyed form. "How the hell do you do that? It's 5:18 and sixty-three degrees on the nose. Get up you slacker. Anyone who can get shot twice in a matter of days, once in the head, and still tell time and temperature like some digital device at the North Pole should be up and moving."

"Come back to bed for a poke, Princess. I'll tell you my secret and give you a backrub so you can get a couple hours more sleep before work. I'll take Jim and Ellen to school."

Stacy gasped and dived back into bed. She began snoring lightly after our fervent interlude which I'm sure would have made anyone under sixty nauseous. I caressed her shoulder and as ninja like as I could, slipped out of bed to wash, shave, and throw on some jeans and a t-shirt. My inspection in the mirror revealed only a slight strip over my stitched wound, miraculously without swelling. I took care in washing my hair and body of hospital, sex, and the usual fragrance of being old.

Jim awaited me in the kitchen. The movies he'd made so far with all their long hours and demands had changed my young grandson as sure as any drill sergeant. He learned the demands of his new trade well, but without the damn DIs screaming in his face. The end product interested me far more than the trail that led there.

"Hello, young Jedi. How is the Force this morning?"

"A lot better seeing you moving around in one piece, and being awakened by G-ma's cries, signaling the lie to her claims of your sexual prowess."

"Gee… thanks for that. There are a few rules in this house, young Jedi. Anything of a sexual nature will not be discussed at the breakfast table or anywhere else unless it deals with flagrant violations of the trust I've put in you. Your G-ma and I are old and not to be subjected to young yuppie larvae critiques. Do we understand each other?"

Yeah… I brought him up short. "Sorry, Pa."

"Never apologize unless your apology means something to someone who cares. I enjoy every moment with you. What you say, I hear. If I need to make a statement of my own in response, I will. I just did. I respect your judgement enough to know I'll never have to

82

repeat myself on this subject."

"I understand. One thing you don't do is 'make nice' with me. I shouldn't have said what I did. It won't happen again. I'm glad you and G-ma are together. I should never have made light of it. Could I have coffee this morning?"

"Sure." I moved to the coffee pot and installed the filter element. After explaining how much coffee in scoops to add, I poured a pot of water in the coffee maker reservoir, and closed the hatch. "Anytime you beat me out here to the kitchen, feel free to make coffee. We have different flavors of coffee and any sweetener you have in mind."

"I'm so programmed with the movie shooting schedule, I'll probably beat you out here occasionally. Thanks for understanding. I never meant any disrespect when I talked to you."

I hugged my adult thinking grandson, trying to remember he was only fourteen, not twenty-four. "I know that. We interact by not only choice, but by rule. What I do is not to be hidden between us. My advice when someone approaches you about me is I recommend sullen one syllable answers – none of which has anything to do with the subject."

"I can do that, Pa. You and Aunt Lo are a rightful justice no one else can copy or even talk about. Our world is... I don't know... falling apart around us in bits and pieces. You and Aunt Lo set things right. You don't mask your beliefs or your actions."

"We want you with us, Jim. What we don't want is someone espousing our take on things but not believing the same way. If you doubt anything you see, come to me. Speak it without hesitation. Nothing you say can alter our relationship. Now... what would you like for breakfast, chipmunk?"

Jim laughed. "Fried eggs and bacon, Pa. I don't want to tax your abilities without purpose."

Why you little yuppie larvae clone. Yeah... I would have probably echoed his sentiments in the same venue. "Understood."

I got the frying pan out.

* * *

Oh crap. Jim started laughing. I should have been amused in the same way. I wasn't. I wanted to pop out of the GMC with weapon in hand to find out how many of the vagrants wondering around the front of the school actually had any purpose other than to piss me off. Signs claiming Islamophobia and racist leanings in a Black Lives Matter manner were being trooped on the sidewalk. The signs read 'No American Anthems', 'Respect Islam' and 'Stop The Killings' with upside down flags. I turned to Jim and Ellen with no nonsense orders.

"You two will go through the crowd out here and enter the high school. I will be on your six until you reach the doors. Anything that happens in between now and then is my rice bowl. Do you understand? Say that you do or I get angry."

"Understood, Pa." Jim took Ellen's hand and waded through the sign bearers without a glance either way.

Once past the line on the sidewalk, security guards lined the way, guaranteeing student passing in safety. I walked them to the safe zone and called Bill. He thought I was calling for a pat on the back.

"Hey Rick. Nice work on the Mercal bust. I heard you're out of the hospital. How's the head?"

"I'll live. There's a problem at Jim's high school. A mixed bunch of demonstrators with Islamophobia and Black Lives Matter signs, I guess protesting their usual crap, are in front of the school. My name's not on the signs, but I think this may be related to my wild weekend remotely. Is it legal for them to do this without a permit?"

"If they stay on the sidewalk, it's legal to hold a rally or demonstration. If it turns violent, that's a different story. I'll send a car around so they see a police presence. I'll contact the mayor's office and see if he has the guts to call it against the public safety.

Jim's at Patrick Henry High, right?"

"That's the one. I'm going to hang around in my SUV and make sure these folks don't try to get inside the school. They have five security guards but I doubt they're trained to handle a mob."

"You're not trained to handle a mob either, Rick. The only thing you know how to do is shoot everyone in the head."

I listened to Bill enjoy his witticism for a moment. "I was a good boy yesterday."

"I'll give you that and your letting McLaughlin off the hook earned you points. I'm not forgetting you kept that asshole from spraying us with an Uzi either. I'll put it to you this way. Please don't shoot anyone."

"Unless they attack the school, I'm not moving out of my SUV."

"Why don't you go ask the principal if the school wants to hire Madigan/Cantelli, the P.I. firm of the stars, for security? I'll call you with what the mayor says. I'll leave your name out of it."

"Thanks, Bill." I disconnected. He did have a point about maybe offering help. We were on stand down anyway, trying to allow everything to cool off. The crew was out making the rounds of the businesses under our protection.

I walked over to the nearest security guard. "What's in the school these people are protesting against?"

He was a guy about my age, carrying an extra twenty pounds. He wiped the sweat off his face with a smile. "You don't want to know. It'll probably just make you think you've been alive too long."

"Now you're teasin'."

"The BLM and Islamo-nitwit group got together wanting to be a part of the new anti-American fad some of the NFL idiots are promoting. They've upped their game though. They want to end playing the national anthem before any school games. They also want Islam sensitivity training for all the kids attending classes in schools."

"You're shitting me."

He smiled. "I warned you."

"You're right. I have been alive too long. Thanks for the details."

"Be careful going back through the meatheads."

"I will." I waited for an opening in the dozen or so marching morons, with the hope to possibly be able to slip through without any interaction, as I did following Jim and Ellen.

A couple of teenage girls in short skirts tried to pass by the banditos on their way in. One of the Isis beards blocked their way, gesturing at the girls' clothing.

"Soon you whores will be covered from head to toe!"

"We just want to get in to school," the blonde girl said, pulling on her friend's arm to ease around the hand waving clown.

Another of the Isis beard freaks moved nearer, reaching out to grab the blonde's arm.

"Touch her and I light you up!"

He stepped back slightly. The girls made a dash for the security throng. The security guards moved to open a gap so the students could pass. The beard wasn't done with me. Both of them moved into my airspace shouting in Arabic. I sprayed both of them in the face with my Eau de Mace special formula, guaranteed to make your eyeballs feel like they will pop right out of your skull. Needless to say, that exercise was entertaining. After watching their buddies screaming as they rolled around on the sidewalk, the other demonstrating jerks gave me a wide berth, as I waved my spray canister. The security guards were stifling laughter as they kept the students' way clear.

I made a call to Bone while the screamers were doused with bottled water by their friends. Bone answered on the first ring. "Rick... you okay, brother?"

"I'm at Jim's high school. Are you and Steve nearby? There's a bunch of demonstrators out in front of the school."

"Let me see. Patrick Henry is about five minutes away. Want us to come over?"

"Yeah... if you don't mind, I'd like to make sure these demonstrators don't decide to try anything inside the school. Bill has a patrol car in route to show a police presence. I see another van driving by right now. It's unloading four more knuckleheads."

"What's all that screaming, Rick," Steve asked.

"A couple of the beards tried to grope a couple girls. I gave them some eye wash to clean their mucous membranes."

"Damn... Rick," Bone exclaimed. "You used that military shit on them, didn't you?"

"What's your point?"

"That stuff is nasty."

"They seem to be enjoying it immensely. Here comes the patrol car making its round just in time to prevent my having to get my toaster out for some barbeque. I suppose you don't like our new stun-guns either, huh Bone?"

"It's all good as long as we don't have to put the Mace victims in our car. We'll be there shortly. Don't shoot anyone."

"Bone? You texted Lois?" The silence at my question answered it. "She'll fly over here on her Gorgon broom and grab me by the ear. I was going to call her."

"All done. You know I'm in thrall to the Gorgon," Bone replied. "Anything, Steve and I participate in, has to be shared immediately if we don't want to watch a building for eight hours."

"Yeah, Rick, think about someone else besides yourself when

87

you do stuff like Mace innocent demonstrators."

"Shut up, Henpeck. I didn't even think you'd be allowed out today after participating in our sting yesterday. Kris probably gave you a spanking for taking her to the movie debut last night."

To his credit, Steve laughed. "You're right. Kris sure as hell didn't like the Terrorist addition to our evening. She knows I'm making more money than I could possibly ever make anywhere else."

"Good news, boys. Jamile and Terry got the call from Bill. That helps. Talk to you when you get here." I disconnected while waving at Terry, driving next to the curb. "Hey, guys – thanks for stopping by."

"Why are there already two bodies in pain on the sidewalk, Rick?" Jamile leaned over from the passenger side, pointing his finger. "You better not have Mace victims to be transported or all that good Karma you got from saving my black ass yesterday goes right out the window."

"They're good, Whiney. They tried to do an Islamo-thug grope on a couple of high school girls so I gave them a taste of the good stuff. The rest of the Isis types and your brother BLM's have been eyeballing me ever since, but they don't want a taste."

"If I didn't know you could kick my ass, I'd get out this car and put a whoopin' on you for calling those jackasses my brothers."

"Sorry, J."

"Liar."

"The Captain called us out special, Rick. He wanted to know if you'd killed anyone yet," Terry explained. "He says you're in another death cycle and we have to do an around the block scan before we go near you. How's your head?"

"Pretty good. I'll have another scar. Big whoop."

"What's the demonstration about?"

"You don't want to know, Terry. You and J would simply ride around the rest of the day cussing my ass out for telling you."

"You're probably right, but the Captain told us not to leave until we know. He's going to add it to his report at the mayor's office," Terry replied.

I explained what the security guard had told me. They didn't take it well. Terry grabbed his partner before J shot out of the vehicle with rage guiding him. "Where the hell you goin', J?"

"I'm gettin' me a piece! I want to hear all about their retarded complaints. I'm sick of this shit. If they don't like the flag, the Banner, or separation of their crap bullshit religion and our schools... then get the fuck out! As to those other BLM bought off stooges, they're doing the work of liberal globalist fat cats. The only thing they accomplish is getting the Blue killed and rioting, all the while using their damn lies about Ferguson and that shithead, Michael Brown's 'hands up' lie. I want to Tase them, bro."

Terry latched on to his partner. "We can't, J! Calm down! We'll leave Rick alone with them for a while. He'll shoot them all in the head and it'll make you feel better."

Terry's gem hit Jamile just right. "Okay... okay... Jesus... this is what we served in the Gulf for – so these lunatics can come over here and shit on our nation?"

We all absorbed Jamile's statement question with uneasiness. We were broken out of our reverie by another Isis beard, running at the police car with his sign. I measured him, stepped a few paces to my right away from the patrol car, and delivered a beauty of a strike right to his nuts. Oh baby... his sign dropped on top of his wheezing, high pitched whine of monumental discomforted body. Terry, Jamile, and my reinforcements arrived with weapons ready. Bone didn't even draw our weapons of choice, which were Tasers and Mace. He grabbed the first of the bunch heading toward the squad car and dwarf tossed him in the air. Bone's adversary landed face first on the patrol car hood, and slid like gelatin down to the road surface out cold.

One of many reasons I hired Bone is because he can control a situation like no one else can. His toss stopped all movement toward the squad car. Bone smiled. "I have Killer Cantelli next to me. If any of you idiots reach for a weapon, he'll shoot you in the head before you can blink. Anyone wantin' to come at us with hands, will end their day like the punk on the road."

Terry stepped forward then, letting Bone know he was moving around him. "All of you will disperse immediately, or be arrested for endangering the public safety. Collect your people and leave."

The mob was done. They not only knew what Bone and the rest of us would do, they also knew five uniformed security guards were at their back, moving into position. After their fellow idiots were dragged toward waiting vehicles, the same van driver who had dropped off the newbie trouble makers that had attacked us arrived for pickup. I told J. He and Terry went after the driver once he was parked. Lo arrived with Trish and Meg. The Blue had backup. Terry ripped open the door. Jamile snatched the driver out and put him against the vehicle.

"Spread your hands on the van and assume the position!" In moments, Terry and Jamile had the van driver in the backseat of their patrol car.

The sidewalk emptied after that in a matter of moments. Lois was unhappy. She thoughtfully kept her angst in control as she intervened on behalf of Madigan/Cantelli. "Want Rick and me to find out what that troglodyte in your backseat knows?"

Terry took a deep breath, while looking at his partner, who was nodding in agreement to put the driver under our control. "I can't do that, Lo. I'll let you know all the details of who he is though. He's coming in for questioning."

"That'll have to do, Terry. Thanks." Lo moved closer to the Blue. "Rick and I want to make sure this demonstration incident is just 'Thugs Gone Wild' rather than these assholes carrying on from our bad weekend."

"Understood," Jamile said. "If he hints at anything other than the usual crap, we'll call you. I imagine the movie debut, and Rick's night visitors, have you watching each other's backs big time right now, huh?"

"Indeed, J… indeed," Lo replied. "I have a feeling though the bearded pricks think they can trash the Blue here like they do in Europe without a response. That ain't happenin'. They don't know what a rampage is yet."

Terry and Jamile exchanged an odd look Lo picked up on right away.

"Okay… you boys are beginning to annoy me. What's up? Madigan/Cantelli is on your side at all times."

"We've heard rumors of more ambushes like the BLM have done," Jamile answered. "It's the main reason the Captain wanted more info on this demonstration when Rick told him a mix of BLM and Islam's thugs were together on this."

"Bill should have told us, J. Rick and I used to specialize in ambushing ambushers, especially in the Middle East. I'll give him a call. Pass it around, kiddies. If someone gets a call they think is suspicious in a place ripe for an ambush, call me."

"Lo's right," I added. "We're at war. Lo and I are packing FBI/Homeland Security IDs. As she explained, we can consult on any situation."

"Don't call the Captain, Lo. Let us explain it to him," Terry said. "We have SWAT but they practically have to request the Governor's permission to get called out or to take a shot."

"We don't want any of you ambushed like happened in Dallas, Milwaukee, and Baton Rouge," Lo said. "We'll take the shots. We can spot an ambush if given situational intel in a heartbeat. You guys know when a call seems like a death sentence waiting for a place to be carried out. Take a chance on us… anytime… anywhere. We'll take the heat for whatever we do. We can be concerned citizens in the right place at the right time. Feel me?"

91

"We'll convince the Captain," Terry said. "You and Rick have backed us before, just like yesterday with the Uzi killer. The fact you two tamed 'Logan Heights' for the entire time needed for the movie shoot was damn impressive. J and I will call if we think we're getting dicked. Count on that."

"Good enough," Lo replied. "Thanks for letting us in on what's rumored. It helps on a few levels. There are brass amongst some of the feds that would cover anything to save the Blue in any situation."

Our group on the sidewalk watching the patrol car drive away turned to interact with the security guards. Lo handed the guy I had talked to our card. She showed him her FBI identification. "Call me if you need help in any situation, especially having to do with third world troglodytes."

Lois was a hit with the security guards. We adjourned to Lo's vehicle. She didn't waste time with politically correct talk. "This stinks. So as not to get called names, the damn mayor avoids embarrassing the Islamic/BLM media enablers. Instead of backing the Blue, he issues warnings to avoid being politically incorrect. That means everything we have is at risk to savage vandals. I know I speak for Rick when I say we stand with the Blue. He and I will take the hit when consequences arise. Anyone here not in all the way best walk away from Madigan/Cantelli now. As Rick said, 'we're at war', thanks to the pansy terrorist enablers in DC. Separation pay will be very good but I want an answer now."

"I want these bastards!" Meg wore the Blue. "Anything… anything I can do to help count me in."

Trish chuckled. "I'm a killer. I'm not going to pretend to love cops, or even America, like Rick and Lo. I ride for the brand. Movies be damned. I'm only sorry I didn't get to kill some of those sign carrying assholes. I give my word as a psycho - I will always protect what Madigan/Cantelli wants protected."

"I'm in all the way, Lo," Bone stated. "I love this damn goofy nation so much with all its faults there is no way in hell I'm turnin' my back on it or the cops. The Blue could have shot my stupid ass any number of times after I got home from overseas, all full of Sand type crap. Hell... I don't know why Rick didn't just shoot me in the head when he had to punch my warrant ticket. I gave him plenty of reason."

"I don't shoot any member of my 'Band of Brothers', period. You were lost for a while, Bone. Lo collected me when I was lost. You're with us, brother. What about you, Henpeck. Lo and I will retire you with severance pay Kris will be very happy with."

"Fuck you, Cantelli!" Steve shrugged. "I hated it when I left before. I'm not leaving again. If what J said is true about the rumors, we'll all work to confirm anything on the streets we run across. Those ambushes to kill cops made me think we are close to losing everything. We can't let this shit happen right in our own city."

"Good... we're all on the same page," Lo said. "If any of you change your mind it better not be in the middle of an op. Those rumors of police ambushes means Madigan/Cantelli is officially out of hiding. Tomorrow we hit the streets, back to basics. We've been off the collecting tickets market for a while. We're back on the skips from now on. Rick and I picked up a lot of tips when we were doing bond work. We find the perp and we collect him or her with full backup. We ain't doin' a reality TV show, but I don't want anyone in danger by being the Lone Ranger."

"Now you're talkin'," Trish said.

"Don't give me any crap, Skipper. You call in when the perp's found. Rick and I will be in on every skip trace and apprehension. We're going to make some contacts as we did in the old days. Small time pests will do anything not to go back into the system. We'll establish our own confidential informants with our lawyer's help. Chosen assets will provide us with insights, we can either pass on, or act in our own way to prevent."

"You two old bats are really going out swingin', huh?"

I gestured Lo not to answer Trish's rhetoric. It was a fair

93

question. "I'll take that one, Sis. I know you youngsters think old age is a promised blessing of easy times and lying in the sun like a snake. When you make a mark on life no one can steal away, you have to decide while you're in shape and breathing if retiring from something you believe in is an option. Lo and I have decided to go out with our boots on. We don't retire well."

"We know you two have our backs in all things," Bone said. "You don't hide anything from us that has to do with our survival. We know this business is not some assembly line job. I don't know if I'll feel like you two do when I get to your age, but I hope I do."

Lo patted Bone's shoulder. "The lectures are over. Let's get to work. The day is young. I'm thinking a special night at the restaurant is in order since Rick couldn't do any of our usual routine. I'll have Shelly handle the details of a limousine ride to the restaurant for all of us who wish to go. The weekend's coming and I don't know what it will mean for any of us in terms of the past week. We'll do what no one would anticipate and have a great dinner with entertainment at the Casablanca."

There was a welcome agreement for the plan except for Steve. I grinned at Lo who also noticed. "Too soon after the movie debut fiasco, huh Steve?"

"Can't do it, Rick," Steve admitted. "Kris won't go anywhere near 'Rick's Casablanca'. Let's go, Bone. I have a few places in the barrio to make some connections. I know how to do it. What's the expense account dictate for our ongoing operation, Lo?"

"The sky's the limit," Lo replied. "Rehearse the good cop/bad cop role with Bone. Make it clear we're not cops. I'm not sidling up to gangbangin' murderers to protect cops. If any of us find targets to extract info from beyond deals - that will be for Rick and I to make them see the light. Please don't mince words with me if any of you find a target of opportunity. I'm not PC. I maim and mangle the PC. Tell us the facts. Let us take it from there. That's good input, Steve. You're a native Spanish speaker. I don't plan on paying a fortune out to illegal thugs on the hunt for their next buck, but I know we have a huge Latino populace here that don't want the borders thrown open to terrorists and Cartels. I trust you to make good deals."

"We can make my folks proud," Steve offered. "Bone and I will only pick hard interrogation subjects from the bunch carrying Mexican flags around. My parents came in through the front door legally after years of waiting. You can only imagine how much they enjoy the thought of amnesty."

"I think we can make them proud," Lo agreed. "Remember the mission. We're in this for gathering intel on assaults to law enforcement. I'll have Shell text you all with your assignments for skips. I don't want to hear any whining. The lowlifes hear bits and pieces. Don't dismiss anything. Record what you hear. I'll determine the veracity and relevance."

"Let's go to work then," I said. "We stay on alert from now on."

"Does that mean you'll stay out of the 'Nite Owl' and the drunk tank?"

"My... what a lovely parting gift, Trish." I didn't think it was all that funny, but apparently, everyone else did. Lo, of course enjoyed it inappropriately.

Chapter Five
On the Hunt

Lo and I sipped coffee at the beach house with Stacy before she went to work. The balmy stillness of the ocean with very light breeze cleared our heads. We conversed amiably enough with Stacy before she left. Afterwards, the silence stretched comfortably while we watched the waves moving sand back and forth in a rhythm nearly magical in soothing even the most horrific thoughts. Lo's phone buzzed. She put it on speaker.

"It's Shell. Go on. Rick's with me."

"The police band claims Bev Segar and Johnny Rich are in our area. A store clerk called a sighting in from near the San Diego Zoo. It's probably a mistake. They fled the state down into Honduras, right? I only called you because if it is true, I knew any rumor would be important to you."

"You did right, Shell."

"I texted everyone with the latest pictures we have of the two. Trish texted me with a report on what went down this morning. I haven't paid much attention lately to the police band. I'm with you two on all of this. I'll update anything the police get about Segar and Rich the moment I hear it."

"Good. We'll check in once an hour too. Text everyone with the same directive."

"Okay, Lo. Talk at you then."

Lo called Van Carmichael immediately, still on speaker.

"Lo? How's Rick? I received reports this morning on you two. I'm going to transfer out there so I can stay abreast of Madigan/Cantelli news."

"Rick's okay. He was creased by a cop. We're keeping that

fact on the down low. We have something else. I know you would have called me otherwise, but have you heard Bev Segar and Johnny Rich are still alive?"

That comment gagged Van for a moment. "No fucking way!"

"We heard they died in Columbia by Company hand a year ago. I crossed them off our list. I don't like it when I find out two assassins with a personal grudge against Rick and me suddenly make their way into our area on the police band instead of a Company update."

"You have me at a disadvantage. I'm looking at the report as we speak. They died in a drone strike with collected DNA match and pictures. I had assets in the area collecting final proof. There's not much left after a hellfire missile direct hit. How accurate do you think the sighting is?"

"We're going to check personally right now. I'm calling Bone. Put him on the permission list for assets. I'll have him scanning the area in minutes around the sighting, with expanding parameters."

"Done deal. I'll work it from this end too. Thanks for the rumor, Lo. I won't waste your time explaining how bad Segar and Rich being alive would be. They know our entire network in South America after hitting our place in Bogota. We hit them with the drone strike within hours of their assault on us. Why wouldn't they have revealed our network down there to the highest bidder?"

"I'll ask the assholes during the time I have them before their demise."

"It could be they lost what they collected in the assault when the hellfire hit, but weren't actually in the vehicle," I suggested. "They could have added their DNA to the scene in a number of ways. Remember, in Afghanistan, when that one Mullah Akhand carried around a pint of his own blood to add at a scene where he was suspected to have been killed?"

"It could be all of that, Rick," Van conceded. "We'll talk

again."

Van disconnected. Lo switched to messages and programmed the GPS to the sighting location at Oscar's Mexican Seafood on University Ave to her phone. "A waiter supposedly from Columbia works there. He's from Bogota, but I'll bet there's more to him than that. I hope he was smart enough not to have tipped Segar and Rich off. His name's Charlie Sapphire."

I laughed like hell. Lois only allowed my amusement for a moment before she popped me on the back of the head. That shut me up. "Hey… you do know I was wounded in the head, right?"

"If you don't want a matching one on the other side, you'd better start talkin', Peeper."

"Charlie Sapphire is our old buddy, Carl Santiago. He told me the alias when we were playing in the Sana'a sand."

"Shit… I should have told you the name before calling Van. If Carl made the report to the cops, it's legitimate. It also means Van assigned his ass to watch us."

"Or he's working for some other department. Van can only have Company assets working in the USA illegally. Self-contracting consultants like us are the only ones he can work without his ass being in a sling. Van wouldn't do anything like set young Carl on our tail anyway."

"You're right," Lo conceded. "I'm ringing his private line but he's not answering. We'll get the straight score from him. He's not stupid enough to get tossed by those two."

"I thought Trish was too smart to get plucked with Sam right out of her own bedroom too. C'mon. We need to get over and find Carl. I know where that Mexican Seafood place is."

      * * *

Lois drove, so all I had to do was make sure my seat belt harness kept me glued to the seat. Ten minutes later we drove in and parked at the small mall parking lot where Oscar's was located. We decided I should go in with my ball cap on and find Carl. It didn't take long. My buddy seated people while working the greeting desk. I asked to see a menu. Carl kept handling people on their way in for a meal while I perused the food offerings. I shook my head as if undecided whether to stay or not.

"It's okay, Rick," Carl told me in a hushed voice without his lips moving. "I figured you and Lo would get the message. Take this."

I accepted a small ranging GPS from him. "Nice. You always get great gadgets."

"I tagged their vehicle while they were eating. I'm shipping out for Columbia aboard a tanker. Bev and Johnny have reached the end of their rope with the Cartels. I'll turn on my phone. Call me in fifteen."

"Will do." I handed the menu back, making a reference to returning later.

In our GMC, Lo waited in calm fashion until I belted in. "Carl's on his way to Columbia tomorrow aboard a tanker. I think he wants to take a couple bodies down there with him by way of the sea for introduction references."

"One hand not knowing what the other's doing." Lo called Van back on speaker. "It's Carl Santiago that spotted the dolt duo, Van. Are you all keeping secrets from one another again?"

"Good one, Lo. Call you right back." Van didn't waste time on chitchat. Five minutes later he called us back. "He's undercover for the South American branch of NSA. He's never been seen down there, speaks the lingo like a native, and has the savvy to survive after working Sana'a with you two old goats. I'll make discreet inquiries. He wants to use Bev and Johnny as intro tickets down in Columbia."

"He gave us a tracker. Can we do this or not?"

"Like you'd listen to me if I told you no," Van groused, his displeasure at the prospects noticeably uneasy. "Think of it from my perspective, Lo. I just found out Carl is out there in your area, on his way to an infiltration job in Columbia. He had a lead from our Columbian assets about where Segar and Rich would be entering the US. They gave him a name for a worker at Oscar's who would be meeting the assassins, providing them with money and IDs to proceed East. They are to become contractors for the Muslim Brotherhood. If he needs something and you and Rick can help him, that's great. We dropped the ball. We thought they were dead. Period. I'm not dumb enough to make up dialogue with you, Lo, and wind up with my car wrapped around a tree in the middle of nowhere."

Van's reference to a certain Company head, who decided to screw us on a mission, provoked the needed amusement.

"We're on the same page," Lo said finally. "Rick and I will take out Segar and Rich when we find them. All I need from you is will it get Carl in trouble if we do as he says? The kid probably knows exactly what he needs in Columbia. We're not up on operations in South America. Those two will be dead. Carl's department obviously did a good intel job getting him placed to ID Segar and Rich. I hope Carl has orders for the Muslim Brotherhood contact. If you want them given to Carl for shipping, thy will be done. If not, we'll go fishing like we did with a serial killer you'll never hear about and give them a burial at sea."

"Eric Stargie," Van muttered almost in an apologetic voice.

"You son-of-a-bitch! You knew about Stargie and didn't stop him or tell us to stop him?"

"Look… you know the Company has assets everywhere on the continent. We can't target civilians or give intel to locals. We look for ways to get intel to local law enforcement through safe channels. Otherwise, we'll get stripped of everything we've gained. Why do you think I've included Floyd in this dangerous fucking game? He's a patriot. Floyd doesn't want a guy like Stargie killing people but if I give him intel on Stargie, he and I both could be wiped out in the Washington DC bullshit, PC avalanche."

I gripped Lois's wrist, shaking my head. She remained silent, her mind filtering everything in a clinical way. I watched her features gradually rescind from murderous intent to acceptance of reality. I secretly harbor the view Lois would authorize bombing the Congress like in a Tom Clancy novel.

"Lo?"

"I'm here." Lo breathed in deeply. "Erase Stargie from the blotter. A fourteen year old girl did what the Company was afraid to do – tell hunters where to find their prey. Back to business – bodies on a sea voyage with Carl or on a sea voyage with Madigan/Cantelli?"

"Give them over to Carl if it can be done. I'll work the details with the South American branch. We actually have someone with common sense and logic there."

"We want read in on Carl's op," I told him. "If we don't get read in, there's going to be trouble, Van."

"Understood. I'll work on it all." Van disconnected without a goodbye. Results were better than a kiss on our butts.

My recruiter, sister in all but blood and my most trusted ally for decades, spoke from the heart in a moment neither of us have had to face. We evolved with the political structure in America. We exited it to allow the status quo to right itself through elections and citizens realizing they were being duped by a globalist mentality to surrender their nation to chaos. She and I looked into each other's eyes knowing that would never happen. Through the public-school brain washing of our kids, and foreign interest money in the billions of dollars, America had been bought. It clung to nationalistic principals through rough folk, who would die before they allowed the enemies of our nation, both foreign and domestic, to enslave us to a Death Cult of Islam. The Death Cult never assimilated into civilization, or had any goal other than world domination. I reached over and gripped my sister's hand.

101

"We can't do it all, Sis… but I think we're at the root hog or die point."

Lois slammed her other hand on the table. "I'm sick of placating the DC minions of the Death Cult, and their media enablers. We need to stab this Islamic vampire in the heart, Rick, while we can."

"Agreed. After hearing about Segar and Rich adventures, I'm certain those bastards are working for the Death Cult in their chosen field of endeavor. I hope we can apprehend at least one of them for interrogation."

Lois patted my hand. "You and I both, brother. They'll need their pedophilia God, Mohammed, when we catch and interrogate them. Unbelievers, like Segar and Rich, don't care about shit. They'll proselytize for anything with a money connection. The Islam Death Cult uses them… so will we. Let's go collect them, partner."

I stood. "Yeah, Sis, Let's gather the tools we'll need. The hunt is on."

* * *

"I'm not leaving this damn place without eliminating those assholes!"

Johnny Rich tried to glide his hands in a gentle up and down, calming motion along his long time partner's arms, which she shrugged off violently. "Please listen, Bev. We barely escaped with our lives the last time we went head to head with those two CIA dolts. They don't hesitate… even for a split second. They don't care about collateral damage or any kind of external surroundings. Think about it. What would we do when we face off with them? We're assassins. We kill people through intricate planning. Fuckin' Madigan and Cantelli kill just to watch their damn victims die. We're good at what we do… damn good. We're only alive now because the shitheads stopped long enough to kill everyone in our safe house before looking for us. They don't knock on doors and say come out, come out, wherever you are, and be served with arrest

102

warrants. We need to make our way East, before anyone knows we entered the states alive again."

Bev Segar, a middle thirties, lean figured, pinched faced, cold blooded killer stared back at her partner with a condescending look of utter disdain. "For God's sakes, Johnny... will you for once grow a pair? What the hell do you think happens once they get word we're still alive? We have a once in a lifetime opportunity to get them when they don't know we're comin'. We're done in South America. In another few moments down there, before we got a private flight to Juarez, we'd have been doing a 'Butch Cassidy and Sundance Kid' imitation. I ain't dyin' in that third world rat-hole. We're in the states now... and damn if it don't feel hell-a-good, partner!"

"We should never have taken the assault job on the CIA assets in Bogota. Some of their damn agents are like the Israelis. They live by the feud. Crossing paths with Madigan/Cantelli in Lebanon put us on their list. I knew it was a bad idea to take the hit on them."

"No... it was a bad idea not to get the job done," Segar retorted. "We lost everything in our safe house. We barely made it into Syria with those hotheads on our tails. Fuckin' Cantelli took the damn shot from a moving vehicle nearly three quarters of a mile behind us and almost ripped your shoulder off."

Rich unconsciously massaged his previously wounded shoulder. "Exactly the reason I want to head East. We have our money and IDs. The Muslim Brotherhood has a place for us in Islamberg no one will dare hunt for us. We can work carefully out of there for a long time. The locals fear saying anything about the place. It's a Sharia Law No-Go Zone, perfect for us. We're on a roll right now. The exchange at the restaurant went without a hitch as did our arrival here. Why not ride our good luck into New York?"

"The Muslim Brotherhood promised us a hundred grand if we could do Madigan/Cantelli before driving across country. They have a place rented right across from their office. Our contact is staying there until we decide to do the job. It won't hurt to take a look at the setup. Once you see those two old bats wandering in and out of their office, you won't be able to resist."

"Do you think we can trust that Perry Monsour guy? He was professional enough at the restaurant. No one noticed the handoff at all."

"He's Muslim Brotherhood," Segar replied. "Our new passports and New York driver's licenses are perfect. I say we go over today and scope the place out."

A shiver ran along Rich's spine, remembering the .50 caliber hollow point tearing a piece out of his shoulder. He was a professional. Revenge meant very little to him. Segar would torture him all the way to New York if he didn't agree to at least profile the job. "Okay, Bev. Call Perry. See if he can meet us there in an hour."

"We're going to get those bastards, Johnny. They won't know what hit them."

       * * *

Perry Monsour, an Albanian national in the country illegally, stopped at the back break room to talk with the new greeter. "Charlie… I'm not feeling well. Can you cover for me this afternoon?"

Carl Santiago smiled. "Sure. I'm off break in a couple minutes. It's slow today anyhow."

"Thanks. I'll make it up to you."

"Yeah, you will, buddy," Carl muttered under his breath, watching Perry leave. He took out his phone. "Perry's heading for his little place on the corner across from your office, Lo. I'll text you the room number and location. Thanks for this."

"No problem, Carl. You may have saved our old asses."

"I doubt that, but my help will make it a bit easier for you and Rick to help me ship them on my tanker cruise."

"We'll be in touch, kid. Are you sure you want to do this Columbia operation."

"I'll be fine, Lo. You and Rick went on a lot hairier missions than Columbia. Rick told me about Bangkok."

"If you need help down there, you call us... hear me?"

"You'll be the first. Thanks. Do you want me to give you a hand on this?"

"No. Rick and I have to get this done on our own. Talk to you when it's over. Get your transport ready. Do you want all three or just Segar and Rich?"

"I'll take all three. I've done my research on Perry. He's been all over Europe at the Muslim Brotherhood's order. Anything you collect out of his place, I'll make sure gets to DC. I'll hit Segar and Rich's place the moment they clear it."

"Sounds good. I'll be in touch."

* * *

Monsour unlocked his apartment door, stepped in, and grew Taser needles. The juice Lo gave him rearranged the neurons in his brain for sure. "He's cooked, Sis."

Lo collected her needles. "The new Taser knocks the crap out of them. Drag him in the bedroom, Rick. We'll ask him a few questions after the other two get here. There's no use in getting into a rush and missing something important."

I did as told. After gagging and securing our new apartment dweller, I dragged him to the indicated bedroom and put him in the closet with something to help him sleep for now. Then, it was the waiting game. Lo and I had a lot of experience with ambushing apartment dwellers. We already had a plan for our two assassins. I would bark out for them to enter in Arabic. Lo and I wanted an interrogation session to find out just how much our deaths meant to someone. That fact would color a lot of other aspects of what we do.

105

Bev and Johnny arrived right on time. Lo waited behind the door. I waited by the balcony. Each of us held both a silenced automatic and one of our new Taser guns. We would take no chances. If they came in, weapons drawn, which is what they should do, we'd immediately erase them from the dimension. They arrived slightly early for the party, all the better. The light knock sounded. I called out from the place I planned to use for enticement in Arabic.

"Come in quickly. I am by the balcony watching Madigan/Cantelli!"

As the door began to open, I moved to where Lo awaited their entrance. They came in as casual as a couple of farmers inspecting the hen house, hands empty, and looking for Perry on the balcony. The Taser needles settled one of the premier assassin teams down in a split second of blinding pain, followed by Lo's St. Vitus electronic dance for Bev.

See... Lo heard rumors Bev Segar thought she was the baddest woman assassin on the planet. Bev let it be known we got off lucky the last time we crossed paths and she planned to take out Lois personally. I gave Johnny all he could handle until he passed out. Lo, however, dialed Bev up and down so as to keep her flopping on the hook, still conscious, with small yipping sounds of horror. Sometimes, we have to give partners their freedom. Lo cuts me plenty of slack. I went about the business of securing Johnny while watching the barbeque with interest. Lo was a master. She played the Taser controls like a maestro directing the Boston Philharmonic. We had a live one so I left her alone to work out her issues.

Lo finally dialed Bev down, taking a deep breath and issuing an audible sigh of satisfaction. She glanced over at my smiling mug. Lo gave me the wave off. "Don't say it, Peeper."

I made a comical zipping of my mouth. I handed her the Taser needles off the vibrating Bev. I cinched her into unmovable limb form and dragged Bev into the bedroom. Johnny followed with my careful tugging. I propped each of them against the wall with duct tape over their mouths next to Perry, who was conscious, and not liking the scene at all. Lo and I sat down on the bed facing them. Lois, always the entertainer, showed them her set of click-clacking pliers and propane torch. They were less than enthused, especially Johnny and Perry. Bev was sullen, showing remarkable recuperative powers, much to Lo's delight.

"There's my bitch." Lo knelt down to pinch Bev's cheek with fondness, while shaking it like an old maiden aunt on a Christmas time visit. "Oh baby… when I heard what you were going to do to me when our ships passed in the night again… I just got all tingly inside. Rick nearly decapitated poor Johnny on your flight into Syria from one moving vehicle to another. That sniper shit fills him up when he nearly makes an impossible kill shot. I got the Charlie Brown 'lump of coal' in my stocking. No matter, dearie, we'll make up for our lost time together now. I'm going to take your duct tape off. If you make a sound, I jamb this up your pussy and light it off."

Lo fired the electrodes on the most powerful stun-gun in existence. "Do you understand or do you need a demo?"

Bev was getting very fond of Lo quickly. She nodded her head virulently in the affirmative. Lo looked at me with disappointment. "What the hell, Rick?"

"Don't take the cave-in personally, Sis. They're assassins. Bev knows the three of them are dead. She wants to help so as to pass on into eternity with the least pain. Let's grant their wish."

Lois shrugged and ripped off the duct tape from Bev's mouth. "Okay… but this better be real good. We have all the time in the world. If your answers don't light a fire of truth in my soul, I'm going to toast you, honey. Rick and I are like human lie detectors. We know when you lie… and I admit… sometimes when we're unsure, we get violent and make mistakes. Be convincing, Bev. You'll only have one chance at it."

Bev did her best. She looked down away from Lo, spouted a convoluted series of events leading to her and Johnny arriving in San Diego. That on the surface, if insulting our intelligence and contacts would have been the main point, Bev did a bang up job. Reality was

107

a horrid mistress within my partner's grasp on interrogation. Lo patted Bev's duct tape back over her mouth as Bev's eyes widened in horror, realizing unfortunately for the first time that there would be consequences for her actions.

Lois stripped Segar of pants and panties to her ankles and rolled her tops up over her belly. I turned the music onto a classical station at a volume which would cover some sound without getting the neighbors up in arms. Lo pulled away the duct tape while I pinched Bev's nostrils off. I anchored her head in place. Segar's mouth opened to scream but Lois reached in with her pliers and extracted her two front teeth with a firm grip on horror and her pliers. She then patted the duct tape back into place over the wide open, screaming mouth of Bev Segar. Lo lit the propane torch while kneeling on Segar's legs. She ran it slowly at a distance over Bev's stomach and groin and back again. Bev was insane with pain. Lois smiled. Bev had been our example. Her Segar illustration worked impeccably. For the next hour, Johnny and Perry spilled their guts in detail no one would ever conceive as illusive. We received confirmation on a few key points from Bone before I readied their eternity shot.

"I told Bev we should have gotten the hell out of here the moment we received the IDs," Johnny muttered. He had looked away from Segar as I relieved her of all pain. "That was a hell of a shot in Lebanon, Cantelli. I wondered why you didn't fire an entire magazine."

I gave the sobbing Perry his shot and shrugged at Johnny. "I had my old Barrett M82. It's good for nearly two thousand yards. I didn't want to chance missing as we closed on the Syrian border. Lo and I had to turn around. We knew you had contacts on the border."

I moved over to him. "Ready, Johnny?"

"One other question. Why do Bev like that, Madigan?"

"Example," Lo said simply. "Some trash talk got back to me after you and Segar made it into and out of Syria. Besides, we were going to let you off easy, but then Bev decided to play hard to get. It was business then. You and Perry did good, which is why I didn't toast the two of you for the hell of it."

Rich nodded. "I wish she had just told you everything. I'm ready. Give it to me."

"Adios." I sent Johnny Rich into oblivion.

Lo fixed Bev's clothing. She took pictures and collected DNA samples while I bagged everything of an electronic nature. We waited for Bone and Steve to bring the body-bags from our office along with a luggage carrier on wheels we kept in the storeroom. I had Bone pass them to me through the door. "Do a walk through to the street front, guys. Observe what kind of attention we have. I'll call you when pickup is due to arrive."

"Okay, brother."

I closed the door. Lo and I deposited Perry, Bev, and Johnny in the bags. Lois called Carl. "We're ready, Kid. Where are you?"

"Five minutes away, Lo, parked and ready to move."

"Wait five and drive out front. We'll be ready for transfer."

With Bone and Steve's help, we stacked the body-bags on the carrier and transferred them down by elevator to the front entrance within seconds of Carl arriving at the curb. We threw the bodies into the back of Carl's transport van along with the bag of electronic goodies.

"Call us if you need us, Carl," Lo told our compatriot. "That's some bad business you're getting into."

"It's what we do. My three tickets in the back will help cement me in with the faction I'm trying to recruit down there against the Muslim Brotherhood. They had big plans for Segar and Rich. The ripples from their deaths will be felt on the 'Dark Web' for a long time to come as speculation will be rampant as to what happened to them. Perry Monsour was the Muslim Brotherhood's key facilitator. Where were Segar and Rich heading next?"

109

"Islamberg," I answered. "We will get someone interested in that place or else. Perry told us the IDs were made in the compound. Rich told us they would be operating out of the Islamberg compound."

"I've researched the Muslims of the Americas place there. Seventy acres at the base of the Catskills. Quite a place for storing underground bunkers for nearly anything under the sun," Carl replied. "I better get going. Thanks for getting this done. I know it's a little too close to home."

"It was that, Carl." Lo closed the door and waved. She turned to the rest of us. "Let's get over to the office. I'll forward a report to Van and send what we found about Islamberg to Floyd too. Maybe HS can take a closer look inside that damn compound. He must have someone who can get in there that knows how to find things. Sometimes, I think we'd all be better off if we shipped the entire Death Cult back to the Sand. With the State Department having already made citizens of people they were supposed to be deporting, it makes me wonder how badly we've been infiltrated all the way to the top of the political food chain."

Trish and Meg met us at the office. They had assumed Bone and Steve's patrol duties while they helped us. We had coffee and some lunch, compared notes on what our plans were, and to continue the confidential informant routine. The Segar/Rich bust with a Perry Monsour bonus would earn Madigan/Cantelli points. We needed to do everything from now on with deliberation. With everyone guided on their way, Lo and I left Shelly to handle the phones and coordinate. We went into Lo's office with more coffee. It had been a long few days for all of us.

"What do you thing about going after Setteridge?"

"Not much. She's too big for us right now. Maybe in a month or two we could go have a talk with her, Lo. Ally's not untouchable. If you're thinking to go against her right away, we can do a few things with Cleaver in a legal sense. He can file an harassment charge to piss her off. We might even win it."

"I was thinking more of what I did to my old pal, Bev."

"If that's what you have in mind, we'd better have Cleav working on Ally so there's a case on file when she gets admitted to the hospital. You are planning on her surviving our talk, right?"

Silence, with Lois playing with her pen.

"Do you know something I don't, Sis?"

"Something smells with Ally's sudden continuation of our feud. She's been burned twice now. I'll agree we need more background on everything she's been doing financially. We're at odds politically. I'm certain of that. We need hardcore facts though to face her down with so we can find why she's hounding us again."

I chuckled at that. "First off, she hates our guts because we faced off with her. Secondly... I think you're right. There are so many Islam dogs bought off and barking on command, I believe we have to assume she's in debt to someone. Her decision at this time after two harsh setbacks convinces me Ally's received a direct order. Let's put Bone on her ass with our newly acquired information permissions. He's excellent at spotting glitches. You and I are proficient at following a glitch trail."

"I'll text him immediately. He and Steve are hitting a couple neighborhoods for street intel. I told him to take his satellite laptop everywhere. I think you and I should stop by 'The Nite Owl'. I'll drive. You deserve to have a couple of pops after the crap you've endured. Is your head okay? I know we have a workout and a Casablanca Night later."

"My immediate response would be no way, no how do I take on a workout and Casablanca Night after even one pop. With everything that's been happening, I think I'll take you up on it. Can you drop me back home afterwards? I'll have enough time to walk over to the school and retrieve my movie star grandson and Mars Bar."

"Done deal," Lo replied. "I hope one of your acquaintances is serving now. They have a pool table over there too if I remember right. We'll recruit someone you know or play a little pool while you sip a couple until someone you know comes in."

"God... Sis... that sounds like heaven after Segar and Rich. If I try to have more than two, light me up."

Lois grinned. "Count on it."

* * *

Luckily, my 'Nite Owl' prior acquaintance in the barkeep business had only minutes ago come on duty. Her face showed a real enthusiasm at my appearance. "Rick! God almighty... I've been reading about you in the papers nearly every day since you last stopped by. Killer Cantelli? Jesus... did you really kill ten men in the last few days?"

Oh boy... and then some. "Hi Lacey. It's great seeing you. This is my partner, Lois Madigan. You probably have read her name interspersed with mine."

Lacey and Lois shook hands. "Any friend of Rick's is a friend of mine." Lacey looked around the bar. "You two look real grim. Are you here to take in a bond skip? I don't think anyone here isn't a regular."

"It's good meeting you, Lacey," Lo replied. "We're not really looking for anyone in particular. Rick's already vouched for you. We need a confidential informant in this neck of the woods. It pays five hundred a month and all you have to do is give me a call if you see or hear anything interesting or weird. Would you be interested?"

Lacey leaned forward over the bar with a smile. "I'll have to turn it down if it includes Rick's bar bills."

Oh my, did the ladies yuck it up over that gem. As Lois and Lacey ended their laugh-a-thon at my expense, I went over to the digital music machine. I plucked in my money to keep the hits going while I shot a little pool and sipped a couple of Bushmills. When I returned to the bar with 'House of the Rising Sun' playing, Lo handed me a double.

112

"Here… I like your friend so much, you can have two of these. I have Lacey's address and phone. I'll send her first check tomorrow. I have a couple of iced ginger ales for us to play pool with."

"I'm in, Rick. Thanks for thinking of me. I can use the extra dough."

"You'll do well, Lace. We appreciate you keeping an eye out for the strange at this time. You have a great ear for people. That's what we need. Lo wants to kick my ass in pool, so I'll try my best to alter her goal while sipping this wonderful elixir. Your sound system is the best, my friend."

"Enjoy. Lo told me you have your old love with you… the one who saved you from the tank the last time you stopped by. Congrats."

"Thank you." Lo and I went over to the pool table. I racked them after a satisfying sip of my elixir. "Lacey's perfect."

"She is indeed. They get a surprising number of tourists in here, along with regulars. This is a great bar."

"We'll have to do a 'Nite Owl' night with you, me, Frank and my designated driver, Stacy."

"I'd like that, but are you sure it's a good idea to expose Stacy to bar environments?"

"It's best to find out in our sight rather than out of it, Sis." I racked the balls.

"Good point. Eight-ball or straight, patsy?"

"Let me go with blind luck and pick eight-ball, Sis." I sipped while watching my partner. She beat me, giving me only one shot which I missed. We were enjoying the hell out of the second game where she missed putting anything in on the break. It gave me a small chance.

"Nice shot," Lo said as I put in my fourth straight striped

113

ball. She smiled while I took aim at my next ball before blurting out, "way to go, sniper!"

I missed and put the cue ball in the pocket. I laughed at how easily Lo had messed my head for the shot. I drained my shot and went over to get my second and last. Lacey had been watching us and inappropriately enjoying my defeat. I held up my glass before placing it in front of her with a flourish.

"Are you letting her win, Rick?"

"Uh… no. Lois is the most dangerous woman on earth I know about. Believe me when I say I would never… ever let her win. Who cares anyway, right?"

Lacey stared into my slightly inebriated eyes with clarity. "If you say it, I believe it, Rick. What's she done?"

"Like in the old 'Top Gun' movie, if I tell you, I'd have to kill you." I smiled and patted her hand while retrieving my refill. I moved to the pool table with my drink and luck in mind. I missed.

Lo beat me like a red headed stepchild. I sipped my drink as Lo did her victory dance of pumping arms and swaying hips. "Good one, Lo."

We laughed together, a part of being joined in all but blood. Lo knew I would try my best to kick her ass in pool, but without an intervention of God, I'd probably never do it. It was nice shooting pool in the nearly empty tavern while listening to my favorite songs. Then, we returned to Cantelli land. In walked 'Grasshopper' from the night Stacy introduced me to my grandson and talked me out of spending the night in the tank. I had worked the old 'Kung Fu' TV show trick on the big young punk walking in, with a dice cube from Lacey at the bar. He couldn't snatch it out of my hand, but I easily snatched it out of his. He didn't like it and almost got himself killed. Lo had laughed like hell when I told her the story of Stacy saving me from the tank in the bar.

I kept my eyes on the pool table, hoping 'Grasshopper' wouldn't notice me as he sat at the bar with his two friends. No such luck.

"Why's that young stud at the bar eyeballing you, Peeper," Lo asked. She noticed him without giving any indication of it. Lo finished me off with a bank shot of the eight-ball.

I moved closer as I grabbed the rack. "That's 'Grasshopper' from the night I saw Jim for the first time with Stacy. Ignore him. Maybe he'll go away."

"That's so cute. You actually think the land of darkness and shadow will let the sunshine seep in with warmth during your new death cycle, huh?"

"One can hope, right?"

Lo, with winner's break, put in two solids, leaving what looked like an open table to my defeat once again. "Heh...heh... no such luck, Peeper. Here they come. We can probably keep the police out of it if you get him to take it outside where I can zap the shit out of them."

"Or I could finish my drink, watch you run the rest of the table, and glide out of here."

"Good luck with that."

"I've been hoping to run into you here, Cantelli," Grasshopper told me.

"Hello there, Grasshopper. This is my partner, Lois Madigan. I never did catch your real name."

"My name's, Sam Cornwell. Don't call me 'Grasshopper' again. These are my best buds, Dereck and Roger. I see the old lady's kickin' your ass at pool."

"She sure is. Nice seeing you. I'll let Lo get back to kicking my ass at pool." I turned to the table with Lo immediately going to work again running the table. Unfortunately, our audience didn't leave.

"We're not done with you, Cantelli!"

115

Lo cackled as I dropped my head down in defeat. "Done with me in what way, Sam?"

"None of your stupid tricks will get you anywhere this time."

"Hey you, Dobey," Lacey called out from the bar. "Leave those people alone or get out of the bar. One more word out of you, harassing them, and I call the cops!"

Grasshopper's friends yanked him toward the bar. They wanted to drink. I gave Lacey a small wave of thanks. Lo went to work on me once again on the pool table while I sipped my drink. I began to believe a ray of sunshine eased away the clouds for a time in Cantelli-land. I smiled at Lois. She was all business with the pool cue. I could tell Sam and his friends disappointed her by going to the bar. Lo decided to stir things up.

"Let's play darts."

No one beats me at darts. Lois had never beaten me. "You're on a winning streak playing pool. Why go over to the dartboards and get your soul crushed?"

She enjoyed my rip of her ability to beat me. "You've had a couple, Rick. I'm feelin' the burn. Today's the day you're going down in 'Darts'."

I shrugged, walked to the digital dart board, put in the money, and promptly put all the darts dead center into the board. I pulled them out and brought them back for Lo. "Good luck."

"Next game, I'll blindfold you."

"It would be fairer... considering your dart throwing ability."

We yucked it up over that ace too. I threw left handed, right handed, and even over both shoulders. Four games of darts and Lo gestured defeat.

"Damn snipers."

"We should return to the office. We've recruited Lacey and avoided any barroom brawls. I'll catch a few hours' sleep before

116

working out. Casablanca Night will be fine then."

"You're planning on hitting both places early too, right?"

"No doubt about that, Lo. I need to change my rhythm patterns." We waved to Lacey on the way out, avoiding eye contact with Sam and his boys. Outside the bar, it was cool and quiet. We amble toward our vehicle in the parking lot feeling pretty good, only to have Sam and the boys run out around us.

"What do you think, Rick?" Lois grinned at me like a cat getting ready to pounce on a wounded canary.

"I don't know. What do you want, Sam?"

"I want to kick your ass, Cantelli. If you don't make a lot of noise, I'll kick your ass and let you and the old lady drive away."

"You don't read the papers much, do you, kid? Rick killed ten guys in the last few days. It's on every front page in San Diego," Lois explained. "A few of the headlines read 'Killer Cantelli'. That's what the press calls him."

"Shit... you're that Cantelli," Derek asked, uneasily looking around the parking lot. "He stopped a damn terrorist attack, Sam! Cantelli killed four terrorists that night and his partner killed one. You're Lois Madigan."

"I am," Lo answered. "Six gangbangers decided to ambush Rick at his house too. He killed them all, two shots apiece. They got one shot off."

"Bullshit!" Sam looked incredulously at his cohorts. "You're not really buying this load of crap, are you?"

"It's on the front page, Sam," Roger added. "How the hell did you do it, Cantelli?"

I drew my extra .45 Colt before they could blink. I handed the Colt to Lois. "That's how. My partner will hold onto my Colt. I'll give Sam a shot at me. He's not going to like it. You two stay out of it and my partner won't have to rearrange your attitudes. Last chance to avoid this, Grasshopper."

Sam literally foamed at the mouth. "I am going to make you cry, old man. I want the old lady's word she won't shoot us when I beat the shit out of you."

Lois started cackling while I took off my jacket and tie. "This is so much fun, Rick! Damn... I figured a little info, drink, and humiliate you shooting pool."

Lois sighed and waved the Colt. "I won't interfere. I will give you this advice though, Grasshopper. Don't try a takedown. Rick doesn't like it. If you try it, he'll break stuff on you."

"Thanks, hag. I'll be careful with the old prick."

"Rick!"

I took a deep breath. "Yeah, Sis."

Lo smiled. "Did you hear what he called your sister?"

"I have to work out later, Sis," I replied, loosening my arms and attitude.

"You'll have a long enough nap to get ready for that, Peeper. I'm only asking for a few extra minutes of pain."

I put my fists up. I don't pretend I'm Bruce Lee. Over the decades of training, I've become proficient at a number of martial arts. I enjoy starting in a familiar boxing stance. I was the heavyweight boxing champion of the Navy a long time ago. I fought professionally until the Seals found out about it and ordered me to quit. I bludgeoned so many gangbangers when Lo and I first had to establish a reputation, for a little while guys in the know got the hell out of my way when we walked on scene at a business Madigan/Cantelli protected. They knew I'd beat perps down and Lo would spray, toast, and shoot anyone who faced us off.

"Okay... but that will definitely mean some time at the bar during Casablanca Night."

"I'll be there, Peeper. We can entertain Frank with our

118

adventures today."

Tired of hearing Lo and I talk, Sam threw a roundhouse right at my head. I blocked it, and rotated inside his reach, slapping him across the face. Oh boy, he didn't like that or Lo's enjoyment of his bitch slap. He came at me all business then, elbows pumping up and down, fists floating around. I smashed a jab right into his nose that busted it and sent blood shooting out. The punk forgot he was in a fight. Sam grabbed his spurting nose as if someone called timeout. I looked over at Lo. She shook her head in the negative. Rats. I backed away while Grasshopper remembered where he was. He didn't know what to do. He wasn't used to taking a punch. His buddies were giving him grief but he wanted to quit already.

"Walk away, Grasshopper. Forget you ever saw me. If you walk into any place I'm at, pretend like you don't know me… but with respect. Otherwise, I'll tear your spleen out next time."

Sam saw the smirks on his friends' faces, watched Lo cackling inappropriately as she egged him on without saying anything. He mouth breathed while coming at me, no longer taking any air in through his busted nose. I saw the fear in his eyes. If he didn't try to tackle me, I'd work him without any further damage. These young turds should have done a stint in the service. It would have wiped away all that aggressive nonsense movie-land and video games had ingrained in their minds. They didn't understand reality between 3D combat with a controller and getting your face punched in.

I moved in on him then, working the body while beating away his strikes. Each punch he threw at my head I blocked and countered with sharp half power shots to his body. After only a couple minutes of that, he lost all discipline while gasping for breath. Don't let anyone tell you a broken nose doesn't mean anything in a fight. Only untold hours training and fights can make you into a fighter if you have the drive to do it, capable of getting past your nose being flattened on your face. Sam threw haymakers, hoping for a miracle. I whipped a left hook under his ribcage that crumpled him like a blowup doll with a major air leak. I walked back a few steps, listening to him sucking wind while rolling on the parking lot surface. I turned to my handler over the decades.

"We done, Sis?"

"Very nice, Rick," Lo answered, while gesturing at Sam's friends. "Get him out of here. I know you probably won't listen to reason, but you don't have a fighter's heart, pussy. Rick could have broken your ribcage into pieces while you held your nose like a two-year old bumping their head on a door. Get the hell out of here, poser. I should charge you for the lesson."

Derek and Roger maneuvered Sam to his feet, still gasping for breath. Lo and I stood off to the side, letting them go their way. Sam, to his credit, kept his eyes down at the path he had to walk and his mouth only gasping, rather than forming words. I put on my tie and coat.

"Good workout, Rick. A quick nap and you'll be ready for Jadie's gym. I know you. The banter as those young turds moan and groan through an aerobics exercise makes you smile. Admit it."

"It does. The fight was a walk in the park. I knew if I was getting my ass kicked, there would have been three young dolts writhing around on the parking lot with our pro formula spray and electronic stimulation."

"Yep." Lo hung her head. "I'm so ashamed."

"You were praying for it, Harpy!"

The cackle sounded a final acknowledgment.

Chapter Six
Brutal Reality

After some much needed hours in the sack, I checked in with Shelly to make sure nothing fell apart at the office while I slept. I ate a hardboiled egg and a banana, my pre-workout meal a couple hours before I go to the gym. I admit to some reluctance in driving to the high school from the beach house. I wished I was walking it instead from home. It wouldn't be safe for Jim though. We kept Temple in the dark about intercepting the serial killer stalker, Stargie. She didn't ask and we didn't tell. A bright spot appeared on the horizon as I drove in front of the high school – no demonstrators. I did a quick around the block check, making sure there were no odd-looking people hanging around in or out of cars. Jim and Ellen awaited me inside the front doors of the high school. I cautioned them earlier not to leave the entrance until I got there.

Parents with under the driving age teens arrived to get their kids like me, while hustling teens with cars trekked to them doing the zombie shuffle with their mobile phones. I don't know how they walked anywhere without bouncing off each other, or stationary objects like a pinball game. They seemed to be mutating, developing a sixth sense for items blocking or walking in their way. A few narrowly missed me but swerved expertly without their faces ever leaving the phone screen. When I left high school long ago, an undercurrent of excited conversation always accompanied students leaving the school at day's end. Now, instead of talking, they texted each other, even when walking next to the companion they communicated with. I half wished sometimes that Jim and Ellen would keep their eyes focused on a phone screen. I recognized the purely selfishness of that wish. I spotted the two of them inside the entrance, watching every face and mannerism going by them. They did have a passion for detecting people and items out of place.

"What new threat on the horizon did you two notice today?"

"Jim had to readjust a senior's attitude in the lunchroom," Ellen answered.

There's some good news. "Oh crap." Jim shook his head in the negative at his partner in crime. I reassured them. "I can't help if I don't know what happened."

"It was nothing. The guy's a bully. He's playing the offended Black Lives Matter card every day at school now. Until today, he was all mouth."

"His name's Jesse Martin," Ellen said. "He took a swipe at Jim's shoulder bag. Jesse got mad because Jim made him miss knocking it off his shoulder. He did one of those sliding movements, ending chest to chest with leering face inches away from Jim's. I told him Jim was Killer Cantelli's grandson, but that only made him madder."

"How very resourceful to mention me, after the demonstration and them knowing I killed six of their BLM mob. I wish I could think of something that wouldn't end in violence during a face to face like that. Having been in a number of them, when I attended school during the stone-age, I never had much luck exiting from those situations without a violent response. You're still in school so I assume you found a way to end the confrontation without a riot."

"Jesse tried to sucker punch me in front of a security guard entering the lunch room. I reversed it into the finger-lock we've practiced constantly, Pa. I held him on his knees while the security guard kept his friends off me. The guard took Jesse to the office. The friends were not happy, but by then there were three more guards on hand."

"I've seen the Facebook and Twitter stuff Bone sent me on the BLM propaganda sites," I explained. "If their parents encourage the BLM behavior at home, reinforcing the lies, the problem will expand into their own kids' heads. The BLM will become their foster parents, inciting riots, looting, and pillaging. The pictures I've seen with a score of black teens posing with automatic weapons in gangbanger style will only lead to more tragedy. Let's go. We have a workout and dinner later."

"What can we do though here in school?"

"Be wary, Ellen. If sanity doesn't return, we may have to get you into a private school or tutored. Pretending nothing's wrong won't work. I will not lie to you and tell you just ignore it and it will go away. Remember, school is a learning institution. When it becomes unsafe to attend, it's useless. Adulthood has nothing to do with the crap you see going on around here with kids acting out as gangsters. I don't plan to allow Jim's life to be ruined or lost and I'm certain your parents feel the same way. We can't remove the hate fomented by racist groups like the BLM and C.A.I.R. Many lives are at stake. I believe in one truth. Take care of your own family, and keep them off the street. I know cops around this city do not hunt down blacks. I have a theory about why the blacks are turning traffic stops and confrontations about the law into killing fields. Leave it alone for now. C'mon."

Outside the school, I became more wary of people passing by giving me looks not compatible with good feelings. "I think I'm going to pay Bone to pick you two up for a while with me. It may eliminate some of the bad temper around here."

We walked out to the GMC, quietly contemplating our surroundings. I could tell Jim and Ellen missed nothing, but also revealed nothing, as they accompanied me. Lo and I spent quality time in 'Logan Heights' during the movie shoot, teaching them how to observe without being observed. It was a hard reality lesson when Stargie spotted them more than once. I spotted the two coming toward us. So did Jim and Ellen.

"Cantelli! A word please."

"Uh oh," Ellen muttered.

"Stay to the side of me, kids." I turned to face a determined black man in a suit with his hand around the back of his companion's neck. "Hi there."

123

"My son Jesse has something to say to your grandson. Go on, boy!"

Jesse straightened. "I'm sorry about trying to do a beat down on you, Jim. I won't make excuses for what I did. I hope we can start over from here on."

Jim walked forward with his hand out. "I'd like that a lot, Jesse."

The two kids shook hands. I could tell his father was embarrassed. It seemed likely he found out through this incident a lot more than he knew before. I held out my hand to him. "I'm Rick Cantelli, Mr. Martin. I'm happy to meet you. This is my grandson Jim Bishop and his good friend Ellen Buford."

Martin shook my hand, and then Jim's and Ellen's, with some relief. I guess he was expecting something else. "Just John will do, Rick. Jess has been suspended for three days. He deserved more but part of this is my fault. I jumped to conclusions about the recent events, made some dumbass remarks about cops, and Jess expanded on my mistake into places on the Internet I'm embarrassed exist. This Black Lives Matter crap is all a false divisive poison, foreign owned, and media backed with lies and coercion. It's a damn shame the way I was duped by the media stories. I do have friends at work... thank God... that made me look at the facts."

Well... well... another ray of sunshine. "It's really tough when the news-people make up the news to suit whatever agenda they're pushing, John. Mistakes happen in law enforcement, sometimes tragically, but I agree completely with you about the BLM."

I shook hands with Jesse. "You are a lucky young man to have a father who cares this much, kid. Stay far away from the gangs. They never have anything in life but prison terms or death. If you want to find out disturbing stats, check out the way Blacks kill and wound other Blacks in Chicago, the gun control Mecca of the country. BLM cares nothing for them. That alone should reveal the agenda they have to you."

"I've read about your adventures over the past few days," John said. "I see you're carrying a scab at the side of your head from it. Can I ask what happened?"

"You can, and I'll explain to the best of my ability." I gave John and Jesse the shorthand version of the drug dealers Lo and I collected, using the 'Logan Heights' details we were worried about. I explained the terrorist intrusion, including the fact the terrorists killed the drug dealers. I did my best to explain what happened on my lawn. "When men draw on me, I don't hesitate for a second. Do I look into my victims' childhoods, and beat my breast because they decided to kill me – but got killed instead – no."

"I sense the truth in your words, Rick. I know from the papers about the training you've had. I'll bet they don't have the facts about a lot of it. I did a stint in the Navy during the Iraqi War. I want Jesse to serve. He doesn't understand completely what's at stake. When jets fly off the aircraft carrier you're stationed on to exact deadly justice on the enemy, nothing else matters – not the media, liberals or traitorous fifth column minions. They fly to support American citizens in combat."

"I'm joining the Marine Corps," Jim said. "My Pa was a Navy Seal. I know I can be one, once I become a Marine. I'm not certain if I want to be Marine Recon or a Seal yet. I'm training with Pa to become whatever I want."

"That's how you put me down!" Jesse turned to his Dad. "Can I train with Jim if Mr. Cantelli will teach me?"

John looked into my eyes. I nodded assent. "Okay... but if you ever try using what Rick trains you with for the gangs, you'll have to kill me first. Is that clear?"

"Yes, Sir." Jesse hesitated for a moment and then hugged his Dad. "I did it, Dad. I...I heard you and saw the news and-"

"Some things in life we put behind us, Jess," John told him. "This is one of them."

"I'll help in any way I can. Jim and Ellen need good friends.

I'm sure you know about Jim's new movie crap. Take my word for it. He's above all that. Jim trains, does school work, and interacts with friends in a topnotch manner. Welcome aboard, Jess. If you want, we'll take you to a special workout we do at a place called Jadie's Gym. We go there Monday, Wednesday, and Fridays for working out. Afterwards, we have a restaurant nearby we all get together at. You and your family would be welcome."

"Yeah! Come with us," Jim enthusiastically reinforced. "You can meet Hollywood Stars and have a great time with me, Ellen, and Temple."

"Temple Donavan from the TV and movies?"

"Yep. Temple's always with us."

Some of the mistrust surfaced in Jesse. I liked the kid because he instinctively knew there was no such thing as a free lunch. "There's no fee, Jess."

"Uh… yeah… but why didn't you all ask me before?"

"Why should we?" Jim was confused at the question. "You never said hi to me or Ellen before. Why would we have asked you to do anything with us? You're a senior. We stay out of your way and hope we don't get noticed. That's the way it works."

Jesse laughed. "You're right. I been so full of myself lately, I probably would have attacked you for asking. I'd like to work out at this gym you go to."

"Do you have a car, Jess?"

"Yeah."

I handed him one of Jadie's Gym cards. "Meet us there at 6 pm. My friend Bone will be at the door tonight because it's Friday. I'll leave word you're working out with us."

"How will I know this friend of yours?"

"Brother Bone's lost a bit of weight, but he's black, six/four, and weighs around 270 pounds. He works for me at

126

Madigan/Cantelli Security."

"I guess I'll see you tonight then."

John shook hands with me again. "Thanks for your understanding. I'm happy to have met you, Rick."

"Same here, John." I gave him one of my business cards and a card for the restaurant. "I don't know what your plans are for the evening, but as I told Jess, your family would be welcome to join us."

"I'll talk to my wife. We only have Jess. If Tara wants to come, what time should we be there?"

"We usually get there a little before eight. There is a slight gimmick to our Friday Casablanca Night. There's a forties fashion you'll see most of the customers in, and I wear a white jacket."

John grinned. "You play Rick from the movie, Casablanca?"

"Guilty. We have a great piano player and the restaurant is done in classic form. Wait until you see Bone and his wife, Carlene. Bone in a black zoot-suit is incredible. Forties costuming is optional."

"I'll remember that. Thanks for the invite."

"That was great, Pa," Jim said while we watched John and Jesse walk away. "I'm surprised you agreed to train Jess and ask his family to Casablanca Night."

I shrugged. "I'm sick of all the BLM crap. A family avoiding the media agenda of making thugs into heroes is a good thing. Besides, I like John."

"You wouldn't have liked Jesse earlier today," Ellen said. "He played the thug real well."

"It's like his Dad said though, some things you just put behind you," Jim replied. "We can use a senior friend at school. Because of the movies, kids already look at me like I have a third eye."

"The girls don't. You should see the player in action, Robin… I mean Rick."

"Oh… Mars Bar, you are dangerously close to the precipice. Now… what's this all about with the girls, player?"

"Mars Bar is exaggerating. It's the usual celebrity stuff," Jim replied. "I'm polite."

"They all want in his pants. If Temple attended our high school, her head would explode. He can barely walk down the halls."

"Smart idea for a senior friend. My experience is girls love to cause trouble. Mars Bar is an excellent example. Keep on as you're doing. Be polite, friendly, but distant without being seen as arrogant." How about that? Dr. Cantelli is in."

"Good advice, Pa, if I could do it all at once, that would be great," Jim replied, while chuckling at my zap of Ellen, who was steaming.

"I do not cause trouble."

"I could list all the times I know of, but we're almost at your house."

The kids said goodbye at Ellen's place. "I'll be picking you up early for the gym. I have to start varying my routines. Be ready to go by five."

"Okay. Say hello to Batwoman for me." She ran inside.

"Trish doesn't actually wear a Batwoman costume, does she?"

"No, she simply insults me in civilian clothes."

* * *

We drove around our area at the beach house, making sure we didn't have any unknown visitors. Inside, I headed for the bedroom. "Do your homework, Jim. If I can help I'll do so after I get some sleep."

128

"Ok, Pa."

When I woke, Stacy entered the bedroom. "I came in to wake you. I should have known that automatic inner alarm clock of yours would make it unnecessary. We're going early, Jim said."

"Yep. Did he have time to explain his adventures at school?" I got up and put on my workout gear. Stacy slipped out of her uniform with me annoying her.

"Stop it." She slapped my roving hands. "Yes, he explained his new method of acquiring friends. If everyone comes tonight from our group, we'll have a big crowd around the table."

"I have a feeling Bill and his wife will skip tonight. He's taking a lot of heat for my adventures."

"Cheech said he's coming for sure. He stopped in to talk with me about the store. He gave me another raise."

"Congratulations." I gave her a hug. "That's the third since you started. You're damn good at running the store. You were professional as hell, setting up the ID princess. Did you like doing it as much as you thought you would?"

"More so. I'll be glad to do it for you and Lo anytime. Do you think there will be trouble at the gym or restaurant tonight?"

"I think we'll be avoiding it going in early. Bone is working the door at Jadie's. One look at him, and most anything of a thug nature will keep whatever they're planning outside."

* * *

I stretched inside Jadie's Gym where the equipment was. Jadie and Stacy talked off to the side. Jim and Ellen worked out on the bench press machine. It felt good being there early. Wonder of wonders, we didn't have to walk through a gauntlet of demonstrators. I watched Jim bench pressing a hundred fifty pounds, doing reps of five. Then I spotted Bone waving at me from the doorway. He had a slightly worried look on his face. We met in the middle.

"You look uneasy, brother."

"There's demonstrators forming outside, twenty by my last count. Their signs have 'Killer Cantelli' and Islamophobia stuff on them."

"They can't demonstrate anywhere here except out on the sidewalk. I'll get Jadie to call the cops. We don't need to get into it. I did put my big mace dispenser in my gym bag."

"I like your thinkin' on calling the cops," Bone replied. "I'll let you lead if we have to face them down. I called Lo already. You don't want to know what she said."

"It probably had something to do with machine guns and grenades."

Bone chuckled. "You can read her mind too, brother."

Bone followed me over to where Stacy and Jadie were talking. I gave Jadie a quick rundown of events. Then another solution surfaced in my head. "Hey... why don't I just leave? I can pick up Stacy and Jim after the workout. Jim's new friend is coming over so it's a necessary thing for him to be here."

"No way, Rick. I'm calling the cops!" Jadie had her phone out like a drawn weapon. "We can't give in to these assholes! I want them off my property and my parking lot entrance kept clear or I call political contacts."

I exchanged nodding glances with Bone. Jadie is a major business owner in San Diego. Sometimes you have to allow citizens to stand up for their rights and make our protectors serve in official form. Jim and Ellen drifted over, sensing something beyond workouts going on. We all waited silently as Jadie finished her conversation.

"They're coming to make sure the demonstrators know they can't screw my business into the damn ground! I want some! What the hell is this? Are we living in a banana republic?"

"I appreciate your support, Jadie. Bone and I are going out to

130

make sure Lo doesn't arrive with machine gun and grenades. I can't apologize for what I did on movie debut night. That clown was going to shoot indiscriminately into all of you."

"I know, Rick. Go ahead and recon my parking lot."

"On it." Bone and Jim followed me. I turned to point at Mars Bar. "You stay here!"

After we reached the front entrance I could definitely see why Bone was worried. This was a mob, and I could see they had been joined by a few BLM activists. I spotted Lois trekking into the middle of the idiots with signs. I breathed a sigh of relief she only had her gym bag with no automatic weapons in sight. One of the demonstrators tried to block her progress from the parking lot. He paid for it. His writhing body on the pavement shocked the rest away from her. Bone and I hustled over at her back.

"The cops are coming, Sis. These jokers will have to move to the sidewalk. This is private property."

One of the crowd recognized me to his quick regret. He ran at me with Isis beard, and pointing finger. "It is the 'Killer Cantelli'!"

I admit to being fired up. I waited for him to veer off as Lo shielded Bone away. I dropped him with an uppercut that I have no doubt broke teeth and jaw. I could hear sirens on their way. I plucked my Mace spray bottle out. "No more! The police will be here to escort you retards off private property. Anyone approaching gets a taste of the good stuff. If you're looking for a weight loss formula, keep coming. I've got you covered right here!"

The crowd proved to be a little on the stupid side, so I gave them a quick sample. When their front running cohorts hit the pavement in a pile of very unhappy people with the aftermath of my military formula Mace causing distress unheard of amongst these troglodytes, they ran away out of range. The police arrived shortly after. The bodies on the ground were in abject misery, which Lo and I enjoyed. Bone wasn't at the human commiseration point we were at. He went inside, retrieved a bucket of water, and put it amongst them. They took advantage of it to dose eyes and faces as the police spilled out onto the scene.

Lois met them without any hesitation. "These people attacked me as I came to work out. I want them out of Jadie Wentworth's parking lot right now! This is private property which still means something in the USA. I have my lawyer on speed dial if there's a law question."

The officer hid a smile as he surveyed the parking lot. "That won't be necessary."

He addressed the forlorn demonstrators with the facts. "You must move off of private property immediately or be arrested. If you block access on the sidewalk to the parking lot, you will be arrested and fined. You all have five minutes to take this to the sidewalk or be arrested here. I will not warn you again."

The policeman then moved to the bucket brigade. "The five minute warning applies to you bunch too. Move quickly, or you will be arrested."

The ones subjected to my Mace answer helped the wounded to transport for a hospital. I didn't know what the fallout was from this, but damn, it sure felt good. I shook hands with Officer Gilbreth. "Thank you. We did not foresee this reaction."

"You're Rick Cantelli. You wasted those bastards that killed LA Blue. We ride with the folks who have our backs, Rick. I'm putting a squad car on duty here. These people will not block access to your parking lot... period."

I shook hands with him. "Thank you. Bad things are on the horizon with the BLM and Terrorists. We have the Blue's back all the way."

"Captain Staley said as much. He's the best ever in charge. He bleeds Blue. At this time on the streets, I'm sure you know how important that is."

"I do indeed. Thank you." We waited outside until all the cretins vacated the parking lot.

Jesse Martin walked to the entrance from his car. He shook hands with Jim and me. I introduced him to Lo and Bone, explaining we knew the Martins from the high school. "Jesse wants to work out with us and do some training with Jim once I get my house back. I met his Dad. I invited the family to Casablanca Night. I'm hoping we don't have a continuation of this Islamo Nazi mob acting out."

"Come early like you did here tonight, Rick," Lo told me. She pointed at the limousine driving near us. "There's Temple. I'm glad she took our advice about having her driver take her everywhere for the time being."

Temple's driver, Pete Boardman, popped out to open Temple's door. He shook hands with all of us. Temple drifted immediately over to Jim where he introduced a stunned Jesse Martin. "I'll be back in an hour. You've had an adventurous few days, 'Killer'."

"Yeah, Pete, and I was on a peaceful roll there for a while. Be careful driving near those jerks with the signs. There's a lot fewer of them now but if they try to block you or anything else, you have us on speed dial. We'll be right out."

"I saw the signs. They're blaming you for just about everything. A few of the signs are blaming you for the attack by terrorists on the theater you and Lo stopped. Pretty soon they'll be claiming you initiated the attack."

"Nothing would surprise me about the Islamo Nazis. Good seeing you, Pete."

"Take care."

We made sure Pete cleared the crowd before angling toward the door with everyone. I noted Jesse found his voice. He asked Temple about her TV show. She told him the show was on hiatus until the producers decided whether they wanted to go on with an older teen scene. Temple explained they would not be renewing Alex

133

Winton's contract no matter what.

"I confess I've only seen a couple of the TV shows. I hated Winton's character. I did see your two movies: 'A New Beginning' and 'Here and Now', mostly because I was dating a girl who wanted to see them, especially since Jim attends our school, and he was in the sequel. I liked them more than I thought I would."

"Their two costars work out with us too, Jess," I told him as we cleared the entrance. "Trish Medina and Karen Bastille will be here too shortly with their husbands. Trish's real last name is Rocha. She works with us in the security business too."

"I read Hollywood rumors about Trish Medina having been a contract killer of some kind. Is that true? I know she did some prison time."

"She does have a past we don't talk about," I answered carefully while Lo snorted amusement. "Trish partners with an ex-police officer. It's a confusing story."

The rest of the introductions went well, much more subdued after the prior demonstrations. Everyone liked Jesse. Temple, Ellen, and Jim introduced him to the humorous part of our workouts. They entertained each other along with the rest of us. Lois and I exchanged some updated information we learned apart. I explained the incident behind the Martin family invitation. Lo told me Van contacted her.

"He put Floyd on alert for anyone moving in and out of the Yemen embassy in San Francisco. They have an FBI office there, so Floyd did his Homeland Security thing, assigning an agent to watch the office. So far, Van says everything is normal."

"How long do you think we should wait since it doesn't seem as if Saleh suspects anyone knows who sent the killers?"

"We need to stretch it as far as we can, Rick. There will be an uproar, even with the patsy we have picked out to set up."

"Any rumor of an attack though and we move on him,

134

agreed?"

"Agreed," Lo answered. "I like the Martin kid. He's entertaining, but keeps his mouth shut and listens too. He has good instincts."

Lo's iPhone buzzed. She glanced down to read the short note while we were doing mat work. "It's Bone. He says the demonstrators got so much flak from passing cars, they left, but not before doing an interview with a local TV station. Be ready tonight at the restaurant. You don't seem to have much trouble annoying the hell out of them. Why not really piss them off? Then we can spray the idiots with Mace attitude adjustment wash when one attacks."

"I like the idea. Let's hope they didn't like the taste of our action before the workout."

"I liked that uppercut you threw tonight, Peeper," Lo complimented me. "All this damn action has you honed and ready. All your old quickness is back. Stacy and Jim have knocked the rust off your old ass."

She was right. "All the workouts, and training Jim, has definitely restored my timing. If I'd been slightly off with that punch tonight, it would have meant broken fingers or hand. I can't afford that. It feels great to be mixing it up again, but I have to knock that crap off. I'm a bad example for Bone. I have to use the tools: stungun, Taser, or spray."

"Agreed. We have wet work to do. I can't have you at less than a hundred percent until we deal with Saleh. We're not going back into Yemen to get the prick. We have to get it done here. God knows how many of the un-vetted Islamic horde our idiot leaders will let in to do Saleh's bidding from afar. Part of this is my fault. That clown today at the bar was just too tempting to pass on. I would have blitzed him and his partners but you may have sustained an injury before I did. It's a bitch always having to worry about what we do because of age."

"True. On the other hand, you and I can make small talk

through a workout like this while the younger set is huffing and puffing. I have to get you back into your Harpy form again."

"Yeah, this shit's boring as hell without the undercurrent of insults and subterfuge. Since you're with Stacy and Jim, I'm having a hard time establishing new targets."

"You haven't lost your touch putting down bad guys, Sis."

"Yeah... I have to admit I was waiting for one of those cretins to try and lay a hand on me. I couldn't let you have all the fun. We're a pair, Rick. That's for sure."

"I'm hoping to keep a low profile though so the mayor doesn't exile me from the city."

The workout ended with the kids and our regular exercise bunch interacting with the stars. Their sequel 'Here and Now' set box office records for a romantic comedy. I could hear them talking about 'Logan Heights' with Jesse listening raptly through it all. I could tell he enjoyed the entertainment world celebrity discussion, especially when Trish and Meg explained how Lois handled the gangbangers. Shelly broke away, telling Max to stay put. She hurried over to us with her office manager face on.

"Hey Shell, what's got your wig in a bun," Lo asked.

"I forgot with all the excitement. Carmen's Bail Bonds in LA called the office after hours. I have all the calls routed to my cell so I took it before heading here. After everything else going on, with Bev Segar and Johnny Rich unexpectedly popping into the area, I didn't know if this case would appeal to you. Stoner Gordio's in our area. Carmen called me personally on the chance we'd take him."

"Stoner? I thought he was doing a dime at Atwater," Lo said. "Why the hell would Carmen care anyway?"

"Carmen fingered Stoner when he didn't show up for his court date on the armed robbery charge he was convicted of that they sentenced him to Atwater for. She knew he planned to head into Mexico. Stoner put up the huge bond the judge allowed in spite of his flight risk. Carmen took the bond. She admits it was because she knew he'd skip and one of her guys knew where Stoner would go immediately. He has a cousin in San Diego. Carmen tipped off the police and they nabbed him."

Lo grabbed Shell's arm, guiding her off to the side of the room with me collecting our equipment bags. "You're giving me a bad feeling, Shell. What's happened?"

"Stoner escaped. He faked an appendicitis bursting, screaming and the whole smear. During the transfer, with him writhing in pain, the guard didn't handcuff him to the gurney. Stoner killed the guard and driver with the guard's weapon. He abandoned the ambulance in LA. Carmen's place was blasted in a drive-by with automatic weapon half a day later. She doesn't believe in coincidences. The drive-by seriously wounded her guy who knew Stoner. Carmen doesn't have any dog in the hunt, but she says you and Rick have history with Stoner so she sent me all his hangouts and the cousin's address."

"How long ago was this?" If the guy would be heading to Mexico, he probably already crossed the border.

"He hit Carmen's place today. She believes he'll hide out in LA somewhere, before heading down here, because the US Marshal's Service is already on the case. Carmen gave them everything she's giving us. She also told them her suspicion he would hang out in LA to see if he got another crack at her. She's making sure he doesn't. They are in lock down."

"She suspects Stoner will head for the border in the next day or so then," Lo said. "I'm not sure I want to be in competition with the Marshal's Service. They don't take interference too well. If they find me and Rick snooping around Stoner's trail, all the federal badges in the world won't keep them from making us the target."

"Stoner was on our list. We archived him when they put him in Atwater," I said. "We put him away a while back, before he moved his operations to LA. He told us he would blow up our houses, kill everything we loved... the whole stream of crap punks like him spurt. It's an interesting challenge, Sis."

"Say no more," Lo cautioned as if I fell off the vegetable truck yesterday. "Text Carmen we appreciate the Stoner update. We'll decide about looking into his case over the next day. She doesn't need to know any more than that. I know when Carmen said they're in lockdown, it means exactly that. Stoner won't get her or their people. Thanks, Shell. Send everything you have to me and Rick. We'll handle it from here."

"Okay, Lo."

After Shelly was out of earshot, Lo turned to me. "Give me some parameters, Peeper. I say we have some fun and smack Stoner down long range. We need a practice session before we do Saleh. Look over what Shell sends and we'll discuss it tomorrow."

I didn't like that prick Stoner. Lo toasted his ass real good, when we plucked him out of the bar he was hanging around at. We asked him nicely. At the time, we were collecting him for a no show on a petty theft bond. One of our informants spotted him and called us. We swung by for retrieval. He made it personal and got lit up. We collected on his ticket and gave him no more thought other than our list for idiots making threats.

"Okay, Lo. We'd have only one real option though other than hunting in the dark. We'd need to stake out the cousin's place. You can bet the Marshal's Service will be doing the same thing. Do we let them have him?"

"He killed a guard and an ambulance driver. I say we pop him."

"Agreed. The Marshals get on escapees really fast so what if they get to him first?"

"We let him go, Rick," Lo replied. "With a couple of deaths on his ticket, we won't be dealing with him anyway. I think we need to look into the cousin's holdings. I'd bet money Stoner's not stupid enough to stay at an already known location. He'd know the Marshals are on his tail."

"Good plan. That's where we'll start. I'll take a look into it when I get home from the restaurant." I started to walk over with the kids. An idea hit me about a way we might be able to garner some more points with Bill. "Lo. What do you think about doing the research and trapping Stoner for Bill?"

Lo hesitated while following me. "I like it. If we get him in one of his hangouts it would be doable. He has nothing to lose. If cops go after him, I think the Blue will take a hit because they'll be hesitant to put the Stoner mongrel down. It would be a great plus for us with Bill if we can do this in concert with him."

"Let's find him first. If we have him in our sights, I'll walk next to him and zap the shit out of him."

"We need Trish and Meg on this if we're going for the capture. He's never seen them. They could playact until near him and get the deed done. If there's any trouble, we know Trish won't hesitate."

I planned to be with Stoner either in my sights or within quick-draw distance. "You're right. No way Stoner has forgotten us. We'll talk it over with Trish and Meg tonight at the restaurant when we can get them alone. I have to get home so I can get to the restaurant early. I want to be on hand inside the entrance to greet the Martins."

"Understood. Don't go rogue on me with Stoner, Peeper!"

Damn! I'm sick of being mind swiped. "We'll work from now on as we did in the past, Sis. We're on a war footing with the crap we're facing now. We move carefully with intel and back anyone we hold dear to the max. After our meeting tomorrow at the office, I'll take Steve with me for surveillance of anything having to do with Stoner. We'll do the grunt work while you and Bone expand on our intel."

"I feel deceptive vibes, Hooterville. I like your plan. Don't alter it."

"I won't. Let's get back into this escape from reality with our

139

movie façade."

"Yep. Let's do it, Rick. Don't forget what I said. I will toast you if I smell a rat."

"Of course you will."

* * *

"I'm telling Pa." Jim whispered to Ellen.

"What the hell? It's a guess. We're working it until we can bring Rick and Lo into it. We've learned our lesson." Ellen could tell she wasn't budging Jim. She also saw in Temple's eyes that her bestie would follow Jim on any questionable op she dreamed up. "I spotted her! Let me guide this surveillance."

"If you're right, and I'm not denying your instincts, this is when we bring in Pa and Aunt Lo," Jim stated.

"Look... there's something wrong with that lady we've been working out with. She drifts. She hovers around, gathering info. Let's engage her and find out what con she's working. You've always known this Jadie's Gym workout is a hotbed for the rumors circulating about anything and everything dealing with the movies and Madigan/Cantelli."

"So what?" Jim guided Temple toward the women's locker room with Jesse paying apt attention to everything. We can't ban the paparazzi no matter what we do. All we can do is piss them off so they snap pictures of us in bad taste."

Ellen looked ready to explode, fists clenched, and body tensed. "She showed here in the class only six weeks ago, in place of a friend she said. Jadie let her stay. Rick and Lo verify everyone who comes in and out. I'm telling you they missed this woman. With all the tips on our movements and pictures away from the gym shortly after our work outs, I'm telling you she's the one doing it."

"Ellen." Temple grabbed her friend's hand. "If you suspect something, tell Jadie. It's written into this class's bylaws. No one can give information of any audio, visual, or hearsay rumor to the press in any way. What would you have us do? Even if the woman's guilty of everything you say, the most we could do to her is turn her in."

"We'll trap her. What if she did the entire thing we suspect her of? Jadie will ban her. We won't ever find out what she's spying on us for."

"Money, Ellen," Temple said. "You can't blame her. They're offering a fortune for shots of us in embarrassing or awkward poses. I've seen a couple of me out there when I've readjusted my outfit or fell on my knee. I knew the pictures were taken at some time in here. Let me help you understand the situation. Think of you making an ass out of the woman in some elaborate way. Payback on audio/video between a celebrity and a camera crew, or fan, always reflects badly on the celebrity when it hits the social sites. No matter what kind of connections a celebrity has through their agent or PR firm, the celebrity will lose when a bad interaction hits the public. The person responsible can portray the disagreement with any spin they want. Fans or paparazzi have no consciences. We can only limit the damage."

Temple paused for a moment before going on. "We've done incredibly well, accumulating serial stalkers, drug lords, and possibly in this case, a woman reporting on us for money. The serial stalker made me fear for my wellbeing and rethink doing goofy stunts. Can't we just watch her a while longer. We can report the times we believe she's investigating us to Jadie. We can then show Jadie some actual hard evidence. She'll handle it. We would be able to reveal the reporter in our midst that way with proof. News or pictures, published in the entertainment venues the day after our workout, can be investigated at that time by Rick and Lo. They can determine if there's a pattern."

"It's not my place to say but that seems the best course," Jesse added. "Those social sites are vicious on celebrities striking back in any way. I'm into the celebrity thing a little. No one pays attention to a funny picture or outfit flaw. Even random remarks or rumors get shed quickly in public. When a celebrity acts out on a fan or paparazzi, even legitimately, they get hosed."

"Okay… I'll keep anything I do on the down low for now," Ellen agreed. "I saw her talking to you a couple of workouts ago, Temple. Did she introduce herself?"

Temple hesitated, glancing at Jim. "Why?"

Ellen put on her Lois Madigan interrogation face. "Out with it Shortcake. I want answers. Did she give you her name?"

"That's not funny, Mars Bar."

"What's the name? Don't make me get out my pliers and torch."

Temple sighed. "Cindy Daniels."

"That's better. We'll have to get Jesse's info and give him a nickname."

"If my friends ever hear you two calling me by some nickname, I'll get blasted. Count me out, Mars Bar."

"Don't call me that," Ellen directed. "I'm Elementary, Temple is Tempest, and Jim is Cross. You can be something cool. How about Shaft?"

"I have to admit. That's a good one, but-"

"We won't ever use it on you in school, Jesse," Jim said. "The nicknames are only for emailing each other. We're under observation because of a couple unsanctioned investigations we stuck our noses in where they didn't belong. Ellen and I are learning the private investigator trade. We're on restriction too with what we can do on our own."

"I'd like to hear more at the restaurant. I better get going. My Dad and Mom are coming. Do you think we can sit next to Bone and his wife? He mentioned telling me how Rick recruited him. He said it was funny."

"I don't know if funny is the word for that action," Jim replied. "Bone's telling of it is a lot funnier though. No matter where

142

you sit, you'll be able to hear him. He'll make you cry from laughing when he tells you about his takedown at the Nite Owl."

"Lookin' forward to it. Nice meeting you, Temple."

"Same here, Jess."

After Jesse walked to the exit, Ellen went into the women's locker room to shower and change with Temple. They both wanted to cut some time off from getting ready for Casablanca Night. Inside the locker room, Cindy Daniels awaited them. She pointed an accusing finger at Ellen.

"I saw you watching me the whole workout you little bitch. What's your problem?"

"Not a thing," Ellen replied. "You looked so lovely tonight, I may have had a staring problem. Sorry about that, Cindy."

Cindy reached for Ellen's shirt front, only to have her wrist snatched by an iron grip. Trish twisted Cindy away from Ellen, easily forcing her to a kneeling, painful position. Trish shook her wrist with a smile.

"No touching the kids. What's this all about? If you have some issues to work out, I'll be glad to help."

"Let me go! I'll-"

Trish twisted harder, drawing a yelp from Cindy. "It's not a good idea to threaten me, Pumpkin. I take threats seriously. Ellen apologized. Run along before you get any more annoying."

Trish released Daniels who slid along the floor a few steps before getting to her feet and rushing for the exit holding her arm. Trish watched her until she cleared the door. The crowd which formed quickly at the interaction, disbursed with some amused mumbling. Trish turned to Ellen.

"Well... Mars Bar... what have you done now? Don't double talk me or I get Lois involved."

"I...I suspect Cindy Daniels is the one who has been taking

pictures and spreading rumors the last six weeks about the movie stars. She could be the one letting people know the likely time Rick arrives for the workout."

"Interesting. What was your plan?"

"I was going to nag Temple into following her one night when she drove herself to the gym. I thought maybe we could learn who she sells the images to."

"Not bad," Trish replied. "I'll tell Lois. It will make her head explode that you spotted something she didn't. Your surveillance technique needs work. You wouldn't have been dopey enough after that serial killer fiasco to let Mars Bar put your ass in a sling again, would you, Shortcake?"

Temple blushed, much to Trish's amusement. "That would be a yes."

"I could have said no," Temple muttered, "but then either you or Lo would have beat the truth out of me."

"All Lo has to do is stare at you for ten seconds and you start singing like a canary on crank. Go get your showers. We'll talk later. I'll see you two at the restaurant."

"Thanks, Trish," Ellen said.

Trish shrugged. "No biggie. I think you might be right. It's a good catch. C'mon, Megaphone. What the hell are you doin' back there?"

"I'm brushing my hair. I'll meet you outside in two minutes," Meg called out.

"Don't forget to put some panties on," Trish zapped her as she walked to the door.

"Thanks for that, Skipper!"

Ellen and Temple enjoyed the interplay amongst the two partners along with most of the locker room occupants. "Trish is a badass," Ellen said.

144

"Maybe it would be a good idea to talk with her first when you notice something. She might give you more tips and leeway than Lois."

"And she'd enjoy baiting the Harpy too."

Chapter Seven

Surveillance

Lois and Trish arrived earlier at the restaurant than I did with my crew. Sam sat next to Trish at the bar while Frank sat next to Lo. Meg stood near the middle with arms folded. They all enjoyed the discussion except for Lo. Ellen gave me an intricate recounting of the locker room interlude along with the reason for it. Jim took Ellen's arm and steered her toward our table. Stacy squeezed my hand and joined them. We did a firehouse type clean and dress at the beach house. We still didn't beat all these interested parties. I joined the group at the bar. Jerry smiled at my approach with Bushmill's in hand for me. You have to love an excellent bartender like Jerry. I took it from him with pleased anticipation.

"Mars Bar strikes again, I hear."

"I'm being upstaged by a damn teenager," Lo griped. "Then Skipper draws the short straw to tell me all about it."

"That's her second, Rick," Frank told me. "Ellen's adventures have driven Lo to drink."

"I figured her head would explode," Trish added. "Imagine my disappointment. The kid has skills. She covered her ass with Daniels too. It was an apology, although a little over the top without enough surprise. What do you want to do about Daniels?"

"I'll let Jadie handle it with the facts we learn. Mars Bar is right. Daniels could be the leak we've been searching for. Not that Rick and I have to change our routines like in the old days. We've gotten complacent, like when Skipper decided she didn't need to turn on her security system, and managed to let her murderous ex-partner kidnap her and Sam. She had us to save her ass. Rick and I have to change our habits."

Oh my. Lois lit Trish up with that one. First, Meg nails Trish on the deadly security oversight, and now Lo. Even Sam chuckled as

Trish's features went from relaxed arrogance to open mouthed outrage for a split second. To her credit, she just lowered her head in acknowledgement to her life-threatening miscue.

"It's beneath you to pile on, Wombat. In my defense, I didn't let anyone do anything. Chet and his boys were only a heartbeat from death. Sam can tell you."

"Trish kicked the crap out of one trying to get to her gun before they Tasered us." Sam confirmed. "She was fighting and I was barely awake."

"Good epitaph for a tombstone, Skipper. 'They were a heartbeat from death' before they zapped and tortured me to death," Lo retorted. Even Trish laughed at that zinger.

"I'm never livin' that one down."

I held my glass for toasting. "I for one am glad you and Sam are still around. Getting there late would have haunted me and Lo no matter what she jokes about."

Lo was the first to clink my glass. "Yeah, brother. We did the deed that day. You fixed old Chet but good. We need Skipper. In this day and age we can't take anything for granted. Security protocols, routines, and bad habits have to change in this day and age. I want to have a bunch more Casablanca Nights before I punch out. The next few months may be tricky with some of what has to be done. My kids are moving down into the area. That fact puts new perspectives into place. Rick and I will be journeying to San Francisco soon. We'll check in with the kids then."

"I want to go with you two old farts," Trish said. "We all know damn well your trip only has a small part to do with the kids."

"We appreciate the offer. This one has to be done by Rick and me alone," Lo replied. "We need you here in the area with our assets while we're gone. We include you in everything we can. This isn't one of those times."

"If we need you in an emergency we encounter, we'll call

147

you, Trish. Believe that," I told her. "For now, let's concentrate on what's in our area. The Daniels' angle will have to be followed by all of us. Mars Bar aced us all on Cindy. We dig deep for her background, financials, and anything else that touches her. That faceoff in the locker room is a key pointer. No way she would have initiated a confrontation like that on a fourteen year old unless she lost perspective. She's not a pro but she could be selling to a pro endangering us."

Bone and Carlene approached us with big happy smiles and dressed to the nines. One look at our faces at that moment and Carlene sent Bone into our midst without her company. She waved at Stacy and went to join her and the kids.

"Did something happen?"

Lo patted his arm. "Nothing happened, but we need you to help us with an unknown element from the gym crowd, named Cindy Daniels. Are you allowed to drink tonight?"

"We took a cab over. I figured with all the limousines normally used, it would be a good idea to arrive by taxi without stirring any excess observation."

"You perceive the situation very well, my brother." I passed a double Bushmills over to him. "We have a few ongoing problems you're well aware of. They can wait. We're enjoying a Casablanca Night without assaults."

"Amen to that." Bone sipped his drink with relish. "Oh my… that tastes good. I heard you invited a new family into the groove, Rick."

I nodded. "I am absolutely positive you'll like the Martins. They're real. Jim had some trouble with the son. I played out the string when the Father arrived at the school, making the son Jesse apologize for his BLM affair with the dark side."

Bone waved me off while sipping. "I talked to Jesse. He's a good kid. I may have promised to tell him all about your recruitment of me into the fold though."

148

Oh... there's some good news. "So you're going to do the takedown at 'The Nite Owl' for laughs?"

"That's the plan," Bone replied to much amusement.

"In that case, I think I'll stay at the bar until it's time to go home. Too bad Steve's not coming tonight. He could have filled in all the parts of that episode."

"I called him on the way over. I told him what I was going to do at the table tonight. He said he's coming, with or without Kris."

"Oh, you dirty rat." I shunned him, hand shielding my face. "Dead to me."

"I don't think we've ever had the story done from both sides," Lo added. "If Steve's coming, this ought to be a classic retelling of a favorite story of mine."

"Let's get over to the table. There's Jesse at the door with his folks," Trish pointed out. "We need to get them seated near Bone... damn... there's Steve and Kris. C'mon, Timothy, let's go meet and greet. We'll intro them to our Casablanca Night pianist. Don may have to come over to listen too. He and the Killer spent tank time together too."

I let my head plop on the bar as the quite amused group moved to meet the Martins. Jerry came over. "Are you going to the table, Rick?"

"Nope," I answered without lifting my head. "I'm staying here until the laughter at the table dies down. Between Bone and Don, I should be able to join them in another hour."

"It can't be that bad."

"It is when Bone tells it, especially with Henpeck Steve adding the details after he finished off the attacking Bone with the Taser. By that time, Bone was out cold on top of me."

"Oh my... sorry, Rick." Jerry gestured for our usual waitress, Katy, to come over. "Get Bone to record the Madigan/Cantelli table

149

during his recital of the takedown at The Nite Owl bar."

"Is that why Rick's over here with his head on the bar?"

"Yep."

"I'm all over it," Katy said. She patted my back on the way to the table.

I straightened and called out after Katy. "Thanks a lot, Katy."

She waved without turning.

I sipped the last of my drink. Jerry immediately refilled it. "That helps, but don't think I'm letting you off the hook. Oh well... I guess Stacy and the kids will be up to speed on my recruiting techniques."

"Do you know what Steve will add to it?"

"Yep. He's going to tell them all about the crowd, gathering around us, as he pushed the unconscious Bone off my unconscious body. He Facetimed Lo during my out cold period. When I came to, somebody in the crowd asked, 'why didn't you just shoot him, Cantelli'. I told him I was trying to cut back."

Jerry enjoyed that one for a moment before remarking, "how many people have you killed, Rick?"

As Bone's bass voice and loud laughter assaulted my ears, I said, "apparently, not enough." I thought his question over and decided maybe the newspapers were right nicknaming me Killer Cantelli.

Jerry walked away, stifling laughter, to serve another group at the bar. I continued sipping while cringing at the party going on at our dinner table. Lois trekked to the bar as the table quieted to normal conversation. Katy followed her with a phone in hand.

"Jim videoed the story for me with my phone. Great kid." Katy giggled and joined an eager Jerry as he finished serving drinks.

"It's all over, Peeper," Lo told me. Jerry broke away from Katy for a moment to serve Lo a drink before returning to her phone movie. "Stacy's ordering for you. The Martin's loved their intro to Madigan/Cantelli. Don hadn't heard the Bone takedown story yet either. You can imagine his enjoyment of it, adding his own tale of tank recruitment for everyone's listening pleasure."

"Wonderful. I could hear Henpeck laughing all the way at the bar here. I'll bet he filled in the dramatic moments when both Bone and I were unconscious."

"Oh yeah, he did. I should have interrogated him harder when he came back to the office the next day. Steve remembered the gathering crowd and all their comments, before and after you and Bone awoke from your dual zapping."

"Gee, that makes my night, Lo. Thank you for that. I guess I've made both the Nite Owl and the tank famous in my older years of senility."

"You'll get over it. Stacy and Jim enjoyed the hell out of it." She gestured at the very entertained Katy and Jerry, hunching over the phone so they could hear but not bother the customers. "I guess those two think it's pretty good too."

"Jerry asked me how many people I have killed."

Lois toasted me. "Not enough."

"Damn it! You snatched that right out my head." I toasted with her. "To the end of the current death cycle."

"Not yet, Peeper. We have a-"

Lois was staring at the front entrance. I glanced that way just as she returned her eyes to the bar. "Well that takes the cake. Aga drove down to test us."

"He brought four bodyguards that look like ex-Yemen Secret Police," I replied, also studiously avoiding the arrival of Aga Saleh into our Casablanca. "What happened to us always being sold out on Fridays?"

"I imagine we'll have to talk with our security guy at the

151

front desk. Aga's got balls. I'll give him that. The fact he'd risk visiting San Diego, and come here to front us in our own place, makes me think if we play our cards right, we'll be able to gather a lot more information on this prick."

"Maybe it's the booze, but I was wondering what his chances are of returning to San Francisco outside of a body-bag."

"Put your game face on, Peeper. Here he comes. That eliminates any chance this was a coincidence. We have an excellent metal detector at the front. If our greeter let them get in here packing, I'm going to toast him before I fire his ass."

"Agreed." I watched Lo reach over the bar. She retrieved a white bar towel, putting her Glock under it on her lap. I loosened the Colt under my jacket.

Saleh stopped in front of where Lo and I sat turned away from him. "You are Lois Madigan and Rick Cantelli?"

We turned slowly toward him. Lo wasted no time. She squinted at him a little with furrowed brow while scanning Aga and his men. "I'm Lois Madigan, and this is my partner, Rick Cantelli. Who the hell are you and why should I care?"

To say Lo's words stung the hell out of Saleh would be putting it mildly. Dark complexioned, Saleh's face changed to a fiery in between color. Lo grinned over at me. "Do you know this guy, Rick?"

I shook my head with a big smile. "Nope. I haven't finished my drink yet either. If you have a point to interrupting our evening, you'd best get to it, Pokey."

　　　＊ ＊ ＊

"Those guys at the entrance look like bad news," Jim whispered across the table at Trish.

She turned, her brow knitting. "Jesus, God in heaven… that's Aga Saleh, the Yemen ambassador, stationed in San Francisco."

152

Trish chuckled, watching the nearly unnoticeable alterations Rick and Lois did at the bar. "The old farts see them coming."

"Shouldn't we go over there, Trish," Bone asked.

Trish grinned at Bone. "I'm a poor one to ask that question. The idiot's approaching two cold blooded killers, thinking he's some kind of Middle East potentate. The newspapers labeled Rick, Killer Cantelli. They weren't joking. Let's stay ready to help. If it gets physical, maybe we get involved so Lo doesn't have to shoot the guys who try to interfere, when Rick engages with one of the idiots."

"I knew we shouldn't have come." Kris grabbed hold of Steve's arm. "We'll be ducking under the damn table in another moment."

"Quiet, Hon... let go of my arm," Steve whispered. "Trish is right. I've seen Rick and Lo in a gunfight. Those five don't have a prayer, if they reach for weapons. I'm hoping Hal at the front wasn't stupid enough to allow... wait a minute... Trish, I'm checking on Hal."

"Good call, Steve. Meg... go with him in case they brought boys we can't see."

Steve forcibly removed Kris's hands, patting them into her lap. He moved quickly to the front where he spotted a very frightened Hal backed against the side wall in the entrance. Two men gripped his arms, acting as if they were with him. Steve stopped before they noticed him. "Shit... Meg, this is for real. Do you have your stun-gun?"

"Do bears shit in the woods. What do you have in mind?" Meg had followed Steve at Trish's direction without a word or hesitation.

"We laugh a little, smile a lot. We move to Hal as if saying goodnight to him. I'll toast the guy on the left. You get the other bookend."

"On it." Meg took out her stun-gun from the evening purse

153

she carried. With it held in her right hand slightly behind her back she put an arm through Steve's.

Steve nodded, shifting his stun-gun to his left hand. "Good one, Meg."

Shaking each other with light laughter, the couple made their way to a spot opposite Hal and his bookends. Steve acted as if noticing Hal for the first time. "Hal! Meg and I are leaving, buddy. I wanted to tell you-"

Steve zapped the guy on the left with a steady arc, never paying the slightest attention to what Meg was doing. She reacted slightly slower, but caught up in a flash. Her target did the electric polka until lying vibrating on the floor. Hal caught a little bit while being held. He collapsed to the floor. Steve grabbed his chin, shaking it.

"Hal! Did the metal detector go off? Answer me now!"

Hal's eyes blinked with determination. "No... I stopped them because we're full. Then... these assholes grabbed me... shit... he stabbed me, Steve."

Steve and Meg went to work on Hal while Meg called a 911 call into an emergency EMT and police presence. Meg pulled Hal's jacket and clothing away from the wound on his side. Steve did a search for the weapons and IDs on their perps. Meg gripped Hal's chin.

"It's not bad at all, Hal," Meg lied, gesturing for Steve to hold the clothing tightly against the wound. "We did a 911. We'll get you on the mend in no time. Sometimes a wound makes you go into shock. I need you to talk to me, my friend. Let's chat. How's the family?"

Steve heard it all, and clamped the clothing against the wound. "Get the killers involved now, Meg... now!"

Meg wasted no time. She lurched to her feet on the side. Meg screamed above the music and conversation. "It's a trap! They're not

154

armed! Mission unknown!" Meg shut up as she saw an eruption of physical assault was ending at the bar.

* * *

"You have no right to insult me, woman! My son was executed in Sana'a by…by this monster next to you! After the executions in the theater of legitimate protests, I will have you both put into prison!"

The bodyguard on our left nearer to Lois reached for her arm. I struck with a half power, pointed hand jab to his throat. He crashed, gripping his throat. I kept moving. When it's party time, there's no use in not going all the way. I put a left hook into the throat victim's buddy behind him, that sent him crashing into his buddies, and then unconscious to the floor. Lois grabbed Aga by the throat with her Glock next to his temple. We heard Meg scream out from the restaurant's front entrance, outlining action at the front desk.

"Call off your dogs or die, Pokey!"

Outrage, annoyance, and even slight displeasure disappeared from Aga's features. To his credit, he recognized he would die within the next second if he didn't follow her order.

"Obey her instructions!"

I grabbed the third guy still standing by the throat with Colt pointed at his other bodyguard companion. "Any sudden movement and everyone dies. Nod your mutant heads if you understand!"

The confrontation ended as Bill Staley, who had been protecting his wife at that point, moved next to us with weapon drawn. Trish and Bone backed him.

"I'm a Captain of Detectives in San Diego. All of you still capable, get on your knees with hands laced behind your heads. You will be restrained and marched to the front."

I repeated the order in Arabic. They followed directions. Lois and I always have plastic restraints. I did the restraining. Bone and I revived the unconscious one. He and sore throat man were helped to

155

their feet and restrained. The restaurant customers remained in hushed silence. I gestured at Don.

"Play it again, Sam!"

Taking my hint, Don nodded and went to work on the piano. Jim, Temple, and Karen joined him. They sang an old hit Don played, 'I'll Be Seeing You'. Aga kept his mouth shut. I had expected him to start yelping about diplomatic immunity. At the front, Meg had already restrained the two goons there, who were vibrating slightly, while moaning out of their zapped state. Steve kept pressure on a wound at Hal's side. Police and ambulance arrived while Steve explained what happened. The EMTs did emergency triage on Hal.

"You did very well, Steve," Lo said. "It would have been a damn bloody mess without you and Meg taking care of the front."

"I'll never get Kris here again. I can tell you that much. It was a great night with Bone retelling the Nite Owl tale. What the hell did this Aga guy hope to accomplish?"

"We'll let the police handle that," I answered. We needed to put some distance between us and Aga for now. "He'll be pulling the diplomatic immunity card soon, I'm sure."

Bill instructed the police officers who arrived to take charge of the prisoners. They bagged everything the men had in their possession. Three squad cars answered the call, enabling the police to take all of them without calling for a meat wagon. Saleh spoke before being frog marched to a squad car.

"This is not over!"

Lois grabbed his cheek, shaking and making cooing noises. "You're just the cutest thing."

Once the police escorted the prisoners away and Hal was loaded for transport, Bill turned to us. "Do you two know why this guy came here?"

"He shouted something about his son being killed in Sana'a,"

156

Lo replied. We knew Saleh was testing us to see if we knew he had hired the killers. Bill didn't need to know that. "He also complained we killed those poor terrorists in cold blood without reason. Same old murderous Moslem bullshit."

"They are all complicit in an attempted murder on Hal," Bill said. "I'll see this through tomorrow with the diplomatic immunity stuff. I know you all are willing to testify. We know which one used the knife on Hal."

"We may as well eat," Lo said.

"I'm with Steve. This will probably be the last time we come here if my wife has anything to do with it," Bill said. "Your new guests probably got more than they ever bargained for."

"You're probably right about that," I replied. "Let's go smooth things over while Karen and the kids are singing. Why don't you join them for a while, Trish?"

"I think I will. We worked on a new number together last time we didn't shoot up the joint. They haven't sung that one yet – 'What Becomes of the Brokenhearted'."

"I like that one a lot," Lo said. "We'll go smooze a bit, while you and the others sing. At least we didn't have a gunfight, but that shit with them stabbing Hal requires a response. That guy better pray the DA imprisons him."

The rest of the evening progressed with some uneasiness when we returned to the table. Between the live entertainment though, and another jewel by Bone, describing when he and Trish went out on a surveillance gig together with me, made everyone forget the confrontation. I used a military type stun grenade, and Trish was wounded. Oh boy, they had fun with that retelling. I could tell the Martins were seriously reconsidering being around us. Kris, and Bill's wife Sue, calmed down to the point during Bone's laugh riot, they might return with their husbands. Shelly and Max arrived after the police and ambulance left, due to a PTA meeting at Shelly's teens' high school, luckily. Meg's date retry was a wipeout though. I could tell in the guy's face, he wanted nothing more to do with us. I didn't blame him. Lo and I agreed to meet at the office on Saturday morning, so we could check what happened with Saleh and his gang, while we planned what needed done. Movie producer, ex-gangland boss, and owner of 'Godfather's Cell', Cheech Garibaldi absorbed the entire evening to the end with a smile. He shook my hand afterwards.

"Another great party, Rick. Take care of my stars and store manager."

"I will do so, my friend."

* * *

I arrived at the office nearly the same time Lo did at the 10 am hour she had suggested. As usual, the info whore badgered law enforcement into a detailed explanation of what would be happening with Saleh. They had already released Saleh as we figured. The DA agreed to only move on the attempted murder charge. The knife man was held without bail. Thanks to our HD security cams at the restaurant, we were able to get high definition images of Saleh's men, and supply the police with a complete showing of what happened. The DA's office received a formal complaint from the Yemen Embassy. That, in itself, was significant. They would have stayed away from their ambassador's personal score if they weren't backing it.

"I wish we could do the bastard while he's in town," Lo remarked. "I think we did pass his test. I doubt he believed we knew about his hiring of terrorists."

"I agree. What do you think of taking him out along his route back to San Francisco? If we collect our patsy, we could get him on the return trip without much trouble depending on the route he takes."

Lois sighed with regret. "I wish. If anything happens to the prick, we'll be up shit creek without a paddle. It's one of the reasons I now believe is why he faced us off in the restaurant in front of so many people. He covered his bases. I still think we fooled him about not knowing he hired the killers. Aga also cemented the fact we're now adversaries. Even Bill would issue a warrant for our arrest if something happened to him. They won't buy the patsy no matter how we set him up. When we head north, we'll need the perfect place to take him out."

I had to admit it seemed Aga screwed us. "You're right about the way he did this. He'd have no problem sending people to kill us at any time he wants. No one could touch him because he'd make sure it was hired guns. He never thought we'd torture the shit out of his minion."

"It's a problem. That's for sure. We may have to forget about the patsy, and make him disappear. Floyd wanted Gabriel Paria and I'd like to keep him happy. That ten acre compound, Paria's using to import illegals from the Sand, wouldn't be missed. Any huge destruction of the place would open the door for the authorities to inspect it. How much you want to bet Paria's storing explosives there."

"Two old farts taking out a terrorist compound with heavily armed guards, huh? Why don't we blow the hell out of that Sharia No-Go Zone in Islamberg too while we're at it?"

I chuckled. "One impossible mission at a time. Want to take a look at Paria's compound? If the government won't shut him down, even if we kidnap him for our purposes, the compound will still be there."

"We need him in one piece." Lois rubbed her chin. "If we could pull something like that off, I have an idea how we could use Paria to do Aga. I wonder if Paria has any suicide vests in stock at his compound."

"Oh my... that's just scary good. Even if they don't have a readymade vest, I can make one. We can use a cell-phone detonator. If we find a place Paria will be going, we can plant the explosive Paria there."

159

"We need to make sure he's wearing enough explosives to get the job done for sure without collateral damage. Damn… Rick, we're doing shit we didn't even do in our youth."

I shrugged. "The homeland is at risk. If the compound looks impregnable for us, we'll have to settle for snatching Paria as we planned before. We have the element of surprise. Paria thinks he's untouchable since the Department of Justice disallowed Floyd from raiding the place. His guards will be lax. They will not, however, be standing outside waiting for me to shoot them. We'll have to go in for close order combat. What do you think of reading Trish in on this if we check the compound and our plan looks feasible?"

"Let me think about that. Trish has too damn much to lose. She'd jump at the chance, but if we got her killed, I don't want to think about facing Sam. We'll recon the compound and make a decision then."

"Agreed. We'll have to read Bone in on this. We have permission to use satellite assets but if we assault the compound, we need real time scanning."

"Lot's to think about once we decide," Lo replied. "No use putting it off. I think we need to take a peek tonight. I've checked the street views of his compound. It's set pretty far back from the road. I've picked an approach I like."

"So you did consider obliterating the compound. I like it."

"How do you feel about crawling in on your belly while I watch your back?"

"Been there, done that," I replied. Lo and I reached an arrangement a long time ago. If we have to do close order combat, I want her at my side. For long approaches to take out guards without alerting the target place's inhabitants, I do it alone. "Can Frank drive us? I looked over the street views too. Across the road, it's empty, and a great place for you to set up."

"That's how I figure it too. I know Frank will drop us off. You're a little long in the tooth for this though."

"I can't argue with you there. We're only taking a look tonight, but since I'm not going all the way in, maybe I should make an approach while you map me."

"How's your head doing?"

"It's fine, Lo. The swelling's gone and the scab's ready to pop off anytime. I'd rather spend the time on approach tonight. I've seen how much open ground I have to cover. I don't want to do it on the night we assault the place. Thank God they've added the GeoMine platform so I don't have to worry about these assholes mining the place."

"I checked first thing when we received the go order on Paria," Lo replied. "You'll still have to worry about motion sensors and trip wires. These bozos know how much animal life there is around that area. No way would they take a chance of alerting locals with explosives. Sensor alarms are another thing. You'll have to take the hand detector if you're really serious about going tonight."

"I guess we better get some rest. I estimate an approach like that to take a minimum of three hours."

"If you don't detect any sensor array, I'm thinking you can do it in two. Why don't you kill something tonight to make them queasy about each other?"

Now, that was funny. I enjoyed the joke until I saw Lois simply grinning at me. "Oh, come on, Sis. You can't be serious. They'll be on alert if I did something like that."

"I'm serious, Flipper. You approach and slit a throat. It will freak the zombies out. In a few days, we'll go back and you slit another throat. They'll be at each other's throats when we go back in for real."

"You do know if I screw up, it will be a major gun battle, right?"

"If it weren't for us needing Paria alive, I'd use our XM-25 Punisher grenade launcher on the compound."

161

Oh boy. I could sure see her doing exactly that. "Cool. Let's bring it just in case."

"No problem."

"We'll have to put Stoner on hold until Monday. We didn't get to talk with Trish and Meg about him at the restaurant with Aga testing us. We have too much going on," I added.

"We stay careful, Rick. We take nothing for granted. I don't want that asshole doing a drive-by on us or our loved ones while we're tiptoeing through the tulips."

I shrugged. "One fiasco at a time during the death phase cycle, Sis."

"I'll put out a notice to all our contacts at the bars around the area with Stoner's mug shot. I'll put out five hundred if we can get him with info provided. Our contacts know better than to screw with us."

"It'll be worth it. We'll talk about plans for tomorrow after we get through tonight."

* * *

"If you keep going at that speed, Flipper, we'll be here all night."

I couldn't get into a discussion with the Harpy in my ear, so I had to take anything she dished out on me. Frank dropped us off a quarter mile from the compound. We both trekked along the vacant underbrush across the road until we found a hill area with excellent vantage point. Lights at the compound made our target an easier plotting point for Lo and I to map the way I would make the approach.

They employed one guard if you could call him that. He sat in plain sight on the extended porch, smoking. Lo would be watching my approach with detailed recording. Since they lit the compound at night, I left my night vision gear with Lo, taking the lighter weight ocular. Strapped at my back so it would not get in the

162

way, my Ruger with silencer felt comfortable, but still in easy reach. Nothing I wore would rustle or catch on anything. A slight cool breeze rustled brush, while helping to cover noise from my approach. My other weapon, a stiletto, mounted in a pouch at my waist, was to be used only if I could make the approach as silently as we hoped.

I didn't need to be quiet until I reached the other side of the road at the entry point we decided on. Lois had already cleared the approach for anything giving off an electronic signal at all, sensors or otherwise. I wore tight black material from head to toe. The famous sniper Ghillie suit works perfectly for stalking in a stationary spot well camouflaged, but rustles. I'm moving at night, with a hoped-for end result of a silent guard kill. Once full length on the ground, I closed my eyes, feeling everything under me: the slight softness of the ground, the brush surrounding me, the smell of night dampness mixed with breeze, and how my old carcass reacted to a young man's game.

"Get your geezer butt movin'. What the hell are you waiting for, Rick? Remember, this isn't a water approach. You can't swim to the porch, Peeper. It's all clear, sweetie. Will you start crawling for God's sake, before I get too old to track you?"

I knew this was payback for my returning to our boat in too leisurely of a manner after a beautiful hit on Teddy Alvarez's beach house a while back. Lo had me. She planned to torture me the whole way. I could tell. I opened my eyes and began moving with care, but at a steady pace. When I reached a point fifty yards from my target, I would slow to a more silent pace. Lo would let me know if the guard showed any sign my approach attracted his attention. After forty minutes of nearly nonstop insults, Lo paused from her verbal assault.

"You lucky bastard! The dumbass took out his phone and stuck his earbuds in. He's looking around guiltily. Now he settled into his seat with his head nodding to the music. I thought these Moslem morons weren't allowed to listen to music. Anyway, change your approach to the left, and get the lead out. I'll let you know if

163

the Music-man notices anything."

I did as instructed, moving at a careful pace, but much faster than I had planned. When I reached the fifty-yard mark, Lo tracked me in audibly every step as I stayed low, but no longer crawled. As I reached the far-left side of the open porch, I crawled toward the guard, hugging the wall, paying close attention to squeaking boards. Staying next to the wall also puts the stalker where the boards have a more solid attachment, and thereby less chance of noise. Three quarters of the way to the guard, I straightened to my feet, becoming one with the wall. With stiletto in my right hand, I hesitated at my attack point, waiting for Lo.

"Do it, Rick. Pluck him. He's ripe and ready for Virgin hunting."

I rushed behind the nearly oblivious guard, yanked his head back with left hand over his mouth. The stiletto blade plunged in under his ribcage, smacking all the way to the hilt once, twice, three times, and the fourth strike made no impression on the guard's quieting body. I then gave him a final poke through his eye into the guard's brain. I took his phone and earbuds off. After depositing them in my front waistband, I repositioned the guard with head down, and hands clasped in his lap. So far, his clothes absorbed all but a small amount of blood. Stopping the heart as I did, cut down on its pumping ability much faster. I cleaned my blade off on the guard's pants.

"Quit playing with him, Flipper! Let's go home. I'll meet you on the road. I already texted Frank. He'll be here shortly."

I stayed far to the left, staying low, but moving toward the road at the fastest pace I could move without breaking my neck in the dark. I reached the road, waiting until I spotted where Lois emerged on the other side. I moved to a point opposite her. "I'm across from you, Lo."

"Frank's a minute out."

I stripped my thin gloves off, turning them inside out, careful

164

not to have any of the guard's blood come in contact with my clothing. We'd wipe the car down anyway tomorrow before breakfast in the beach house garage. We'd keep our heads down through Sunday, watching satellite feed of the compound. Seconds later, Frank slowed to a stop where Lois directed him. We entered the vehicle from opposite sides, Lo into the front passenger seat with the equipment bag, and me in the rear driver's side. Frank eased away from the stop, increasing speed without excessive engine noise.

"I take it your initial sighting was a success?"

"Yeah, brother, except for your wife verbally torturing me the entire time when I couldn't speak." I entertained him with Lo's ongoing zingers from the approach on the way to the beach house.

Frank patted Lo's knee, enjoying the one-liners during a deadly op. "You were in rare form tonight. I never thought to get a text this fast. The guy really guarded the place with earbuds, listening to music?"

"We did the unexpected," Lo replied. "I half expected them not to have a guard at all. They're complacent."

"I have his phone. We'll have to stop soon and take a look at it for anything we can use. I doubt they'll think to check for his phone, but no use in taking a chance of a trace. It's an iPhone. I'll take the chip out of the holder at the side after I see what's here."

"I have the kit for emergency disassembly and battery replacement in my bag." She fooled around in her equipment bag and retrieved the little red toolkit for taking apart the iPhones we use. "Your eyes are better than mine. Here's an iPhone memory drive. Download everything onto the drive before you take it apart."

I accepted the drive, turned on his phone and transferred everything to the memory drive. I handed it back to Lo. She held the bright mini-light on my operation. I'd taken enough of ours apart for battery replacement to know the procedure. Lo held a plastic bag underneath to catch the small screws and retainers. After separating the halves, I disconnected the battery. We'd save everything as is in case the data transfer didn't take.

When we reached the beach house, I put on my windbreaker with hoodie up. "I'll see you two tomorrow. If you want, take a taxi over. I'll cook something for us while we sip a few, after I wipe down the car. We can check our satellite laptop for news on those poor terrorists and their compound. We have Stoner Gordio on our plate now too. If we can, let's see if at least Trish and Meg can join us for brunch. I liked the idea of us finding Stoner and getting Trish and Meg next to him for a quick zapping."

"So do I. I'll text everyone when I get home. I'll wipe the car down myself. That sounds good though. We need to go over the next phase on all fronts, including Stoner. I'll check over the phone data tomorrow morning. How's eleven sound?"

"Perfect. See you then." I waited until Frank drove away before approaching the house. Stacy told me to be noisy when I came in. I did exactly that after disabling the alarm system. I'd had enough ninja practice for one night. Although I wasn't overly noisy, Jim popped out for a moment to greet me. He waved.

"Hey, Pa. Did everything go okay?"

"We learned what we needed to. How late did Temple and Ellen stay?"

"Until one. Temple's driver took her and Ellen to Temple's house. Ellen asked for permission to stay overnight with Temple. Can I ask them over tomorrow?"

"Sure. Lo and Frank will be over at eleven. I'm going to make brunch for us all."

"Great. See you in the morning."

"Okay, Jim." I went in the main bathroom and stripped out of my clothing. I put on a robe and slippers. I walked out to our laundry area to load my clothing in for washing. After starting the washer with heavy detergent and cold water, I cut my gloves into tiny pieces. I soaked them in chlorine bleach, drained the bleach, and went out to our fire pit. I burned the pieces.

Stacy awaited me after my chores and shower. "Hi there. I've been anxious for you to get home. I had a bad feeling about tonight."

I slipped into bed, running my fingertips along her leg to the swell of her breast, eliciting a shuddering response. "Everything went very well. Do you need something to help you sleep?"

She moved into me, taking my hand and kissing it. "Yes, please."

Chapter Eight
Complications

Stacy and I made veggie trays with Jim's help. We had plenty of my favorite ready to grill hotdogs and hamburgers. We made deviled eggs, put different chips in bowls with dips, and covered everything for later attention. Frank and Lois arrived as Stacy and I finished the preparations. The day was a little cool but without any wind other than the usual subtle ocean breeze. Jim paced around, anticipating the arrival of his female company until I told him to sit down or I would tie him into a chair.

Lois inspected our preparations. "This looks great. Shelly and Max can't come. They have some family deal planned. Everyone else is coming except Sam. He flew to Chicago on business last night. Bone's bringing his special gear for discussion with satellite streaming. I did a bit of that myself. No news and no reports on what happened at the compound."

"Why don't you two go talk in the kitchen," Frank said. "Bring me an Irish Coffee if you would, brother."

"You got it. I'll be back. Do you want anything, Stace?"

"Nope. I'm anxiously awaiting Jim's female brigade to get here. Temple always has the entertainment world insider updates. Jim doesn't pay enough attention to his new career."

"I'll work on my interest more, G-ma."

I left them to it. Lo followed me into the kitchen where I made three Irish Coffees and took one out to Frank. We killers took our coffees to the kitchen table. For now, we had the house to ourselves. "They buried their own then?"

"That's my hunch, Rick. It makes sense. They don't want the authorities of any kind snooping around. I'm hoping they fell for my subplot. They could be looking at each other with the suspicion it's an inside job."

"It won't make another approach any easier. You can bet the guard or guards won't have earbuds and music on."

Lo shrugged. "Who cares? We go take a look. If you can make another quiet assault, you'll really ring their bell. If not, when we make the real assault, we'll go in hot and heavy after you take out the guards."

"I'm still fuzzy on the purpose of last night's excursion. I was all for taking a look at the place and mapping an approach. I don't see what alarming them did for us. Hell... even inside the compound, if they do suspect it's an inside job, they'll be armed with one eye open and one hand on a weapon."

Lois let her arrogant smirk pop out at me. "You take the guards out. Trish and I float into position. Then we open the door, you call out in Arabic to defend the front. We fire randomly inside the door and wait. Once we get a bunch of them together near the door, we throw in a couple of military bangers and military strength tear gas canisters. We'll have our oxygen breathing apparatus on to finish by going inside and throwing some more tear gas. The hunt for our familiar face will be ongoing. Once we have Paria with us, we kill everyone else and make him tell us where their weapons storage is."

"You do realize that even in a remote acreage like that we won't have much time before the locals descend upon us. Explosions and automatic weapons fire does attract attention rather quickly."

"That's the beauty of my plan if it works," Lo said confidently while taking a big sip of her Irish. "Damn... this tastes good."

"Agreed. I looked over the compound's blueprints. The housing is in the main building where the guard was. Did you get a chance to go through any of the surveillance feeds?"

"They rarely go into the two outlying buildings and stay for any length of time. One houses their vehicles. The other appears to be strictly storage. You can bet there's some kind of underground vault for the weapons. We need Paria alive. My count is eleven men besides Paria. They do not have women and children on site. The faces change as they get a new arrival. We know from Floyd's files they use the facility as a training ground for freshly arrived agents."

"This op is beginning to rival some of the ones we did in our ill spent youth," I replied. "I'm thinking we won't have the time we need to set the scene. What do you think of wiping them out and waiting? After a couple of hours without any cops showing up we could take our time. If we clean the place reasonably well right after the battle, Trish and I could play dress-up with any police arriving on the property to check what's going on. Floyd could make sure we're not interrupted by any feds."

"I like it. Just putting Skipper in a burka would be worth the whole operation. You could pretend to be a real imam and beat her when she spoke out of turn."

Lois could barely get the whole zinger out with me laughing my ass off at the first couple lines. We enjoyed that one for a time until the doorbell rang. I checked my screen in the kitchen. It was Temple and Ellen. I let them in, barely beating Jim to the door as he jogged toward the entrance from the back. They were all smiles, probably about the direct hit Ellen made about Cindy Daniels, another loose end we would have to address. We needed to figure out who her contacts were.

Ellen came in, looking all around. "Where's Lo? I'm wondering about moving on Cindy Daniels. A spy in the gym could be giving out all kinds of information to bad people."

"Never mind, you little wart," Lo cautioned, coming around the corner from the kitchen with her finger pointing at Ellen. "Nice catch on Daniels. That's as far as you go, Mars Bar. We'll handle the Daniels' problem. Keep your eyes open and remember Daniels should never have made you. If you hadn't been so obvious, we could have been brought in on your suspicions before you tipped her off. No harm done, but you need seasoning, kid."

Ellen nodded. "I'm glad I was right. I was too obvious once I noticed her. Do you think she'll come back to the gym?"

"It depends on who pays her to spy on us. Trish said she was a little hard corps to be a paparazzi plant. Cindy may be getting paid by the people we're having problems with. I want her to forget all about you kids. If she comes to the next workout, pay her no mind. We'll do all follow-ups. Is that clear?"

"Yes." Ellen's mouth tightened. Lo grabbed her chin.

"Don't go off the rail. If I even suspect you're pulling one of your Mars Bar undercover screw-ups, I'll yank your club membership so fast it'll make your head spin. I don't want you killed, or for you to get your minions hurt."

"I understand, Lo... honest."

Lo released her, getting into Jim's face next. "I'm depending on you, Jim. Rat her out."

"In a heartbeat," Jim confirmed. "I'm not letting anything like that serial killer stalker happen again. He could have killed Temple before we even knew he was after us."

Lo smiled and moved on to the already cringing Temple. "And you, Shortcake. You need toughening. Mars Bar's using you like an old gym bag. Don't make me have to put you into the Madigan boot camp for careless minions."

Temple's eyes widened as I saw Jim turn away, stifling amusement. "Madigan boot camp? You can't do that, Lo."

"Don't test me, Shortcake. You're under our protection. If you want to stay there, you need to listen to me and not Mars Bar."

"Okay...okay... but no boot camp."

"We'll see. Run along. Rick and I have more to discuss before Trish gets here. I need another of these, Rick." Lo pushed her empty coffee cup at me. "Hurry, before we get an attack of the killer tomatoes or something."

171

I traded a knowing glance with Jim. He took Temple's arm. "C'mon, Ellen, we have great food in the back."

Trish and Meg arrived at nearly the same time we sat down with our fresh coffees. I checked the screen and opened the door for them. Trish gestured behind her. "Bone and Carlene are right behind us."

"Good. We need a meeting." We waited until Bone spotted us. He immediately hung his head, as if going to see the high school principal, much to Carlene's amusement. "It's okay, Bone. I see you brought your tools. Come in the kitchen with us."

"Go on, Timothy. I'll go in the back. I hear teen laughter already. Temple always has the new movie news."

Bone kissed her and followed us into the kitchen. "I called Steve. He's making things right with Kris. I promised to brief him on any new plans he's involved in."

"I have the big urn going. Does anyone want an Iris Coffee?" They all wanted one, so I made more to go around. "We're checking on info from the compound. No news and no reports, so they're keeping our visit on the down low."

"I'm sure Shelly texted news about a takedown requested by Carmen's Bonds. Stoner Gordio tried a drive-by on her place. They're in lockdown. The Marshals are on his trail. Rick and I need him off the streets. He has a grudge against us too. I took him down hard when we collected him the last time."

"I have something for you on that front, Lo." Bone had already opened his satellite laptop. He pointed the screen toward me and Lo. Trish and Meg moved so they could see the screen. "The cousin hangs out at an upscale place called The Tipsy Crow. I'm thinking we need to drop some seed money in there. I don't know how popular the cousin is though."

Trish nudged her partner. "I see your pretty pink blush. You took the pom-poms to the Tipsy and got laid, didn't you?"

172

"Damn it… Trish!" Meg was now fire red with Lo gobbling every morsel.

"Good exchange. What do you know, Meg?"

"I used to live near the Fifth Avenue bar in a one room apartment. I was within walking distance of the Crow. I might know a couple waitresses we can trust, if they're still working at the place. No more talk about my night life while living near the Crow."

"No need, girlfriend. Your face says it all," Trish replied. "I'll yank it out of you later."

"You will not!"

"I like your idea, Bone. We may not have much time. Maybe the Marshals will get lucky and nab him near the cousin's house. How'd you get the bar tip, Bone?"

"I crashed in on Cousin Walt's financials. He runs credit card tabs at least three times a week at the Crow."

"Damn good. Let Meg see if one of the waitresses' names is on his slips matching one of her waitress friend's. Do the receipts show initials or anything?"

"Yeah, Lo… give me a minute." Bone scanned to the credit card slips. "Uh… Becky, Natasha, and Corey… and Ned."

"Oh my." Trish shoulder hugged Meg. "Meg the Peg Rider knows Ned, huh girlfriend?"

"I see that," Lo said. "Ease off, Skipper. Are you on any kind of friendly basis still with this Ned guy?"

Meg pulled away from Trish. "I broke up with him. He's a bartender there. I don't recognize the other names. We were getting along good but then I found out he was doing Oxy. He knew I was a cop. I stopped going to the Crow. A couple months later I moved into the place I'm in now. Ned understood my breaking it off with him but he was pissed at the way I found out about the Oxy habit."

"You went through his medicine cabinet," Lo said. "Always

173

a good idea when getting involved with anyone, friend or not."

"Yep. He tried to say it was for an old injury playing basketball. We've all heard that story. I told him great, show me the prescription. We went our separate ways. I can try and recruit him. We didn't part as enemies. I'll go over to the Crow tomorrow."

"Screw that. Let's do brunch, and have a girl's night at the Crow," Trish said. "I'll be your wingman. I see Bone already has a bunch of photos of the place. We'll check exits, and the way we may have to take down Stoner. Did you have a plan, Lo?"

"It involved you and Meg doing a low key approach. Once near the Stoner and Walt, I'd like you to take down both of them. Rick and I will back your play and move in for collection. Then we give him directly over to Bill Staley for the ticket with Rick acting as his CI."

"I'm in," Trish said.

"I...I guess it's a workable plan, Lo. I don't mind taking Trish over with me tonight too. There are three bar areas in the place, The Main, The Lounge, and The Underground which is a dance place. It's possible if we can take pictures of both Walt and Stoner with us, we'll be able to learn which area Walt normally frequents."

"Stoner's killed before. I don't want collateral damage. He doesn't know you so if you spot either him or Walt, finish your drinks and leave unless the situation looks ripe. No matter what, call me with how the scene looks, with number of people and where our targets are sitting."

"Do you want to take them inside or outside the bar," Trish asked. "I see in Bone's picture the Crow is on a street corner. That makes it more difficult to take them outside."

"I would rather do it outside, but I think you two could zap the two right at a table, or at the bar as quickly as Steve and Meg took down the two bozos on Friday night. Rick and I will move in fast, showing our FBI credentials, to secure and transport them, so we don't disrupt the place for long."

"Meg and I will check out the Crow. When do we move on our other situations," Trish asked. "I understand it's important to keep last night's playtime on a need to know basis, but having that Aga guy moving on us puts everyone at risk. Even I know he screwed us by making an obvious feint at the restaurant as a smokescreen."

"We'll handle that operation as it unfolds," Lo replied. "Keep security in mind at all times. Stoner is an immediate threat. You're in the mix with us on our compound op when it happens, Skipper… if you want to be."

"Hell yeah, I want to do it. You two old coots can't take that compound quietly without help. It's important for my rehabilitation to ease away from past deeds slowly. It's a process."

"What about Bone and me?"

"We can't include you two in our compound and Aga Saleh problems," I told Meg. "We need people on the outside during some of our extracurricular activities. You and Bone will be in all the way on the Stoner deal. We need a capture to stay in the good graces of our police captain and the mayor. I'm taking a Bushmills into the back and sip while I barbeque. We have a great spread. Let's eat. That's enough shop talk for now."

"I need to have an aside with Megaphone about the wondrous Ned," Trish joked, ducking a back of the head slap from Meg.

* * *

Jim, Temple, and Ellen strolled along the shore, inspecting objects in the beach sand after brunch ended. Ellen was the first to speak. "That was fun today. I'm glad your movies are doing great. What do you do with all the money, Jim?"

"Pa and Lo's lawyer handles the money, investing it for me in municipal funds, Roth IRAs, 401Ks, and diversified stock funds.

He's the same one who takes care of Temple's investments. Pa makes me look over each investment. Even though he and Lo trust Cleaver completely, he told me to never give over control of my investments."

"How do you like the celebrity part so far? You don't talk about it much."

"What's there to talk about? It's not like anyone is recognizing me on the street. In school, I'm polite. The school kids don't care."

"Except for the girls," Ellen corrected.

"What?" Temple stopped for a moment, gripping Jim's arm. "What about the girls at the school?"

Jim patted her hand. "It's just Ellen trying to get a bite. Don't give it a thought. You know how it is when guys recognize you. It's much lower key at the school. The girls flirt. I'm always polite, just as you are with the guys who talk with you."

"You're a guy. It's different," Temple said. "I know Mars Bar is baiting me."

"Lo ate your lunch, Shortcake," Ellen replied. "Madigan boot camp? I don't think so."

"I'm not finding out. I need Rick and Lo. I'm not screwing around and getting voted off the island. They like your initiative, but Lo will toss you under the bus if you keep plotting behind their backs."

"You're my minion, not hers. We can't stop our side investigations over nothing."

"Jim will rat your butt out," Temple declared confidently. "I trust Jim. You can't tell me what to do. Anything we do together will be discussed with Jim."

"You are carrying your Lo act too far, Ellen. We're not your minions," Jim told her. "We have fun together when you don't push things too far. Temple drives us everywhere. She goes along with all your goofy plots, some bad, some good. You have charisma. You had Jesse contemplating following your direction. Pa and Lo don't want you to stop because you have potential. Rein in your Lois Madigan mimic side until you have the experience and skills to handle situations like she does."

By the time Jim finished, Ellen's tight lipped mouth and blushing features indicated his input caused outrage instead of contemplation. "Maybe you're right about everything. I admit it. You two piss me off... always wanting to play it safe. The world's not safe. If you want to get anywhere, you have to take chances. I have to do what I think is right."

"Even if it means getting us all killed," Jim asked.

"Teens used to do all types of dangerous things without dying in the old days. I'll bet Rick and Lo turned their old fifties and sixties worlds apart when they were teens."

"Our world is different. People know everything we do, no matter how private we stay. Every person has an HD camera with instant digital communication on a device capable of sending out images and movies for the whole world to see. Gangbangers think they can play knock-out games against people for any imagined slight. Political idiots beat people if they have an election yard sign going against their wishes. Police officers get assassinated as they try to enforce the law. All that is where your imagination goes on vacation, Ellen. This ain't the fifties, sixties or any other old decade. It's a world of Death Cult terrorists, racist thugs striking out at anyone in their way, and killers who think death is a game."

"Jim's right on all counts," Temple stated. "That was awesome. I grew up playing a teen detective, but I knew the difference between reality and fiction. I'm not sure you do, Ellen."

Ellen knew she hovered close to the point where her two best friends would think they needed to leave her behind. School friends, workouts, movie premieres, training – all would be gone. "I'll take my passion down a notch but I don't have to like it. You two don't really think I'd put you both in danger on purpose, right?"

Silence.

Ellen stopped in her tracks, watching Jim and Temple keep walking. "That's just... wrong!"

* * *

"Meg! It's been a while. You look great."

"Hi Ned. It's good to see you. I had to move to another area. This is my friend, Trish."

Ned shook hands with Trish. "I'm Ned Cochran. You look very familiar. No matter... any friend of Meg's is welcome. What can I get for you two ladies?"

"I'll have a glass of Beringer's. Nice to meet you, Ned." Trish liked the looks of the lean, dark haired, six footer. He didn't look like an Oxy addict, but she was well aware of the painkiller addiction. It was very hard to distinguish.

Meg picked The Lounge bar area because Ned worked there the last time she saw him. The Lounge's popularity with regulars made it the logical choice for the cousin. Located upstairs, it would be a bar to frequent away from casual sightings. Meg and Trish arrive at 6 pm to possibly meet with one of the waitresses or Ned before the bar filled. Only five other people were in the room and they enjoyed cocktails together at a table. Meg wasted no time.

"I'm not a cop anymore, Ned. I work for Madigan/Cantelli Security. Trish is my partner at the firm. You may have seen some of the headlines about our firm's involvement in violent episodes lately."

"I sure have." Ned checked to make sure the table guests were happy and then returned behind the bar, leaning over it closer to Meg. "What's this all about? Cantelli's the ex-Seal that wasted ten guys this past few days. I know your partner too. I follow the entertainment page. You two escort celebrities and Trish Medina's a star."

178

Trish showed him pictures of first Walter Palinsky and then Stoner Gordio. "The first is the cousin of the second. He runs a tab in here under the name Walter Palinsky. The second guy is the one we've been hired to bring in. Stoner Gordio killed two men in an escape from Atwater Prison."

Ned straightened away from the bar but kept his voice low. "I'll be back with your Beringer's. Is that what you'd like too, Meg?"

"Yes, please... and a little more talk. I have an offer for you."

Ned filled two wine glasses with Beringer's and brought them over. "On the house. What's the deal? I know Walt. He's a regular. I've never seen the second guy. You believe he's coming in here?"

"Walt's his cousin. He's helped Stoner before," Trish answered. "There's five hundred dollars in it if you'll call us when or if they come in."

Meg passed Ned her card. "That's my personal number. Are you interested in helping us?"

"For five hundred in nailing a prison break killer, I don't think so." Ned smiled. "For you, and to get Stoner off the streets... yeah, I'll help. Only on one condition though."

Meg blushed, amusing Trish. She looked away from Ned. "What's the condition?"

"You give me another chance. I've missed you. I don't do Oxy or anything else. I haven't touched anything since you broke up with me."

"I...I... uh..." Meg stammered, earning a head slap from Trish.

"It's a deal, Ned," Trish told him as Meg gasped. "She's already wet thinking about it."

"Trish!" Meg hissed.

179

Ned enjoyed the exchange, covering Meg's hand with his. "Just dinner and a movie or something. You can come over and inspect my medicine cabinet."

"Okay... I-"

Ned glanced suddenly at the room entrance and then back at Meg. "Hold that thought, Meg. Walt just now walked in, but he's alone."

A big, sandy haired man, wearing black jeans, black open necked shirt, and black leather coat walked in, taking a seat in the first chair at the bar. His trimmed beard and tied back hair gave Walter Palinsky the look of a biker. He nodded at Ned as the bartender moved swiftly in front of him to take his order.

"Hi, Walt. What can I get for you tonight?"

"I'll have a Black House Stout. I'm meeting someone. Run a tab for me, Ned."

"Sure thing." Ned served Palinsky, staying down at his end of the bar, away from the middle where Trish and Meg sat.

Meg and Trish sipped their wine without paying attention to Palinsky. "I should never speak to you again. What kind of partner slams her friend like that?"

"Oh, calm down, Meg. I did you a favor. Ned knows what you do. He's not afraid of killers and he wants to get in your panties again. What's not to love? He said he'd let you inspect his medicine cabinet."

"Wonderful." Meg leaned closer to Trish. "The cousin's meeting someone, probably Stoner. What should we do?"

"I vote we call the coots and take these guys down now. Let me call them and see if they're coherent. Rick and Lo tossed a few back earlier." Trish called Lo.

"Yeah, Skipper?"

"The cousin's at the bar at this moment," Trish told her.

"He's waiting for someone, but we don't know who. Very few customers are here now. It looks good for a takedown. Want to gamble and collect Killer Cantelli for a party?"

"We're still at Rick's. It's a good gamble. We'll enter as the bent over old couple like the night we took down the drug dealers on the pier."

"Some disguise."

Lo growled. "Be there in twenty."

"See you then." Trish disconnected. "Lo said they'll be here in twenty. They'll come into the bar all bent over and feeble like they did when we hit the drug dealers on the pier."

"This would be perfect," Meg replied. "Should we zap both? We don't know what the connection is between Palinsky and Gordio."

"We do it as outlined by Lo. You're thinking too much like a cop. We toast them until they stop moving. Get your head in the game. Think about the Ned love machine on your own time. Did you wear panties tonight?"

"Not funny," Meg replied through clenched teeth.

"Ned looks good. I say give him a chance. Here's what we do. The moment Rick and Lo sit down at a table, you and I saunter by them. We turn and zap the crap out of them. You take the cousin. I'll take out Stoner."

"Okay. I'm glad the coots have FBI credentials. Zapping people on public property is probably not the best of ideas."

"It's a good time for it. There's not many people here and we've informed Ned about the escaped killer. He'll be glad not to have them in the bar," Trish replied. "Well... well... Stoner walked in just now. He's sitting at Walt's right, so I walk out first."

* * *

With my cane and bowler hat, I slouched toward the table

181

directly behind Stoner and Walt. They sat exactly where Trish said they were sitting. I gripped Lois's arm as she too made her way to the table, slightly ahead of me. She wore a tied down bonnet. We were adorable – two old coots as our underlings like to call us, out for an adult beverage.

Imagine our surprise when Trish called to let us know Stoner and Walt decided to have a meeting at the Crow. Neato. Lo and I had been sipping coffee ever since the earlier belts we drank while eating and visiting. It had been a great day at the beach house, with movie conversation, intricacies of detective work, and Bone giving the kids a lesson on filtering out gibberish while digging for information.

Now, here we were, sitting right behind a high profile target. Lois called Bill Staley to put him on alert about a possible apprehension of killer, Stoner Gordio. To say he was excited at the prospect of a live fugitive, guilty of killing innocents, would have been a tremendous understatement. Bill promised to have local law enforcement ready to take custody. Lois eyed Stoner Gordio with Harpy talons ready. I knew she wanted to Taser him right into the floor. I had reminded her of the importance of FBI credentialed backup on this, coupled with the fact we supplied the enforcement end if other unknowns decided to interfere. Lo gave Trish the nod.

Trish and Meg, dressed attractively, moved with the grace of debutantes at a ball. They laughed, teased the bartender, and sauntered suggestively toward our targets. They achieved their goal of attracting attention. Walt and Stoner gulped the hook like two big guppies. Stoner started their downfall by wrapping an arm around the passing Trish. He may as well have stuck his hand in an alligator's mouth. She hit him with the juice until he collapsed off his chair doing the six million volt jitterbug. Meg missed Walt who lurched away. Lois shot the needles into him belt high. She got her happy on until I put a hand on hers. She sighed and cranked it down.

I held my FBI credentials out to everyone in the bar. It had been filling gradually with customers. "Our prisoner is an escaped killer. His buddy is an enabler. We're taking custody of them for transport. Please enjoy your evening. We will be leaving shortly. We apologize to the 'Tipsy Crow' for any inconvenience, but this is a very dangerous man."

My announcement quieted the usual gasps and yelps of surprise and anguish. I then went to work on our prisoners, cinching them securely with plastic restraints. I got them to sitting positions on the floor while Lo, Trish, and Meg watched my back. It took a few moments to get the duo into coherency. They were not happy. I helped each one to his feet, grinning at the declarations of innocence and mistaken identity. I grabbed Stoner's chin, knocking my bowler hat off.

"Hi, Stoner. It's me, Rick Cantelli. That's Lois Madigan next to us in the bonnet. We're collecting you again. My advice is stay in prison. It won't go well for you the next time we see you. If you'd like, I'll give you a demo of how you'll be going into the afterlife." I held my stun-gun to his nuts. He squealed like a rat when the trap slams on its hind quarters.

"No! Take me back... I'm done."

Lois faced him, tearing off her bonnet. "If it were up to me, I'd fry your ass until the eyeballs in your head popped right out of your skull. Do anything even hinting at resistance and we'll take you somewhere quiet and teach you respect. Nod if you understand or I start your lessons right here."

Oh... he nodded. Walt was a problem and an enabler. He assumed he'd be let go after all the commotion died down concerning his killer cousin. Ah... no... that's not how we operate.

"I'll own your asses for this!" Walt's mind flipped into unreality. "Stoner's my cousin. We met here because I hadn't seen him in a long time. I don't know nothin' about no jail break or killings!"

"You're harboring a known murderer," Lois said formally. "Save your legal protestations for the police. They know how to deal with accessory crimes. Come see us if they don't get you situated

183

properly. Rick and I will see you get treated to just exactly like you deserve. Now, let's all walk quietly down the steps to the front door. I've already contacted our local constabulary. They'll take you two cousins into custody in a more formal way. Don't forget to fill out our 'how do you like us now' cards after booking."

"I'm not recommending you assholes!"

Yeah, we all enjoyed that Walt statement. Lois patted his cheek. "You're just adorable. I hope they let you out, Walt. You and I will have some fun then."

We marched them as inconspicuously as possible to the exit. In the lower Main Bar section we encountered what Lo and I think of as collateral damage, meaning if our exit is interfered with, we get violent until everyone understands the circumstances. A big bruiser of a guy rushed at us from the side.

"Hey! You ain't takin' Walt anywhere!"

I faced and waited for him, measuring all the ingredients with decades of expertise. I dropped him with a perfectly timed uppercut that I'm sure some dentist will have to repair. He landed heavily, blood seeping from his damaged mouth. I once again showed my FBI credentials in a professional manner.

"Relax folks. Captured killer here. Enjoy your evening. Sorry about Walt's buddy here, but Walt's in federal custody." I spoke while Lois did a quick search of identity and weapons on the downed intruder. She took a quick picture of his license.

"We're good, Rick." Lo gestured for Trish and Meg to continue to the exit.

Plain clothes cops we recognized from Bill's University Precinct awaited us on the curb. The black detective, Art Moorer, grabbed Stoner in a less than professional way. "I knew the guard you killed, you piece of shit! Play me at your own risk to the station. I'd just as soon drive to the side of the road and slit your fucking throat as look at you!"

184

I put a hand on his arm with care. "Easy, Art. We need you on the force, buddy."

"Damn, Rick! Clyde had two little kids."

"I got him, Art." Stu Gillespie extracted the terrified Stoner from Moorer. He helped him into the backseat.

Art took Walt in hand and placed him next to Stoner with grim featured purpose. He took a deep breath. "I'm sick of this shit, Rick - BLM imbeciles, Stoner freaks, illegal alien terrorists... how in hell do you and Lo cope with these freaks? I've been on the damn job for two decades and I still can't get used to any of this shit."

"You're not supposed to, Art," Lo replied. "I'm sorry about your friend. Rick and I don't get used to it. We channel everything for a later date. I know you and Stu have been together for a lot of years. It's the main reason Bill sent you to collect these two. Stay on point. There's a lot more of us common people with you than you ever hear of."

Art nodded. "Yeah... I know. I have your number. If this turd gets free, you'll be my first call."

The cackle sounded like when I was young. "Oh baby... we'll have some fun then. You won't have to worry about Stoner again. Rick and I will drop everything until we get him. I'll send you a postcard. It will be on the down low though. We can't have deserved justice actually visited upon these pillars of society, right?"

A slow smile spread across Art's features. "I know what you and Rick have done... at least parts and innuendos. It's a damn shame the police are now the scapegoats for everything."

"That's how we see it too, Art," Lo replied. "Call me if you need anything, be it advice or a final solution."

"I sure will." Art hugged Lo and shook my hand. "I'm damn glad you two old killers are around."

"Keep that to yourself, my friend," I told him.

Art and Stu both chuckled at my admonition. "Will do, Rick."

After they drove off, the four of us were left to face the fact we took a damn killer off the street, and he was alive. Trish stared at us for only a moment before dancing around, pointing her fingers at us. "You two old has-beens! You wanted to torch Stoner so bad I bet your teeth are aching."

Lois breathed deeply and smiled. "Right on all counts. If we hadn't needed some brownie points, no one on earth would have ever seen Stoner or his cousin again without a séance. I kicked myself for not using you two as backup so I could fry Stoner's balls off. Thanks for giving me some closure on the cousin, Meg, you incompetent worm."

We enjoyed that zinger, Meg most of all. She shrugged. "You can leave, Trish. I'm rejoining Ned at the bar and pay my debt."

"You little minx!" Trish hugged her partner. "Ride him until he begs for mercy Peg-Rider. Yippie ki-yay, Meg!"

"I'm going," Meg said. "Goodnight. If I stay out here any longer, I'm going to toast Trish until her voice box burns."

We watched Meg return to the 'Tipsy Crow' with varying degrees of amusement. Trish enjoyed the interchange more than I would have thought normal.

"What is it with you and Meg?"

"Nothing, Rick. We enjoy spiking each other. I'm better at it than she is. That's all."

"How much do you know about this Ned guy," Lo asked.

"He's dreamy. Meg better overlook any of his flaws. That guy's the real deal and he cares for her. Ned was carrying a torch for her. We owe him five hundred by the way."

"It appears we'll have a messenger to get it to him," Lo remarked. "This has been one hell of a good day, kiddies. I'm done.

I won't be in the office until ten."

"Ditto," Trish said. "I wish Sam was home."

"Here," Lo handed her five hundred dollars. "Go give that to Ned. Tell Meg she can take the day off tomorrow. That should get you into her good graces again."

"Good one, Lo. See you two in the morning." Trish turned to hurry back into the Crow.

"It's still early, partner. Stacy's driving. Let's go back to the beach house and throw down a few more pops while we listen to the kids blather on about detective work and the movies."

"Perfect," I replied. "I think the kids had a slight falling out."

"Who cares? It probably had to do with Jim telling Mars Bar to behave or stay home."

"Agreed."

Stacy drove alongside at the corner. I opened the door for Lo to get in on the passenger front, before I slipped in on the rear side. "I saw the police take those guys away. That must be a relief to take down Stoner so fast."

"It happened smoothly with very little commotion," Lo replied. "It's definitely a bonus to get Stoner. I'll text Carmen and let her know Stoner's off the street. When we do get in tomorrow morning, let's work the Cindy Daniels angle right away. If she's harmless, no big deal, but if she's spying for some entity we don't like we can handle her Monday night at the gym."

"Yeah, let's not put her off any longer. We can go through everything in her life. I believe Ellen's right though. Although I watch my six when driving places, it may be we're underestimating Daniels. Maybe she's competent enough to be shadowing us. That would not be good at all. I hate to say this, because we're never this complacent, but we haven't checked our vehicles for bugs for a long while, probably before Daniels' first gym appearance. I think we should start with the simple first before we tear into OnStar and cell-phone traces. Daniels could have decorated every one of our vehicles on a single night at the gym. The range would make it possible for her or accomplices to follow us without discovery."

"You're right, Rick," Lo muttered. "We had that period of peace after the Logan Heights' movie and serial killer catch where we may have relaxed a little too much. We're in Staley's 'death cycle' again. If we find bugs on the cars, we'll need to trace them. Anything sophisticated enough to provide range have a limited number of shops specializing in stalking gear like that. We know a few."

"Daniels may have her prints on something too if she did plant them. We'll get on the case tomorrow. I'll check our vehicles at the beach house. We have one of our RF and GPS signal detectors at the beach house. I'll inspect ours when we get there. I'll do Temple's too. Pete drove her and Ellen. I may as well do all the ones still at the beach."

Lois growled. Not a good sound. "Wouldn't it be nice if they had someone on our case today? We might be able to back-trace them if they're close enough. I forget. Do we have one of our hidden camera detectors at the beach?"

"I believe we do," I answered. "We'll inspect every inch of the gym too. It's time to get our tech mojo going again. I doubt we can back-trace anything unless it's an obvious RF signal from an older device. That's unlikely. Was Bone still at the house, Stace?"

"Yes. He wanted to hear how things worked out with Stoner in person."

"I wonder if he'd be interested in a bit of surveillance tracking."

Chapter Nine

Detecting Work

I came in the house with my three teen shadows after our vehicle inspection excursion. All of our vehicles grew expensive transmitters at some point in the past. The kids loved every second watching my sophisticated signal detector. Our past training sessions involved security components and in Jim's case, actual installations. They understood how OnStar worked. I explained the difference between Radio Frequency signals and GPS transmitters. I set the transmitters I had removed on the kitchen table from my gloved hands. The kids watched Lois expectantly. She put on her nitrile gloves and examined them before handing one to Bone, who also was gloved.

Lo gestured at the surveillance treasures. "This removes all doubt what's been happening to us. No way some paparazzi wannabe shells out the money for these babies. Forget my 10 am crap, Rick. Can you get to the office early?"

"Sure. I agree with you. Let's get to work on our electronics first thing. Stace has to be at work for inventory. I'll drop the kids at school a little early and come in. How about it, Bone? Want to help us with some tech tomorrow."

"Count me in, brother. We need to do Jadie's Gym right after the office. This baby only takes maybe an hour to go over the entire place." Bone held our hidden camera detector in one big paw for Carlene to see. "Madigan/Cantelli has the best tech toys known to man… at least for a private sector company."

"This spy stuff is creepy," Carlene said. "I hope this isn't as serious as you suspect. Wouldn't the paparazzi invest big money for stuff like those transmitters too? I mean… they get thousands of dollars for one compromising photo, don't they?"

"It can be a lucrative and creepy way to make a living," I

189

admitted. "We can only go on hunches right now. Our hunch is something more sinister than paparazzi. We'll get it fixed quickly and find out who it is that's behind the surveillance."

"I wish we could skip school for the hunt," Ellen complained.

"Not happening, Mars Bar," Lo replied. "You kids don't skip school for anything."

"If it would help, I'll have Pete take them to school, Rick," Temple offered. "We can have a light breakfast in the limo on the way."

"Thanks, Temple. That would help," I told her. It would probably be a good idea not to drop Jim and Ellen off at the door in the limo. You can have Pete let them out a block or so away so as not to feed the teen trolls looking for reasons to terrorize their classmates."

"Great! Mornings are boring for me when we're not filming. Maybe I'll drive them. I need to do something besides read scripts. It seems like I'm either working 24/7 during movie making or wandering around the house," Temple said. "I'm looking forward to starting college for spring quarter."

"We'll have to work on your disguise skills so we don't have to have Secret Service level protection for you," Lo said. "Your last three movies have made it nearly impossible for you to run around town without some form of appearance alteration. The same goes for you, Jim. One more big hit and you'll need to grow a beard, coupled with hats and hoodies."

"I'll pay more attention from now on. I've been careless too, considering how close that serial killer got to me," Temple admitted. "Anyway… it will be nice to have a diversion tomorrow morning. I'll text you two around 7 am, and see how you're doing."

"Hey… you haven't mentioned anything about a new script you're considering, Temple," Carlene said. "Oh… I see it in your eyes. You have been looking at something."

190

"It's silly. Quincy Wolf wants to try his hand at directing one of those apocalypse type movies with me and Jim, surviving minute to minute with a pit bull puppy. He gave me the script to read. Quincy told me if I liked it to give it to Jim. It's violent and sweet, all at the same time. I'm telling him I won't do it though, because they kill off the dog."

"Agreed! I hate movies like that where they kill off the dog," Jim said. "I saw 'Old Yeller'. The ending sucked."

Ain't that the truth? "I'm with you on that one, kid."

"Rick had a mutt dog growing up named Tick," Stacy dredged out for everyone's instant attention. "He passed on of old age when we were seniors. Rick used to tie a belt around his hind quarters so Tick could go outside at the end."

"Gee… thanks for the lovely memory, babe."

"Well I'll be damned!" Yep. The Harpy was engaged. "You never told me you had a dog in all these years, Rick. Why didn't you ever get another and why is it this is the first time I've heard of it?"

"None of your business," I replied. "I didn't ever want a dog after Tick died. That's the whole story in a nutshell. It isn't an 'Old Yeller' story. Tick was fifteen when he passed."

"That's the truth," Stacy bludgeoned on into storytelling land. I could tell in her eyes I was going to get hosed. "Boy… if you wanted to get your ass kicked back then… just mess with old Tick where Rick could get at you. Remember when Tick was on the front porch, Rick?"

Bingo! "I could use a drink. How about you, Sis?"

"No… I don't want a drink. I want to hear about Tick on the porch."

A chorus of 'me too' erupted with Bone leading the call.

"C'mon, brother. I had me a big ol' dog named Reno. I never got another dog either because of him. We get too damn close to

191

them. When they pass… it's like losin' a family member. I don't have a porch story though."

I stood and made myself a drink at the sink. The memory of Tick on the porch that day stabbed me right in the damn heart. It was the day realization arrived I was going to lose him. Fuck Stacy, Lo, Bone, and the rest. I wasn't telling the story.

"Were you there, Stace?"

Stacy blushed at Lo's direct question. "Yep. Rick's parents went away for the weekend. We were sixteen and already doing what we weren't supposed to. It was like paradise that weekend. I made up a story I was staying with my girlfriend, May. She agreed to cover for me. Tick loved the front porch, lyin' on his mat, watching anything happening on the street in front."

"Don't do this, Stace."

"Pa!" Jim had to get involved. "We want to hear it!"

I turned to the window over the sink and shut up. What's the use? When you bond again with the love of your life from decades ago, shared memories from the past seep into a haunting miasma I believe follows into all the years ahead. I wanted Stacy with me. I better damn well get used to our past.

"Rick loved the shit out of that dog," Stacy continued. She would have barked like a dog if Jim demanded it. "He helped Tick to the front porch in his favorite spot. Then… well… ah…"

"Oh for God's sake, Stace!" Lois was not enthused with the suddenly chaste Stacy. "Get to the story. We all know what you two horn-dogs were doing."

Stacy chuckled over the reprimand, took a deep breath and went on. "Everything was peaceful until Rick suddenly launched to a standing, listening pose. Then I heard it too – sharp thudding sounds and Tick yelping in between barks. Rick jammed into his jeans and tennis shoes in seconds, raced out of the bedroom with me behind him, throwing his robe around me."

192

"Rick threw open the front door as a rock smashed into the porch floor near Tick. Three teens our age chucked rocks at the porch, laughing as they tried to hit Tick. I saw a couple rocks hit Rick as he charged into the three. He ran over the one in the middle and kicked him in the head. The fist fight following the kick seemed to last longer than I know it did. One after another, the other two went down. Rick didn't stop there. He began methodically kicking the shit out of them. I yelled at him that Tick was okay. I finally screamed at him. I thought he was going to kill them. Rick stopped and backed away as some neighbors came out. I ran into the bedroom for my clothes. When I returned to peek out the door, Rick was holding Tick. The neighbors clustered around the three downed teens until the police and ambulance arrived, glancing at Rick in surprise, horror… or probably both."

"In our town back then, the police didn't arrest the person defending his property. They looked over the porch and Tick. They saw where the rocks hit Rick on his way to the front. There was a bloody streak on his neck and a big bruise swelling on his chest. We gave them our statements. I told them I was visiting. The ambulance took the teens away. One of the cops gave Rick good advice. He told him to come with them just as he was and have his picture taken along with filing charges against the teens. I stayed with Tick while Rick went with the cops. He was only gone an hour. We cleaned Tick up. Tick loved the extra attention. The rock hits he took only hurt him with direct contact. The teens had an assortment of cracked ribs and broken faces."

Lois needed more detail, of course. "Why the hell did those punks do it… just for the hell of it?"

"My Dad was in a beef with one of the kid's fathers." I sat down. What was the use? "Dad fixed cars on the side for extra money. Kenny Boyer's Father thought our front looked like a junkyard. Thinking back, sometimes Dad did have two or three cars parked on our lawn. Our house probably looked like the redneck roadhouse sometimes, but neighbors weren't jammed into each other in Twin Falls. I've heard the population now is approaching fifty

193

thousand people. Back when Stacy and I lived there, it was less than half that. Kenny's Father, Kyle, stopped one day and told my Dad he'd have to quit working on cars in the front. Dad stuffed Kyle into his car and told him to go home."

"Kenny admitted later he rocked our porch because of hearing what Kyle said at home. He didn't know I was there even though he saw Tick on the porch. Kenny claimed he didn't mean to hit Tick. I agreed not to press charges. We didn't pay the hospital bills. All the parents were pissed, but between the pictures and police report, they didn't have a chance to do anything else."

Stacy chuckled. "Rick's reputation was cemented in stone. After breaking that guy's jaw who was going to slap me, and putting three guys in the hospital from the porch event, no one in the town screwed around with the Cantellis. I was grounded for a month when my folks found out where I had been. Rick's Dad put him in the Cantelli slave labor camp for a month, doing every crappy job he could find for Rick. He even hired him out for digging jobs and such. We were forbidden to see each other."

"Damn good story," Lo said. "Cantelli snuck into your room at night after the grounding, didn't he?"

"How… never mind… yeah, he would climb the trellis to my window."

"I see you grinning over there, kid." I pointed the warning finger of fate at him. "Don't get any ideas. I'm nailing your bedroom window shut and putting extra cameras focused on Temple's windows."

Temple gasped. "You can't do that without my permission."

"It's a very good idea," Ellen stated.

"Ellen!"

"We're all kidding, Shortcake," Ellen replied. "Rick knows he couldn't stop you two no matter what he did. He has to take Jim's word for it."

"Oh," Temple said, looking away from Ellen. "After that story, I'm thinking of doing the movie. I'll make it part of the deal that the dog doesn't die at the end. The trainer told Quincy we'd have to live and work with the puppy they pick out for the role so the filming will go smoothly. The dog has too many parts to not be completely trained. If I get them to agree to that, would you want to do the movie with me, Jim?

"Sure. I'd love to do an adventure movie again. What will we be surviving, anyway?"

"A nuclear war's electromagnetic pulse shuts down everything. On top of the casualties from the war, survivors battle for everything. Our characters lose their parents. We set out on our own into the mountains. I think they're using Wyoming for the scenes."

"I'll read it. I like it already as long as the pup doesn't die. If it was real popular, they could make sequels with the dog aging naturally into a badass sidekick."

Temple gripped Jim's hand. "We'll have to make the first movie do well first. I'll call Pete and have him take us home after Rick checks the limo for bugs, Ellen. That was a great story, Pop."

"I don't want a dog."

"Jim and I will take care of it and do all the training if we get the deal done."

"You two don't even have time to take care of yourselves," I retorted. "Dogs take a lot of care. They're not like cats. They love people and attention. They have to be walked a couple times a day."

"We know all that, Pop. Don't worry about it. Besides, we may not get the movie deal at all. They might tell me to shove my demand up my butt. The dog lives at the end or we don't do it." Temple called Pete for a pickup. "He'll be out front in fifteen minutes."

The kids said goodnight and split apart after I checked the

limo for bugs. It didn't have any so I figured her personal car probably did. I would have to check it tomorrow. Lo and I sat with Stacy and Frank in the kitchen once again. Jim went to his room to finish his reading assignment. Frank was the first to speak. Bone stayed with Carlene to have one for the road because Carlene was driving.

"I liked the dog story. Lo and I thought about getting a dog but like you said, we never have any time either. I bet you'll love the dog."

"Like Bone said, we get too close. It's brutal."

"I'll help with the bugger," Bone said. "I can keep my distance then. I can be like Uncle Bone to the dog. I wonder what they'll call the dog in the script. I can't put it off. I have to ask."

Bone phoned Temple on a Facetime connection, "Temple? I know they'll want you to call the puppy by its movie name while you two bond with it."

We watched as Temple clapped her hands as she sat in the limo with the back Bluetooth iPhone screen on. "Yes! I can't believe I left that out. Kull. They call the puppy Kull in the script. I had to Google the reference. Kull was a barbarian from Atlantis, Robert E Howard wrote about."

"Great stories," I said. "I like it. Dogs react better to consonants in their names."

"You read Kull, huh brother?"

"I read everything Robert E Howard ever wrote. He created Conan the Barbarian too. Anyway… it's a great name for a dog. I'm surprised a script writer would pick a great name like that and then kill off the dog."

Bone smiled. "I can picture a pit bull named Kull. They're cute as hell if people don't screw them up."

"I like this new movie idea if they change the dog part," Lo said. "People don't care if you kill fifty people, but if you kill the damn dog, it will turn off the audience forever. Make them change it, Shortcake. I want to see Rick with a puppy."

"I'll try, Lo. Goodnight." Temple disconnected.

"Thanks, Lo… crappy input." All the Tick memories were already flooding my brain in waves of sharp, biting remembrance of the greatest dog I ever saw. I poured another drink at the sink. Stacy came over to put her arm around me.

"Sorry, Rick. I thought Tick was far enough in the past to talk about."

"Don't sweat it. I remember the time when Tick and I were young. I wasn't real popular in the neighborhood with the kids. I spent a lot of time with him, traipsing around the woods near our house, pretending all kinds of things. I have those memories too."

I sipped and said my goodbyes to my guests. Lo gripped my arm on her way by.

"Tick must have been a hell of a dog."

I took a deep breath before answering as my throat constricted. "He was indeed, Lo."

After everyone left, I refilled my drink and went out to the back beach house railing. The breeze blew in gently from the ocean with a chilling salt taste to it. Stacy joined me.

"I shouldn't have brought up Tick."

"Yeah… you should have. If we don't share our lives with the kids they'll never know what the hell ever brought us forward to where we are. You saved me from prison that day on the porch. I was going to kill the three of them. Your scream yanked me from the abyss."

"I know. It's why when you came back from the police station, I…I… couldn't keep my hands off you. You were a killer. I could feel it. Everyone since then has been a fake. I admit I'm a sicko."

"We're a very weird pair, babe. It's best not to get too deep about the reasoning behind us standing here together. You're the reason I never married. I felt the heat when I came back from the police station. I never forgot the moments after... ever. That day on the porch jolted me into the realization of what I was. Life changed forever when you appeared again in my life. In spite of all the negative crap, I knew there could only be one for me to share the rest of this life with. We're old together. I never wanted anyone younger. You know me inside out. I know you'll never question anything I do because you have a darkness within you too."

Stacy grabbed me so as to look into my eyes. "I love you so much. You and Jim have given me life again. I don't give a shit if you kill a thousand people. I guess you know that about me. I know because of you I'm not a complete sociopath. I will be with you forever, Rick. Come to bed."

I ran my hands along her sides, staring into her eyes until she shuddered under my touch, with the cooling ocean breeze caressing our souls.

"Please... Rick."

I journeyed then into a youthful moment from long ago without regret or nostalgia. We joined in a white hot recognition of everything we were and hoped to be.

* * *

Temple drove her car in spite of any bug that might be on it. She figured it would be safe to drive Jim and Ellen to school. At the beach house, Jim saw what she was driving and went back inside. He came out with the detector. After his inspection, as she awaited the results, Temple conjured other thoughts with a cloud of guilt descending. She knew Stacy worked an earlier shift at 'Godfather's Cell' that morning because of a business meeting. Rick left earlier to meet Lois at their office. Jim proceeded to do an intense inspection of Temple's vehicle, taking more time than needed from his observation of Rick's doing it the night before. When he straightened, and glanced at Temple, her blouse was open under the jacket she wore.

Jim scanned the area around them uneasily. "What are you trying to do, Shortcake?"

"What do you think I'm trying to do, Hooterville Jr? We have the beach house to ourselves. I came early because I knew Rick and Stacy would be gone already." Temple moved against Jim, feeling his entire body tense at her contact. "I want you."

Within seconds, Jim's attention to detail with his scanner collided with Temple's seduction ploy. He was lost, and Temple knew it. She led him towards the beach house. "Don't say anything. Don't think anything. Make love to me again like the first time in the movie set trailer."

* * *

Ellen looked at her watch again. She had called both Temple and Jim, only to have her calls go to voice mail. When she returned her attention to the street, Temple's new black Toyota Highlander drove into view. It both thrilled her Temple listened to Ellen's advice in buying a mainstream vehicle, and made her slightly envious her friend could buy anything she wanted without a thought. As she entered the Toyota's backseat area, Ellen noted Temple's hand pulling away from Jim's thigh. Ellen controlled her breathing, mad because she also envied Temple's affair with Jim. She could tell instantly the two had once again escalated their togetherness into the physical realm.

"Well, this explains why you two didn't get here early like I expected."

Jim didn't look around. "Careful with your mouth, Mars Bar."

Temple remained silent. Ellen could see her face in the rear view mirror was bright red.

"I'm just sayin' one look at Temple in the gym and Lo will have her ear twisted into a pretzel. You're okay in the casual mode,

Jim, but it won't do any good when Lo mind melds with Temple. I think it's what makes Temple so well liked in her movies. You'd have a hard time being a villain, girlfriend."

Temple sighed as she drove toward the school. "It was my fault. That story last night Stacy told about her and Rick was so romantic. You're probably right. Lo's going to torture and lecture me and I don't care. I know you're right about my inability to play a villain. No one would believe my attempt at acting a part like that. I have to think of my parents whenever I need to express rage for a scene."

"Maybe we could rehearse enough like you do in the movies so facing Lois wouldn't be such a dead giveaway," Ellen suggested. In spite of being upset over the physical aspect reemerging between Jim and Temple, Ellen wanted to be able to fool Lo at least once in a while. "I want you with Jim and me, doing things on occasion, without vomiting it up to Lois the moment she looks at you. I don't know much about acting. Is that possible?"

"I'm not sure. I can act seriously for parts. Maybe that would be a way to throw the Harpy off my scent. When she gives me the Medusa stare, trying to rip facts out of my head, I can be prepared to discuss something serious. I'll practice at the gym. Otherwise, my goose is cooked."

Ellen's brow furrowed as Jim chuckled in appreciation of the idiom. "Where the heck did you get that saying?"

"I research idioms like that when I'm acting. I suggest them to the writers on occasion for a funny line or even a serious one. That one came from a fourteenth century Czech priest who was burned for religious reasons. His name was Hus which translates loosely to goose, hence 'your goose is cooked' meaning you're in trouble or a mess."

"I have to say, it's great being your friend, Temple. I'm always finding out something else about you I would never have expected. I like your idea of cooling Lo off with some serious fact from your life as a question to her. You'll have to be able to spew them out when needed though. Any hesitation and it won't work for a second."

"Agreed, Ellen. I need to work on my game face big time. Part of it is... hey! Check out that white van!" As Temple slowed her approach toward Patrick Henry High School, a block away from Green Elementary School, a white van parked near two school girls walking toward the elementary school.

Three horrific masked clowns in full head to toe costumes leaped from the van to surround the screaming girls, gesturing and grabbing at them. Jim jetted out of Temple's Toyota before it came to a stop. He launched a sidekick into the first clown's leg that buckled the joint. Jim followed through the kick, tackling the second clown as Ellen and Temple arrived. They stun-gunned the third clown to the sidewalk. Ellen added a long blast of pepper spray in the clown's face. They both ran to Jim, who was pummeling the second clown into the cement with elbow strikes and forearm blows.

"Jim!" Ellen shook her friend's shoulder, while Temple used her camera to film the van driving away from the scene.

Thinking he was being attacked from behind, Jim ducked and rolled forward over the second clown, turning with fists in a fighting stance. When he saw Ellen and Temple, Jim dropped his hands. The first clown was screaming in pain from his shattered knee joint. Jim kicked him in the face. Temple and Ellen hugged the two terrified girls, calming them. Jim Facetimed Rick.

"Pa! We have trouble. Creepy Clown attack... if you can believe it." Jim scanned his iPhone over the area where three miserable clowns were in different stages of distress. "They tried to attack these two girls."

After showing Rick the two targeted victims, Jim acknowledged something and disconnected. He went over to the girls and his friends. "Lo's calling the police for us, explaining the situation. We'll need to keep the clowns here. Can you two girls stay until the police come? They'll need to know what happened to you."

Both girls nodded. Ellen could tell they were afraid to do anything other than wait for the police. Ellen was the first to speak. "I've been reading about these Creepy Clowns. I never thought I'd see one or get a chance to pepper spray and stun-gun one."

"What do you think they were going to do?"

Jim put a hand on Temple's shoulder. "Probably just scare the hell out of the girls. I'm glad we didn't need to find out. I hate clowns!"

Ellen smiled at the broken and maimed clowns writhing on the sidewalk while the one she pepper sprayed cried, sobbed, and threw up in the grass. "Yep. It was a bad day for Bozo wannabes."

* * *

I held the phone for Lois and me to assess the clown carnage. Lo immediately called Bill Staley and put Cleaver on alert. "Hang tight, kid. We're on it. Lo's getting the sirens moving."

"What is this phase, Rick? Did you see that one clown's face? Those are elbow strikes."

"Jim knows not to let an attacker off the pavement. The other one probably won't be walking around the same way ever again with the angle his lower leg was at. Boo hoo."

The cackle sounded. "I think Ellen might be the catalyst. We can label these the Ellen phase. Let's get going. Maybe we can survey the damage before it gets hauled away."

Lo's phone buzzed with a message. She pumped her fist. "Yes! Shortcake filmed the getaway van complete with license number."

"I see those beady little eyes of yours and fingers tapping at a streaky pace. What are you doing?"

"Can it, Peeper. I'm working here. I'm texting Shortcake not to give the video over of the van until I see if it's registered or stolen." Lo proceeded to find answers to her question as I grabbed a

Go Bag for our trip to the scene of Creepy Clown reeducation. Her dance signaled the cops may not get a chance to investigate much into this.

"You've learned the van wasn't stolen, and Shortcake acknowledged not giving the number to the cops."

"I texted Bone. He's on it too. Maybe you're not as senile in the head as you seem, Peeper."

"Gee, thanks, Sis… I think."

"Hurry up! I want to see some maimed clowns. I've been keeping track of this new idiot phenomena of 'Creepy Clowns'. I had hoped to get the first sighting of this shit in our area. Good Lord! I would have toasted their nuts off!"

I enjoyed Lo's perception and hoped for handling of the Creepy Clown phenomena. It only took moments before we were heading to the scene of the clown catastrophe. I had seen the videos of the 'Creepy Clown' incidents across the nation. They needed to be ended before every terrorist group used the phenomena as a cover. That some of them hadn't been shot yet was a mystery to me. This was better though from our point of view. The kids reeducated the clowns, and we received a license plate number we could investigate. Maybe we'd luck out and find a 'Creepy Clown' conclave to torture into submission or boat trip. If those assholes were using this façade as a way to actually grab kids off the street, our discovery would not end well for them. Lo and I can't be everywhere; but we will end a pedophile clown ring in secret, and not break a sweat.

We arrived at the scene of clown crime in time to see the EMTs working over the clowns, much to Lo's amusement. We showed our FBI credentials to get onto the scene with Lo scoping out each clown's injury prognosis with enjoyment. We spoke before joining the kids and target girls at the sidewalk's side.

"Oh my, Rick… this is just so much fun."

I had to suppress the appreciation for Lo's pronouncement

with will power. "I don't know yet what these mongrels expected to accomplish. We'll find out shortly. I'm really interested in the race of these guys. You saw the features on the clown the girls stungunned and pepper sprayed. He'd cried or wiped away most of his makeup."

"I saw it. The prick's Middle Eastern. It would be a perfect play for those pedophile assholes from Islam to latch onto something like this. They'd defend it as their right by Sharia Law to do anything to the infidel."

Lo jabbed her finger into my chest. "You're baiting me and I don't like it."

"Sorry. I did in a way. We have the opportunity to get to the bottom of this singular cesspool. Let's do this. We'll go through the motions here and bring the crew in on the discovery and action phase immediately."

"You're reading my mind now, Rick. Let's do it." Lo led the way over to the kids. There was no reason to talk with the police yet. We could make up for any slight they felt later.

"You kids were exceptional," Lo stated. "I'm jealous of the clown clubbing. You've all earned the right to give me a thought on this. Do it quick and concise."

"I saw Moslem in the one Temple and I blitzed," Ellen said.

"I saw terror, Lo," Temple added. "They meant to make a statement and get away with it. They were going to take those girls. They wanted others to see the taking."

"Damn good insights, girls," Lo complimented them. "What about you, young Hooterville?"

Jim didn't pretend. "I saw those clown faced bastards attacking the girls. All I wanted to do was kick the shit out of them. I admit I didn't give much thought to anything else, Aunt Lo."

Lois hugged him. "Don't give it a thought. Your Pa worked the same way. That's why weapons have handlers. They act and react in a heartbeat. Handlers make sure the initial interaction goes only so far. You girls kept Hooterville Jr. from killing. I can see it in your faces. Well done. I had the same problem with Hooterville Sr. They're seldom wrong when they force a mission. Keep that in mind. Handlers guide and infuse data. When the rubber meets the road, we do exactly what you two did – maim and kill until the op is done."

"We'll see what the police plan is for the clowns and witnesses. Did they talk to the girls already?" The parents and girls were grouped together about twenty feet away.

"No," Jim answered. "The parents arrived a few minutes ago. The girls are really shaken up. I heard the police tell them to relax for the time being. They took our statements and confiscated our stun-guns and pepper-spray. Do they ever give our stuff back?"

"Probably not," Lo answered. "They may look the other way that you three were armed with the tools. Stun-guns and pepper-spray are illegal for minors. It's sixteen to eighteen with adult permission on the stun-guns and eighteen and over on the pepper-spray. We may have to get Cleaver involved if the police on scene make an issue of it, or the clowns do."

"I don't like the clowns' chances." We would need Bill Staley to identify the clowns for us if Lo and I couldn't get anything from hunting down the van. "We better talk to the police and see what they have in mind for the kids."

In an hour's time, the matter of who did what phase ended. Bill arrived on scene to check on things. The kids' use of force did not enter the conversation. Self-defense did. Thanks to Bill, the kids went on to school without a detour to the precinct station. The parents wanted our roughnecks recommended for sainthood. Their happiness at how the event ended went a long way to the unanimous decision to allow the kids to leave.

"Jim's infected with your DNA for trouble, Rick," Bill said. "I guess you and Lo already know about the illegality of Jim and Ellen having pepper-spray and stun-guns."

"It's better to see them alive at the end of the day than worry about the law," Lo replied. "We trust them to make the right decisions or we wouldn't have armed them."

Lo pulled Bill over further away from the other police presence. "We don't hide from you anything that may be important later. We have details on the clown van. One of the clowns for sure was Middle Eastern. Rick and I want to check the van before we release information to the police or even if we need to."

"Lo... those three clowns in the hospital will be tried. The DA will bring charges. There will be a trial unless they take a plea deal. They will press them for information on their getaway van. It's in the statement the girls they targeted made to the on-scene officers. You won't have much time to conduct an investigation."

"We won't need much time. I will text you as to what we find."

"Understood. I'll text you with the identities the moment I receive them. I better get to the precinct. I'll also let you know if there are any problems with identification."

"Okay, Bill. Make sure you warn the guards on the clowns at the hospital of the potential danger until we can find out more information about these people."

"Will do." Bill smiled. "Those kids are really something."

"Yeah... they are," I replied. We shook hands and Bill walked away. "Do we have an address, Lo?"

"Bone texted it to me. He's seeing if we have anything in space we can pluck real time images from on the place. I'm open to ideas. I saw you brought a go bag."

"We do a drive-by after Bone gives us an idea of what's there. I was thinking of doing our old census bureau knock."

"Dangerous, but it's either that, or hand it over to the police. The 13th Street address Google map picture looked like a regular house, one story, single garage, and nothing remarkable about the entrance. You drive. I'll open the laptop so I'm ready if Bone can get some real time images. Do we have any bangs left?"

"I have two in the bag." We rode in silence toward the address. Bone called us five minutes away from the place.

"I'm streaming to you, Lo. It will be on delay. I've been watching. Infrared shows two people inside. Both are male and have emerged, loading stuff in the van. It looks like they're getting ready to bug out. They're inside right now."

"Thanks Bone. We're only a couple minutes out. Let's test our communications. Wait one." Lo gave me my com unit. "Do you hear me?"

"Loud and clear, Lo. Keep me on. If anything happens on your approach, I'll see it."

"Understood," Lo replied.

I parked four houses from the house front. We went to the back of the GMC and put on Kevlar. Each of us took one of the silenced Ruger 9mm handguns from the bag. With two inside, we wouldn't use the bangs. Once outfitted, I drove us to the address front. We exited quickly, jogged to the door and rang the doorbell. I waited a moment and rang again. Lo opened the screen door and used the lock at the hydraulic closer to keep it open.

"I have infrared imaging, Lo. Someone's coming to the door. He's holding something."

The door unlocked, opening slightly. I busted the door back into the greeter, leaving him for Lois. I went through, catching the second man, still partially in clown makeup. I hit him dead center, gripping his legs and driving him into the wall behind as I heard Lo's stun-gun's arc at my back. My partial clown carried a handgun he tried pointing at me as he hit. The wall ended his attempt, as the gun hand hit the wall, and his weapon cascaded down to the floor, luckily not discharging. I flipped him to his stomach, not wanting to leave any evidence if we decided to hand over the operation to Bill. I whipped murderous left and rights into his kidneys. He screamed

207

with each blow.

"I have your back. Cinch the clown." Lo chuckled because the clown was crying. "Oh you poor thing. One more shot, Rick."

I obliged. The clown sung out in high pitched agony as I plastic tied his wrists. "How are we doing, Bone?"

"Good, Rick. No movement anywhere around the front area. I have the police channel monitored. No calls. You and Lo can take your time. Did you catch a clown?"

"We have one, Bone," Lo answered. "He'll be pissing blood for a while. I want us to stay in contact though. If these turds are expecting anyone, I don't want to get surprised. Can you hang on while I toast one of them?"

"They were going to snatch a couple of little girls. Light 'em up."

"It won't take long," Lo assured him. "I'll make this clown pussy tell us everything we need in moments."

Lois and I incorporated patterns and methodology in the field. We seldom strayed far from it unless revenge was involved. We waited until our two perps regained their composure. They babbled about rights, they were innocent, and we had no right to break in. I took my time anchoring them into straight backed chairs Lo retrieved from the kitchen, slowly acclimatizing them to the fact we were not the police. Halfway through my positioning, the whimpers of acknowledgement filtered out, mostly because when a perp meets the Harpy stare, they know something more than their names would suffice. I gestured at Lo with a hand to remain silent. She smiled, because of course Spock-ella had mind munched my intent.

"You fools!" I switched to Arabic on a hunch because I racially profiled these two assholes. "What kind of idiocy is this? In broad daylight you idiots try and kidnap two young girls? Explain before we cut your throats why you would do such a thing?"

208

Talk about shock. Lois and I remained in neutral outraged form, awaiting an answer. I had no idea if my interjection would work or not. Who cares? They actually glanced at each other with utter ignorance. Then we heard the jewel.

"We received our orders!" The clown suddenly was miffed. "We acted exactly as ordered. Why have you Kaffirs done this?"

Lo gave the clown a taste of high octane electronic arc to his nuts. When he was coherent, she pinched his nose for a moment, shaking his face back and forth, before answering in Arabic. "Do not question us, dog! I will have you gutted on the floor and your throat slit like a sacrificial goat!"

The clown's comrade broke. "We did as ordered! Please… call Gabriel! He ordered us to do it. I spoke with him personally!"

"Oh my." Lo put her hands on hips, expressing doubt and threat in the same gesture. "We have come to torture every traitorous item in this cell's grasp from you two. Speak!"

Our ill-dressed clown acquired a glint of hope. "Gabriel has been attacked. His compound was assaulted and a guard killed! We are to direct attention away from the compound! Surely, you have received orders."

"Other than torture and kill you surviving idiots from this morning's disaster, we have no other mission to complete except end the two of you."

Lo's matter-of-factly stated execution hit these two tools to the heart. She projected a façade of absolute indifference to their pleas and explanations. They bought the program completely. "I will call for your sakes. One thing must be done before anything else happens. I want everything of an electronic nature in this place, including passwords and location… quickly. Otherwise we extract the information from you with pain you cannot envision."

The next half hour included a treasure trove of information we didn't anticipate. I pulled Lois aside. "Good Lord in heaven, Sis. The kids kick the crap out of a trio of clowns and we hit the mother

209

lode."

The Harpy cackle sounded, disturbing our playmates. "Did you get that, Bone?"

"I did, Lo! For God's sake, what in the hell do we do with these two?"

"That's not in your purview, Bone. Thank you. Lo out." Lo and I removed our ear pieces. Everything after this discourse had to be discerned by her and me. "What do you think, Rick?"

I grinned. I walked behind the so far silent minion. I broke his neck as his compadre screamed. I walked behind our clown and gripped his head in the same manner as his compadre. He was so wronged, so compliant, so ready to tell us anything to stay alive. Over the next half hour we took him meticulously through everything Lo could think of. Then... I broke his neck. Lo and I are not in the nice business. We only have one ending for the enemies of our nation. The three, luckily in the care of police custody, would be on the list. Each one would die upon release unless both of us perish in some way. I can live with that. Police Captain Bill Staley... probably not so much. Too fucking bad. Lo and I ride for the brand: America.

"I'll check the garage. If it's empty, I'll put our GMC in there and load the bodies. This screws our day a little, but we sure received some nice leads."

"You don't know the half of it, Peeper. Check this out." Lo held one of the phones she was inspecting so I could see the contact screen.

"Damn... Cindy Daniels. We have been under observation. The kids are making us look bad. First they uncover the Daniels plant. Now, they beat some clowns up and connect a ring of Middle Eastern gooney birds."

"Get the vehicles switched," Lo ordered. "We'll cry over our shortcomings later. I'll finish scanning through the phones before we load everything in the van. I'm not comfortable with these

210

interconnecting threads leading to Gabriel Paria. He's becoming a bigger pain than Aga Saleh. Maybe we should have rocketed his compound."

* * *

Two hours later we fed the fishes out beyond ten mile point. We drank a coffee and tried fishing for a little while after Lo moved the boat. The Cindy Daniels thread haunted our morning out on the waves. The tablets, phones and laptops revealed the links between the compound and the clown cell. We closed and transferred the money in their account to our own off shore stash. We hoped when our shark food guys were discovered to be missing along with the cell's money, it would further cast suspicion on someone within these Muslim Brotherhood splinter groups.

Paria's plans to kidnap the girls in broad daylight would have led to massive manhunts and missing child Amber alerts. Later, after the initial uproar died down, they planned to dump the girls' bodies outside Balboa Park. Lo was the expert at intelligence but we could not find any indication concerning the reasoning or possible misdirection behind the killings. It appeared we needed Paria alive for more reasons than we had known.

Lois started the engines. "We need to return to port. It appears we'll have to do this one step at a time. Daniels is the logical choice to question next. She's one of those self-loathing liberal enablers the Death Cult attracts. I'll figure something to draw her into conversation tonight at the gym as a stall. I'm glad I didn't talk to Jadie about Cindy yet. We'll send Trish in to check her locker and gym bag. If Skipper finds something interesting, we'll take Daniels with us after the workout. If not, we'll stay with the investigation for the time being, and hit the compound again on Wednesday night."

"If Trish could clone her phone, it may be worth it to leave her alone until after we do another night assault on the compound," I suggested.

"It couldn't hurt," Lo replied, steering the Sea Breeze for our dock. "We had better get a look at the compound's guard system

211

since you killed the music lover on their porch. Frank and I will swing by the beach house tonight. I'll find out if we can get a viewing on their place."

"Hey, Sis, ever wonder this week if we upset the Karma Gods or something?"

"We're still alive and so is everyone we care about. On the other hand, a lot of bad guys are dead. I'd say we dealt the Karma."

I chortled a bit over that one. "You're right. Between the kids and us, we turned into the Karma train. One thing… what if Daniels doesn't show tonight?"

Lo glanced my way with a slight smile. "Then we go get her. I don't know why but I have a hunch about Daniels. I wish we had the three clowns in our custody. I guess we should have kept our two Bozos alive until we scanned the damn phones. I've already texted Floyd that the Clowns Bill has in custody are part of a Muslim Brotherhood cell. I'll overnight everything we have from their place."

Chapter Ten

Tombstone and Extortion

We were almost back to the office when Shelly called. Lo had her on the Bluetooth. "Lacey called from the Nite Owl. She told me there's two bad lookin' dudes asking about you and Rick. They're paying cash and drinking ice cold Vodka. Lacey told them you sometimes stop by."

"Thanks, Shell," Lo said. "We were almost to the office after some business we had this morning. Rick's with me, so we'll head over there and check them out."

"Why don't I have Steve and Bone go over there for you," Shelly suggested. "I'm sure they can learn whatever motive those two have for wanting to find you and Rick. You two coots have been in enough crap this week."

Shelly's small crack at Lo and I drew a few laughs from both of us. "First off, Bone must be shielded from unknown messes. He only fills in as muscle when we have a logical situation we're aware of in advance. Secondly, I don't want to lose Henpeck. It would be just our luck he'd get scratched in the bar and Kris would yank him out of Madigan/Cantelli like a big tuna."

After Shelly enjoyed Lo's explanation, she did one parting shot. "We can't afford to lose you two meal tickets either. Bye."

"Shelly's getting mouthy."

"We can take it. We need her. She's not trying to get out into the field any longer and she's the best office manager we'll ever get, not to mention she knows where a lot of bodies are buried... so to speak," I replied.

"True. Who do you think these two punks are looking for us?"

"Lately, I'm not in the mood for guessing. At least they

didn't wait for Casablanca Night on Wednesday. Are we still going over for our extra dinner night?"

"We sure are. We can't drink before our compound assault but there's no reason not to have dinner and listen to Don playing piano with whoever we can get to sing. You're right about not ignoring chumps so we get blindsided at the restaurant."

The Nite Owl parking lot, nearly empty, but for four vehicles, became the practiced starting point for us. Lo checked the DMV records for each one. The little Toyota Corolla was Lacey's. When Lo checked the Chevy Silverado, the cackle sounded.

"You'll never guess this one, Rick."

"Don't tease me."

"Ben Sokolov."

Holy shit! "Russian Ben? What the hell? He got ten to fifteen at Atwater. It's only been a couple years. No wonder he came to the Nite Owl looking for us. We plucked him out of here back then."

"Ben's holding a grudge, shooting his mouth off, and drinking Stoli vodka. I'll check and see if he's out on parole or if some idiot lawyer got the prick's sentence thrown out. Hold on." Lo went to work on the satellite laptop keyboard. "His lawyer got his conviction thrown out for evidence tampering. What a crock. The prick's a killer. What do you want to do, Rick? We don't need this crap."

"Like you said, he's been throwing down Stoli in a few places. Once he got his nerve up, he juiced his companion into hunting for us. He doesn't expect us to show and ruin his drinking day. Let's go ruin it."

Lo clapped her hands. "I was hoping you'd say that. This shit is like a shot of adrenaline. Are you sure you want another bout, champ? How's your hands… and don't lie to me?"

I flexed them. "Real good. If he goes for a hideaway, I'll pistol whip him."

"Good call." Lo got out of the vehicle while checking her Taser. "If the buddy moves I will light him up like Christmas Eve at the White House."

"I never doubted that. What do we do with them afterward though?"

Lo shrugged. "Sometimes you have to let the deal play out. I'm not getting back in the damn boat again though. I could endure a drive to the desert. Eventually, it may come to that. We toasted Russian Ben until he sizzled like a shrimp on the barbie."

"You toasted him. I was an innocent bystander."

"You pistol whipped the guy with him. He ended up in the hospital with a concussion."

Oh yeah... that's right. "Uh... wasn't he wanted too?"

"Lucky for you, Peeper. Get your game face on. I'm going 'Tombstone' on Russian Ben. I'm feelin' the flow."

I grinned and loosened the Colt at my side. "Oh yeah. I have your six."

Lois barged into the Nite Owl with Harpy stare scanning all around. "I heard someone's looking for me. I'm your Huckleberry! Ah... there's my bitch, Rick! Hey tulip... did you miss me?"

Oh man... I watched the macho shit drain out of Russian Ben's face like hot water in a vortex. Lo walked into his air space, smiled, and told Lacey to bring a double Bushmill's Irish. Lacey rushed over with a double while the four of us eyeballed each other in much different attitudes. They wondered how the hell we got there and we wondered who to kill or maim first. Lo threw down her Bushmill's, sighing with a rapture I immediately was envious of.

Lo stared into Russian Ben's eyes. "Well... are you going to pull those pistols or whistle Dixie?"

"Listen, Madigan, I-"

Lois bitch slapped him. "That's Ms. Madigan to you, poser!"

215

God almighty, the only thing I wished was I could have streamed this to the office for safekeeping. The Stoli, his size, his bad guy image... nothing could get Ben's balls out of his stomach where they had retreated. His friend couldn't believe what was happening. He reached for Lo and I smashed him right between the eyes with my Colt's grip. Then it was on like no movie ever made. Lo pulled out her Ruger in a split second, jamming it against Russian Ben's forehead while I examined the identity of the companion.

"Pull your piece and let's play, butt-munch! Keep your finger off the trigger, and pull that hog-leg out. I'll give you the time. We'll settle all your grievances right the hell now!"

Ben glanced down at his groaning partner and lifted his hands in an openhanded gesture of surrender. "I'm done, Mrs. I'm done."

Lo grabbed his lower lip in an iron grip. "Hear this, sweet-pea. If I see you or I hear of you asking about me, I will end your pathetic life, no matter where you are. Nod your understanding, get this companion piece of shit on his feet, and get the fuck out of my sight!"

Russian Ben nodded. He helped his agonized buddy to his feet, guiding him toward the door, as I watched for any movement I didn't like. I thought we should have killed them on the spot. I confess to being wired wrong. I trusted Lois. Maybe we wouldn't have to hunt our bar intruders down. They would be on the list... forever until they were dead... or we were.

"Have another, Lo," I told her. "You can observe tonight at the workout. Your 'Tombstone' was the best of all time."

Lo smiled, signaling Lacey over. "I will accept your offer, Hooterville. I'll have another one of these, Lacey, and thanks for letting us know about those two."

"Uh... no problem," Lacey said, understanding for the first time she was in the presence of a killer without peer. "Damn... you two are scary good. I was terrified of the ones I called you about. I see now, there are realms of bad-asses unknown to me."

Lois sipped and then chugged her double. "Rick and I have been around blocks not listed in any map guide. We appreciate your help and your input. We will never turn your bar into a gunfight zone."

"I figured the gunfight would start just now."

Lo contemplated Lacey's observance. "Uh… okay… let me amend that to we won't do so without thinking every detail through. How's that?"

I could tell Lacey didn't believe anything of a violent avoidance in Lo's declaration. She nodded her acceptance though. "I'll keep you informed, Ms. Madigan."

Lois patted Lacey's shoulder. "It will always be Lo to you, Lacey. Thanks for the tip."

I waved at Lacey and followed Doc Holliday Lo out of the bar. I kept hand on Colt leaving the bar but Ben's Silverado was gone. "That was so much fun, Lo, I'm almost at a point where I wish we could do 'Tombstone' every day."

Lo waved me off. "It would get obnoxious facing down posers like Ben. He'll think about it in the time ahead. We'll have to kill that scumbag, Rick. The only thing we accomplished was add his friend to our list."

I smiled at her perception of our 'Tombstone' episode. "Agreed, but it blended nicely with the way our days have been going lately, including today."

"I can't argue with you there. Maybe we can make it all the way to the office with this attempt. Bone and Steve should be there by now. Other than helping out on info gathering, they're establishing informants for us, right? What else did we have for them?"

"They're on security patrol too. Bone mentioned something

about an install sale he was suspicious of having been scared off by a protection racket bunch. The owners of the herbs, teas, and spices shop are Chinese. They also cook specialty dishes for takeout. Did he talk to you about it?"

"I told him to hold off on any action," Lo replied as we drove toward the office. "I sent him and Steve to make a few placement diagrams according to the owner's wishes. They were hot to get the new system installed, but when Bone arrived with Steve, the owners gave them the fast shuffle about making a mistake."

"We're not the cops, so it's probably a bad idea talking the owners into something they don't want. Is it a commercial area we could sell a lot of systems in if we get the account?"

"It's next door to a lumber yard on Commercial Street," Lo answered. "There are a couple of small store malls on the other side. I believe we're being restricted by a bunch of thugs running a protection operation they think no one can touch. I'm feelin' the buzz, Wyatt. Do I have to get a lecture about drinking and facing off with hoodlums if it comes to that? We're on a roll today, partner. You remember what we used to do when we were on a roll in the old days."

"Yep. We rode the damn wave right into the rocks. No lecture from me. You're very entertaining on a buzz and I'll back anything because I'm jealous of the buzz. Let's stop at the office, gather Bone and Steve. We'll have a nice look see as to what's happening on good old Commercial Street. We can make a decision then on site."

"We may as well. We're not gettin' any younger, Peeper."

At the office, Bone, Steve, and Trish who had clocked in were waiting. Trish waved. "I think Meg got lucky. I didn't feel like taking the day off. I heard you two bandits and the kids stirred up creepy clown land, followed by a boat cruise. I might have known if I took a few extra hours off, you two would turn San Diego upside down."

Trish approached, pointing at Lois. "You've been drinking. I

218

see Rick's sober as a judge but wearing the same silly 'I fucked the neighbor's cat' look. Where have you two been?"

"Sit down, Trish. Lo and I stopped by the Nite Owl on the tip from our CI there. Lo did a 'Tombstone' on a couple of bad guys at the 'Owl'. We had fun. Relax, and I'll do the storytelling. I wish we'd had a movie but we couldn't risk it."

Trish enjoyed the hell out of that. "She really did 'I'm your Huckleberry'?"

"Yep. Grab a chair, because today ain't over yet. We're going to recon the Chinese herb shop this afternoon, without announcing our intentions to the owners."

We all got coffee, including Lo, who made hers Irish because she earned it. In five minutes, I had them all in a trance, listening to the story, with Lo's lines drawing much amusement. Shelly passed the latest report over to Lo about the herb shop. She scanned over it at Lois super speed, in spite of the liquor.

"Okay... I think I have a good understanding of this. You guys were right. This looks like someone stopped by and warned off the Zhoas. Rick and I were discussing possibilities. Do you think we can recruit the lumber yard business and those two little shop malls into our security network if we fix the Zhoas' problem?"

"They're scared, Lo," Bone said.

"Like we reported in the file, they were glancing worriedly out the windows while we stood there," Steve added. "It pissed me off. I knew cheap pieces of shit with their pants' waist down around their thighs, probably came in and tortured the Zhoas back in line. If you think we can stop this, I'm in all the way. I hate how the Zhoas were cringing while we talked to them."

"Good input," Lo said. "I'm the Chinese branch of this business. Rick's passable in Mandarin and a few other dialects. I handled most operational interaction though on scene. I'll speak with the Zhoas and see if I can get them to reconsider."

"Damn, Lo, you speak Chinese, huh?"

"Yeah, Skipper, I do." Lois launched into a tirade of Trish jokes in mainline Chinese I couldn't stifle all amusement from. "How was that, Rick?"

"Native as usual, Sis." I translated the jokes, leaving Trish red faced at first, and then laughing at the end."

"You two shits are too much for regular killers to handle. The damn CIA really does employ some bad ass assets when they can separate themselves from the pantywaists in DC. Good Lord, how many languages do you fossils speak?"

"Rick's the Russian bureau," Lo replied. "We both speak French, Spanish, Arabic, Pashto, Mandarin, and a few dialects of Chinese. We've been in crash courses when we moved in Italian, Czech, or a couple other places. Rick speaks Vietnamese because he did time in the Seals at the end of Vietnam. It was that time the Company got interested in him. The Company recruits all they can from special-forces with language skills."

"You two piss me off," Trish said. "It's no damn wonder the two of you trashed my contract killer career. The thought I had any chance against you two old pricks was shit on a stick. How many fucking foreign country ops have you two been assigned?"

"So many, it's stupid nostalgia to recite them all, Skipper," Lo replied. "We inform you bunch as needed, at this time, depending on our own interests. Right now… let's go see what we can do for the Zhoas."

I sat listening, reliving in a flash flood of visions, the times Lo and I entered territory we might never leave in one piece. I glanced around at our small family of people we cared about. Only Trish probably suspected in a small way how much Lo and I had been through. No one could imagine it all. In our prime, we were the deadliest duo on the planet. I think some of our adventures, since Stacy came along and lit the bonfire of past instances, we two old coots grasped the old danger like a life buoy, remembering what we

220

once were. That we wanted to hold on for the ride meant danger for anyone around us.

"Lo and I have your backs. Remember the option to get clear from us old killers is always available. We will make your severance pay enough to last for a long time."

"I'm never leaving this damn outfit," Trish stated. "I'm no movie star in reality. It's all fiction. When I'm here on stuff we shouldn't be doing, my happiness meter pegs. I know you two old goats regret the danger quotient for the rest of us. For me... forget about it. I'm into anything you allow me in."

"I'm in," Bone said. "I'd be in prison or dead if not for Rick. I get to use skills I learned I never dreamed would be useful in civilian life."

"Although I'm Henpeck now for derision, I hope to God I can continue on here."

"Well okay," Lo said. "Time to go over and see if we can make life a little better for the Zhoas. We'll take two Terrains. I want you monitoring the police band, Shell. Bone and Steve ride together. Trish... you're with us. We scope the situation out, do some surveillance in case we get lucky, and then move to conversation with our hoped for clients."

* * *

"We need to teach the Zhoas a lesson."

"They caved and sent the security assholes away. We good, Pete."

"We need to make sure they ain't backslidin', Drey. We own this, dog! We ain't lettin' any pussy Hollywood security shits put us out of business."

"I hear T-Bone Griffin works for them," Drey replied. "Believe me, brother, I don't know about the company, but that bad boy mixes with anybody."

221

"I saw him and some Cholo with him. We need to make the Zhoas understand that they die if a security crap firm gets a foothold in our territory. Enough time's passed. We stir the Zhoas up now and they don't ever think about puttin' no security on our asses ever!"

* * *

"Well, looky here," Trish said, looking through the range finders. "What is it with you two? You get in the mix and shit just falls into place."

"Shut your face, Skipper! We're working here. You'll learn if you live long enough that most ops depend on immediate follow-ups. Bone? You listenin'? We all go in if these two dolts heading for the shop go in."

"We're ready, Lo."

"We saw that lead prick on our way out, Lo," Steve said. "This ain't no coincidence."

* * *

Kel and Drey glided inside the herb shop, hoodies in place with sunglasses on, hitching at their pants. He motioned at Chen as she remained motionless behind the counter, looking away. "Hey baby... Drey and I wanted to check on security. After that misunderstanding earlier, we don't want you folks takin' heat. We got this, baby. No need for outside people. Neighborhood looks after itself. You feel me?"

"We...we want no trouble... only do business," Chen replied quietly as her husband joined her.

Kel gestured with his forefinger in jutting acknowledgement. "See? That's what I'm talkin' about. We doin' business. Black lives matter, baby. Remember that... we got no problem. We have to collect a bit extra though because of that earlier misunderstandin'. I think fifty will make things right, huh Drey?"

"Yeah man... that do for now." Drey turned as the door chime rung.

* * *

"Let me do lead, Lo!" Bone sounded off, already striding toward the shop within seconds after our gangster targets headed in. Steve paced only a couple steps behind him.

"Hold for us you blockhead!" Lo and I hurried out with Trish chuckling at Bone's enthusiasm.

"Let Bone lead, Harpy," Trish directed. "Just the sight of him will throw off those butt-nuggets."

Lo nodded reluctantly. "You lead, Bone. Steve? Get your hand on your damn handle."

"On it," Steve said on our com.

Bone barged into the shop, drawing both thugs attention as we caught up with them. He saw the lead punk reach and rushed him. Bone caught his wrist and broke it with a two hand snap. His perp dropped with a scream to the floor. Steve covered the companion with his Glock pressed against the stunned companion's head. The only thing Steve's thug had in his hand was a phone. Lo and I walked in with Trish, wondering if we even had the right guys. Shit happens. Bone went with his gut. We'll cover his play. I was certain he had the right guys anyway. I saw the one still standing glancing at his phone while thumb texting very adroitly. I took it off him.

"You too late, man," the texter informed me. "Best you and yo' troops get the fuck out of here. We doin' business. Let us go. Maybe we don't cap your asses when backup get here. They on the way."

We enjoyed his threat for a few moments while Bone and I restrained our two extortion racket specialists. The Zhoas watched us in stunned silence. The thug with the fractured wrist stopped sobbing. "Damn… brother… why you do me like that?"

Bone held the plastic bag of wallet, weapon, and drugs for him to see. "You reached for your piece, punk, and I ain't your damn brother. Shut your face with the cryin' like a little girl, or I'll kick you in the nuts so you have something to cry about."

"Okay... cupcake," Lo said firing off an arc with her stun-gun before jamming it against the texter's balls. The discharge gave him a nice wake up call. "Who the hell did you call? Answer fast or that little discharge jolt will be like Sunday morning sunshine compared to the zapping I have in store for you."

"Don't! I called our boss. We got an emergency line. Nobody mess with our collections. We own this area. Best if you find your own place quick. We got killers on the books."

"Thanks for the warning." Lo turned to the Zhoas and spoke to them in mainland Chinese. "How long have these two been robbing you? Answer in Chinese so these two cannot understand us."

"It has been six months. They claim to be collectors for the 'Black Lives Matter' group," Richard Zhoa answered. "They increase their demands nearly every other week."

"Thank you." Lo returned to the guy she questioned first. The rest of us were on watch for new arrivals. "Who is your boss?"

He cringed as Lo jutted her stun-gun against his crotch. "Dekay Kesson!"

"That bastard runs all the mini-riots we've had lately," Bone said. "He led that street blockin' business the other day, stopping cars and harrassin' people."

"What do you think, Rick?"

"Let's take them all. We'll gag the two idiots here and stay out of sight until they get here. After they get inside the store, we'll light them all up, and toast them until they're well done. We'll see what kind of a ride they have before we decide the ending to the story."

"I like it. Steve? If they arrive, and leave a driver with the car running, can you take him?"

224

Steve nodded. "I'll move the GMC closer to the scene and wait for the arrival. What do I do if the driver goes with them?"

"Wait until they get inside and we start the party. Join in. Once we get their vehicle keys we'll restrain them. If they have a vehicle with enough room, Rick and I will take them for a ride. We'll need an install done for the Zhoas. We'll need to keep an eye on their place until we sort this out. You stay on lookout while Bone and Steve do the install, Trish. I don't want anything happening here that we don't plan first. Let's get ready to rumble. Go on, Steve, and get set."

"But…but what about those killers comin' to get us," Trish joked.

"I do love a good barbeque, Skipper," Lo replied while Bone and I gagged the two extortionists out of sight.

* * *

The Chevy Tahoe parked in front of Zhoas' Spice and Herbs shop. Dekay Kesson glanced over at the three black suited men with him pulling black silk masks over their faces. "Go find out what this shit's all about!"

"What about the Zhoas, De?"

"Take 'em in the back. We need an example of what we protectin' everyone else from. You get me, Bras?"

Bras nodded. "What you want done with Kel and Drey?"

Kesson waved him off. "Bring those two idiots out. I'll decide later about them. Lock the place after you fix the Zhoas."

Kesson watched his three men strut into the Zhoas' shop. He grinned. *I needed an example anyway.*

His driver's side window smashed into pieces, raining small nuggets all over him. The stun-gun, so powerful he broke a tooth when it arced into his neck, jolted Kesson out cold across the shift console. Steve opened the driver's door. He shoved Kesson over the

225

console and onto the passenger side floor, upside down. Steve ran around to the passenger side door, paying no attention to the electronic noise coming from inside the shop. He gagged and restrained Kesson, hands and feet. After brushing the window glass pieces off the seat, Steve waited with his prisoner.

* * *

Our Taser needles hit the three killers as they cleared the doorway in their face masks. The barbeque escalated into a toasting of epic proportions. I didn't call a halt because I saw Steve wave from the Chevy Tahoe outside. Lo was having a lot of fun, varying voltage, randomly juicing her target at intervals opposite Trish.

"Ladies? Can we cinch these guys so our installation doesn't take until after work hours?" Bone and I needed some time to load these guys.

Lo and Trish quit reluctantly. Bone and I went to work on restraints and gags as Lo talked calmingly to Richard and Chen Zhoa in Chinese.

"Hey, Rick," Bone called out by his man. "This guy looks older. Maybe he's that Kesson guy."

I finished wrapping my prize and came over to check Bone's capture. I lurched away a couple steps as if someone had traipsed over my grave. "Lo! Come over here!"

Lois wasted no time. She excused herself and hurried next to me. She gasped in recognition a split second before the familiar cackle erupted. "Oh… my… God."

Trish finished gagging and restraining the guy she and Lo toasted. She peered over Lois's shoulder at the guy Bone cinched. "Do you know this gooney bird?"

"As I live and breathe… this… this is so special," Lo muttered. "Oh Rick, our ship has finally come in. It's the last of the holdouts."

"It's Dingo Salvatore," I explained to the very curious Bone

226

and Trish. "Dingo was a CIA contact in Bolivia. Lo and I went after a Hezbollah assassin wanted for attempted bombings of our embassy in Saudi Arabia in 1992. We traced him to La Paz, where we were put in contact with a supposed CIA asset named Dingo Salvatore. He ratted us out to the assassin, Momar Ahmadine, who tried to ambush us in the mountains near Caranavi."

"Rick and I weren't a couple of fresh picked fruit. Something about old Dingo didn't sit well with me, so we varied the approach Dingo suggested," Lo added. "I created a diversion on the road. Ahmadine and a few guys took the bait. Rick shot the driver through the head from his nest we'd picked in advance, but the damn jeep they had flipped over the cliff. We had to go down and make sure. It was a bitch of a jungle rot mess. After camouflaging our ride, Rick and I went down the mountain and took care of business, including pictures and DNA samples. Dingo was waiting for us at the top. Rick nearly got him from half a mile away."

Lo bent down and grabbed Dingo by the nose, moving his head sideways. A bald furrow glinted in the room light above his temple. "Rick ended the two with him but by the time we got to the top, Dingo was gone. We had to get the hell out of there. The USA wasn't on good terms with their President, Jaime Zamora. Dingo went on the list and we reached the extraction point on the Peruvian border."

"Damn," Bone muttered, looking down at Dingo who was regaining consciousness. "I don't think you'll have to worry about the list anymore, Mr. Salvatore."

At the mention of his name, Dingo looked up at a smiling Lois, and screamed behind his gag. Lo patted his cheek. "Ah... that's so sweet. He remembers me, Rick. I bet Dingo has a great story to tell us about how in hell he came to be in the BLM extortion ring here. I don't know that we have time to hear it though. I'm good to drive so let's get this show on the road."

With Trish, Bone and Steve watching out for gawkers, we loaded our new found friends into the Tahoe and GMC cargo areas.

Kesson did not like his trip from upside down into back cargo area where he was stacked like cord wood with his underlings for transport. Lois showed the Zhoas her FBI credentials and told them the gang would be going into federal custody. She explained we needed to install security to make sure there weren't any remnants of the gang left to come calling on them. They were very happy. We would send Steve and Bone around the area, along with Meg and Trish, to sell some commercial security systems since the protection racket was about to be closed for all time.

I drove the Tahoe after Steve and I wiped down the inside with Clorox wipes. Lois followed me to a grassy, tree-lined spot we knew of on Loma Paseo. I guided each one of our guys into a seat, put a plastic bag over each one's head until they freaked through their last breath. I then put their masks back in place, released them and buckled them into their seat belts. Safety first, I always say. I also folded their hands over their laps, posing them like little altar boys in the backseat. I saved Dingo and Kesson for last in the passenger and driver's seats. The little gangbanger boys in Lois's GMC would be taking their journey in the Tahoe cargo area. Lois was having some fun with the Dingo and Kesson, poking and prodding while I made arrangements for them.

"I wish we could help Dingo to the other side in a special manner but we just don't have time. Even the questions don't thrill me anymore."

"I know, Sis. It's been nearly three decades. The prick's probably been up to no good the whole time. Maybe we should stash him and take Dingo on a boat trip tomorrow."

"Don't tempt me. We have too much on our plate. Take him. Let bygones be bygones, I always say. I'll entertain Dekay until you finish with Dingo. We still have the two dingle-berries in my GMC too."

I helped Dingo to his feet, but kept my killer finger hold on him until he was belted in securely on the front passenger seat. I put the plastic bag over Dingo's head slowly, letting him feel the caress of plastic before tightening it around his neck. Dingo still had a lot of kick in him but like the other two, I was standing on his feet, hunched over holding the bag in place.

"See you later, Dingo. Your Bolivian buddies are all waiting in hell for you. Say hello for Lo and I."

When I rejoined Lois with Kesson in the back, she took off his gag. Oh boy, he was really mad. "I think DeKay is upset, Lo."

"I noticed." Lois played him. "Are you the big boss controlling the extortion games in the area, De?"

"You're damn right I am! Where are my boys?"

"They're up front, waiting for you," I told him. "We needed to warn you we are taking over Commercial Street. I'm afraid we'll have to relocate you and your boys."

Kesson snorted in derision. "Bullshit! I been workin' the street for six months. I ain't givin' it up to two old crackers. You two goin' to be sorry you were ever born."

"Gee, Rick," Lo whispered. "Maybe we shouldn't have messed with DeKay. Whatever should we do?"

"You best leave me and my boys alone. Next time I see you, you're dead! Hear me?"

Lo sighed. "I guess you better put him in the driver's seat, Rick. We need to send him on his way. I think he means business. I'll bring the GMC alongside so we can load his two gangbanger minions. They were noisy as hell in the GMC cargo bed. Be right back."

"Okay, Sis." I helped DeKay out of the cargo hold with finger hold pressure he didn't like. "Easy there, big fella."

"Don't! You bendin' my damn fingers too hard!"

I belted him in the front seat. It was then he noticed Dingo next to him, staring sightlessly out the front window.

"What the fuck is this!"

229

The bag went over his head and I anchored him down with my body while he went on his journey to hell. After a while, I removed the bag and posed him with his hands at ten and two on the steering wheel. I left the keys in the ignition but kept the vehicle unlocked. I still had some cargo to load. "You guys have a safe trip now."

Lois drove next to me in the GMC. I opened the two cargo hatches and transported the two wide-eyed punks, Lois nicknamed dingle-berries, from the store. They started their day of pillage and plunder early today. Now they get their reward. Lois parked in back of the Tahoe to block any traffic view. We did a quick dual bagging while sitting on our bound dingle-berries. I removed our restraints and gags. Kesson had an old bed cover in the back. I arranged the two BLM gangbangers in the cargo hold in a spooning position and tucked them in under the bed cover. I clasped my gloved hands together.

"Ah... aren't they cute?"

"Quit playin', Peeper. You're driving."

I slammed the Tahoe hatch closed. In the GMC driver's seat, I stripped off my Nitrile gloves. I put my seat belt on, because as I remarked earlier: safety first. "I'm going to miss old Dingo. I wish we could have asked him what the hell he was doing in San Diego. Dingo wouldn't have told us anything without you making a mess out of him. That would have spoiled our crime scene."

Lo nodded in agreement. "They'll have a field day when they investigate the Tahoe."

"Yep. The police will have fun, especially when they check their rap-sheets. We have all their personal stuff. We can go visit their places and see if we can work the puzzle for a while."

"Too chancy. If we can't get anything off their electronic gizmos, we'll leave it alone." Lo glanced at the clock. "We cut this a little close. We'll have to go directly to the school to get Jim and Ellen. We could call Temple to pick them up but I don't want Jim to get any ideas."

I enjoyed that wishful thinking as I drove toward the school destination. Jim and Ellen knew to stay inside the school, until someone familiar to them arrived. "It was a shocker this morning with the clown attack. Otherwise, I would call Temple and ask if she wanted to be designated driver. We'll check with Bone about notoriety from this morning's heroic kidnapping intervention. I keep forgetting Temple and Jim are huge stars right now, at least temporarily. I did check the 'Logan Heights' movie sales. They're through the roof."

"With everything going on I forgot to tell you Cleaver's getting requests from all the talking head shows. He's leaving the decision to Cheech and Quincy whether to let the kids go on them. He's afraid the age difference will be harped on at every visit."

Lo paused for a moment as if thinking about the situation for the first time. "He's probably right. If Cheech and Quincy want them to do a promotional tour like that, we'll have to coach the two of them through it. They had Trish and Temple stay away from the talking head shows and allowed Karen to handle the promotions with their male costars for the two romantic comedy movies. They can't do that with the 'Logan Heights' movie. Cleaver thinks they're nearly ready to film the third movie in the 'A New Beginning' trilogy."

"From killings to movie talk, Sis – we're livin' the dream."

* * *

"What are you two waiting for? You're not ambushin' clowns again, are you?"

Jim and Ellen both laughed at Jesse Martin's remark as he joined them near the front door. Jim answered. "My Pa gives us a ride to and from school because of the cases his security firm is handling. Your Dad's amazing, talking the principal out of suspending you. Are you coming to the workout at the gym tonight?"

231

"Are you kiddin'? Count on it. The principal was swayed by you going with Dad to explain it had been a misunderstanding. I never thought she'd drop the suspension either. Do you think there'll be protests again tonight at the gym?"

"I wish I knew, Jess."

"There have been so many gun battles and confrontations at the gym and restaurant, including a sniper attack, it's amazing anyone goes to the workouts or Casablanca Nights," Ellen said. "My folks allow me to go with Jim. I think they're trying to get rid of me."

Jesse and Jim inappropriately enjoyed Ellen's disparagement of her parents' concern for her. Two black students slid over to Jesse. It was obvious they were Jesse's friends. He smiled and gestured at Jim and Ellen. "Hey... I want you guys to meet Jim and Ellen. They-"

"Fuck that, dog! We want to know what the fuck you thinkin', you Uncle Tom traitor! Suckin' up to whitey!" The taller one in the front, jabbed a finger in Jesse's chest, so enraged, his hand trembled, and spittle flew."

"Yeah, Jess... you sold us out!" The second so-called friend wasn't as enraged as his companion.

"I didn't sell out anybody, Greg," Jesse gestured with open hands. "I learned a bunch of stuff I didn't know before. We've been lied to. Wealthy whites created BLM! My Dad-"

"No you don't... you don't talk shit about..." Greg shouted, pulling a knife. Jesse backed away quickly. Greg followed, his face a mask of deadly intent as he jabbed forward.

Jim remained still. Greg jutted the knife blade at Jesse. Jim, who had been on Jesse's left side, launched a full power left hook, striking Greg flush at his temple. He dropped as if shot, his knife clattering to the hallway floor. One of the security guards who had seen the interaction from down the hall was already running to the group.

Jesse stared in disbelief at the friend still standing and gawking at the unconscious Greg. "Jay! You guys wanted to cut me? What the hell?"

"No… Jess… I didn't know Greg had a knife. He was pissed. I-"

The security guard arrived. He was black too. "I saw what happened! You're comin' with me too, Jay! Don't you move!"

Bending over the fallen Greg, the security guard with Dennison on his nametag put the knife in a baggie after putting on Nitrile gloves. He then turned the snoring Greg on his back, patting his cheek until Greg began to groan. "I'm going to help you sit up, Miller. I saw you pull that knife on Jess. I don't know what your problem is, kid. I called the cops. They'll be here to collect you."

Jim, Ellen, and Jesse moved away to give the security guard room. Dennison helped the groggy Greg Miller to his feet. "You in big trouble. Jay? Empty your damn pockets on the floor."

Jay did as told. There were no weapons. Dennison gestured for him to retrieve his belongings. He then searched Greg and found a baggie of pills. By then a squad car arrived at the school front. Dennison took Greg out to them, motioning for the other teens to follow. Fifteen minutes later, having heard the story, including Jay saying he didn't know Greg had a knife, the police officers loaded a restrained Greg into the backseat.

"Oh shoot. Here come Rick and Lo," Ellen said.

Chapter Eleven
Oh Cindy

"What the hell is this," Lois asked. "A damn cop car out in front of the school, police officers, Jim, Jesse, Ellen, a security guard, and two black kids, one being loaded in the back."

"I swear this damn death cycle is threading its way through everything." Lo and I parked. We hurried over, noting the police weren't loading anyone else in the car.

Jim waved. "It's okay, Pa. The police are handling it. Officer Dennison told them what happened."

"Yeah," Ellen added. "Greg in the police car tried to stab Jesse. Jim knocked him the hell out."

Jesse started laughing, but Jim stared at Ellen with furrowed brow. "Way to calm the situation down, Ellen."

"Killer Cantelli?" The woman police officer smiled up at me. "I'm Peg Dixon. I was one of the officers on scene when you and Ms. Madigan shot it out with the terrorists that killed two of our cops transporting Tonya Stuart. You two are becoming a legend. Is Jim Bishop your grandson?"

"He is, Officer Dixon." I shook hands with her and an Officer McNab next to her. "This is my partner in Madigan/Cantelli Security, Lois Madigan. Did this Greg guy say why he wanted to stab Jesse?"

"They think I'm a sellout, Mr. Cantelli," Jesse answered for Donovan. "Greg and Jay are supposed to be my friends."

"That's the way it happened, Mr. Cantelli," Officer Dennison added. "I heard Greg screaming at Jesse and pulling the knife."

"What did you sellout to?" I'm a little behind the times on the whole racist sellout game if everyone simply wants to be an

American.

"He a House Ni-" Jay got Lo involved.

"Shut your pie-hole! I detest that word and I don't give a shit who says it." Lo walked into Jay's face. "You have no self-respect, no honor for the men and women who fought to make that word and all its connotations evil, and you shoot your ignorant mouth off about Jesse? Why? Because he has a Father teaching him we're all Americans and not race baiters? You should be ashamed of yourself, you young toady!"

Lois shut everyone the hell up. Jay tried a stare down and ended ignominiously with his head down. "You live in the greatest country on earth. Instead of reaching out, and becoming the best at a career, here you are trying to be a BLM gangster. Wise up, dummy! All you'll end up doing is going to prison for killing innocent people, and the police trying to protect them. Looting and pillaging is not a career, nor is working the system for entitlements! Damn... Rick, sometimes I just think we've been alive too long."

"I think you made your point, Lo. Is it okay to drive the kids home, Officer Dixon? We promise to bring them in for instant testimony to back up Officer Dennison, or to press charges formally against the knife guy."

"I think we're done here," Officer Dixon answered. She addressed Dennison then. "What would you like done about Jay?"

"I'm taking him to the office. They're not gone for the day. I want him punished, but I'll let the Principal decide. I don't believe he wanted Jesse stabbed, but he's into the same BLM crap as Greg in your car is."

We parted from the cops. They drove off and Officer Dennison grabbed Jay by the shirt. "Come along with me you young idiot. I just saved you from a year in prison. Ferguson was a lie, dumb-shit! I'm black, but I have enough brains to pursue the facts. The lies were exploited by rich white liberals and idiots! BLM is a hoax and now a dangerous, terrorist organization. They kill police officers, loot, pillage, and terrorize our own neighborhoods. Get yo' damn head out of your ass!"

Dennison waved at us while guiding the reticent Jay towards the office. The small crowd around us erupted in applause for Dennison. He grinned and nodded his thanks. Lo's speech struck home, but having Dennison reiterate the cold hard facts energized the crowd. Lois gripped Jesse's arm.

"You call us if you get any kind of threat whatsoever, Jess. We'll see you over at the gym."

"I'll be there." Jesse shook Jim's hand. "Thanks for my life, brother."

"Anytime, Jess. See you at the gym."

The small crowd of onlookers parted the way.

"You two certainly had a busy day," Lo said. "We have to arm you both for self-defense again. I know the pepper spray and stun-guns are illegal for you two, but having them in a situation like that knife incident could mean the difference between life and death."

"Jim really popped Greg," Ellen said. "He started snoring the moment he hit the floor."

"How's your hand, Jim?" I know something about hitting people with bare fists. If it's not done just right, it can mean fractures.

"Good," Jim answered, flexing his hand. "Those workouts with you using the mitts to catch my punches helped. Does Greg go on the list along with Jay?"

"They sure do," Lo replied. "I'll have Bone get all the arrest specifics with our clearance, along with any rap sheets they have. That stupid ass was really going to stab Jesse just because he was hanging around with you two?"

"He stabbed at Jess," Ellen said. "It will be an exciting day at school tomorrow with all that happened today snowballing through the rumor mill. Did you hear anything about Cindy Daniels?"

"We had to shelve her for the day because between clowns and convicts today, Rick and I were too busy to play with her angle. We have a plan for her tonight at the gym though. You mind your business, Mars Bar. Watch her, Jim. If she screws around at all with anything else today, I'm putting her in restraints."

The kids enjoyed Lo's threat. We dropped Ellen off. After which, it was time for us coots to rest before all the crap we planned for tonight started.

* * *

"They're at it again, Rick," Stacy remarked.

"It looks that way." Another menagerie of morons picketed on the sidewalk with signs claiming the gym was Islamophobic, Killer Cantelli was a racist, and Jadie's Gym was offensive to Allah. "If they try to stop us, hold onto something."

"Rick! You can't make them into speed bumps," Stacy cautioned as the kids hid amusement.

"Says you." The morons weren't quite as dumb as they looked. They didn't block our way. They shouted some unkind words at me in Arabic. I rolled down my window and answered with some gems of my own in the same language. A couple of them ran after our car as I speeded into the gym's parking area. "Stay in the car for a moment. I see Lois heading our way with Trish next to her. This won't take long."

"Cantelli!" The big one in the front, complete with Isis beard and no mustache, pounded toward me. "You are a racist, Islamophobe!"

"No, I'm not." Lucky for him and his buddy they stopped ten feet away from me. I was in the mood for a good pistol whipping. "Islam's a death cult of pedophiles, slavers, misogynists, and non-assimilating parasites. It's not a race, so I'm not a racist."

237

He screamed and charged. Too bad he must have thought Lo had her hand behind her back in deference to his misogynist belief system. When the Taser needles hit him dead center in the groin, he danced a different tune. Lo went to work with enthusiasm. She gave him a rising and falling hummer that literally changed his screams in tone and volume until he passed out. His buddy saw what happened and ran for the street. Trish, of course, was laughing her ass off, watching the maestro at work. Lois sighed, dialed down, and retrieved her needles.

"Jadie called and told me we had company with signs. I knew you had to pick up Ellen, so I called Trish to see if she wanted to come early and discuss our Cindy plans. It worked out, because Sam had business in LA tonight. I picked up Trish. We tried everything to get the idiots on the sidewalk to attack our Terrain. What the hell did you say to garner this one into the zap zone?"

"I spoke to them in their native language. I believe goats, dogs, and Mohammed were mentioned in my brief retort to them."

Lois and Trish loved that explanation. "Well done, Peeper. I refuse to admit how much the barbeque on this one satisfied my cravings. You were going to do something brutal like pistol whipping him, weren't you?"

"Yep." I opened the door for my first love princess as Jim and Ellen exited the vehicle. "You three go inside and stretch. I'll be along in a few."

"Don't get put in the tank tonight, Rick," Stacy urged.

"He'll be fine to rock your world later, Stace," Lo guaranteed. "We have a little side op we're working. We need to talk with Trish about it until I can bitch slap Mohammed's turd into consciousness."

"Sure, Lo. I'll take the kids inside. That was a very entertaining toasting."

Lo sighed as she knelt to bitch slap Mohammed's turd into coherency land. "It sure was, girlfriend. See you all inside once I

238

find out what we have to do with Rick's issues and our Daniels' problem."

I began walking toward the sidewalk. I was a Navy Seal for many years, and a CIA agent/assassin under Lo's guidance for decades after. What I wasn't... a pussy that allows terrorist scum to intimidate me. Since these assholes don't know where to put their Mohammed Sharia Law, I'll shove it up their asses myself. Workouts are boring anyway, except for the chatter.

* * *

"Where's Rick going, Lo?"

Lois looked after Rick's striding figure with a grin. She shrugged. "The usual, Skipper – trouble."

Lois straightened near her reviving Taser target and kicked him in the face. "We're doing Tombstone, Skipper. Want to come?"

"Best jog along, Lo, before someone takes your place." Trish jogged after Rick.

With a short cackle, Lo followed.

* * *

One of the beards ran at me with his sign. I clocked him with the Colt gun butt. I spread my arms with Colt in hand. "I'm your Huckleberry, rubes. If you want a piece, start reachin' now."

I holstered my Colt and waited. Trish and Lo arrived at my sides. It was time for a little fun. I began bitch slapping all the troglodyte males in the crowd. Lo and Trish joined in on the women in their slave costumes. We had us a party. It didn't take long to disperse the crowd to parts unknown. They ran for it. They had no sensibility toward my movie reference. Only one thought he was Johnny Ringo. He tossed his sign down, beckoning me on. He was a big one... a Goliath with an Isis beard. I'd had enough of this politically correct bullshit to give me a bad taste every time I looked at one of these mutants. I put my Colt on the sidewalk.

239

"Let me light him up, you old coot," Trish called out.

"Stay out of this, Skipper! Watch his six with attitude and silence or go on back in the gym!" Lois pulled her Ruger with intent. Trish shut up and drew her Smith and Wesson.

"I will crush you... then I get shot?"

"Nope. My friends protect my back from you back-stabbing third world toilet bars," I replied in Arabic. "If you want to fight... fight. No one will harm you, little goat."

He ran at me. I dropped one foot back and snapped a forearm blow into his face that broke his nose. I stepped in and threw hooks up under his rib cage as he gripped his injured face. Those were blows to maim and kill. He collapsed, gasping to fill his lungs with air. I kicked him in the side of his head, relaxing him a bit. I picked up my Colt and holstered it.

"I guess we may as well talk out here, Sis, while we wait for Shortcake to arrive. Maybe Cindy will drive in too."

"Agreed." Lois spelled out our plan to Trish, emphasizing it would only work if Lo could keep Daniels occupied long enough on a polite basis for Trish to clone her phone.

"First off... you damn coots are walking hand grenades. It doesn't take much to pull your pins. I'm in. I'll watch for you to engage Cindy, then head for the locker room. I know which one is hers. Do you have a plan for keeping her talking?"

"Yep. I'm going to speak to her about the rules she signed concerning any kind of picture taking, reporting to the media, and misrepresentation of why she's there. I'll keep it formal and polite. If she gets testy, I'll bitch slap her. That should get you an extra twenty minutes while she cries and sobs."

Trish and I enjoyed the hell out of Lo's final ploy for more time. Temple drove into the lot, saw us and stopped. She ducked her head out, gawking at the man in misery at our feet. "Hi. Is it okay to go in? How's Jim?"

Lo's eyes furrowed, her whole body tuning into Shortcake's mental processes with Spock-ella speed. "Okay… what have you done now, cougar?"

Temple yelped comically. Her features drooped into submission for a moment. Then her lips tightened. "You're mean. I seduced Jim when he checked my car out at the beach house. So there, you old bat."

Temple surged into her Toyota and screeched into the parking area. Lois laughed her ass off. My partner, the mind munch, had once again stripped away everything in a human's soul and ripped out facts not in evidence. It took many moments for Lois to regain speech. Trish shook her head and walked toward the gym. I prodded Goliath until he groaned his way into flexibility.

"C'mon dummy. I'm not standing here all night waiting for you to get your ass off the pavement."

"I…I am hurt. Call an ambulance."

Lo knelt down where he could see her smile like Jaws at a fish fry. "You can get the fuck out of my sight or I can give you one of these on your nuts." She fired an arc next to Goliath's groin area with her stun-gun.

Oh my, did Goliath move then. "You do have the night off from workout, Sis."

She waved me off. "I know. It's just that I want to be next to Shortcake while she senses my presence. We'll leave Cindy to arrive on her own. Jesus… did I nail Shortcake or what?"

"You got the two horned-toads dead to rights," I admitted while we walked toward the gym. "Even I can picture it happening now. Temple drives to the beach house. Stace is gone. Sir Galahad hurries out to do a sensor check on Shortcake's Toyota, looks up, and Temple has rearranged her clothing for better viewing. How am I doing?"

Lo nodded. "Pretty damn good. I bet that was a wild muskrat

241

love scene in the beach house before school. No wonder Jim had the hots for clowns this morning. His testosterone level shot through the roof. Then, to top it all off, he gets a deadly situation with his partner the minx Ellen, on his six, and he ices a knife wielder. I have to play nearby tonight, Peeper. I'll fake some of the boring parts."

"You earned it. Damn... you nailed Shortcake in a split second."

"I own her. She's in thrall to the Dark Lo."

Now that was funny.

* * *

Inside the gym, Temple joined Stacy, Jim and Ellen. She began her stretching exercises after the initial chaste greetings. Only a few of the workout group milled around. They walked over to say hi to the young stars. Jim and Temple signed anything and everything presented to them by the regulars at the gym and restaurant, as did Karen and Trish. Ellen stared at Temple, knowing instinctively something was off about her flushed friend. Trish watched the teens trading furtive glances too.

"What's happened, Temple?"

One glance into Ellen's eyes prompted Temple to turn away. "Lo nailed me outside while I drove in. I ducked my head out to see if everything was okay. She ripped my inner thoughts out like they were Cheerios in an open bowl."

Trish laughed, while Jim and Stacy exchanged looks with Stacy smacking Jim at the back of his head. "You two tempting fate and the law are going to be in deep trouble. A couple more movies as romantic leads and no one will care one way or the other."

"It was my fault, Stace," Temple admitted. "Ellen thought I could fool Lo by talking to her immediately about something serious. It's useless. All she has to do is look at me."

"We'll do better G-ma," Jim promised. "I read the script already for the new movie Temple emailed me. It's incredible. Great

242

story, action, suspense, Kull the puppy, and the two of us surviving against all manner of danger."

"It's a good thing, Shortcake," Trish said. "The media will learn they can manipulate you the same way as Lo if you don't get a game face."

"This will help too." Ellen held her iPad for everyone to see. It was a news site where Jim was being heralded as a hero for saving a classmate's life. "It even says Jim took out the attacker with one punch. They didn't cover our clown story though from earlier in the day. I wonder if that turned out to be more complicated than a bunch of pedophiles."

"Lo has the video I sent her of the getaway van. I think her and Pop were going to investigate more thoroughly. I called Quincy and told him my script demands. He didn't argue for a second. He liked the idea of letting the dog live and be in a sequel if the movie is a hit. I get the puppy tomorrow from the trainer."

By then, Lois and Rick came into the gym.

"Step up your game, Shortcake," Ellen warned.

"Would if I could."

* * *

Karen and Danny drove in as Lo and I walked toward the gym. Shelly and Max were only a few seconds behind them, so we all waited to walk in together.

"Baby Lo's going to be in the new movie, Cheech told me," Karen said excitedly. "We won't have to spend any time apart. How are things with you, Sis?"

"Busy. Rick and I kicked so much ass today, Karma had to install new tracks for the Karma express train to retribution. I'm glad you'll have my baby niece with you. When my kids get moved down here, we'll have some nice family get-togethers."

"I hope you two plan on a night's rest," Shelly told us. "You

243

would not believe what busy means to these coots."

"We're in a bad phase," I admitted. "It will hopefully end soon when we fix a couple threads leading to Cindy Daniels."

"The one Trish gave an attitude adjustment to in the locker room?"

"That's the one, Karen," Lo answered. "We better get inside."

"It's nice not having the protestors out front," Shelly's husband Max remarked.

"I'll second that," Shelly agreed.

Karen's husband, Danny, smiled at Lo and me. "I have a feeling these two had something to do with that. There's no dead bodies and police, so that's a good thing, right?"

"We decided to negotiate with them tonight, Danny," Lo replied. "We pointed out some flaws in their thinking and at least for tonight they went home to think it over."

"How's the teen romance triangle going?"

"I got Shortcake good tonight," Lo replied to Karen's question. She went on to tell them what happened to Temple the moment she entered the parking lot as we entered the gym.

"Everyone stopped talking the moment we entered the building." Max gestured at our workout area. "I think Temple has been updating the crew."

"Mars Bar probably dragged it out of Shortcake," Lo observed. "I get to work out behind Temple."

"Cindy just walked into the locker room, Lo," Trish informed us as we joined them. "I'll take my stuff in there now. Once she steps out, I'll go to work. I have my tools. You can engage her then. Maybe you can get Jadie involved in the conversation too. She mostly wanders around until class starts anyway."

"True. With Jadie, I'll have a voice of authority in the

244

conversation. Rick will keep watch. How much time will you need, Skipper?"

"If you can keep her busy for about ten minutes, I shouldn't need more than that."

"Can we get near enough to hear how you do with her, Lo," Ellen asked.

"Nope. Any thought you kids are involved will piss her off. This way, with Jadie at my side we can get this done easily, especially if I can get Jadie to have our little meeting in her office. What you and Temple can do is go in the locker room with Skipper. Shield off what she's doing if anyone is in there, or walks in."

"Okay, Lo." Ellen and Temple went with Trish. I could tell Temple was relieved not to be the center of attention.

Lois left to corral Jadie. They spoke for a moment and Jadie followed Lo to a spot where they could intercept Cindy as she walked out of the locker room. Our small deception unfolded perfectly with Cindy surprised but willing to talk with Lo and Jadie in the gym's office. Less than ten minutes went by before Trish, Temple, and Ellen emerged from the locker room. Lois and Jadie returned with a tightlipped Cindy, who immediately went to her old position. Jadie called the class to order. Ken joined her at the front to lead the exercises.

"Quincy agreed to the script changes," Temple told us as we took our positions. "Little Kull will be delivered tomorrow. Jim and I are supposed to get acquainted with Kull and start training sessions right away. It will mean Jim has to move in with me until at least after the movie is done."

While the rest of us appreciated Temple's zinger immensely, Lo gestured with a threatening finger at our young starlet. "Don't think for a second I won't run over there and box your ears, you little imp."

"I can't wait to see the dog," Jim commented. "We'll do all the training so Kull will be incredible in the movie. I'm going to buy

245

the dog from the trainer. He'll sell because he won't know how well the movie will do anyway."

"Yes! I'll call Quincy tonight. Great idea, Jim," Temple agreed.

I could see how happy the kids were with having the dog. I had no intention of raining on their parade, although Stacy stared at me with that 'don't you dare ruin this' look. We proceeded through yet another workout with snide remarks about the 'Creepy Clown' apocalypse I requested Ellen relate to the others. She has a storytelling side to her. Where someone else would relate events in an informational way, Ellen could make her listeners believe they witnessed the event. Her description of costumed child predators attempting to kidnap young girls on the street stirred the hell out of everyone in listening range. The teens clown intervention provoked many cheers from Ellen's audience.

Lo enjoyed the story so much she forgot about raking Temple over the coals which was just as well. "Good story, Mars Bar. It nearly got us all the way through this tedious crap to stay in shape."

A woman named Tracy near us asked about the teens' later deadly encounter. "Jim... did you really stop a killing today. I heard on the news you prevented someone you go to school with from getting stabbed."

"He did," Ellen answered for him. "The guy tried to stab our friend and Jim knocked him out. The guy hit the deck snoring with his knife clattering to the floor next to him. Hey... where's Jess. With all the other events since we got here, I forgot he was supposed to join us. I'll text him in case his parents didn't want to take a chance allowing him out after what happened."

"Do that now," Lo ordered. "Let's make sure there isn't some other element in it."

Ellen stopped at the point where we were doing the loosening exercise at the end of the workout. She texted in rapid skill. A few moments later, her phone dinged. She smiled. "It's okay. Jess says

246

his parents were freaked out. They went out to dinner together and to a movie. That's a relief. We'll see him in school tomorrow."

Lois retrieved her phone Trish used to clone Cindy Daniels' phone from the equipment bag. Her features darkened. "Sidebar, Rick! You too, Trish!"

Over at the side of the workout room, she showed us the text Daniels had sent to none other than Aga Saleh. She reported the lecture given by Lo and Jadie, explaining her cover may be blown. Cindy also mentioned the GPS trackers weren't working correctly. That was, of course, because we had stripped them off of the vehicles. She mentioned meeting at her apartment in San Francisco when he returned there.

"Oh my... I think it's time to move on this, Sis," I told Lo. "Aga's in San Francisco again. If he meets his honey there, we'll have the perfect opportunity to use Paria."

"Agreed. It's just as well Sam's away on business. No more fooling around at the compound, trying to make their heads explode. We need to move full bore on it tonight. If anything, hearing about the aftermath will keep Aga in place. I'm thinking it's time to take Cindy into our circle too. What do you think of sending Trish with Cindy to her place in San Francisco, while we gather Paria from his compound?"

"Damn good and damn chancy," I said as a hundred different scenarios flowed through my head. "What do you think, Trish?"

"I love it, but I want a piece at the compound. That's a deal breaker. We take Cindy tonight, and stash her in the trunk if we have to. Rick and I move on the compound as you two originally thought of as a joke. I'll put on the fuckin' burka and we face off with the guards, requesting a meeting with Paria. Hell, with Rick's language skill, he could throw this whole deal right into our hands. All we have to do is get past the guards with an open door. We toss in the military bang grenades you reprobates have and Lo streaks in with the GMC to join us."

247

Lo smiled. "I like it, Skipper. You want to kill something... you little viper."

"Hell yeah," Trish whispered fiercely, looking around guiltily. "I'm not some fuckin' girl scout. Let's do it all now. I'll kill everything in my sight and on mission. Then I'll greet Sam with a big smile when he gets back from his business trip like a Rolling Stones' groupie."

"Done deal, Skipper. How would you like to take Cindy? We need to do it here."

"She's visiting right now with our workout buddies," Trish pointed out. "I'll walk her to her car on some pretense like I'm really offended by the rules. When I get her near the car, it's a late model Chevy Impala, I'll stick her or zap her. Do either of you two have a knockout shot?"

"Did you just insult us, Skipper?"

Trish chuckled. "Let me have it. I'll take care of Cindy. I'll belt her in the front and take the bitch to my place until we move on the compound."

Bone walked in then. After doing his usual security patrol, he swept the gym for bugs while Cindy Daniels worked out. He was smiling. "All clear. Are we having dinner at the restaurant later?"

"We have some work to do tonight, Timothy," Lo replied. We'll make it up to you when we return. We have a vital trip to San Francisco planned. I'd like you, Steve, and Meg to work from home, doing whatever paperwork we have left. Shelly will be at the office if you need anything."

"You're taking Trish," Bone responded. "That means loose ends get taken care of. You reapers be careful. I'll go see if Carlene wants to go try a different restaurant for the fun of it."

"Keep your eyes open, brother. We're not out of the woods yet."

"I will do that." Bone walked away with a wave.

248

"I'll text Meg. I forgot to tell you she called me earlier to let me know she was working out in a different way," Trish told us. "I think Ned rang her bell again, the little minx."

"Good. I was wondering about Meg but figured the reunion probably shifted into high gear," Lo replied. "Give her a hotshot, Rick. Trish needs to go corral her pal."

I retrieved our bags, Lo and I always keep near us. I handed off a syringe to Trish. "This will keep her comatose until we see how Aga reacts to Cindy's offer for a meeting at her place. It's a bitch of a drive. When we go, we'll stuff Cindy in the GMC cargo hold and take turns doing a straight through drive."

"Sounds good, Rick. I'll bring my Hip-Hop and Rap on the iPod."

"Great... you won't live to see San Francisco but we'll think of some way to fill in for you, Skipper," Lo promised.

* * *

Cindy Daniels glanced at the young teens laughing and joking after the workout ended, surreptitiously watching to see if they paid any more attention to her. She politely conversed with the people around her while walking toward the locker room. Cindy spotted Trish walking toward the locker room too. She hesitated, after their confrontation before, but Trish smiled and waved.

"Hey... Cindy, I hear Lois and Jadie made sure you knew the rules about pictures and talk outside the gym. They were a little harsh, I'm sure. Don't worry about it. I told Lo the kid was imagining things. Ellen thinks she's Veronica Mars, teen detective. We call her Mars Bar."

"I overreacted, Trish. I don't want to get kicked out of the workout sessions. I do modeling in LA and San Francisco. These workouts really keep my weight down."

"That's great. You do modeling too. Do you have a portfolio? I could show them to our producer and director. We're making the third movie in our romantic comedy trilogy. Quincy's always looking for new faces."

Trish had her, body and soul immediately. "Quincy Wolf? I'd love that! It's brutal getting any kind of a break. I have my iPad in the car. It has my complete portfolio, including a couple of video clips of a shoot. Would you like to see them?"

"Sure," Trish replied. "Let's get cleaned up and I'll walk you out to your car for a look see. If they look good, we can go over to the restaurant across the street and have coffee while I call Cheech and Quincy."

Cindy could hardly breathe. "Oh my God... that would be wonderful. You'd really do that for me?"

The cold blooded killer smiled reassuringly. "I'm always glad to help a friend."

* * *

Cindy opened her Ford Explorer cargo area hatch, threw in her gym bag, and bent over to retrieve the iPad with her portfolio on it from the computer bag. She felt a pin prick at her neck, batting at it. Her eyesight immediately blurred to a grainy image of everything. Trish glanced around quickly. Seeing no one nearby, she confiscated the Ford keys and shoved Cindy into the cargo hold, and slammed the hatch closed. Trish slipped into the Explorer, started it, and drove toward home.

* * *

This turned into the longest day we'd had in quite a while. I followed Trish home in her vehicle of choice for doing errands, a Honda Accord. We needed room to store the vehicles. Sam's mansion incorporated a huge garage with four separate automatic doors for vehicle entry. Trish opened two of them. I drove her Accord into one. She entered the other with the Explorer. Trish nudged me as I inspected the Explorer.

"What are you thinking about, coot?"

"I was wondering if the Explorer would be comfortable enough for the trip north. I was also wondering if Cindy has a garage. What if after we question Aga and Gabriel, we put all three of them into the Ford, inside the locked garage?"

Trish grinned. "I get it. We can pipe exhaust fumes into the cab with something like clothes drier ducting. We let it run until it stalls out from no gas, check the passengers for life, and leave it as is. I'm good with this. I'll drive the Explorer with Cindy in the back. You and Lo drive north in the GMC with Gabe. The driving doesn't mess with my mind like you two coots."

"It would solve our discovery scenario. We'll use their hands to inject three hotshots into their arms, leaving the syringes near them, and wait it out just as you suggested. A three way interlude after Paria's compound is destroyed could provide deception and a half-assed explanation – a suicide pact."

"That's pretty damn good, Rick. All the bases covered and we can make the compound nearly as messy as we want. I hope the neighbors don't get antsy with our using those military concussion grenades."

"We'll have to take that chance. We'll play this out all the way by driving over there tonight in the Ford Explorer. I'll have you take a video of me all in black near the Explorer shouting 'Allahu Akbar', and a few other choice pieces of crap in Arabic, a moment after we finish torching the compound."

"Lo's going to kick your ass for creating a scenario like that."

"Yep," Trish was probably right. "She'll be here in a few minutes. Let's get Cindy bound for the trip. We'll have to make sure no telltale signs ruin our scenario like bruised wrists."

"I'm sure you've done that before. I know I have. Let's get busy."

By the time Lo arrived, Trish and I had our unconscious princess bound comfortably to limit movement for now if she wakes while we're handling the compound. We will put her in a tightly wrapped blanket with duct tape for the trip north, making it impossible for her to move while in transit. I went over my plan with Lo. "What do you think?"

"I think I'm getting sick of being beaten to the punch by teeny-boppers and Peeper has beens. We do it as you outlined. It covers everything, including a Yemen ambassador's death. We have to bring the cleaning kits along and dress appropriately. Thanks for agreeing to the drive, Skipper. It's a bitch. Maybe it's because Rick and I have had to do it in the dead of night so many times."

"I figure we'll get ahead of this and gamble a little," I replied.

Lo brightened. "I see where you're going. We hit the compound before confirmation from Saleh, fix things there, and head directly for San Francisco. Skipper can transport Cindy. We'll take Paria with us. I'll question the prick as you drive. I bet I break that pussy in the first five minutes."

"I wouldn't touch that bet," Trish said. "Do you two old goats ever get tired of cleaning the messes for the idiots in DC, selling out the country every day for pay for play cash from the Sandpit and billionaire globalists?"

Lo patted Trish's shoulder. "We've covered this before, Skipper. Nothing gets in the way of us and America. Rick and I got bored and pissed, playing the part of a couple old coots while the nation disintegrated in our lifetime. We're just happy to play a damn part in this last stand against the 'One World Order' assholes. If you're looking for a safe-haven, we ain't it. We risk family, friends, and our own futures, without knowing there will be any other payout at the end, other than dying with our boots on."

"I want a piece of the action as always. I know you two include me in any ops you can. That's all I ask. We joke about that fuckin' slave costume the Moslem mutants want to put women in, but to me, that's war. I'm going to wear that piece of shit tonight and waste mutants. If it fits in with your agenda, great. What can we use to party with?"

"Silenced Uzis. We're not fooling around. I'm hoping the bangs will silence opposition until we can get inside and party until only Paria's left. You and Rick will be the key to that part. It's going to be dangerous as hell at first. Rick has to keep his hands in plain sight. You're his backup. You have weapons free under the slave costume. Keep your head down in deference. It allows extra room under the burka. We're not playing. If you see a situation you don't like, kill everything in sight, including Paria. We can only fix mistakes if we're still alive."

Trish smiled. "That's what I like to hear. I already have the black slave costume. I'll go put it on. What about you, Rick?"

"I have what I need in my bag. I can't look like an Isis asshole approaching the entrance. I'll have on the black jeans I have on now, black t-shirt, and black windbreaker with scarf. We may launch within a second of getting out of the Ford. Remember not to make any sound if our initial meeting isn't questioned. Lo and I know what you are, Trish. We don't pretend. We kill people and we're damn good at it. In this instance it's for a good cause, but frankly, we don't care. It's like the excellent way you played Cindy. I'll bet she was bonding with you by the time you stuck her with the syringe."

Trish patted the unconscious Cindy. "Yeah... Cindy and I are real close. She's a model, with not only a deadly sand troglodyte as a boyfriend, but also aspersions to star in my third movie venture. Heh... heh... I don't like her chances."

I admit it. We three killers chuckled over Trish's ending of Cindy's existence. Trish didn't have to mention Cindy sold out her country, us and all our friends, to embrace a death cult who would enslave the stupid bitch under Sharia Law. We realized all the implications of her helping Aga Saleh towards his goal of terror crap. She was a puzzle piece that now would be fitted in with the rest of her fellow terrorist pieces. Lo and I don't take you to court when we catch you betraying everything we love and believe in. We relieve you of all your earthly attachments and then we metaphorically piss on your grave.

"I feel the old urge boiling up, kiddies," Lo said. "Let's get to this. I'm an info whore. I see the BLM dogs burning our nation down over lies, Moslem mutants parading around in major cities chanting 'Death to America', and politicians licking their asses while taking pay for play money to sell out their nation. I feel the need for speed. Violent justice is the only damn thing that's going to put me in a good mood on the way to San Francisco."

"I hope Paria does what the rest of these mutant leaders do: hide while someone else fights," I said. "That way we won't have to worry about killing the prick."

Chapter Twelve

The Last Day

I drove into the compound in the Cindy Daniels' Ford Explorer. I hoped it might be possible the guards had seen it before. Such was not the case. The two guards leaped to their feet with weapons ready. "I've got one chance at this Trish, and then it's game on."

"Understood."

I parked. With scarf covering my lower neck and chin, I know I looked dark enough to fool the guards if they didn't shoot first. I ducked out the driver's door, shouting out in Arabic immediately. "As-salamu alaykum! I am here to see Gabriel Paria. Aga Saleh sent me. He made a woman bring me the information with one order: she is only to speak with Gabriel Paria."

The guards stopped pointing their weapons at me. One of them gestured me to come forward. I opened the Explorer door for Trish, who demurely left the passenger seat. She kept her head down and hands inside the burka, clasping the silenced Uzi, I hoped. I led the way with Trish following to my right side, slightly behind me.

"We were not told of anyone's arrival, especially not a diplomat's emissary," the guard in front of me said. "You will not be allowed inside."

"Agreed. Can Paria come out on the porch and receive the message this woman has. Ambassador Saleh told me his communications are compromised. This woman arrived today. She will tell me nothing of the message. It was not explained by the Ambassador either."

"Wait here!" The guard I talked to went inside.

"Perhaps this slave can entertain us once this message business is ended," the other guard said, smiling at Trish.

"That is acceptable. If Paria wishes, I shall leave the woman with you. I do not know what she looks like under her clothing."

The guard stepped down from the porch and approached Trish. He gripped her chin, tilting it back slightly. He looked into Trish's eyes and laughed. "This one has an attitude. We will welcome her properly later. I will speak for her to Gabriel."

I heard the door open. I didn't have to worry about Trish. Gabriel Paria strode onto the porch wearing slacks, sandals, and shortened white 'Arab thobe top'. He matched his pictures perfectly – six feet tall, short cut black hair and Isis style beard without mustache. Paria approached us, leaving the porch with his guard on his left. The guard closed the door behind them. Nice. I drew my Colt, pistol whipping the guard to the ground, before grabbing Paria with Colt barrel under his chin. Trish didn't waste bullets. She jammed the Uzi under the guard's chin and fired a round up through his head.

In seconds, Trish and I were at the door, dragging Gabriel over the porch, listening for commotion over the silenced round Trish had fired. With the Colt barrel still jammed into his throat, Gabriel wisely remained silent. Minutes passed without interference from inside. I motioned Trish to take care of the guard I put down. She moved to his side and again fired a single round through his chin into his brain.

"Join us, Lo."

The GMC roar escalated as it shot into the compound approach. I plastic tied Gabriel's wrists behind his back, followed by his ankles with two ties to hogtie them together, and then gagged him. Lo parked, ran onto the porch, opened the door and threw in one of our military grade concussion grenades. She waited, as screams reverberated from inside the building. Lo pitched the second one much further in than the first one, before passing helmet masks to Trish and me with sound dampeners. Trish handed me the other silenced Uzi she carried. Lo already held hers, ready to go in. Once we had spare magazines positioned for instant use, I charged through the door to the right, firing into each body I came across. Lo and Trish slipped in left, repeating the firing into bodies.

We used the grenades in each interior room where we were unsure of occupancy. The concussion grenades worked their magic, leaving only disorientated goons, bleeding from every orifice. Firing short bursts into each acquired target while covering our asses, we proceeded through the living quarters until we accounted for the body count given to us by Bone using live satellite surveillance. He would be the final arbiter as to the operations conclusion. Lois kept watch while Trish and I dragged each body out into the main area into a pile after I coated the flooring with flame retardant. Gathering electronics, mobile phones, and computer laptops. I found only one desktop computer which I hauled to the GMC with the rest of our loot.

"Outstanding," Lo spoke for the first time. "Twenty minutes from start to finish. Any movement or calls for help to police, Bone?"

"Nothing Lo. No action anywhere on the compound grounds. I'm monitoring all police bands. There is no indication of a disturbance. I'll sing out if I see or hear anything."

"Thanks. We will be done shortly." Lois walked over to a very frightened Paria. Eleven dead men kept him company in their pile. "I don't have time for a lot of crap."

She held her stun-gun to his nuts. "This is a Vipertek VTS-989 Stun-Gun. It packs a fifty-three million volt arc. You tell me where your safe is, all your passwords, safe combination, and where we can find your weapons cache. Go ahead. I'm recording."

Gabriel's lip trembled. He didn't know for sure if Lo would singe his balls off. He did, however, know he didn't want to find out. Lois recorded everything. We emptied his safe of its contents which turned out to be quite a haul in cash and precious metals. The weapons storage area underground, twenty-five feet from the building, shocked the hell out of us. We had to have a sidebar.

257

"Jesus... God in heaven..." Trish muttered as we stared together at the underground storage area that seemed to have everything but an atomic bomb. "I know you two are used to this... but damn!"

"We're not used to this, Skipper. What now, Rick. I figured we'd firebomb the compound and weapons, but I think we'd probably blow up half of San Diego."

I looked around, grinned, and shrugged. "I think we should go shopping, lock it up again, use the magnesium flare idea on the main room after we coat everything around the bodies with fire retardant as we planned. We'll overnight the keys to the weapons kingdom to our buddy Van and let him and Floyd battle out the details. They asked for it. Let's give it to them. We'll still make our video of me as Paria screaming 'allahu akbar' and a few other choice items while the room burns."

Lois smiled. "Let's go shopping. I see a bunch of items I like. We only have to make room for Gabe. The rest of the space can be taken in both vehicles with our plunder. I have plenty of room in my safe room. Let's do it. You come with me, Trish. I know you're good with weapons, but I don't want only everyday items. Rick will fill his bill competently on his own."

"On your six," Trish said. "You lead. I'll follow."

We spent the next half hour stocking our own arsenal with weapons we would have a very hard time obtaining. We refilled many items we had used on previous missions along with gaining rocket launchers and ammo for them amongst other very formidable types of grenades and explosives. It was Christmas time in Cantelli-land. Loaded down would be a weak word for our two vehicles.

Then it was time to stage our Paria scene. It would be messy, rotten business, just like the members of Islam's Death Cult are famous for. Unfortunately for them, they came to the wrong nation and met us. We give back in kind. When we retaliate, there's nothing left for the Virgins. I sprayed down all the walls, ceiling, and flooring around the bodies heavily with flame retardant. I inserted

258

the flares amongst the bodies after lighting them off. I got the bonfire of the vanities going real good. Then I posed in full Isis, AK47 waving madness with black mask and Isis flag draped around my neck. I shouted 'allahu akbar' while cursing incoherently in Arabic with Trish recording it all. It was then time to get the hell out of Dodge before the neighbors called the fire department. Once clear of the area, I used the throw away phone to call it in to 911 myself using a voice modulator, letting them know that I, Gabriel Paria, lit the traitors' bodies on fire using magnesium flares. We didn't want our fire department people hurt.

After depositing our plunder at Lo's house in the safe room, we returned to Trish's mansion. We shed all clothing and sign from the compound, depositing it into a bag for disposal later. We all engaged in an hour's power nap, took showers, and hit the road with our prisoners. Cindy got a booster shot, and wrapped tightly in a blanket, duct taped around to prevent movement. Gabriel had assigned seating next to Lo in our GMC backseat for the trip. Bone came back on line with us for the interrogation. We needed instant checks in some places. As Lois suspected, Gabe wanted no part of any kind of torturous ordeal. He talked... and talked. Unfortunately, we didn't learn much new information. He did confirm Aga Saleh's involvement with his halfway house for terrorists. Lois reported in to Van at our on-line drop, letting him know we would be sending him the key to the compound's arsenal and all the specifics. He acknowledged but said he wanted to send a messenger directly to us. Van called Lois on a secure line.

"I know you don't want this, Lo, but the faster I get a key to your locker at the compound, the better for Floyd and us. Is it okay if I send someone to retrieve the package?"

"Okay by me. Send your minion to the entrance to the Santa Cruz Beach Boardwalk. I'll meet him or her alone. Make sure your minion has a picture of me. I'll wear a red scarf."

"Understood. This was bad, huh?"

"Worse than you can imagine, Van," I put in over the speaker.

"Can you give me an ETA when you get close?"

"Will do," Lo replied. She disconnected. "I think we frightened Van."

"I sure as hell hope so." The hour's power nap had recharged me because of the mission ahead. My mind filtered through various scenarios for Cindy to reconnect with her creature from the Sand: Aga Saleh. Naturally, the Harpy plucked my thoughts out before I could even voice them myself.

"You're scheming in that Peeper has-been head of yours for a way to pull off this caper with Cindy and Aga. Don't sweat it, Rick. We'll go with the basics. Trish and I will make Cindy lure the Aga into her home. Once he arrives, we set our scenario, see it through, and stop by for a quick visit with the kids undercover."

"He will have bodyguards, Lo. That prick won't journey forth from the embassy without his palace guard."

"Oh no... whatever will we do?" Lo's sarcasm lightened the situation a bit. "Seriously, I think we'll have to kill them and take them on a boat ride on The Sea Breeze when we get back to San Diego. They can't show at our crime scene in any way, shape, or form. Otherwise, our scene disintegrates with the first look by the cops."

"No shit... thanks, Lo, I would never have figured that out."

The cackle sounded for a moment. "We take them north. I hope he only has a couple. We only brought two body-bags."

"We could dump them in the salt marsh near the bridge on that old access road, like we did that MS-13 clown who threatened Kim."

"Not bad," Lo replied. "It's a bitch though in the marsh. I have an alternative though. They'll have a car. We'll shoot them in the head, drive the car to the access road, cut their heads off peaceful Moslem style, and throw a couple mag-flares in with them. Nothing can catch fire down in the damn marsh. We can use Cindy's Explorer for picking you up so no one spots our own vehicle. Then we set the Aga scene of death in the Explorer and drive away."

"I like your alternative better than mine. When Aga's car explodes, it will draw attention too, which can work in our favor. We'll be in the house with Cindy and Gabe. When Aga arrives, we'll explain his options. He'll call his men in the house. We'll make them do the dance electric so there won't be any slugs to be found. I'll give them each a hot shot and cut their heads off at the marsh as you suggested. I can mag-flare them then. Using the Explorer is a good idea. I think we have a good plan. I'll drive by our old marsh access road on the way to Cindy's, just to make sure it's not blocked off."

"Yep," Lo agreed. "No use chancing a run around the city with dead bodies in the car."

* * *

At the Santa Cruz Beach Boardwalk, I watched Lo's back from a distance. We don't take chances of any kind on a covert mission. With our knowledge of government leaks, and outright treason with classified data, we made sure our asses were covered so we can seek the necessary retribution. To our surprise, Van Carmichael came in person.

"Damn Lo, that's Van approaching on your right with a couple of men," I spoke in her ear. We had our com units in with Trish waiting as our driver outside the pier area.

"I see him. He must be as sick of being hung out to dry as we are." A moment later, Lo greeted Van. "Well, looky here. How are things on the home front?"

"Untrustworthy with all the Moslems in our State Department. We've had some mysterious betrayals of data lately. I caught a military flight from DC. I'm taking it to San Diego where I'll meet Floyd. We're doing a joint task force on the compound. Only a couple of my guys are coming with me. It will be mainly a Homeland Security operation. I have a list of questions for Saleh when you finally have him in your hands. I didn't want to chance

261

sending it either."

"Understood," Lo replied. "Give them to me. I'll make sure to get answers. Paria didn't know much."

"I'm sure it wasn't because he was holding out on you."

"That, you can be sure of. He was sent in directly from Syria in the very first load of Moslem infiltrator/refugees. The State Department lost track of a disturbing number within weeks." Van handed Lo an envelope. She handed him the keycards we found for entry to the compound's arsenal. "I will let you know when we return to San Diego."

"See you in a few days. Thanks for doing this, Lo. We'll get Aga Saleh soon."

"I'm sure you will, Van. Rick and I will help after we visit with my kids."

"Of course. Good night."

I watched Van walk away. Lois met me at the entrance to the Boardwalk. I knew we'd never get a chance to visit the kids but at least Van didn't know what we planned yet. "Were you tempted to tell him?"

"Hell no," Lo replied. "He'll be okay with after the fact explanations. He'd be relieved. Van has other worries about security if he's doing hand deliveries and pickups. Glance to your right, Peeper... two o'clock."

"I see them." A gang of four hoodies measured us from a distance, skulking around, and it wasn't even dark yet. Separate from them, another punk worked his phone camera. "They're interested in us. That's for sure. You're not thinkin' of playing with these kids, are you?"

"Don't ruin this for me, Rick. They haven't been watching long. They just got our scent. Hold onto my left arm and trudge along like we did at Meg's bar the other night. We'll do the oldster trick."

This wasn't good. I bent slightly. "C'mon, Lo. We may have to kill a couple of them. How does that fit in with our plans for this evening? Think about it."

Then they decided for us. One of them ran straight at me, readying to drop me with a looping right roundhouse. Lois tripped him. He hit the pier deck. Lo did a football kick at his head that nearly snapped his neck. She ran right to the camera guy, zapped him with her fifty-three million volt Vipertek. She confiscated his phone. Lo threw it on the deck and did the Mexican Hat Dance on it. The other three headed for her. I intercepted them with a nice dose of military grade anti-thug spray. We walked away from the Boardwalk with only curious stares following us on our way.

"Was it good for you?"

"Shut up, Peeper," Lo retorted. "You used to know how to have a good time. You didn't even save me one of your three to zap."

"We needed a diversion. Thugs throwing their guts up and rolling around screaming acts as a wonderful crowd magnet."

"That's true. There's Trish." Lo led the way to Cindy's Explorer. Security police were running by us. We acted like a couple of octogenarians, leaning on each other for support.

We got in the Explorer. I glanced at the cargo compartment where we stashed Cindy and Gabe. "Did they stay quiet, Trish?"

"Gabe's out cold but I think Cindy's waking." Trish drove away. "What was all the commotion on the Boardwalk?"

"I think there was some kind of altercation between thugs with a camera and some geezers," Lo replied. "If the one geezer hadn't sprayed the last three and hogged all the fun, I could have had another toasted imbecile notch on my new Vipertek."

Trish enjoyed the hell out of that explanation. "I might have known it was you old coots."

"The Harpy made me do the old man walk with her to bait those poor kids, Trish. It...it was horrible. Oh... the carnage... she

263

drop kicked this poor hoodie while he writhed on the pier from her face plant trip. Then she viciously ran at their camera guy, innocently recording what could have been another classic 'Polar Bear' attack against defenseless citizens, and destroyed his camera phone. Do you think we should turn ourselves in?"

Oh yeah… my companions snorted appreciably through the rendition of events while I heard the first wakey/wakey sounds from a groaning Cindy. We were close to our destination but not close enough to listen to 'groany' for a couple hours.

"I think we should unwrap our little Cindy. Lo can entertain her while prepping our Aga Saleh bait scene. This won't work unless we have her ready to bait our hook."

"Yep… Rick's right," Lo acknowledged. "Find us a dark spot, Skipper. I'll work her all the way to Cindy's house in the city."

"San Mateo," Trish corrected. "It would be better to arrive with Cindy primed to act out this venture. I know it's a bitch, but why not stick to Route 1 all the way? We won't have to chance crossing a toll bridge then."

"Good input," Lo replied. "Let's make the switch. We'll keep you on-line with us if you want."

"I'd like that, if for no other reason than I suspect the ambitious model/actress mask will slip. I'm curious about the little monster underneath who does the bidding of these Sharia Law mutants."

I glanced at Lo, who was nodding her head. "I want to experiment with that too. It will at least be an entertaining journey the rest of the way."

* * *

Cindy sat sagging against the passenger window. I watched her regain consciousness while negotiating the windy coastal journey. The beauty of the rocky coastal classic route stirred the soul. At the later hours of the day, many parts of the route remained untraveled during this weekday traffic period. I carefully did my inspection in split second glances. Anyone who has traveled the beautiful Route 1 knows not to let their eyes wander for very long from the curvy road of wonder. Cindy perked up in intervals. She recognized her predicament with secured wrists at her back and ankles restrained together. I saw then the unchained psychopath beneath. I grinned. Oh... yeah.

"Did you see it, Sis?"

Lois chuckled appreciatively while patting Cindy's face. "Oh my... yes... I did. You nailed it, Skipper. Cindy has awoken to her new temporary world. To her credit, she's pretending disorientation as we speak. She's all in."

"I'm glad you're doing a video," Trish replied. "I have to watch this damn road. I'd forgotten how treacherous it was."

"No accidents of any kind, Trish," I warned. "I have her in my backseat and it's hard as hell not to watch every second of this."

The Harpy predator of life emerged during Cindy's last awakening ploys of fierce fear and disorientation at her surroundings. Lo stroked Cindy's cheek with slow, feathery touch of absolute vicious intention of evil... evil for Cindy anyhow. "Hello there, sweet cheeks. I know so much about you, my little munchkin. You fooled me, when I diverted attention away from Trish cloning your phone. I'm not fooled often. It always pisses me off... but that's okay, sweetie... it's not your fault. It may be I won't have to torture the living shit out of you, because my red headed stepchild Trish figured you out before me."

I saw Trish's Explorer waver on the road. "Trish!"

"Sorry... I'm good."

I saw the Harpy smile as she nearly caused an accident. Damn... she and I may be the only people on earth so nuts we can drive other psychos to suicidal tendencies. I have had my times, but I admit to never touching the absolute mistress of disaster, my partner for all time, Lois Madigan.

"Why…why am I here? I…I've had an accident."

Lois patted her cheek. "Don't worry about that, kid. That's why we have a blanket under you. We can't stop for the formalities. Here's the deal. We know you've been bedding Aga Saleh, and were stupid enough in your little psycho reasoning to think you could sell out civilization to the Moslem mutants – not on my watch, honey. This is where the cliché of rubber meets the road comes into play. From now on… you're my bitch. The only thing you need to know is I will cause you pain no movie on earth could ever prepare you for. My partner Rick's seen me in action for decades. Tell this little chickadee about my short-comings."

I felt we needed to move on. I was all in on Lo's real-life ploy. I could feel the path of her informational gathering skill. I attempted with passion to save our psycho princess from pain. "Lois Madigan will zap, torch, cut, or pull apart your entire being until she achieves your complete surrender, Cindy. Take this as a warning and cooperate to the end. God help you if you don't."

I saw in a rearview mirror glance the disbelief and cunning stream across Cindy's features. I probably sighed or gritted my teeth or the Harpy plucked my thoughts out.

"She thinks I'm kiddin', huh Rick?"

"I wish I could, for the love of humanity, say she didn't. Cindy doesn't believe."

Lois clapped her hands in enjoyment. "You and that rear view mirror… oh God… this is going to be good. Me and a mean girl, head to head… any bets, Peeper?"

"Who the hell could we bet with, Lo," Trish asked. "Rick and I know what you're capable of without remorse or hesitation. Pick another gambling variable. I get to pick first: four minutes."

"Forty-five seconds," I inputted without hesitation.

"Really, Rick?" I saw Lo taking another look into Cindy's temporarily defiant eyes. "I thought maybe a minute and a half to

266

two."

"Okay... no fair holding back, Sis. I say we go with our original picks."

"I'm good with that," Trish said.

"Okay... fine... but where the hell did you pick forty-five seconds from? Oh... never mind... no more priming the pump."

"It's all yours, Sis." I smiled. I knew Cindy was no idiot. The more intelligence you have, the more willing you are to accept reality. I knew without doubt, once Lo introduced her to reality, she would sing to the heavens above for relief. Unfortunately for her the only relief would be total information gathering. "If I win, I direct operations for a week."

"If I win, I get to do every kill mission," Trish said.

Silence then as Lois inspected Cindy's features, which were wavering between abject fear and belligerence. "Damn it, Cantelli! Let's get this started."

Lois didn't cheat. She got her Vipertek out. "Time! Okay pussy... check this out."

Lois lit off the Vipertek arc. "That's 53 million volts, kid."

Lo jammed the electrodes into Cindy's groin. "Oh baby... with all that wetness... this will be epic!"

Cindy screamed. "No...no! What do you want? I...I'll do anything! I'll set Aga up for you! You can listen in on the phone! I swear to God... I can get him to come to me!"

"I have thirty seconds," I said, glancing at my watch. "She believes you now. Start rehearsing her. We'll be able to find out by her performance. Cindy's smart and cunning. She'd sell out her own mother to avoid a hangnail."

"I should have known better than to try outguessing Hooterville," Trish complained.

"You think you're left out. What about me," Lo said. "No

267

matter. Okay, let's get to work. We have your phone, dodo. I'm going to check all your past voice mails and messaging right now. Start thinking about the lines you plan to use on Aga. If I don't like your progress, I'll start your re-education program. There won't be any takebacks. You'll be screaming then, honey."

I could see Cindy's surprise. She'd never figured Lo would compare how she communicated with Saleh from her actual messages. "You surprised her, Lo. She has stuff on her phone Cindy wishes wasn't there."

Lois listened to all voice exchanges and skimmed through her messages, paying close attention to which ones were to Aga. She smiled at Cindy. "I have your tone down perfectly. Impress me now. I don't mean just get the words right. I want to hear the same sickening passion in your voice I hear on your messages to the mutant."

I grinned in the mirror as Cindy's lips tightened to suppress the angry retort Lo's declaration tempted. To her credit, Cindy's internally rehearsed endearments and charming invitation to come over impressed both of us coots. "That sounded real good, Lo."

"Yes it did. Let's start again. I'll answer as Aga and feed you some excuses why he can't come and play. Make your replies cordial and accepting if he's not willing to come. I know he'll want to see you by the messages and voicemails he's left you about calling him the moment you get home."

Lo grabbed Cindy by the ears, going eyeball to eyeball with her. "How often does he visit you? Glance away from me one time while you're answering and I light you up with old sparky."

It gave me something to do while driving toward San Mateo where Cindy lived. I listened intently to the conversation, picturing it taking place on the phone. Lois added Aga to the conversation in a convincing pattern of avoiding the subject directly without giving away identity or purpose. Cindy seemed shocked at Lo's perception of how the banter would move along in real life. By the time we drew near to Cindy's home, I thought Lois captured everything in the rehearsal.

"Sis... you nailed it. Cindy follows your script and she will have a visit from Saleh without doubt if he can possibly make it."

"It sounded perfect, Lo," Trish added. "I'm thinking ETA in fifteen minutes. Did you check her place out? I've never been on Forge Road or near it."

"My daughter Kim handled some properties in San Mateo. She always sent me a portfolio of anything she lists for a critique or suggestions. I know she represented one near Forge Road once. I checked Cindy's place with our satellite imaging and street view. It's in the midst of trees with a nice double garage. How'd you manage to buy a spread like that, Cindy girl?"

"I have been seeing Aga for quite some time. He loves me. Before the trouble in Yemen where his son was killed, he spent months in the states under diplomatic cover. After Sana'a, Aga lived in New York for a time before moving into San Francisco, asking for an ambassadorial position there."

"I get it. Aga made the down payment on your house. Now, he uses it as a base when he visits the West Coast. How in hell did you two meet?"

"I... modeled in New York for a while."

Lois chuckled while watching Cindy closely. "That's a lie. For a psycho, you're not a very good liar. What were you doing for real in New York, hookin'?"

"No! Okay... I modeled some, but it takes money to stay in the City. I hired on with an escort service. Aga hired our service for a party. He and I got along well."

"He recruited you." Lo immediately jumped to the proper conclusion by the look I saw form on Cindy's face. "How long ago?"

Cindy shrugged. "Three years."

269

"Aga hired you out for party gatherings, where he could place you near conversation that was valuable." Lo grinned at Cindy's drooping countenance. "That would be a yes. What made him get you a house in San Mateo besides the usual? Oh hell... this is the perfect halfway house for infiltration from the Canadian and Mexican borders. So you know Gabriel Paria... yes... you do. It's perfect for Aga to check on operations with Paria without ever being seen."

"How... shit!" Cindy didn't like Lo's cackle as she trapped Cindy into acknowledging with one word everything Lo surmised.

"Once Aga's son was killed, he really went after us. Is that why he sent you to San Diego?"

"After you and Cantelli killed his son in Sana'a he went insane with rage for a while. That's when he sent me down to make direct contact with Paria."

"You're not bad at the game," Lo acknowledged. "What the hell was Aga's dipshit son doing in a hotspot like Sana'a anyway?"

"Aga thought Sana'a would be another easy propaganda win like Benghazi for Isil. His son, Donar, wanted to be part of the operation. He acted as an intermediary between the military and Isil. All went according to plan until you butchers-"

I shook my head, keeping eyes on the road, while Cindy danced the electric polka for a moment, that probably seemed like a lifetime to her. Even psychos make errors in judgement. I'm sure Lois awaited a chance to show Cindy what any variation in the plan would bring. Cindy accurately described our escape from Sana'a. I sent so many Moslem mutants virgin hunting without their parts, I could probably take the mantel of butcher proudly.

"Hey, Sis... I kind of like the sound of it – the butchers of Sana'a."

"You would... damn if you didn't throw down on a crap load of those assholes that day." Lo began bitch slapping Cindy back from the electronic fog she vibrated in. "It's okay if you want to start name calling again."

Lo put the electrodes against Cindy's groin. "Begin whenever you're ready."

Cindy became aware in a heartbeat Lois was ready to make her dance all the way to the destination. She screamed and then begged. Trish's appreciative amusement could be heard in our ears for a few moments as we neared Cindy's house. Cindy convinced Lo of her absolute obedience to proper protocol when referring to us coots.

Lo patted Cindy's cheek. "Okay, doll-face, I'll hold off on your attitude adjustment. Be a good girl and don't mention that idiotic Isil term to me again either or I light you up. Rick probably blew Aga's son's head off. Boo hoo. I think we have an understanding, Cindy. I see on your phone you have an app for opening your garage door. Neato. Do you have an empty stall for us in there?"

Cindy was eager to please. "Yes! I only have the Ford Explorer. Please... don't zap me again. I'll do whatever you want."

"Good to hear," Lo replied. "If we park both vehicles in your garage, what's Aga's move when he visits?"

"He visits with two bodyguards. They remain outside with his vehicle. It has always been a Mercedes. Aga never spends the night."

"Let's work on that," Lo replied. "I want you to encourage him to spend the night. Let's explore the overnight stay with hints of ecstasy awaiting him. If he only wants a quickie, don't argue with him. Make sure he knows you want whatever he wants, short time, long time, anything... or else."

"I...I understand. He normally only stays for a couple of hours. He drinks at my place because he cannot at the Embassy."

We arrived a moment later. Once we were gloved, Lo activated the garage door opener app. It worked. Trish drove the

Explorer inside. She exited gloved and her hair tied back tightly. I eased the GMC in next to it. Lo worked the app and the door closed. We went to work moving our unwilling cohorts inside, undoing their ankle restraints. We marched them inside, where we made them strip out of their clothes with our Tasers pointing at them. Lo took charge of Cindy, once she showed us where her washer and dryer were. I made Gabriel do laundry after we allowed them bathroom breaks. Soon after, when everything of a human factor had been completed with clothing and personal hygiene, I restrained Gabriel again. He kept his mouth shut and did what he was told silently. He saw the end in sight and decided to plea at the right time for a painless death. Good choice. Then it was time for me to do a professional wipe down of the Explorer. I was considering other options than using the Explorer as a suicide machine if we were able to corral Saleh.

It didn't take much time to network Cindy's already cloned phone so we could listen to everything she and Aga conversed about. Lo shook Cindy's chin, eliciting a yelp. "Listen to me closely, doll-face. One mistake... just one... and when Aga bails, I will torture you to death. Honey... you don't want that. I will keep you alive for a full day of agony beyond your understanding. Are we clear?"

We had taken the restraints off Cindy because Lois owned her, body and soul. Cindy made fists on the table, closing her eyes and nodding vehemently in the affirmative. "I understand! I will not make a mistake... not ever."

Lo released her chin and stroked her cheek. "I believe you. Don't let me down or I will have to show you what nightmares are made of. Let's make the call, girlfriend. Take some deep breaths or whatever you need to do. Don't make the call until you're calm enough to deliver the same performance I saw in the car on the way here."

"I...I won't... honest to God!"

"That's what I like to hear."

Trish and I were networked in when Cindy made the call, but it was laughingly obvious Aga wanted Cindy in the worst way

272

possible. I could tell he had been probably pacing whatever rug he was on. Cindy slipped in the possibility of Aga spending the night with excellent delivery. He quieted for a moment, giving me hope we would not have to deal with his bodyguards' disposal. The problem with bodyguard handling, involved the car we would be disposing them in being traced immediately to the Yemen Embassy and Aga. It would add another mystery to our suicide scene for the police. The mystery marsh scene might also give us extra time getting into San Diego. The separate death scene could also mean extra investigation.

Cindy allowed only the right amount of silence before speaking again. "It's okay. Think about it, but whatever you decide will be wonderful."

"Yes... let me consider it. I will see you very soon, my love."

Cindy ended the call with endearments similar to her past messages. I restrained her in the living room with Gabe, both gagged, with multiple ties at wrists behind their backs and at the ankles. I moved the GMC out of Cindy's garage, parking it around a bend in the road. I left the garage door open. Sparsely populated with spread out housing and heavy foliage, I understood why Aga picked this house and neighborhood. We waited in comfort for our honored guest.

"I like your idea about subduing them all at gunpoint with our FBI credentials," Trish told Lois. "They'll be whining about diplomatic immunity, harassment, and lawyers. Hopefully, we won't have to shoot them. Cleanup would be a bitch."

"We'll see," Lois replied. "It will all be a mystery for the police; but you're right, restraining them without shooting would be best. Rick can load the bodyguards in their car and give them a hotshot to hell. Remember, lots of noise when they walk in."

Aga texted Cindy, letting her know he would be here in minutes. Unfortunately, Saleh said he would spend the night, but his bodyguards would sleep in the living room. We don't always get what we want. Bodyguard disposal now became a necessity. Trish

273

seemed happy with the additional news. Lois texted him back that the garage door was open and to come inside. She added Cindy would be waiting in the bedroom for him. He acknowledged with a wide eyed emoticon and a thank you. Aga was so cute. We heard the car drive into the garage bay. Saleh came through the door, hot to trot with bodyguards trailing him closely. Trish and I jammed our gun barrels up under the bodyguards' chins.

"FBI! You are all under arrest for espionage!" Lois shoved her credentials in Saleh's face with one hand, while covering him with her Ruger pointed at his nuts. "Do anything but get on your knees with hands locked behind your head, and I blow your dick off!"

Aga came unglued while doing what Lo ordered. "You cannot do this to me! I have diplomatic immunity! I have done nothing wrong. Why are you people wearing gloves? What is going on?"

"Shut your pie-hole!" Lois restrained Aga while Trish and I held position. Once he was restrained, Lo kicked him over on his side. She then covered the two bodyguards. "On your knees now with hands locked behind your heads!"

They kept their mouths shut and followed Lo's command. I restrained them with hands behind backs. Trish and I escorted them to Aga's Mercedes, after I used the manual switch to shut the garage door. I seated them in the back and belted them in. They were clearly upset and annoyed, but figured they were actually under arrest.

"Where are you taking us," the second one to be belted in asked me.

I looked over at Trish on the other side next to our first belted in bodyguard. I nodded. We stuck our syringe needles into each one's neck. I patted the bodyguard's shoulder who had spoken, while the light faded from his at first shocked eyes. "We're sending you virgin hunting with all your parts intact. You lucky boys get sent pain free too."

We walked back inside where Lois sat smiling at the pushed over Aga. He chattered away, warning Lo of all the bad things that would happen to her once the Yemen Embassy heard of this outrage. "I see Aga has lost none of his delusional charm."

"He's been quite entertaining," Lo replied. "I think he's threatened me with everything from beheading to a hanging."

"Where are my men? What have you done with them?"

"They're in your car, sweetie," Trish said. "Are you two really going to use the Explorer?"

"It would probably be messy and a little dangerous," I said. "I'm thinking of a more romantic ending."

"Ending! What is this ending business?" Aga began getting curious. "You must let me go free. I am warning you!"

"Should we discuss this in front of him," I asked.

"Sure." Lo answered. "He wants the facts, Rick. Spit it out. I was cooling toward that Explorer idea, especially now that we have the three of them together without any real damage. "

"I want to do all three no matter what you decide," Trish stated.

I shrugged. "I don't have a problem with that. Let's strip them all down to their dainties. I noticed Cindy has a king sized bed. Trish can give them our heroin hotshot, leaving the syringe in place. We arrange them provocatively with Cindy in the middle on her bed."

"Ahhhh… you big softie," Trish kidded me.

"I like it," Lo agreed. "We've been very tidy. Once we have this jerk off our backs, we can concentrate on more important things. Maybe with Trish doing these three, Peeper, your death cycle will end."

Aga heard enough to realize he was in real trouble. He changed from threats to bribes. "I will pay you anything you want.

275

I-"

"Shut up," Lo interrupted. "You've been trying to kill us. Game over. I have some questions for you given to me by my boss. Answer them and I won't have to barbeque your balls. Want a taste?"

Aga jerked away from Lo's Vipertek. "No! What are they?"

Lois read off the questions which encompassed the situation in Yemen at the moment, including terrorist organizations sharing the spotlight there, while I recorded both questions and answers. She gripped Aga by the chin the whole time. God help him if he would have lied. "Okay, Aga... I believe we're done."

Saleh started sobbing, much to Lo's amusement. She fired off her Vipertek which shut him up. "Rick's going to help you to your feet. You'll then walk in and lie down on Cindy's bed after Trish pulls down the covers. If you try anything, I will zap your balls. I wish we could torture the shit out of you for a while, but it wouldn't fit into Rick's romantic death scene."

I helped him to his feet while Lo jammed the Vipertek to his groin area. Trish hurried ahead to fix the covers and arrange pillows. I took off Saleh's shoes, socks, and pants. He had on cute bikini underwear, probably just for Cindy's pleasure. I sat him on the bed with Aga blubbering in my ear. Lo handed Trish one of our heroin hotshots. She turned Aga so she could get at the right spot on his left arm. Trish glanced at Lo.

"He's right handed, isn't he?"

"Yep. I would have stopped you otherwise, Skipper. Cindy's right handed too. Gabe is left handed."

Trish injected the openly crying Saleh, leaving the syringe in place. We waited for the very potent shot to take our buddy Aga to happy land and then dark shadows. Trish and I eased his jacket and shirt away from him. I placed his hand on the syringe, posed perfectly. Cindy was next. Trish treated her with care.

"I'm going to give you something to sleep, Cindy. You have another trip ahead." Trish gave her the shot. She went away as peacefully as her boyfriend.

Lois stayed with the unhappy Paria. Trish and I posed Cindy on the bed in the middle without any clothes, leaning against Aga, her head against his shoulder. We marched Paria into the bedroom with Lois keeping the Vipertek on his groin. Trish helped me double team Gabe until he was completely naked on his lower half. We put him in bed next to Cindy. Trish repeated the death procedure. After watching Gabe get happy and then dead, I helped him off with the rest of his clothes with care not to disturb the syringe. We made some final touches by arranging clothes and shoes as if they tore them off each other haphazardly while getting into bed together.

"It looks great, Rick," Lo said. "It's much cleaner than the Explorer idea. We'll lock the house when we get back. You drive the Mercedes to the salt marsh access road. I'll follow you in the Explorer. Trish stays with our scene until we return. We've wiped everything down so you need to close the garage door with the manual switch, Trish. I don't want the phones or anything else the three had on them disturbed from where I arranged the items. It would be suspicious as hell and ruin everything if we took any electronics with us. I downloaded the contents of everything on the way here."

"Are you two still going to fire bomb the Mercedes," Trish asked.

"We have to," I answered. "We need a mystery at the salt marsh too. It will be late enough by the time I get to the access road. No one will be down there. I'll wear my hoodie and scarf anyway. We'll be back in an hour tops."

* * *

The salt marsh access road was not a tourist site. I drove along it until I found a spot not too far from the main approach. Lois turned the Explorer around near the Mercedes. I hit the switch for the back rear window. I took the two magnesium flares out with me

277

and closed the door. I lit them off and placed them in between the bodies on the seat. I ran over to the Explorer, got in, and Lo drove toward Cindy's house. We didn't need to stick around for the results.

"I wish we could sneak a visit with the kids but it's just too damn late," Lo said. "We'll be able to get away for a San Francisco visit once we get clear of this mess. We'll fly up with Frank, Stacy, and Jim."

"Agreed. I wish we could stop too. The trip back to San Diego will be brutal. I'm glad there's three of us sharing the driving. We can make it straight through without notice. We used cash all the way so we're golden. They won't discover the bodies for a while if Aga didn't tell his people at the Embassy where he went. The bodyguards and car will be investigated first."

"I'll take the first shift driving. Trish enjoyed herself," Lo mentioned with a smirk. "We'll have to put her down like a rabid dog if she ever goes rogue."

"She's got Sam, movies, and our business. Hell, she's still young enough for her and Sam to have a couple kids. It worked well for Karen. Trish is pissed because she knows she's on the list."

"Too bad," Lo replied. "Skipper's on the list forever… period."

Chapter Thirteen

Kull

Stacy and Jim were sitting at the breakfast table. We had made it back before the morning's rush hour nightmare with only one quick gas stop. "Good morning, my fellow travelers in Cantelli-land. The darkness and shadows have lifted for the time being. We'll be able to move back into our house tonight."

Stacy came over to hug and kiss me. She looked really nice in her work clothes. "Do you really think everything will return to normal?"

"I'm not sure about the demonstrations. The BLM gangsters are the ones to watch for. If they've had enough of us, I think the Moslem mutants will move on to some other target. Lo and I talked about it on the way home. We plan to use our FBI/Homeland Security contact to do some investigation into the BLM contingent around here and find out if we can get Immigration to look into the demonstrators' status. Lo and I will take pictures of the ones waving signs at the gym and restaurant next time."

"I'll let you know if I see or hear anything more around school, Pa. That was weird with Jess's friends turning deadly on him like they did."

"Thanks for reminding me, kid. We do need to stay careful with you and school. One more incident like that, and I'm pulling you the hell out of there. We'll either get a tutor or find a private school."

"Most of the kids attend for an education, not fight club," Jim replied. "I hope I can keep going to school with Ellen. Are you taking us this morning, Pa?"

"I thought G-ma or Temple wanted to drive you and Ellen to school."

"I have to go in to work early again," Stacy said. "We waited to see if you arrived home in time before we made other plans. I have to go right now, so I was going to call Jim a taxi if Temple couldn't drive."

"The trainer gave the new pit bull puppy to Temple last night. Kull is the greatest! He is so smart, it's scary. The trainer gave us a few basics to work on with him before he left. We played with him for a couple hours, threading in the tricks. Kull learned them all. He learned the house breaking the best. We took him outside and gave him treats for taking care of business."

"Okay… that's just swell." I tried to be as enthusiastic as Jim. Some downers live with you forever. I lost brothers-in-arms on missions and my 'Killer Cantelli' label fits me too close for comfort. Losing Tick who grew up with me nearly unhinged my head back then.

The doorbell rang. Jim spurted to the monitor. His face glowed so I knew who it must be. Stacy giggled, recognizing nothing we ever did would keep Jim and Temple apart for long other than changing interests. Jim let her in with the damnedest little bugger I ever saw. She shoved Kull into Jim's arms while launching into a sneezing fit. Temple's eyes were as red as her nose. Kull settled into Jim's arms without a peep. Dark gray with a white belly stripe, Kull incorporated all the pit bull facial features where they look like they're laughing at you. He perked up with each new Temple sneeze. She went over and washed her hands and face in the sink.

"I'm allergic! I can't believe it! I sneezed all night long," Temple complained. "I called the doctor and trainer. They both said I would eventually develop an immunity, but it will take time. Can you take Kull until I get over my reaction to him?"

Oh shit. It was four on one giving me whiney, pleading looks, including the dog. Kull tilted his head, wavering between pleading and laughing. Jim really wasn't pleading. He smirked, knowing I had a snowball's chance in hell of avoiding taking the little runt in.

"Wonderful. What exactly do we do with Kull during the day? Oh… never mind… Killer Cantelli is here to save the day. I'm getting your butt up early, kid. Dogs need walks, training, leashes, poop bags and patience. When do the training classes start?"

"Tonight, Pa. You need to go with us, especially since you'll be with Kull a lot." Jim held Kull up for protection as I moved to put him in a headlock. Kull tilted his head from one side to the other, laughing at me in vicious expressions of rancid cuteness.

"Go home and heal, Temple. I'll take Jim, Ellen, and Kull the wonder dog with me to their school. Did you bring all the stuff we'll need?"

"The trainer gave each of us all the supplies we would need because both of us have to be completely comfortable with Kull. It included everything you listed for sure. Thanks for this, Pop. I'll go home and try to dry up before our training session. Either way, I have to go. Quincy wants to start filming in two weeks, three at the most."

"I haven't paid attention to the Hollywood Entertainment section. How are all the movies doing?" I stroked Kull's smooth head. This dog was dangerously cute.

"A New Beginning is now on DVD and Blu-ray. It will be playing on Amazon Prime and Netflix too. 'Here and Now' did so well it's still in the movie theaters. Pre-release sales for the 'Here and Now' DVD and Blu-ray editions are terrific so far. 'Logan Heights' turned Jim and I into an action duo money maker. The new movie already has more money backers than Quincy needed to start production."

"That's wonderful, honey," Stacy said. "I have to leave. Kull is the cutest thing ever."

"Spoken like a true absentee owner," I stabbed her with reality.

"Never you mind, Grinch. You make sure Kull is in first class condition when I get home." Stacy hugged and kissed me while the kids laughed, and I considered what revenge in the way of sexual favors I would visit upon her.

"At some point today, I will need some sleep in an actual bed. Let's go. Everyone out. Let me carry Barfy the furniture slayer."

Temple gasped. "He is not a furniture slayer. The trainer gave him the perfect chew toys. He loves them. I did drive the Lexus today instead of my new Highlander."

"Wise decision. Out." I took Kull from Jim. He grabbed his pack and I grabbed my keys. Jim handed me Kull's leash with attached waste bag carrier. Oh goody. I shooed everyone out the door while Kull observed from the crook of my arm. I set the security to on and we were once again heading into the Cantelli-land of puppies, joy, and probably rainbows. For five minutes the darkness and shadows might withdraw.

At Ellen's house, she ran out to the GMC gasping in joy at Kull on my lap, paws anchoring him on the window frame. "Oh my God... he's adorable!"

"Get in, Mars Bar," I ordered. "He'll jump all over you the moment you get inside. We have to arrive at the school before Creepy Clowns, BLM wannabes, and Moslem mutants assault us."

Ellen got in and Kull pounced. The trainer succeeded in getting some basics done. Kull wasn't a lick the face dog. He liked to prance on laps. He then sat quietly watching the front while Ellen and Jim stroked him. My reservations about the bugger were flying out the window. Dogs have that effect on people. Once the dog gets in your life for whatever reason, your life changes around the dog, not the other way around.

"Moslems hate dogs, Rick. They think they're unclean beasts." Ellen decided to stir me around in the fry pan, baiting me for a bite."

"Thanks for the info. I'm aware of their attitude on hating practically everything on earth - then annoying the hell out of everyone they can't kill about how offended they are by whatever it is. Let's leave the Moslem horde out of today's conversation. We have the gym tonight. What time's that training session for Kull? I want to make sure I don't get too much sleep."

"We'll have plenty of time. The trainer's meeting us at Temple's house at 4 pm. It only lasts forty-five minutes. The trainer said Kull needs to learn in a regimental atmosphere and then have everything he's learned reinforced until the next lesson."

"Sounds good. Maybe we can do the training session, get a nap, hit the gym, get a nap, and then have dinner on our Wednesday Casablanca Night at the Collinswood's restaurant."

"Will you be laying off the adult beverages, Pa?"

"That's none of your business. Your Aunt Lo and I earned a couple pops and a good meal without demonstrations or mutant hit squads."

"I don't want you to keel over after everything you've done lately," Jim replied. "If something happens to you, I'll have to get a dog-sitter for Kull."

Kull liked the sound of snorting amusement. He leaped into the front to find out why I wasn't amused, peeking around at my face while pawing my arm. "Yeah... it was real funny, Kull. I suppose I'll walk him to the school door so you two don't beat up any more innocent bystanders. You'd better heel Kull on the way to the entrance, Jim. I imagine the trainer told you how important making the dog anticipate the owner's intent is."

"He did. You seem to know a lot about dogs for someone who hasn't had one for nearly half a century."

I parked a block away from the school. "Gee, what a lovely parting gift. Maybe we better continue your martial arts practice tomorrow. I think I'll have a couple lessons for you."

Jim leashed Kull as the two teens scrambled out of the GMC. "No thanks, Pa. You're too willing. I think we need to take a few days off so you can cool down."

"Can I train with you guys," Ellen asked.

"I think it would be better for Jim to show you some of what he learns for now. Did Jess come to school yesterday?"

Jim nodded as we sauntered at Kull's pace with Jim making him behave, stopping every twenty or so feet to allow him to romp around smelling everything in sight. "His parents have put him in a holding pattern until they see if the Cantelli-land of darkness and shadow recedes for the immediate future."

"A wise decision. He can join us after his chances of getting maimed and killed in our company lessen to an acceptable level. Kull's doing very well."

"He's so cute! I want to help train him too. Can I attend the class at Temple's house?"

"I'll ask the trainer, Ellen. I think he wants as many people around Kull as we can get because of the filming demands with people on the set everywhere. Temple's allergic to him, so I imagine we'll have any lesson outside for the time being."

Ellen allowed us a glimpse of her cunning smile as she realized there was something Temple wouldn't be able to do that she could. "That's too bad about Temple's allergies."

"Yeah... we can tell how shook up you are about it, Mars Bar," I said.

"Hey, Rick... don't look now but there's demonstrators moving into position." Mars Bar decided I needed a distraction.

She was right. I'd been watching Kull play around and march behind Jim. I made another error in forgetting the school was still having trouble with the offended of Allah. "What the hell are they

284

out here for now? It can't be because of me. They have the attention span of gerbils."

"We heard yesterday representatives from C.A.I.R. stopped in to complain about proper halal meals not being served," Jim answered. "We thought it was a joke."

"Nothing can be considered off the table for those cretins. They're offended by everything and everybody. If they're in their own homelands, they kill each other. They've been doing so for over fourteen hundred years. We need to shut their infiltration off from our country. They're tearing Europe apart. Anyway, for today, let's leave the mutants alone, and not go into zombie apocalypse mode with them."

We approached without making eye contact while the mutants paraded around with 'give us halal meals' signs, chanting some idiocy about food sacrilege. It would have been funny if this murderous cult wasn't trying to tear America apart from the inside out. I glanced down at Kull. He had his laugh face on so he must have agreed with me. We received the usual Isis bearded stares. I could only guess what was under the slave costumes the women wore. I avoided their beady eyed stares from the rectangle hole in the costume for their eyes. One of the beards stopped us as I led our single file group toward the sidewalk leading to the entrance.

"You cannot take that dog on the premises!"

I turned toward Ellen, who tried to stifle amusement. "You did this, Mars Bar. You jinxed us."

"Pa's right," Jim agreed. "You baited him in the car. Now look what you've done.

"Oh sure... blame the messenger. I merely tried to warn you. As for you, hairy-face," Ellen pointed at the guy blocking my way. "Kull the dog has better manners than you do. Isn't that right, Kull?"

The little performer sat with paw in the air when he heard his name. Ellen shook with him while the blocking beard fumed.

285

One of the women in black slave costume stopped to reach for Ellen, who smacked her hand away. "Don't touch me, Salome! I'll slap your lone ranger mask right off your face."

The woman cursed Ellen but stepped back, contemplating using her sign on Mars Bar. She grinned with Jim backing her play, gesturing the woman on. Wisely, what I think was a woman moved away as did her cohorts.

The beard decided to reach for me. I was ready. He shook hands with my Vipertek. One short touch and he was on his back in the grass. I had the Viper in my left hand, watching crowd reaction, with my right hand on the Colt .45 holstered at my back. Lucky for the mutants that they didn't reach for anything. The security force from the school moved on them immediately. The lead security guard gestured us along. He stooped to stroke the happy Kull.

"Cute dog," the guard remarked. "What's going on here. I saw you dust this guy vibrating on the ground. You're Rick Cantelli, right?"

"Guilty as charged." I showed him my FBI/Homeland Security ID. "My grandson has a few moments before school. I'll take a movie of the men's faces."

"You cannot do that!" The beard on the ground stuttered into coherency. "That is harassment!"

"No… you and your friends annoying the hell out of everyone is harassment." I used my iPhone to begin movie making. I could get HD stills off it later. The other mutants involved wanted no part of a video recording. I froze them in place, holding my FBI credentials for them to see. "Do not move."

Once I finished with the men, I pointed at the women. "Get the hoods off so I can film you people in the slave costumes."

The one Ellen had backed off began gesturing and sobbing about being disrobed in public as a woman. I had an answer for that. "How the heck do I know if you're a woman. You could be anything under that bear suit. Tell you what. Leave now, and I won't call the police to help me remove your Halloween masks. If you're back here in the future, I will film you, or you burka people will be unmasked. Make your choice quickly."

I started getting Arabic curses muttered from the men. I turned to return them in kind, ending with, "the next comment and I place you in federal custody. Leave, or strip off the burka masks!"

Hearing my orders in Arabic, my protesting mutants decided 'retreat and annoy' another day would be their course of action. They began walking away as the first bunch of students and parents arrived on scene. "I'll be back every day, waiting for you munchkins. Remember, next time, the Halloween masks get removed."

Kull drew the most attention after the demonstrators went away. He amazingly stayed at Jim's side watching everything with his laugh face. Not even my Vipertek arc with dropping victim phased him. Kull absorbed all the attention with only paw shakes and interested mug face.

"Thanks for ridding us of the protestors, Rick. I'm Ben Hathaway." We shook hands.

"I'll be back to drop off the kids. I meant what I said, I'm getting Homeland Security involved in these goofy demonstrations. These people could very well be testing security precautions, access to the school, and taking videos of the building for terrorist acts."

"Damn... we hadn't considered anything like that," Ben replied. "Any help you can give us on that front would be welcome. Did you hear the news about an FBI raid on a suspected Isis compound near here?"

Apparently, Floyd decided to brief the locals. "I did hear some very worrisome news about an operation that was ongoing. How did you hear about it, Ben?"

"I still have friends in the SDPD. Anyway... thanks for the help."

"No problem." I took the leash from Jim for the impressive Kull. "I'm not forgetting the jinx you instigated, Mars Bar."

"I don't care. I couldn't believe they tried to block our way on the sidewalk because Kull was with us. Do you really think all those things you told the security guard are true about the demonstrators?"

We walked on together to the school with Kull heeling again perfectly. "Yeah... I do, especially with all the interference the Isis/Muslim Brotherhood and C.A.I.R. keep trying to perpetrate on people's everyday lives. Okay, you two, stay out of trouble. I'll go get some sleep and be back to fetch you for the dog training session."

"Okay, Pa."

"You were pretty quiet this morning, Jim."

Jim shrugged. "I wanted to bash all their heads in. I didn't want Kull to get involved."

"He's a good one. Good decision making, Jim. I have every intention of ending these demonstrations. See you later, kids."

I called in to Floyd Randolf and shared my thoughts on the Paria compound possibly being players in this C.A.I.R. crap along with the Isis/Muslim Brotherhood connection. He thought my suspicions about the demonstrations being testing tools for terrorism very close to my own.

"I like your idea, Rick. It's noninvasive and legal. When demonstrators harass people, while in all likelihood, acting as foreign agents for terrorist organizations, they should be at minimum photographed. I'll back your play on this. The worst that could happen is the Moslem enablers in the DOJ tell us to back off, in which case we would be free to report the fact to the media. I'll send you the directive in writing. I have your fax number at the beach house. I'll sneak a signature on it at DOJ and let you experiment."

There's a surprise. The FBI taking an initiative on an

unpopular case with their leaders. I like it. Maybe they were getting tired of being used as a cover for crooked politicians. "That's very courageous of you, Agent Randolf."

Floyd chuckled. "Fuck you, Cantelli. Not all of us can find the bad guys and shoot them in the head. I'll have the signed fax directive to you within the hour. Has Van spoken to you any more concerning Aga Saleh?"

"Nope. We found his girlfriend spy at our gym workout. She went back to San Francisco - drugged, tied, and gagged."

"The San Francisco police found Saleh's two bodyguards, and the car he's always driven around in, burnt to a crisp in the salt marsh. Give me the girlfriend's address. I'll pass it on discreetly. They asked the FBI in on the case, requested by the Yemen Embassy."

I looked it up on my phone and gave it to him.

"I have a feeling, the love tryst between Saleh and his girlfriend ended in tragedy. What do you think, Rick?"

"Who knows what can happen with two wild and crazy kids in love?"

I woke up shortly before it was time to retrieve the kids from school with a dark gray lump sleeping on my chest. I don't want to insult Kull with this comparison, but I do believe we have an example of the 'camel's nose under the tent' cliché. At least he'd have Jim to sleep on at night. I know how rock hard and big these puppies get. I maneuvered him to the bedside. He barely snorted. After my shower and change of clothes, I felt human again. Kull and I went for a walk along the hardpacked sand by the ocean. He wanted to go diving into the surf in the worst possible way. I played alpha dog and heeled him along with me until driving to the school. Wonder of wonders, no demonstrators were annoyingly on scene to disrupt the afterschool retrieval of students.

Kull practiced under my care to heel, slow and speed pace, turn with me, and play when allowed. The damn dog's intelligence began to unhinge me. At only twelve weeks old, he displayed nearly adult intelligence level. The trainer was unquestionably a professional. I knew from Tick if a dog's intelligence shows signs of above average acceptance of training, the more they learn, the better. I admit to being so enthralled with Kull pacing around with me, I didn't see the squad car drive alongside us, until I heard a familiar voice screaming from the back.

"That is him! That is the man who attacked me today."

Yep. It was the early beard who got the worm in the grass doing the electric hula. Fortunately for me, Bill Staley must have taken a hand in this police action. My old friends Jamile Crosby and Terrance Stanley eased out of the squad car, smiling and shaking their heads slightly to tip me off. Kull sat and cocked his head to the side with his interested look. Terry let the complainant out of the rear. I eased my windbreaker to the side, allowing him to see the Vipertek again. He stayed against the squad car, pointing from a safe distance.

"I want him arrested immediately!"

I peered at my friends' shirt fronts. "Officers Crosby and Stanley? How may I help the Blue today?"

"Captain Staley sent us with this gentleman who seemed to know you would be right here. He claims you attacked him," Terry said. He and J were both checking out the adorable Kull. I could tell they both wanted to roughhouse with Kull rather than deal with the jackass leaning on the car.

"He blocked my way toward the school with the kids. He reached for me. Rather than pistol whip him, I gave the gentleman a battery charge."

"This Kaffir meant to walk near the school with that dog! It is unclean!"

J knelt next to Kull as if inspecting him. "He looks pretty clean to me. What's his name?"

290

"Kull. He'll be starring in a movie with Temple and Jim, so Kull has to live with us."

"Arrest him!"

"I have a directive from the main FBI/Homeland Security office in DC authorizing me to investigate the tedious and annoying demonstrations, launched by these professionally offended nitwits. We believe they are a cover for testing and doing reconnaissance of potential terrorist targets such as the school here."

"You lie, Kaffir!"

J pointed at the beard with violent intent. "You seem to think I don't know what Kaffir means. It was a favorite racial slur in South Africa. It is meant by you religion of Islam people as a slur for non-believers. I'm a non-believer. Say it again and I'll let Mr. Cantelli light you up."

That shut the beard's mouth. Terry chuckled. "You said something about a directive, Mr. Cantelli? That is one scary theory, by the way. It fits all the idiotic offended ploys they use to get near and observe."

"I have copies of the directive in my shoulder bag." I stroked Kull while he stuck his face in my opened bag on the sidewalk. I gave one of my copies to Terry while Kull crawled into the bag and peeked out over the edge.

"Holy crap, Rick! They're really looking into these fake demonstrations, huh?"

"If what we believe is true as to the cause, the reconnaissance of potential targets like schools, universities, restaurants, malls... all of the trivial crap demonstrations, would fit potentially disastrous terrorist targeting."

Terry handed the directive to J. He scanned it and opened the rear squad car door. "Agent Cantelli has the authority to investigate any demonstration participants deemed trivial and a cover for a reconnaissance mission. His authority overrides your complaint. Get in the back, Sir, or we will leave you with Agent Cantelli. Believe me... you don't want that."

The early beard that got the worm dived into the back.

"Can I keep this to show the Captain, Rick?"

"Sure Terry. I'm passing them out to the school security. I smell a rat, by the way. This doesn't seem like a complaint Bill would have ever wasted time on. Who dropped a dime on him?"

Terry moved closer to me. "Judge Setteridge issued orders for Captain Staley to investigate the complaint personally. He'll be happy to get your directive."

"Great news about the kids' new movie," J said, while playing around with the Kull in a bag, popping out like a jack-in-the-box. "I saw 'Logan Heights'. Those kids were incredible in it. We better get back. Stay out of trouble, Agent Cantelli."

"Yes... Officer Crosby... would if I could."

By the time they drove off, I managed to empty my bag of its lurker, as the school let out the participants in teen education. I managed to find Jim and Ellen in the flow. I surrendered control of Kull, found Ben the security guard and made him an enthusiastic fan of my venture. On the way home, I explained the police stop to Jim and Ellen.

"Aunt Lo isn't going to like that news, Pa. She hates that judge."

I smiled at Jim. No truer words were ever spoken. "You've heard the term 'last straw', right? I'm afraid Saint Ally burned the straw, haystack, and barn to the ground."

"Uh oh," Jim said.

"Yep."

* * *

Judge Alexis Setteridge regained consciousness in waves of nausea. She squeezed her eyes tightly shut, her mouth a tight slash trying to keep from throwing up. The last thing she remembered was getting into her car. The judge felt the restraints on her wrists and ankles. She could tell a strap kept her immovable on a hard surface. Smelling salt air and hearing the sound of engines throttling into a higher speed, Setteridge opened her eyes to squinting slits. The light cast a shadow over the face of the woman hovering over her. She recognized the face in a horrid moment of utter terror.

"Oh my... it's just so special having you here aboard my boat, Ally."

"Madigan? What the hell are you doing? Release me at once!"

"I'm going to release you, Ally. First, I need to find out how you came to be involved in this dirty business of selling out your country."

"You...you're delusional! I have nothing to say to you! I will see you in prison for the rest of your life for this outrage!"

Judge Alexis Setteridge heard an annoying cackle of a laugh. Then she heard the click-clack of plier jaws she saw in Lois Madigan's right hand. When the propane torch fired into blue flame life in Madigan's other hand, the judge began to scream.

Lois Madigan bopped Setteridge in the forehead with the pliers lightly. "Save your breath, baby. You're going to need it."

* * *

The Hollywood stars sang together at Don Blanco's piano. Even Ellen sang next to her friend with Stacy's arm around her. The rest of our Cantelli-land inhabitants enjoyed the performance from our table. I sported my Rick of Casablanca fame attire with new white jacket. Lois sat next to me holding her sleeping niece at the bar with Frank and I bracketing her. Jerry served us double Bushmills for our first drink since leaving San Francisco with Gabriel Paria and Cindy Daniels. We handled our drinks with hesitant care.

293

The news of mysterious deaths and disappearances from north to south exploded into the news, along with a terrorist compound revealed and assaulted by unknown forces. The only figures who were on a need to know basis, Floyd Randolf and Van Carmichael, accepted the details necessary for their own departments, wisely choosing the 'ignorance is bliss' decision for the rest. Kull hid out in the bag at my feet with a bone from the kitchen.

We raised our glasses with ardent pleasure in the moment. "To the end of the death cycle," Lo announced.

"Amen, Sis," I replied. Until next time.

The End

Thank you for purchasing and reading **Rick Cantelli, P.I. Book V: Blood Ties**. If you enjoyed the novel, please take a moment and leave a review. Your consideration would be much appreciated. Please visit my Amazon Author's Page if you would like to preview any of my other novels. Thanks again for your support.

Bernard Lee DeLeo

Author's Face Book Page -

https://www.facebook.com/groups/BernardLeeDeLeo/

BERNARD LEE DELEO - AUTHOR'S PAGE -

http://www.amazon.com/Bernard-Lee-
DeLeo/e/B005UNXZ04/ref=ntt_athr_dp_pel_pop_1

AMAZON AUTHOR'S PAGE (UK) -

http://www.amazon.co.uk/-/e/B005UNXZ04

Made in the USA
San Bernardino, CA
20 November 2016